SAFE FOR NOW

Bob Howard

ISBN-13: 978-1-945754-17-3

Dedication

This book is dedicated to my readers in the United Kingdom. They have supported me with kindness from the very beginning.

Table of Contents

1

Symone

Southern England - The Beginning

It wasn't exactly a loud noise that woke Symone Tisdal from a deep sleep. It was just loud enough to pull her from the grip of a dream to a level of awareness where she could listen for any of the telltale sounds a mother would recognize. Those sounds in the middle of the night didn't always signal that something was wrong. Sometimes it was just one of the children having a dream of their own. One or two words would escape from a sleeping child's mouth, but they were always loud enough to rouse Symone.

Whether it was a dream or the start of a long day due to an illness, Symone accepted the job as hers alone while Henry was away. She wouldn't take away his dream of living in the International Space Station for a few months by letting the obligations of being a parent interfere. She lifted her head a few inches from the pillow and concentrated on the quiet house. There it was again.

She could tell it wasn't coming from either of the children's rooms. It sounded like something bumped against one of the garbage cans on the back porch. It was followed by the unmistakable crash of a potted plant that had undoubtedly fallen from the railing around the patio.

Symone was already at her bedroom door, pulling on a robe. The children's rooms were further down the hall from the stairs. One reason she had fallen in love with the old country house near Verwood was that the master bedroom was closer to the top of the stairs than the smaller bedrooms. She would check on the children before investigating downstairs, but she was startled, and she felt more petite than her thin, five-and-a half-feet frame had ever felt. Her brown hair was long and straight, so she knew she didn't strike an imposing figure if there was a threat in her home. Her pretty face certainly wasn't going to scare anyone off either.

She peeked into her daughter's room. Emily didn't show any sign that she had been disturbed. Symone debated for a moment whether or not to wake her but decided to let her sleep. It was probably nothing more than an animal from the woods or maybe a cat, but her skin crawled when she heard another potted plant fall just as she pulled Emily's door shut. She waited in the gloom outside the door in case the sound had reached Emily this time. The six-year-old didn't call out after a few minutes, so Symone quietly moved toward the next door. Her bare feet hardly whispered on the thick carpet.

Her younger child, Adam, was sitting up in bed, but Symone knew the lost expression on his face very well. He wasn't quite awake.

"Here, baby. Let me help you with your blanket."

The four-year-old blinked as she brushed the hair from his forehead and gently pressed a hand against his chest to ease him toward the pillow.

"I heard something. Is Daddy home?"

"No, baby. Remember I explained that Daddy will be home soon. Now go back to sleep. We don't want to wake your sister."

Symone was grateful that this was one time when Adam did what she told him to. He let his head burrow deeply into the pillow and was asleep before she could cover him and get back to the door. Adam would likely sleep through it all and probably wouldn't remember it in the morning.

She moved more quickly now. Symone went to her husband's bureau where he kept the small lockbox, but first she got the key from the jewelry chest on her bureau. She opened it and removed the Smith & Wesson her husband had insisted on buying. If he wasn't prominent in the United Kingdom's space program, he might have had difficulty obtaining a permit as quickly as he had.

Symone did as she had been taught. She ejected the empty magazine and racked the slide open. Next, she checked the empty chamber before reversing the process by slipping in a full magazine then releasing the slide. She pulled the slide back one more time so it would put a bullet in the chamber. After she released it, she made sure the safety was still in the up position and wrapped her hands around the weapon with her fingers outside the trigger guard. It was all a ritual her husband taught her so she would always know when the gun was definitely loaded and ready to shoot. She had rehearsed for this moment, and there would be no accidents.

She was aware that there was a faint shudder running through her body as she silently descended the stairs. She had rehearsed it, but not in her wildest dreams had she believed she would ever need to remove the gun from its box. It had all been to appease Henry and his close friend, Adam Callaway. The American astronaut was almost a member of the family, and they had named their son after him, but she had doubted his reasoning when he explained why they needed the gun. Now she understood, but it still scared her to have the gun ready for business.

At the bottom of the stairs, she stopped and listened. There was a faint breeze coming from somewhere, and the goosebumps that popped up on her arms were partly from the realization that she had left windows open for the fresh air. She wondered if she would be standing in the darkness at the bottom of the stairs if she had thought to close the windows for security. Symone was torn between being mad at herself and glad because leaving them open had enabled her to hear what had awakened her.

Her eyes had adjusted to the dark, and she was grateful that the slight glow in the east meant sunrise wasn't far away. A moment of regret slipped in because she knew she wouldn't be going back to bed, but it was pushed back by the unmistakable sound of someone or something blundering around on the back porch. This time there were no crashes from broken pottery, but the thumping of feet on wooden boards didn't sound like anything other than an animal of the two-legged variety.

It was only at that moment when Symone thought about her phone or even the security cameras Henry had installed. Their spotty WiFi had caused her to treat the cameras as an afterthought, but she had left her phone on the nightstand. Now she wished she could at least try to see what was out there using the phone app.

The kitchen was to her left on the other side of the formal dining room, and as she peered around the corner, she focused on the door to the kitchen. From her vantage point, she could see the door to the back porch, but it was still too dark to make out details. Something moved beyond the glass, but it was little more than a shadow to Symone. She would have to get closer, and she momentarily considered retreating to her bedroom to call the police.

The idea of someone getting inside because she wasn't strong enough spurred her into moving again. Keeping the gun aimed at the floor the way Henry had shown her, she moved sideways toward the kitchen door. She didn't know why she was walking sideways. It just seemed like the right thing to do, and it also seemed like she got there faster that way. One more step, and she would be able to see the back porch through the window, but she had to be careful not to give herself away.

Symone drew in a deep breath to calm herself and then took a quick look. She immediately ducked back into her hiding place. She needed a moment to understand what she had seen. She assumed it was a man because of his height, but she didn't just assume he was drunk. She knew he was because he literally fell from view in the brief moment when she had dared to step closer to the window. He had his back to her, so she didn't see his face, and when he fell, it was down the stairs to the flagstones that marked the path through the garden.

Another dash into the kitchen felt like the only way to keep him from coming back to the door, so Symone steeled her nerves and rushed into the room. This time she raised the Smith & Wesson and flipped the thumb safety downward. Following where she aimed, she went to the door and yanked it open using one hand. She was proud of herself for not shaking so hard that she would need to sit the gun down to open the door.

The sun was just beginning to peek over the horizon, and she had a good view of the path. Nothing was there. The pieces from the broken flower pots littered the floorboards of the porch, and a few had obviously fallen in the other direction to the ground below, but there was something else.

Keeping her eyes on the path and the gun ready to shoot, Symone lowered herself to her knees to get a closer look at the dark spot on the top step.

"Is that blood?" she said just above a whisper.

When she lifted her eyes from the spot again, there was more light, and she saw another large, dark spot on a flagstone. The bushes that bordered the garden swayed, and Symone backed into the open doorway as she stood straighter. She didn't know why, but she kept the gun aimed at the bushes. That was when she made the decision to let the police deal with why there was blood on her porch.

Less than ten minutes later, Symone had locked the doors, closed the windows, drawn the curtains, and returned to her place of defense facing the door to her porch. The gun rested on the kitchen counter next to her as she called the police, and as the phone rang, she forced herself to breathe evenly. She listened to it ring endlessly and realized she failed to calm herself with each ring because no one was answering. She hung up and immediately dialed again.

It took almost an hour to finally get the local constable on the phone, and getting angry at him did no good. He apologized for the delay but said they were quite busy and simply asked how he could help.

Symone drew on every bit of the calm she had seen in her husband and told the officer what had happened. He was a bit too interested in the part about her arming herself before going outside, and her temper almost got the best of her. She stopped herself just short of insulting his genealogy and simply asked when she could expect an investigator at her home. He told her it could be later that afternoon and hung up before she could come unglued, and that was what she did.

She was still beating the phone against the kitchen counter when she realized that Emily and Adam were standing at the kitchen door watching her. She discreetly slid the Smith & Wesson behind canisters of sugar and flour.

"Mummy?"

The one-word question from Emily was enough for her to get a grip on herself. Her children were standing between her and the back door, and she suddenly had a fear that something would burst through the door at any second. She moved to the other side of them and shepherded the children into the dining room.

"Let's get you some breakfast."

"We aren't going to eat in the kitchen?" asked Emily.

Symone felt a small flash of pride in her daughter when she realized Adam was dressed and even had matching socks.

"You helped your brother get dressed this morning? Well, you're a big girl now, so we can have breakfast in the dining room."

The truth was, Symone wanted them to be as far from the back porch as they could get, and she surprised them when she further announced they could take their breakfast upstairs to their bedrooms.

******

* * *

It was late afternoon when the sound of tires crunched over the gravel driveway to the Tisdal home. Symone had passed the time getting dressed and then waiting in front of the television watching the news. She didn't like what she had seen. After the previous night, her imagination was connecting dots that created a picture she didn't want to see, but she saw it anyway.

Symone understood the news stories for what they were. A warning about things to come. Most of her friends and country neighbors were the type who would write off the first events as nothing more than tabloid journalism. Things that they had seen in movies that didn't happen in real life but were happening close to home.

The first time she had heard of cannibalism in a major city was when a homeless man in Miami was found eating another homeless man behind a dumpster. He might have been naked, but she didn't read the whole story. It was just too violent and sensational. She had only read enough to know he was strung out on something like meth or PCP, and it had taken multiple police officers to restrain him. In the end, they had been forced to fatally shoot him.

That had been years ago when there had been a spate of such stories. The fascination with television shows and movies about zombies was at a peak, and whenever it happened in real life, people asked the obvious question. Could it really happen? The stories were eventually explained away and forgotten.

There was something different about the new reports. Maybe it was the way they didn't get blown out of proportion. As a matter of fact, they were almost secretive about the details.

An upscale private school in London had enough money to keep some of the details out of the news, but even threats of lawsuits didn't stop all of the leaks, and the public heard enough of the details for Symone to wonder if it might be real this time.

Her husband was a famous astronaut and just the kind of family the school wanted to draw into its fold. The Headmaster had sent stacks of invitations to the Tisdal family, inviting them to bring the children by for a tour of the campus. Symone doubted they would be taking him up on his invitation now that there was the cloud of a murder hanging over the school.

It seemed the janitor had something in common with the homeless man in Miami. Not the drug habit, according to the scant reports, but his preference for dining on living flesh. What caught Symone's eye wasn't the gory details but the fact that it wasn't behind a dumpster or in one of the endless cellar rooms of the school. It was in plain sight with no attempt to disguise the crime.

The short report in the news said it was between classes when the halls were crowded with students, most of whom were on their way to the dining hall. The janitor emerged from a custodial locker feeling ill, and when he stumbled into the river of students who choked the busy corridor, he fell on one young boy at random.

The students pushed at the others around them in a fruitless attempt to put distance between themselves and the warm arterial spray. The brutality of the attack was perhaps what made it appear unbelievable. The fact that it was an isolated incident was what kept it from becoming the warning sign the public needed. If the police had been quick to inform the media of their discovery of the janitor's mother, a few more people would have become as wary as Symone Tisdal, but the connection was slow in coming. Apparently, she and her son were both victims of the same infected person. The partially consumed remains of the mother were strewn around her house, undiscovered for almost two days after the attack at the school. Fear and panic would come much later when it was too late.

The sound of the police car was a welcome interruption to the news broadcasts, and she greeted the officer outside the front door of the house.

"What was it, heavy traffic?" she asked sarcastically.

The first officer who got out of the vehicle caught the brunt of her anger. He was young, maybe no more than twenty-five years old. There was a slightly older female officer getting out of the car from the driver's side. Both kept neutral expressions on their faces, perhaps because they understood Symone's frustration.

"Good afternoon, Mrs. Tisdal," said the young male officer. She barely heard him because he spoke softly and was obviously ready to be attacked. He had his hat in his hands and nervously rotated it by its brim.

The female officer came to his defense.

"Mrs. Tisdal, I can assure you that you would understand our delay if you had seen the cause for yourself."

Symone opened her mouth to renew her verbal assault, but she noticed the female officer had a new bandage on her right arm that extended from below the cuff of her shirt. It had a reddish tint that reminded her of what she had seen on the porch.

She let out an exasperated sigh and said, "Well, you're here now, so we might as well take a walk out back."

The pool of blood that stained the boards had turned black in the hours since she had first examined it. The weather was a bit cool, but there were still flies walking around on it. They swirled away when the trio approached from the garden.

"There was a man," said Symone. "He was on the porch and then went that way toward the woods." She gestured toward the trees that bordered an area of nationally protected forest.

"Can you describe him?" asked the female officer. She pulled out a notepad and pen. "Was he possibly injured and just seeking assistance?"

"I didn't see his face. He had his back to the window when I saw him, but he was either injured or drunk." She pointed toward the bloodstain. "My guess would be injured. Should I have helped him?"

The two officers appeared uncomfortable by her question and shared an unspoken exchange with their eyes. Symone sensed that this was a moment they had prepared for during their drive to her home.

The male officer once again deferred to the female with a glance in her direction.

"Mrs. Tisdal, you did the right thing. We are only at liberty to tell you there were other calls to the police last night before yours, which is why we were delayed in our response to your call. Not all of them went well."

"What does that mean?" Symone was suddenly more frightened than she had been.

"You said you didn't see his face. Is that a security camera above your door?" asked the young male officer. He had been busy studying the bloodstain and smaller black spots on the garden flagstones but seemed to be taking in every detail of the scene.

Symone was a bit embarrassed because she had forgotten to check the camera. Her husband was an astronaut, and she had ignored the simplest of technology he had installed.

"I'm so sorry, officer. Yes, and I had totally forgotten to check it. My husband made sure it would record all the time because some cameras don't get everything if they depend on movement. It automatically erases everything about every four or five days, so it would all still be there."

"Can we see it?" he asked.

Symone led them up the steps and to the back door of the kitchen. They stepped over the dried blood and broken pottery, and she noticed the female officer was glancing in the direction of the bushes that had moved the night before.

"Did you see something?"

"I don't know," said the officer, but for the first time since they had arrived, Symone noticed something she had seldom seen before. The officers were wearing sidearms, and they had both moved their right hands to rest them on the grips of their weapons.

"Mummy? What's happening?"

Emily had appeared in the doorway just as the two officers made a move toward the back of the garden. Symone quickly crossed the porch and gathered Emily into her arms.

"Back inside, Emily. Where's your brother?"

Symone suddenly got a bad feeling about Adam.

"He's looking at the police car," said Emily.

It didn't take much to get Symone into motion, but this time she moved even faster than she knew she could. Something felt terribly wrong, and the officers felt it too. The young male officer seemed undecided about which way to go, and at the last second, he chose to follow Symone.

When they crossed the dining room, they could see the front door at the foot of the stairs was standing open, and they didn't see Adam until they could also see beyond the gravel driveway. There were people on the other side of the police car, and they appeared to be injured. Adam was standing at the top of the brick steps on the front porch watching as the people walked awkwardly toward the house.

"Stay back," yelled the young male officer as he passed Adam and took up a protective stance between Adam and the closest of the strangers.

His hand had gone to the gun again, but this time he drew it and took aim. His target was a man who was probably in his early fifties, and the man was already in need of medical attention. He walked forward with a heavy limp and didn't heed the warning to stay back.

"I said stay back," warned the officer for a second time.

Symone watched in disbelief as the officer brought his weapon down and shoved it back into the holster. The man was so close to the bottom of the steps...close to the officer...close to her son.

She didn't even remember picking up the gun she had put behind the canisters earlier, but she had done it when she ran through the kitchen on her way to the front door. It felt heavier than before, but she found herself automatically going through the ritual Henry had her practice over and over. She verified that it was loaded and that there was a bullet in the chamber. She flipped the safety downward and brought the gun to eye level.

The officer had taken a step forward to intercept the strange man as he stumbled toward Adam. Symone was aware that she was aiming a gun over her son's head, but she had practiced enough to know the recoil would pull the barrel upward. She was ready to take the shot until the officer moved squarely into her sights.

For a third time, he told the man to stay back, but this time he reached out and put his hand on the man's chest and pushed. He was surprised by how easily he could push the man away, but the second surprise was that the man grabbed the officer's forearm with both hands. The officer was pulled forward as the man fell backward, and because there was a gentle slope where the steps met with the gravel driveway, the officer was unable to stop himself from falling on top of the man. That was when the screaming began...and gunshots.

From somewhere behind the house, there were three shots. Symone had forgotten that the female officer had been drawn toward the bushes, and she was sure the shots had come from there.

Emily screamed for her mother and ran from the dining room out to where Symone was trying to reacquire her target. She slammed into Symone's hip, making her pull the trigger. The blast from the muzzle of the 9mm gun was deafening, and all Symone could think was, "Where did the bullet go?"

Adam was on the ground now, and Symone saw that he was only inches from where the officer lay face down on top of the injured man. Blood was everywhere, but it seemed like most of it was across her son's back.

Symone was torn between pulling herself free from Emily or taking her daughter with her. Emily didn't understand what had happened until she saw Adam lying prone at the bottom of the steps, but she couldn't stop herself from grasping at her mother for protection.

The screaming had never stopped. It had only been drowned out by the deafening crack of the Smith & Wesson, but as the ringing in her ears subsided, Symone understood that it was the police officer who was screaming.

Anyone who has ever been bitten by an animal knows that the action is terribly invasive. The victim of a bite has to wrap his mind around the pain, as well as the amount of blood that erupts from the wound. The invasion is compounded when the bite continues. In this case, the strange man had his teeth sunk deeply into the wrist of the officer, and he was pulling his head backward in an attempt to tear away a mouthful of his arm.

Adam lifted his face from the gravel even as more blood flew from the melee that was happening only inches away. He was sprayed again, and he cried out for his mother.

Symone dropped her gun, and in a combination of crawling and falling down the porch steps, she dragged Emily to where Adam had pushed himself up onto his elbows. She didn't even notice when she skinned her knees on the edges of the bricks. She kept Emily under her right arm away from where the officer fought to free himself from the other man, and with her left arm, she scooped up her son.

In a blur, Symone was on her feet and running with a child on each hip. When she was far enough away, she was able to stop. Emily allowed her mother to let go of her long enough for them both to tend to Adam. He was crying uncontrollably as Symone spun him around to the left and the right, running her hands over the places where she saw the most blood. With relief, she discovered that she hadn't shot him, and the blood wasn't his.

It was like coming out of a thick fog. Her skinned and bloody children stood beside her as she knelt on the sharp gravel. The screaming had been replaced by a mewing sound that came from the lips of the police officer. He was on his back now, and the other man knelt over him. He was still burying his face into the officer's forearm. The officer seemed to be watching the man even as the crazed stranger sat back on his heels and chewed. His body had gone into shock, and he was fading fast.

More gunshots rang out from nearby, and the man fell away from the officer. Symone didn't know how she did it, but she somehow forced herself to move again. Maybe it was the sharp interruption of the gunshots, but as she scooped her children up for a second time and ran back to the steps, the female officer ran past her toward her partner. Symone had dropped her gun at the top of the front porch steps, and she put Adam down just long enough to pick it up.

Maybe it was because she knew it was what Henry would do, or maybe it was because something was so different about the attacker, and there were more of them coming, but something inside of her took control. Symone stepped inside the house and put the children down at the bottom of the stairs to the second floor. She put her face in front of Emily's.

"Take your brother to Mummy and Daddy's room. Lock the door when you get there. Don't open the door until I come back for you."

Emily opened her mouth to protest, but Symone put a finger across her lips.

"Your father would want you to be a big girl right now, and I need for you to protect your brother. He's scared."

She only watched for a moment as Emily straightened her shoulders and took her little brother's hand. She led him up the stairs to the second floor, but Symone knew she didn't have time to waste watching them reach the top. She turned back to the open door at the front of the house and rushed outside to help the female officer.

Nothing that had happened from the time she had been awakened during the night to the moment she rushed outside had been what she expected, but if she could mark a moment in time when everything made the least amount of sense, it would be when she rejoined the battle.

There were at least six people in the field on the far side of the driveway, and they were struggling through the tall grass as they walked toward the house. A fence at the edge of the property would slow down their arrival, but judging by their difficulty just walking, Symone wondered if they could climb over the low fence. Her question was answered when she saw another man flip over the wire when he walked into it as if it wasn't even there.

Next was her car with the police vehicle parked close behind it, and there was a woman who appeared to be unable to find her way around them. She was wedged between them, and the harder she tried to get through the gap, the more entrapped she became.

Most confusing of all was the scene where the female officer had gone to the aid of her partner. She knelt at his side and appeared to be doing chest compressions to save his life. At least, that was what Symone thought the woman was doing. It took a minute to understand that she did have her hands on his chest but that he was holding them there while she was attempting to free herself from his grip.

The man who had bitten the male officer was on all fours facing away from Symone, but he was laboriously pushing himself to a standing position as he turned toward the officers on his left.

Symone had seen the way he had torn into the flesh of the male officer, and she had seen the female officer converge on him as she put at least three bullets into him. He shouldn't be getting up was all she could think, but Symone made a mental note that she didn't need to understand it all. She just needed to help.

She felt totally detached from reality as she raised her gun and aimed first at the strange man. Because she was at the top of the steps, it was an easy shot, and the bullet hit the man just above the left ear. He collapsed away from the two officers, and before he reached the gravel driveway face first, Symone was already lining up for her next target.

Looking down the sights of the Smith & Wesson, she saw the young male officer's face, and it wasn't the face of the nervous young man who had fiddled with his hat less than an hour ago. It was feral, and it was the face of an animal. She pulled the trigger, and his head bucked backward. The female officer was pulling to free her hands, so she fell away from him as he lost his grip. Her face was tear-streaked and bloody, and she crab-walked on her hands and feet away from his body. The whole time she kept her eyes on her former partner. Symone didn't see any new wounds on her, but the bandage that had protruded from her sleeve was a deep red.

Guttural growls were coming from the other side of the fence, and the woman by the cars had fallen into the gap where the front bumper of the police car almost touched the rear bumper of Symone's car. Her weight had caused her to become so wedged between them that she wouldn't be getting free anytime soon.

The people on the other side of the fence were all gathered in one spot and leaning against the top wire as if it wasn't supposed to be there. Those in the back were pushing forward so hard that it was forcing the wire to cut deeply into the midsections of those in front.

The shock that had held the female officer weak and immobile broke loose, and she screamed at Symone, "What's happening? Why are they doing this?"

Her voice was high and shrill, and for some reason, it caused the group on the other side of the fence to become even more agitated. They raised their arms in the direction of the officer, waving them at her as if she would come to them if they couldn't get to her.

The man who had flipped over the fence reappeared at the back of the police car and stumbled across the gravel driveway. The crunching of his feet was drowned out by the chorus of groans at the fence, but he was already reaching forward with his hands.

Symone felt calm despite already seeing and doing things that were totally foreign to her. She raised the gun again and fired a shot in the direction of the man. The side rear window of the police car exploded, but the man didn't even flinch. She adjusted her aim to the right and fired again. This time her bullet hit him squarely in the middle of the chest, just as Henry had taught her. The force punched him back the way he had come, and he landed in a sitting position behind the car. Symone kept the gun aimed at him, but she was momentarily stunned into a world that was separate from what was happening around her.

Her hearing was gone. The pounding in her ears drowned out everything.

"This must be what it's like to have a stroke," she thought.

There was so much death in front of her, already more than she had ever seen, and she had delivered some of it. Gunshots had slammed into bodies, and sound had exploded against her eardrums. When Henry had taught her how to shoot, she had worn bulky ear protection, so the violence was a surprise to her. Now she was staring at a man she had shot in the chest, and he was leaning to his right in an effort to push himself from the ground.

Behind the man, there were two people who had been eviscerated by the fence. The wire had cut so far into their bodies that they were only inches from being cut in half, but they still squirmed against the wire. Once it had cut through the material of their clothing, their skin offered no resistance to the pressure from behind, and the sawing motion of their struggles sliced organs as easily as paper.

Symone's hearing seemed to return just as the wire snapped through their spinal cords. She was surprised in a detached way that she could hear it happen. Still connected by muscle tissue, sinew, and clothing, their upper bodies slumped over the fence and hung loosely toward the ground. She lowered the gun and watched as everything seemed to be moving more slowly.

Another series of pops interrupted the distant world where Symone had gone. The female officer was on both knees with her sidearm raised. One by one, her well-aimed shots hit the heads of her targets. Her training had been the same as what Henry had taught Symone, but she was enraged. She aimed every shot at their heads, and every shot was accurate. Her last target was the woman wedged between the cars, but she had one more shot in mind. Symone didn't know why she did it, but the officer put the barrel of the gun to her own face and pulled the trigger.

Symone welcomed the darkness that followed.

2

Shire County Dorset

Southern England - The Beginning

While Symone had been drinking coffee and waiting for the police, the first tourists of the day were arriving at Stonehenge only thirty miles to the north. Around the same time she fainted on her own front steps, reporters and camera crews were broadcasting events from the famous tourist attraction. They were sure the reports would shake the country. Unknown to them during the first hour, similar accounts were filling the airwaves around the world.

Symone awoke to the realization that the sensational broadcasts were as honest and accurate as the reporters claimed. All she had to do was open her eyes to see it in her own driveway. It was ironic that she lived far enough from a metropolitan area that her neighbors who watched the broadcasts might doubt what they saw. They didn't know it was happening practically in their own backyards.

Everyone for miles around heard the gunshots, and some people even tried to call the police. One after the other, they hung up their phones when the incessant ringing went unanswered. Some tried to call again, but they eventually gave up. Whatever it had been, they lost interest and had better things to do.

Symone's next thought was her children, but on the ground only a few yards away was what she had last seen when she passed out. She felt like her heart was in her throat, and before she was able to gather

15

enough strength to get to her feet, her emotions welled up, and she was wracked with sobs. She cried so hard that her stomach was gripped by spasms, and she threw up the little bit of toast and jam she had eaten that morning.

The sobs and spasms eventually subsided, and Symone thought about what she needed to do while still lying at the top of the steps. She kept her eyes open as she thought and took in the sight of the devastated bodies around her. She could see all of them, but her eyes kept going back to the female officer.

"Why did you do that?" she asked. "I still needed you."

Symone had a moment of clarity about her own selfishness that brought with it a massive wave of guilt. The young woman had been so traumatized that she had taken her own life without hesitation, and Symone was angry at her. A psychiatrist or mental health counselor would have told her it was a normal reaction to be angry. The guilt that followed would be expected too. Then their advice would be to get over it and take care of business. Right now, that business was the safety of her children.

She wiped the sleeve of her shirt across her eyes and then her mouth, and she pushed herself up from the cold bricks. Flies buzzed nearby. Otherwise, there was nothing but silence.

Her eyes focused on her own gun, and as she reached for it, she felt like it wouldn't be enough. The matte black Glock belonging to the female officer was about ten feet away. The recoil had caused it to flip in her direction. Symone was relieved that it was closer, but the relief was short-lived because she needed the ammunition too. She had her own supply, but if she needed more guns, reason told her more bullets would be a good idea. Besides, the magazine from a Smith & Wesson wouldn't fit in the Glock even though they used the same ammunition.

It was difficult, but she managed to keep her eyes averted from the face of the officer as she removed four magazines from her belt. Symone forced herself to collect them from the male officer when she was done. She made a pile of guns and magazines at the top of the stairs before going to their car. If she was right, there would be more ammunition in the trunk. Her gun held seventeen rounds, and each of the Glocks had fifteen round magazines. That meant she had well over one hundred rounds in the magazines. She was thinking clearly enough to know it would be a missed chance to resupply if she didn't at least check the car while she could.

It turned out to be a good decision. The case was too heavy for

Symone to carry very far, especially if the three of them would be walking, but she would leave with as much as she could.

"Leave?"

The word hung in the air. Symone didn't realize she had to take the children and leave until that moment. She had a fair supply of food in the house, and there was a well for water, but something told her it wasn't safe to stay. They couldn't just barricade themselves inside the house until help arrived.

"Or could we?"

Symone pictured herself sitting down at the kitchen table with her husband and asking him the questions.

"Should we stay here with shelter, food, water, and weapons? Should we take what we can carry and leave? If we leave, where should we go?"

There were too many gaps in the information for her imaginary husband to give her advice, which answered the question for her. She didn't have to decide yet, at least not at the moment. She decided to pack as many supplies as they could carry, and if it turned out to be a better idea to leave, they would be ready.

Emily and Adam were still sequestered safely in the bedroom. Symone wanted desperately to get out of her blood-stained clothes. Still, she decided to take advantage of the few minutes she would have to get organized without them under her feet.

She first went to the cool cellar and dug through her husband's camping gear. Backpacks, a small tent, and sleeping bags went into a pile. A propane cookstove and lantern were next. When she added the propane canisters and flashlights, Symone stopped and studied the collection. When she mentally added the guns, ammunition, food, and water, she reached a conclusion. They weren't walking.

In the end, she decided the only thing to do was to load the car with everything they would need if they chose to go. They could determine where they needed to go after they ran into the authorities. She reasoned that there would undoubtedly be a coordinated response to whatever was happening. Once they learned she was the wife of Henry Tisdal, she and the children would be whisked away to a safe place.

She would need Emily's help. Although her daughter was highly mature when looking after her little brother, menial tasks like hauling gear to the car induced a flurry of complaints. Symone gave it further consideration after she remembered her daughter would see the carnage in the driveway if she helped. It was bad enough to have to see it herself. Making her daughter walk past the bodies repeatedly was not a good idea. Instead, she announced that the children could have a full day of movies in Emily's room and that she would provide the popcorn. With any luck, she would keep them away from the front door. As an added incentive, she told Emily she would be busy cleaning the cellar. If Emily wanted to join her, she would be welcome. That was all she needed to ensure Emily stayed in her bedroom.

Once the door to Emily's room was closed, Symone knew her daughter well enough to know it would stay shut unless one of them had to use the bathroom. She rushed to her room and hurriedly changed into a pair of jeans, a sweatshirt, and a pair of sturdy hiking boots. The blood stains weren't from her or from her children, so the clothes she was wearing went into the garbage can. After she was changed, she felt less vulnerable and was ready to take on the remainder of the day.

Her leg muscles burned in protest, but she attacked the cellar stairs repeatedly until all of the gear was in the kitchen. She filled the backpacks with canned and boxed foods and organized everything before she opened the back door for the first time since the confrontation had started out front. Then she remembered the first shots she had heard.

The man she had seen the night before was lying on the flagstone path near the bushes at the back of the garden. She didn't need to check to see if he was alive because it was apparent that the officer had been an accurate marksman even from a distance. Symone decided it would be easy to ignore his prone figure as she carried gear to the car. The front driveway would be the hard part.

"To hell with it," she said out loud.

Symone sat down the bundle she had in her arms and walked at a brisk pace to her car. It was a blue SUV with plenty of cargo space, and she would need every inch of it. She would also prefer to simplify the loading process. She avoided glancing in the direction of the bodies that littered the driveway as she climbed in behind the wheel and started the engine.

She cut the wheel to the left without even touching the brake pedal, and she accelerated toward the frail wooden fence surrounding the garden. The woman wedged between her rear bumper and the front of the police car rode with her for a few feet before falling off. The car crushed the gate, and Symone drove straight to the back porch. She saw with satisfaction that she had missed the tomato plants. Tomatoes were hard enough to grow without running them over with a car. They didn't really matter anymore, but Symone felt like it was a small win for her.

It took half an hour to load everything, but Symone turned on the small kitchen TV to keep an eye on the news broadcasts as she went back and forth. The networks played the same video clips over and over again. There were medical and police vehicles driving at high speeds to and from Stonehenge. Still, very little was known about what had happened there. Symone was reasonably sure that she already knew.

Her hopes began to dim when a banner crossed the bottom of the screen. It always seemed that those banners started in the middle, so she had to wait for it to come back around again to catch the whole message. A list of roads that were closed to all traffic except emergency vehicles scrolled by. They included every road she could choose no matter which direction she wanted to go.

She had given it some thought as she carried survival gear to the car. She thought they could go north to the suburbs above London. Her parents had a small place there before they passed away. It was still empty because she had never gotten around to dealing with the emotional chore of clearing it out. It would be cramped, but they would be nearer to services provided by the government. She also wondered if it would be safer to keep more distance between herself and the metropolitan areas because there would be less chance of conflict.

"What am I thinking?" she asked herself. "Look at your own driveway. I'll bet there aren't many people who could say they have over a half-dozen dead people in their driveway."

It was hard to imagine anyone else could be going through something similar, but it stopped her cold in her tracks when she considered it. Of all the people in the world or even just southern England, she couldn't have been singled out for this. Nothing could be drawing these strange, mangled-looking people to her doorstep alone. At one point, she stood on her back porch and faced to the northeast. Her closest neighbors lived in that direction. She wondered how they were doing.

When she was done loading the car, she found herself staring at the TV, not really seeing or hearing the news anymore. The banner continued its path along the bottom of the screen, delivering messages that were becoming all too familiar. Road closures went by again, and Symone saw the banner as some kind of fence that had gone up around her. She couldn't go to her parents' place. The routes toward the Isle of Wight and Weymouth were closed, so she couldn't go to the Isle of Portland. For some reason, she felt like both places were isolated enough to defend.

"Where did I see that?"

So much news had been broadcast already that she didn't know if she had figured some of it out herself. Maybe it was because she had heard her husband talk about how England would defend itself from attack. Still, she couldn't recall ever having this discussion with him. Once again, she asked herself what he would do if he was at home right now.

That thought had just crossed her mind when an international broadcast cut in on the local news. It reminded her that the day had gone by, and the sun was already dipping low in the west. It was the middle of the night in Baikonur, Kazakhstan. She was very familiar with the images of the Cosmodrome, but she had never seen two rockets ready to launch minutes apart. The banner said there were problems with security at the Russian space center and that the launches were threatened.

Symone turned up the volume and caught the tail end of the report just as the network cut back to local news. She hadn't been worried for Henry since the day he had launched into space. He had told her the launch and reentry were the only dangerous parts of the job, so she seldom worried in between. Crews were sitting atop both of those rockets waiting for the most challenging part of their mission, and there was a security problem totally beyond their control. If it was the same thing as what had happened in her driveway, it could only get worse for those crews.

Something made her snap out of her trance. Her husband had told her she could get so deep in thought at times that she resembled a statue, and he fully expected to see pigeons perched on her head sooner or later. She self-consciously checked her surroundings to see if someone was there and realized that wasn't a luxury she could afford anymore.

As if to confirm her concerns, there was movement at the edge of the trees not far from the body she had chosen to ignore. Two men stumbled from the trees. They were walking parallel to her, and they hadn't seen her yet. Even from a distance, she could see they were both horribly disfigured or injured.

The back door was open about six inches, and she wasn't sure if it would attract their attention if she closed it, but she felt too vulnerable without its protection. She took the chance and reached for it as slowly as she could while keeping her eyes on the two men. It swung quietly closed, and it made the faintest click as the lock engaged. There was no indication that either of them heard the sound, but she was horrified to see three more of them come out of the trees. One of them was walking straight toward the house. The other two appeared to be following the first pair.

Symone very slowly allowed her knees to bend, and she sank below the window level on the door. When she was low enough, she crawled from the kitchen into the dining room. Her only thought was that she had to get upstairs and make sure the children stayed quiet. This was one time when Emily couldn't just appear behind her.

Once she was away from the door, she ran the rest of the way and didn't stop until she was at Emily's door. She listened and heard them laughing about something in a movie. That meant she would have time to reach her room and watch the strange men from above.

The master bedroom was over the kitchen, so she could gently part the curtains and see where they were. Four were in the field and moving away from the house. They were going directly toward her nearest neighbors. The fifth man was standing at the bottom of the steps by the back door. As far as she could tell, he wasn't doing anything except standing there. She noticed how much he slumped at the shoulders. It wasn't just bad posture. The man didn't seem to have the ability to stand up straight. She wasn't sure how she knew that, but she was sure of it.

He turned abruptly in the same direction as the other men and stumbled away as if he had simply gone the wrong way. Symone heard a faint popping noise and realized it was coming from her neighbor's house. She also understood that the noise was why the five men were walking that way.

"Oh, no. Oh God, no."

Symone imagined what it must have sounded like when she and the officer had fired their guns. From a distance, it must have sounded similar to the popping noise she could hear coming from her neighbor's house.

Symone ran from her room and found where she had left her cell phone. She quickly pulled up her neighbor's telephone number. She couldn't remember if she had ever called them before, and they had only exchanged numbers once when they had run into each other at the market. They were a lovely old couple whose son was in the military. She remembered how excited they were when they had learned they lived near Henry Tisdal. He would surely be knighted one day, and they would be able to tell everyone they were friends.

Symone had resisted efforts by everyone in the small town to turn Henry into a celebrity, but they were nice enough and typically reserved. Now Symone wished she had put them in her favorites so she wouldn't have to find their number.

The phone rang three times before an angry male voice answered. All he did was yell, "I'm busy," and immediately hung up.

Symone dialed again. As soon as the call was answered, she yelled first.

"Mr. Clark, don't hang up. You must stop shooting immediately. Stop shooting and go to the cellar. Just hide...there are more coming your way. They're attracted to the sound of your gun."

The pause on the other end of the phone gave Symone hope that her neighbor was at least going to listen, but she hadn't considered what had already happened. She was talking to Mr. Clark as if he didn't know what was going on.

"They killed Helen. They killed my Helen. Now I'm going to kill all of them."

She stared at the phone after he hung up again. She could hear the gunshots resume, and she could tell by the shorter space of time between pops that he had more targets. The men outside her house hadn't even reached him yet, and there was hardly a pause between shots.

The realization that the firing was continuous made her count the shots. She mentally added ten to the starting count even though she knew it had already been at least that many before she started counting. She couldn't tell for sure, but maybe it was more than one gun. She hoped so for Mr. Clark's sake.

After a quick glance at the surroundings, Symone raised the window a few inches and put her ear to the gap. The sound of the gunshots was immediately sharper. After a few moments, she was able to reasonably say the gunshots were from different guns, and they were coming from different directions. The advice she had just given to an angry man had fallen on deaf ears because he had already lost his wife. If she had seen them kill one of her children, she would be shooting too.

She hadn't seen that, though. She had seen them converging on her four-year-old. She had seen them kill the police officer, but she had been lucky so far.

"Would I be lucky on the road? Would I run into rescuers or monsters?"

When she thought about it more, she realized she had been luckier than she had a right to believe. She had gone out after the confrontation in her driveway, brought her car to the back door, and she had loaded it. If those strangers…those monsters had come along while she was loading the car, then she would be the one hiding in the cellar as they attacked her doors.

The decision was far easier to live with than she expected. She had to get the gear back inside without being seen. When she loaded the car, she had been barely vigilant. As she unloaded it, she would need to be stealthy. If they couldn't leave, she had to make sure none of those people knew they were in the house.

After a quick visit with the children, Symone went charging back down the stairs. Emily and Adam were only mildly interested in why she dropped by. They were so engrossed in their movie that they didn't want to be bothered.

It took longer to unload the car than it had to load it because between trips outside, she ran back upstairs and spent a few minutes surveying the landscape around their home. The trees beyond the garden were a protected natural preserve. To her left was a series of broad, open fields before another stretch of rolling countryside that was occupied by primarily small trees. Her neighbor's house wasn't visible to her, but she knew it was just barely out of sight.

In the opposite direction where another neighbor lived, the terrain was similar but slightly more wooded. She was surprised that she could hear the gunshots from that direction because the house was further away.

Not seeing movement in any direction, she made another frantic dash outside and gathered together the next armful of gear. She was breathing heavily, but she told herself there would be time to breathe and rest later. After almost an hour of unloading, she locked the back door behind her and slumped down against it. She still had to get everything back downstairs, but she felt like there was more she could do to be prepared.

Symone sat and rested longer than she had intended, and she was startled when she lifted her head from her hands and saw the kitchen window over the sink across the room. The darkness on the other side of the window was foreign because somehow, the nightmare that had begun last night had lasted an entire day. She was sitting on the floor of a brightly lit kitchen with madness roaming around outside.

She practically lunged at the light switch. The darkness of the kitchen was only partially complete, and Symone remembered the porch light was on. She slapped at that switch, and the world was instantly darker.

"Do I have to think of everything?" she asked herself, and she knew the answer already. Yes, because forgetting anything might mean the death of her children, and she was not going to have Henry come home to that.

"Okay. If I have to think of everything, then what next?"

Thinking about Henry reminded her that she hadn't checked the news networks for a long time. In the dark, she grabbed a blanket from the pile of things she had carried in from the car, and put it on the table. She pulled the TV from the counter and stretched the cord as far as it could go until she could slide it under the kitchen table. The blanket was spread over the table so it would block the light when she turned on the TV, and she recoiled at what she saw.

The banner across the bottom of the screen had one horrible message after the next, but the one that struck her the hardest was the message that said the two Russian spacecraft had been destroyed on the launchpads, and the crews had died in the explosions. The heartbreaking news was followed by reports of savage murders and cannibalism. Symone was crying for the second time within the same day.

That wasn't her personality. She cried from time to time just like anyone else, but she usually only let herself cry once, got it all out, and then attacked the problem. It was just that this day wasn't ending, and the problem was attacking her.

She eventually turned the TV off and crawled out from under the table. She felt cried out and weak, but the germ of a plan was forming. Something told her this day was just a taste of what was to come, and if this was the appetizer, she needed to figure out what the next course would be. Most of all, what could she expect from the main course?

******

* * *

Symone decided they had to dig in. If she had seen the whole thing coming, she would be able to use a hammer to nail the doors shut or cover the windows with boards, but she couldn't take that chance. The pounding would be as bad as shooting at them. The thought made her stop and listen. There was no sound of shooting coming from anywhere. She didn't think it was because there were no more targets. From what she had seen on TV, there would be targets for a long time.

The camping gear was back in the cellar, so she took some time to get the children some snacks and get them settled in to watch another movie. As they watched the opening scenes, she discreetly unscrewed the lightbulbs throughout the house. She used thumbtacks and duct tape to seal the edges of curtains around all the windows. She couldn't go outside and test her work, but she was positive she had blocked off any light that could be seen coming from inside the house.

Having an astronaut for a husband meant she had picked up some valuable tips over the years. One of them was to use a red light at night because it wouldn't harm her ability to see in the dark the way a white light would. It wasn't difficult to find the materials to make a red flashlight. All she had to do was dig through the supplies from the last birthday party. A red balloon stretched over the end of her flashlight worked nicely.

Moving quickly, Symone went from room to room, gathering everything she could think of that might be helpful. If she had to consider its usefulness, then it wasn't needed. From her bedroom, blankets, pillows, and clothing were gathered in a pile. When she went to the top of the stairs, she just tossed everything over the railing of the stairs. It occurred to her that they might still be forced from the house, so she tossed suitcases over the railing. She used careful aim to make sure they landed quietly on top of the pile of blankets.

She decided to take a quick shower because she didn't know when the next one would be. She didn't waste a lot of time luxuriating under the hot spray because she worried the whole time that she was missing something. Either that or she was being the idiot woman in a "B movie" plot by taking a shower. At any moment, the curtain would be ripped back, and she would become the next bloody victim. When she was done, the fresh clothes gave her renewed energy, and she lost all track of time. It probably wouldn't have mattered that it was already past midnight because she wanted to be done before it was too late.

Before leaving the bathroom, Symone packed everything into an overnight bag as if she would be away on a long trip. They had a sink in the cellar, and they would brush their teeth and sponge bathe on schedule for as long as they could. She had a suspicion that not everyone would be so lucky.

When she peeked in on the children, she found they had fallen asleep in front of the TV, so it was an easy decision to leave Emily's room for last. She practically emptied Adam's room of clothes, bedding, and his favorite toys. If she could find a way to make him last more than a day in the cellar, she would try.

The kitchen was next. Henry didn't put a refrigerator in the cellar because it stayed relatively cool down there the whole year-round. If she could get her refrigerator down the stairs on her own, she would do it. Symone imagined it would arrive at the bottom the same way as everything else that she simply threw from the top. Fortunately, when she did an inventory of the canned goods in the pantry, she estimated that they had enough food to last a month if she made modest meals. Bread, cheese, butter, and some refrigerated foods would keep long enough to use it all, but it would go first.

Her watch said it was four AM when she finished getting everything into the cellar she could think of. The case of ammunition put a real strain on her back, and she wanted to rest, but she didn't know how much time she had. There was also one last thing she wanted to do. The cellar door was just a door. There wasn't anything special about it except that it opened outward, and her plan had slowly grown throughout the night. If it opened inward to the cellar, the idea would be less effective because she needed to block the door with something heavy.

When she made a mental list of things to remember about the door, the number one item was that nothing could get in, but they could get out when the time came that they should leave. She got a beer out of the refrigerator and sat down at the small table that was reserved for breakfast and meals while Henry was away. When he was home, they felt that it was important that they all sit together as a family in the dining room. As she sipped the beer from the bottle, she studied the refrigerator and the cellar door. They were located directly across from each other.

"This could work," she said.

It really wasn't that much of a plan when she thought about it, but she admitted that was what the coyote always thought when he drew up another plan to catch the roadrunner. Adam was particularly fond of the American cartoons, and his namesake had a lot to do with that.

26

Adam Callaway delighted in bringing her son new copies of his favorites.

The refrigerator sat on four tiny wheels that were surprisingly cooperative. If she could get a rope around it near the bottom, she felt like she could pull the refrigerator to the door until it blocked it. From what she remembered of the day before about the mindless people out front, if they couldn't climb over a low fence or navigate around a parked car, it wasn't likely that they would know to move a refrigerator to get to the door behind it. There was only one problem. The rope and winch were outside in the toolshed.

Henry liked to tinker with his tools, so he had a variety of things that she wouldn't mind having in the cellar with them, but to get the refrigerator across the room, she would need the rope and the winch. As a matter of fact, she could use the winch to keep the refrigerator securely against the door. Getting those things meant going out in the open again, and the shed was at the edge of the property by the trees. It would have to wait until daylight because there was no way she would go out there during the night.

******

Her neck hurt from having nothing but her forearm for her pillow, and the circulation had been cut off to her hand. She sat up, having slept at the table, and shook her arm to get the circulation moving again. The pins and needles didn't bother her as much as the amount of light in the room. If that much sunlight could get in, then any light inside could be seen outside. She needed to be done before dark.

The first thing Symone did was ensure there was nothing happening outside. She checked from every window before going upstairs to wake the children. It was also time to talk with them about where they were going and why. It wasn't going to be easy because she knew she would be forced to frighten them to get them to understand. Adam was too young to really understand anything, including what he had already seen the day before. As a matter of fact, Symone had watched him for any signs of trauma.

It went better than she had thought it would, and there were only a few questions that had her stumped. She didn't know why the people wanted to hurt them, so she fell back on the old explanation that they were bad people. As long as Adam and Emily bought it, she was doing them less harm with that explanation than the one that included the apparent desire to eat people.

After a quick breakfast, Symone made it as much of a game as she could, and they moved Emily's personal belongings to the cellar. Emily asked her once why the bad people wouldn't find them in the cellar, and she had simply told her Mummy had a way of fixing that problem. That satisfied Emily, and after getting the children situated in the cellar, Symone had to face the last big test of her will.

When she stepped out the back door, Symone expected people to come out of the trees, but nothing moved. It was more silent than it should be, and she knew wild animals were quiet when there was a threat nearby. She didn't even hear any birds.

She had to pass closer to the body on the flagstones than she liked, but it couldn't be helped. She tried not to look at it as she hurried to the shed, but she couldn't neglect the possibility that someone else might come from that direction. She made it into the toolshed and was breathing heavily.

"So far, so good," she thought.

Her priorities were the rope and the winch, so she went straight for them. The rope was actually something Henry had called a towing strap, so it was sturdy and strong but not heavy. The winch made her sore back hurt just looking at it, but she looped the strap over her neck and got both arms under the winch. She used her shoulder to push open the door to the shed and stepped outside under the weight of the heavy winch. A man was standing halfway between her and the house with his back to her.

His shoulders were slumped in a way that told her he was one of them. Symone knew that even the simple act of sitting down the heavy winch would give her away. It would crush the gravel under it and make enough noise that she might as well just try to walk past him. Her arms were already trembling under the weight.

She was out of ideas, and even though it was cool outside, she had sweat running down her forehead into her eyes. The sweat made her eyes burn, and her vision blurred. Giving up crossed her mind as soon as she saw a second one appear on the walkway that went around to the front of the house. This one was shorter, and he wasn't having any trouble walking.

Symone didn't recognize her own daughter until Emily threw a rock and yelled at the man.

"Hey, stupid. Follow me."

The rock was a good shot. It hit the man in his left ear. Emily turned

28

and ran back around the corner and out of sight, and the man stumbled away after her.

Symone summoned up every bit of strength she had and walked with shaking legs as fast as she could. As her legs burned and protested on the steps of the porch, the back door swung open wide. Emily proudly held it for Symone to fit through quickly and then pulled it shut behind her. She didn't even know where to begin to thank her. She sat down her heavy load and pulled Emily into a big hug.

"We should hurry, Mummy. That bad man is on the front porch."

Emily said it as if she was showing great patience and telling Symone something she didn't already know.

"Okay, Miss Smartypants. Help me with the refrigerator."

The refrigerator rolled easily on the hardwood floor, and they turned it around and moved it over to the cellar door leaving just enough space for them to get inside the cellar with the winch. They rotated the appliance until the back of it was facing the cellar door, and the front was facing outward. She plugged it into an outlet on the wall next to the door and thought her plan had a chance of working. It was an odd place for the refrigerator, but her hope was that it would hide the door behind it well enough.

Symone looped the strap around it across the vent at the bottom below the French doors and then ran it under the door to the cellar. Once they were securely inside, she turned the wheel on the winch, and the refrigerator rolled up against the door, closing it as the strap drew it tighter. With the strap securely fastened to the winch, the refrigerator wasn't going anywhere. Symone and Emily descended the stairs to join Adam. She had a small TV set up for them and another for herself.

"Well, now. Isn't this cozy? Let's see what's happening in the world."

3

Sparks

Guntersville - Year Eight
From the pages of the journal of Ed Jackson

If he's still alive, Captain Miller has been inside Fort Sumter for a long time, but we haven't been able to communicate with him. If we knew more about his situation, we would also know for sure whether to hope or finally grieve his loss, but for now, we're still just hoping.

We've made some progress with communications, thanks to the people in Huntsville. Gentry Campbell has been a blessing. She established a link with a satellite cluster before the rest of the Mud Island people made it from Huntsville to Guntersville, and we were able to bring the Chief and the others up to speed about the plane I discovered.

Excited isn't a word I would use to describe the Chief's reaction because it didn't do his anticipation justice. He loves to fly, but this thing is a beast that he can fly into battle, and a battle is what he has in mind for the people in Atlanta. They have to pay for the lives of six soldiers who hadn't done anything to them. I think the Chief is still a gentle soul, but he's tired of the bad that has come out of people since the start of the infection.

******

Charleston, South Carolina
* * *

The bottom floor of Fort Sumter felt sterile. It didn't even smell bad after a year of being sealed off from the rest of the shelter. Captain Jim Miller figured it had something to do with the positive pressure he had created in the HVAC system on the first day. Whatever it was, he didn't think he would have survived a year alone if he had to put up with the smell that probably permeated the floors above him.

The infected had found a way onto at least those two floors, and he was still stuck on the bottom floor. He had been busy, though. At first, he was busy working on ways to escape, but everything was a dead-end. What he knew for sure was not much compared to the things he could only guess at. He knew for sure that the white powder didn't have a permanent effect on the infected dead. When it had gotten loose inside Fort Sumter, it had killed everything, even the infected. That hadn't been the end of them. The living people who were killed by the powder were the newly infected dead, and they were roaming the stairwells and hallways outside of the one floor he claimed for himself. There weren't any spiders or anything else out there with the dead, but he wasn't going to take that for granted. It might only be that he couldn't see them.

In the supplies stored on the bottom floor of Fort Sumter, there were a variety of military issue gas masks and HAZMAT suits, but they had never been tested against the agent used by the people who had fortified the Yorktown. At least not until he wore one of the suits at the beginning. Even then, he didn't know if the agent had gotten into the air on his floor of the shelter. A tear in the material of the suit had forced him to risk breathing the air on his floor because he had already worn the faulty suit while he surveyed his predicament.

The powder appeared to be large enough in particle size to be stopped by the filters on the masks, but he didn't feel like finding out by trial and error. He didn't even know for sure if the powder had to be inhaled to be lethal or if it could be absorbed through the skin. That was why he had chosen the HAZMAT suit over a gas mask.

Then there was his test of the HAZMAT suit to withstand bites from the infected dead. It was a miserable failure that left him no choice but the masks, but there was one major drawback to that idea. There would be no way to get the genie back in the bottle if he tried a mask and it didn't work, even though he thought the powder had to be inhaled. That was all a guess, though. From what he had seen, the powder was gone, or it was inert, but testing that theory was not an option. At least it wasn't an option yet. Not until he would run out of food or water.

When he finally gave up on the idea of escape, Captain Miller turned to the next best thing. He was sure the technology inside the shelter had to be something he could reverse engineer, and he had some success before a wisp of smoke drifted up from parts he had cobbled together into a primitive transmitter. He had spent several days constructing the device, but without the proper tools to regulate the power supply, he applied too much current to the contraption and fried the thing after broadcasting for less than a minute. He didn't know if anyone heard him or not, but he had a faint hope that someone had listened to him call out for help.

He returned to his project several times over the following weeks and months, but spare parts were not on his inventory lists, and he couldn't bring himself to cannibalize any of the other systems. The parts he would need to sacrifice would have to come from the closed-circuit security system that allowed him to monitor the floors above him, and he wasn't ready to give that up. As a matter of fact, it wasn't exactly entertaining to see what was happening on those floors, but it was the only real contact he had with the world outside his own floor. It occurred to him that turning off those closed-circuit cameras would feel like he had turned off the lights. With a little persistence, he had been able to monitor every floor of the shelter, and in much the same way some people check their email and text messages, he set aside an hour or two every day to search the upper floors in the hope that he would see a familiar face...preferably one that was still alive.

******

"When did I start talking to myself?"

"A better question would be when I started answering myself," said Captain Miller. He had to admit that he didn't really remember when it had started, but it was long enough ago that he felt like he was being rude if he didn't answer.

"That's not good," he grumbled.

"Then stop doing it," he answered. "Are you really going to do this?"

"I don't see where I have many choices. There's only so much I can take. I have to at least try."

"Are you going to keep talking to yourself after you get out of here?"

He felt ridiculous standing at the stairwell door wrapped in sheets of insulation and duct tape. He used everything he could find to create a bite-proof suit, and he still wasn't sure. It was bulky, and he moved like he had a major rash somewhere below the waist, and he was trying not to rub against it. It was undoubtedly due to the hair that was being pulled out by the tape.

On the other side of the door, there was so much activity that the sound of his voice couldn't be what was stirring the infected into a frenzy. He doubted they could even hear him. When he thought about it, he couldn't remember the last time they had been so worked up. He also couldn't recall a time when so many of them had gathered at the bottom of the stairs.

One had tumbled down the stairs six to eight months ago, and its incessant groaning had drawn others to the bottom floor. They had made quite a racket for a few days, but one had lost interest and crawled up the stairs away from the pack. Captain Miller had watched on the closed-circuit TV as the others had followed it. The crawling exodus continued until they were all on the move, but they had only gone up a few floors before they lost interest. One of them found the open doors of the two floors above his, and the change in the sounds it made from the inside of that floor became the latest attraction. The infected changed directions, and the whole group migrated again. They were back outside his door, just when he needed them to be elsewhere.

Captain Miller felt even more ridiculous sitting back at his work table. He didn't know if he should rip the tape off like a band-aid or pick at it slowly. There were too many of the infected out there for him to take the chance. If he had opened the door, he wasn't sure if the door would have opened far enough for him to step through and then get it closed behind himself. He waited as long as he could before he finally accepted defeat.

Enough time passed that the worst of the tape removal was finished, which meant a couple of hours had gone by. He didn't really care because it wasn't like he had somewhere else to go. He knew that he would eventually get hungry, so he would eat. Sometime after that, he would get sleepy, so he would go to his bunk. He didn't bother to check the time anymore because it didn't matter what time it was. Something told him his break from a normal routine was bad for him, but he had slipped far enough into a depression that today's failure piled on top of every other failure was like a powerful grip that pulled him even deeper. Being on the bottom floor of the shelter symbolically forced him to always be looking upward. Everything he wanted was above him, and every day the shelter became deeper and deeper.

A loud banging noise made him jump. It was sharper than the accidental dull pounding the infected did on the door. There it was again, and this time it was closer. Either that or the infected had gotten the door open so he could hear them better. If they were inside the door, it was only a matter of time before they found him.

The banging increased in frequency as if someone was hammering faster. With a jolt, he remembered his training and knew he had been giving himself alternative explanations for the sound of gunshots. It was something people did when they couldn't conceive of the fact that someone was shooting a gun near them. Those were gunshots, and they were overlapping. There was more than one shooter, and that could only mean one thing.

He didn't even pull on his shoes, and in his socks, he was running so fast that he slid right past the door to the stairwell. When he got himself under control and got his face to the small glass window on the door, it took him a moment to process what he was seeing.

It was something he had seen on TV several times in his life. There were details on the protective suits that suggested he was looking at the genuine articles. Two people in bulky NASA spacesuits occupied the landing outside the door. Each suit had a variety of memorable patches sewn on them. Aside from the big NASA breast patch, he saw the shoulder patches that said International Space Station, and if that wasn't confusing enough, one of them had a shoulder patch that was familiar. It was the patch of the Russian space program. When that person turned a little further, he saw the Russian flag on the shoulder.

He didn't know whether or not to celebrate. He supposed being rescued by the Russians wasn't such a bad thing after being alone for so long, but he didn't like the idea of Fort Sumter being occupied by a foreign country.

The other spacesuit-clad person saw his face at the glass and raised a hand in a friendly wave. The arm came up high enough for him to catch a glimpse of a different flag on that sleeve, and the flag of the United Kingdom was a welcome sight. He also couldn't wait to hear the story of how an astronaut and a cosmonaut just happened to find their way to the bottom floor of the shelter at Fort Sumter.

The astronaut in the UK suit brought his face closer to the glass and gave Captain Miller a broad smile. The face inside the helmet was familiar, but the name escaped him for a moment. Then it came to him. When the world had fallen apart, there was a crew at the International Space Station, and there was no way to bring them home. In a joint military briefing with Navy personnel, they had disclosed that much of their intelligence about foreign military movements came from satellites, but the ISS communications had gone silent. If they had been able to communicate with them, maybe they could have coordinated a rescue at sea. He wondered which was worse, being marooned in space for years with no way to get back or being trapped on the bottom floor of a shelter under a zombie infestation.

"Sorry, Chief, I know they aren't zombies," then he added, "but these guys couldn't have gotten here soon enough because now I'm not just talking to myself."

The astronaut rapped on the glass with a big glove and pointed at his name tag. The name rang a bell as he read it, and he mouthed the words, "Nice to meet you, Henry, and very glad to see you."

He pointed at the cosmonaut.

"Who's your friend?"

He doubted the man could hear him, but the questioning expression on his face was probably obvious because Henry reached a bulky white glove to his companion and pulled the person to the window.

The big, bright smile on Kathy McGinley's face brought a rush of emotion to his chest and his eyes. He pressed both of his hands on the left and right sides of the glass and got his face as close as he could. He didn't feel like he could get close enough. He wanted to kiss her and apologize to Tom later. He knew he couldn't hide the big drops of tears that filled his eyes, but he didn't care. He could see them filling her eyes too.

Henry held up a dry-wipe board in front of the glass with writing on it.

"Hugs later. Let's get you out of there. Don't know if the powder is inert. We have a plan."

He pulled it away from the glass, wiped it, and wrote the rest of the message. While he wrote, Jim Miller just stared at Kathy, not believing yet still believing that his friends had found a way to free him from his prison.

Henry finished writing and held up an explanation of what they planned to do. They had found a way to penetrate the door and give him a way to get out of the safety of the bottom floor, but they had to go back to the surface first. There was an explanation on the dry-wipe board that laid out the process and what he needed to do to get ready. He gave them a thumbs-up and a smile.

The whole process was an ordeal that took almost two hours, but they couldn't come this far just to expose Captain Miller to the agent that had been so lethal. Being an astronaut and an engineer, Henry knew what they needed to do, and by the time they had arrived at Fort Sumter, the group had a plan.

It involved finding a way to get one of the spacesuits to Captain Miller without contaminating the suit or the air he breathed while he put the suit on. While they flooded the bottom floor of the stairwell with something that resembled a heavy rainfall in Florida, Captain Miller put on one of the hazmat suits. The idea was to remove any airborne particles of the agent. Once the area was washed clean, Henry came down alone and erected a decontamination chamber around the door where he was able to leave the Russian spacesuit.

Captain Miller knew the process wasn't one hundred percent certain to work because they didn't know enough about the lethal white powder, but he was willing to take the chance. At least he wouldn't have to fight the infected to get outside.

He heard the three raps on the frame of the door that signaled the chamber had been finished, so he opened the door and retrieved the bulky package. When he opened it and quickly put it on, he noticed the name tag that said, Lebedev.

"Whoever you are, Lebedev, I hope I'll have the chance to thank you."

He walked out through the decontamination chamber and into a heavy downpour. It felt the way he had felt the first time he had walked out of combat. It was a sense of freedom and a welcome to a new life ahead of him, and he remembered the moment the shelter door at Mud Island had opened in front of him. It was what hope looked like.

Henry was waiting for him on the stairs, and he held out a gloved hand. Even though it was through the thick protection of the glove, it was human contact, and he was grateful for it. They walked slowly up the stairs, and as tiring as it was in the heavy suit, he couldn't believe how quickly they emerged into the tunnel that led to the back entrance of the shelter onto Morris Island.

Through the visor of the spacesuit, he saw the most welcome sight he had seen in over a year. Spread out on the sand with the ocean and a bright sunrise behind them was a group of people who he knew would come back for him if they could find a way. His Mud Island family, all smiles, rushed forward to welcome him back to the world of the living. He couldn't help worrying about his ribs when the Chief gave him a hug.

******

Needless to say, there was a lot to tell, and Captain Miller wanted to hear it all. The only entertainment he had since becoming isolated was the antics of the infected dead that were isolated with him.

They had set up a campsite on the beach as a base of operations, and even though there was plenty of time left in the day to travel, the decision was to spend the day and night out in the open. To Jim Miller, it was like being reborn. Plenty of people volunteered for sentry duty.

Even though the infected didn't wash up on beaches the way they used to, there was still plenty of reason to post guards. As the daylight faded, small fires dotted the beach and the sand dunes. The blue crabs were so aggressive that they would follow people walking near the water, and they attacked when they saw the opportunity. The fires apparently made it more difficult for them to see their prey. The sentries stayed inside the ring of campfires and watched the gaps between them.

The first thing he wanted to know was how everyone else was. Ed, Jean, and Bus weren't there, so he had to hear they were all well. Kathy told him they all sent their regards and congratulations for making it out alive, but most of all, they sent their thanks for the way he saved so many people and risked his own life on the day the poisonous agent was brought inside Fort Sumter.

They spent hours talking about what happened in Huntsville. There were highs and lows. Saving thousands of people by getting them into the Operation Paperclip shelters was incredible, and bringing online the communications systems of the super shelter would be a big step in their fight for survival, but Captain Miller was saddened by the senseless slaughter of his soldiers in Atlanta. He could see the smoldering anger in the Chief and knew there would be a reckoning. He wanted to be there when it happened.

Another low was hearing about the officers who allowed themselves to be corrupted by the comforts offered by the Sheriff. In this case, the NCOs stepped up, but they all knew it could have turned out the other way around. It would take a long time to pull the military back into the functional force it had been, but it wouldn't be impossible.

The real story was the return of the ISS crew from space and the Chief's announcement that they were planning to take Henry Tisdal home. He compared it to when the original Mud Island family took Tom home to his wife.

"We did it for Tom, and we can do it for Henry," said the Chief.

Captain Miller kept waiting for the punchline, but it didn't come.

"You were in the Navy, so I know you've heard of the Atlantic Ocean before."

He smiled when he said it, but he kept an otherwise neutral expression on his face.

"I know," said the Chief. "I've thought of that."

"So, you have a plan."

"I'm working on it."

Captain Miller noticed the grin on Henry Tisdal's face, but the fact that the man wanted to get home to his wife and children made him realize that it wasn't something they would be joking about. In the light of their own campfire, he regarded the faces of Iris, Kathy, Tom, Colleen, Hampton, Sim, and Cassandra. They were all smiling because his rescue was cause for celebration, but he sensed they were also excited about what they were going to do.

"Henry," said Captain Miller, "I hope you conveyed my thanks to Natalia Lebedev for the use of her suit."

"I certainly did," said the astronaut, "and she said it couldn't have been used for a more noble cause. She was glad the plan worked."

"Well, I can't help thinking that things might have turned out differently. If you guys would have wanted to, I imagine you could've landed somewhere in the English Channel or close to it."

"We talked about it, or rather I talked about it, but without ground-based telemetry, as Adam Caldwell put it, hitting the English Channel would have been like kicking a one hundred-yard field goal. Even if the power was available, the accuracy would be too risky. Maybe someone will do it someday, but it's not very likely."

Kathy interjected, "But you hit a pretty small target when you landed so close to the Marshall Space Flight Center."

"There was a difference," said Henry. He struggled just a little to put it in layman's terms and settled for another example. "It's like when a friend offers you a ride because he will be driving by your house on his way home. Huntsville meant no significant course changes. The closest we would have come to the English Channel would have been the middle of the Atlantic, and there would have been no recovery ship."

"So the Chief said he can help you get home?" asked Captain Miller.

"He said he can get me up the east coast, and I think I have an idea after that."

Captain Miller appeared to be lost in thought for a bit, and everyone could see it by the way he toyed with the sand between himself and the campfire. He didn't lift his head when he spoke, and that itself was almost as strong as what he said.

"You know what's between here and the northeast, right? Let's say between South Carolina and Greenland. If we're going to find any military presence left in the world, it's going to be in the Atlantic between Greenland and England. We've taken a step back in time, folks. Whoever rules the seas will rule the world."

Everyone had to let that sink in, but the Chief understood it the best. Being a Navy man, it made sense to him, and he put it into clear language for everyone.

"What Jim is saying is that we're likely to run into whatever it is that's left of our military. My guess is that it would be a unified force. Some of Jim's old buddies will be teamed up with Marines and naval vessels. They aren't likely to greet us with open arms."

"Why not?" asked Henry.

"I'm a deserter," said Captain Miller. "My battalion was assigned to a carrier group as the US military tried to become organized enough to get a foothold on land. They tried dropping us into strategically important areas with the idea of taking back the land a little at a time. We kept getting pushed back, so we knew how dangerous the infected could be. Someone got the bright idea that we should bring the infected back to the ships with us so they could run some experiments on them."

"And you didn't agree?"

"I still don't. The Chief and Kathy can tell you firsthand what happens when the infection gets onto a ship."

"I can, too," said Cassandra. "I watched it kill every doctor onboard, and they were sure they were onto a cure before the infection killed them and everyone else."

"So maybe they should try it," said Henry with some hesitation.

Hampton hadn't been on a ship when he was confronted with the infection, but he was shaking his head furiously.

"No, it's not that simple. It doesn't matter if you're on a ship or in a town or city somewhere. If the infection is in there with you, it will get loose sooner or later. It's human nature to protect your family. Loved ones will hide bites, and family members will take risks that get them killed."

Captain Miller added, "Even if it isn't family, people make mistakes, and if that mistake is on a ship, the close quarters will make the results of the mistakes move more quickly, and I saw it brewing, so I left. About a hundred people followed me, so I won't exactly be happy to run into any US forces. Although, I've thought a lot about turning myself in if they'll give my people a pardon."

"Don't even think about it," said the Chief. "You know they would hang you for leaving with military property. The military also has a strict code of justice, and you would be sugar-coating it to call it anything except the highest crime in the military next to treason."

"So you have a plan to keep us from running into them and for me not to be hung?"

The Chief said for a second time, "I'm working on it."

******

They all agreed that an AC-130 coming in for a landing was actually a thing of beauty. For some reason, the design made it appear to be graceful yet deadly, and they all admired the way the pilot landed on a short runway and brought it to a stop. The Chief had reluctantly surrendered the operation of the aircraft to one of their most recent recruits. He was a former Air Force pilot, and he had logged hundreds of hours in combat flying the AC-130. As skilled as the Chief was, he had to admit that the man was more qualified.

His name was Jordan Sparks, and he had been a Captain like Jim Miller. That was where the similarities ended, though. Sparks, as he preferred to be called, was a lot younger than Captain Miller, and he was presumed to be dead by the military. If they ran into any US armed forces on their trip up the coast, there wouldn't be a picture of him with WANTED written over it and taped to any bulkheads on Navy ships.

Sparks looked like he belonged on a surfboard instead of behind the stick of an AC-130. He was lean but muscular and had a head of curly blond hair that would have made him right at home on any beach in California.

When Ed had found the plane hidden away on a small, dirt runway in Alabama, he had wondered how it had gotten there, and even more than that, he wondered why it was in such a good state of repair. He didn't think he would get the answers to those questions, but he knew he had to get it back to Guntersville. He raced back as fast as humanly possible and brought back a large force to claim the prize. The helicopters had been valuable to them, but this plane would be their way of organizing the fight to take back the country from the dead.

Dr. Bus was a skilled pilot, and he was excited at the opportunity to fly the plane, but it felt like such a big responsibility for someone who was his age. Everything about it operated so well that he told Ed it felt like it had been manufactured only a week ago, and if he was excited about the take-off, there was no way to describe how he felt to land it. He would have welcomed the chance to stay in the air longer, but he had to keep in mind the need to conserve fuel. After he landed in Guntersville, he spent over two hours inspecting every detail of the plane. Someone had shown the plane a lot of love.

That "someone" was Sparks, and he showed up at the front gates of the village over Green Cavern two days later. Sparks walked casually up the center of the steep road with his thumbs hooked in the straps of his backpack and a grin that stretched from ear to ear. He was greeted by a burly, armed guard who gave him a grin in return. It was hard not to be amused because Sparks was so cheerful.

"Welcome to Guntersville," said the guard. "We have to take care of a little business before you can enter the town, though."

Sparks' grin shrank just a little, but it wasn't entirely unexpected. He just hadn't considered the possibility that he would be inspected for bites by a big guard with a beard.

As nicely as he could, he asked the guard, "Any chance we could skip it this time?"

The guard was shaking his head from left to right even before he even finished his question. They appraised each other for a few moments, each waiting for the other to make the next move. Finally, the guard had to laugh.

"We've become a bit more sophisticated since the first year when everyone had to strip. Even if you've been bitten, you're not likely to suddenly start eating people. You still have to be inspected, but not by me. I'll check your backpack, and I'll hold your weapons until you've been cleared to get them back. A medical tent is just inside the gate. You'll get a physical and be interviewed there."

"Interviewed? I'm not here for a job. I'm here to get my plane back."

41

The guard was at least six inches taller than Sparks and outweighed him by a hundred pounds. Sparks could outrun him if the need arose, but he wasn't about to try to get by him. He slipped his arms out of the straps of his backpack and handed it over. As he did, he had a chance to check out the walls behind the guard, and he saw a few things he hadn't noticed before. There were more guards at the top of the wall, and there were gun slits at lower levels. He knew he didn't pose a threat, but he could tell these people were prepared for anything.

Once his personal belongings were searched, the guard signaled for someone to open the gate, and Sparks walked inside. He noticed that the place had gone into some kind of alert status. There were streets that snaked away through a neat little town, but the only people he saw were armed and strategically stationed where they could make invaders regret their decision to trespass on this town.

"Who should I see about getting my plane back?" he asked the first people the guard introduced him to.

******

Over the next week, Sparks learned that one of the favorite phrases of new arrivals was that they felt like they had fallen down the rabbit hole. It was amazing what people forgot about from the years before the infection and what they had taken for granted. Just the simple act of not being suspicious of anyone who he didn't know was refreshing. Once he was cleared by the medical inspection, he had undergone an interview by a welcoming committee that had the task of determining how he would fit in. He was told that everyone who found their community was welcome, everyone was encouraged to stay, but the laws that existed before the infection were the same laws inside their town.

It didn't take long for him to draw the attention of Dr. Bus because Sparks kept asking what he could do to get his plane back. Of course, Bus was glad to meet the man who had given the AC-130 the care it needed so it wouldn't rot from lack of use, but giving the plane back was not something they planned to do. Enlisting Sparks to fly the plane was a better idea. In return for his service, they would protect it for him. It was painfully obvious to him that protecting it was something he couldn't do, and it needed a crew to be effective in combat anyway, so it was a deal he was smart enough to accept.

Doctor Bus caught up with Sparks and asked him how he would

feel about a trip up the east coast, and Sparks said he was all for it, but he wondered how they would keep from being shot down by the military. Bus laid out the flight plan, and Sparks saw how it zigzagged from South Carolina into the Appalachian Mountains.

Sparks asked, "What's in South Carolina?"

"That's the first part of your mission. I won't be going along, but you'll be picking up a group of people who you're going to enjoy. They were here in Alabama when we got the news that Ed had found the AC-130. They could have waited for the plane, but they decided they could be in Charleston in two days if they pushed it, and they had something important to do. An Army friend needed to be rescued."

"Sounds like your friends have their priorities straight," said Sparks.

"When you meet them, you'll understand," said Bus.

******

Sparks saw the reception waiting for him on the runway and taxied in their direction. As he did, he couldn't help using the moment to assess the group Bus told him he would enjoy. Some of them stood out from the others because of physical characteristics, but there was something unique about the way they stood or even sat on their gear, waiting for him to reach them and stop.

One man was at the center of the group, standing with his hands on his hips in fists and his feet apart. He had to be the biggest man Sparks had ever seen, but the smile on the man's face betrayed his cheerful personality. Doctor Bus had told Sparks he would know the Chief on sight.

He also told him he would recognize the others. Kathy was the beautiful ex-cop. Her blonde hair was a dead giveaway. Her husband, Tom, had to be the man next to her. Even after years of not playing baseball, he still looked like he could walk back onto a field and pick up where he left off. There was a tall, slender woman with silver hair next to the Chief. That had to be Iris, and Sparks knew from talking with Bus that she had a sharp mind that had saved a lot of people after the infection began.

The African American couple was Cassandra and Sim. Sim would be his navigator on the flight, and he couldn't wait to meet the man who had been the navigator on the flight that had gotten the President out of Washington. Dr. Bus had assured him that the story was worth hearing. His wife, Cassandra, was someone you would want for a bodyguard, and he could see that she was alert by her posture, even though they were surrounded by open runways. The last couple was sitting on the gear shoulder to shoulder, just watching his approach. He had heard that the redhead, Colleen, was as Irish as she could get, but Hampton, the healthy country type in the ball cap next to her, offered a calm balance to Colleen's sharp wit.

Two men stood off to the side, and something about them was immediately recognizable. It was something that military people saw in each other. Both appeared to be around the age of forty, and both had neatly trimmed hair that gave away their bearing as officers. Jim Miller and Henry Tisdal both took pride in their military backgrounds even though they were both separated from those years by time and circumstances.

Something told Sparks this would be an interesting trip, and he couldn't wait to find out why they were going up the coast.

4

Plain Jane

North Charleston, South Carolina - Year Eight

The former Air Force AC-130 took off from Joint Base Charleston within minutes after arriving. Once he had gotten the plane stopped in front of the group, Sparks saw the Chief give him a hand signal that he understood to mean he should keep the engines running, and as soon as he popped open a door, gear was tossed in at him. The Chief gave Sparks a handshake that felt like a bear had grabbed him, and everyone else introduced themselves. Sim followed the Chief into the cockpit and got comfortable behind the copilot seat. This group was ready to go, and Sparks was amazed by how quickly they were ready for take-off.

At a cruising altitude that was lower than the plane would have flown before the infection, Sparks leveled off and turned to the Chief with a questioning look. He had been told they were going up the east coast, they would be flying over the Appalachian Mountains at a low level and would be refueling in Canada. That was the extent of it. He could guess it had something to do with Henry Tisdal, but he hadn't been given all the details.

The Chief gave him a friendly slap on his shoulder and said something about the smooth take-off. Then he slipped out of his seatbelt and ducked out of the cockpit.

"Where's he going?" asked Sparks.

Sim was concentrating on a map spread across the navigator's table. He was drawing lines between points and then doing calculations on a pad. He would check his watch, make a note, then draw another line.

"He said something about playing with the guns," said Sim without looking up.

"Is he going to shoot zombies?"

Sparks didn't understand the blank stare Sim gave him and went back to his own work. At just over four hundred and fifty miles per hour, they would be over the foothills of the Blue Ridge Mountains soon, and he was going to enjoy the twists and turns he would make in order to follow mountain passes. They could fly higher and go over the mountains in a straight line, but Captain Miller had identified the likely locations of spotters based on his old information, and they were hoping to avoid detection.

The Chief and Captain Miller didn't really expect to avoid detection over such a distance, but by flying low in the valleys, they hoped to limit the number of locations that could spot them at the same time. Before one spotter could relay their position to another, they would hopefully be traveling fast enough to be by the next spotter. Their route included a few switch-backs that would have them traveling over the same place more than once. It wasn't fuel or time-efficient, but it could help to keep anyone from guessing exactly which direction they would be going next.

Sim leaned forward and asked, "You named your plane?"

Sparks nodded, "She's Plain Jane."

"Nice play on words, but why that name?"

"There have been several variations of the AC-130. It started out as a cargo plane, so most people make the mistake of calling it a C-130. It was converted to an attack plane, and it went through a bunch of different weapon modifications. The weapons on this one are the standard configuration, so she hasn't been dressed up like the other models."

The Chief chose that moment to arrive back at the copilot's seat, and he was like a little kid with a new toy.

"This thing has a 25mm cannon that rotates so fast it can fire over four thousand rounds per minute. It also has a 40mm cannon and a 105mm howitzer. If something doesn't get her in the first minute of a firefight, they won't see a second minute."

Sim couldn't help himself and asked, "Shoot any zombies?"

The Chief eyed him suspiciously. He knew he was being set up, but he wasn't sure how it started.

Sim handed him a slip of paper with map coordinates and time of arrival on it. He checked the time and passed it to Sparks.

"We're going to Lake Norman? Are we landing?"

The Chief shook his head and said, "Just a pylon pass."

Sim added, "I spoke with Ambassadors Island as we were about to leave Charleston, and they said someone has been trying to breach their main entrance. We might have to deter them."

"I don't understand," said Sparks. "Whoever it is, why aren't they letting them in?"

"That's an easy one," said the Chief. "We learned the hard way at Fort Sumter that it isn't safe to bring everyone in."

Sim continued, "Ambassadors Island can't be breached. The walls of the shelters can withstand practically anything, but the people who want in are trying to force their way in. They were given the terms for entering, but you have to imagine what they're thinking. They can't conceive of the fact that there's a functioning town below the surface. They think it's just a backyard shelter under there, and just like a bunch of criminals or bullies, they're trying to dig out the occupants."

"So, they were offered the chance to come in, but like when I walked up to the front gate of the village, they had to agree to a few things first. I have to admit that I didn't have a clue about what was under the village."

"Right," said the Chief. "Some of the shelters are small, like the one at Mud Island that belonged to the founder of the survival club, and some are immense. If you had attacked the village, you would never have found out about the shelter. You would have just thought that was one tough village, but let's say an army attacked the village. The army would wonder where everyone went, but they'd never figure out how to get inside Green Cavern."

"We're coming up on Lake Norman now," said Sim.

Sparks tilted the plane to its port side and banked into a circle around Ambassadors Island. Out the windows on the left side, they had a good view of the neighborhoods and trees that covered the island and the surrounding banks that lined the huge lake. The island had been an exclusive neighborhood with a gatehouse. Neglect, harsh weather, and even gun battles had taken their toll on some of the homes. Off and on through the years, people had taken refuge in the homes, but the infected had too often discovered them. When the Chief and Kathy had ventured into the homes, they had found them to be occupied by swarms of the infected.

The turn around the island gave them an excellent and consistent view. It was called a pylon turn because it kept the weapons constantly on their targets. The plane rotated around the island, staying at the same angle and distance the entire time. When they passed over the main entrance, they saw the problem.

The people on the ground hadn't seen an airplane in years, and the sight of the gunship rotating around them was something to be admired rather than feared. They stopped in the middle of their project and shaded their eyes against the sun as they watched.

"I have Ambassadors Island on the radio," said Sim. "Putting them on speaker."

The radio came to life, and the voice of a young woman was explaining that they had warned the people outside to cease attempts to excavate the entrance. The woman had chosen her words well because there was a bulldozer poised to push away the entire brick wall and surrounding soil that hid the entrance to the shelter. Having the entrance exposed would mean more and more outsiders finding it.

The message in progress ended with a stark warning to the people outside that the bulldozer would be destroyed as a warning and that people should clear the area.

Sparks said to the Chief without turning away from his stick, "You know those weapons back there are manually targeted, right?"

"He knows," said Sim.

That was when he heard the 105mm howitzer fire once, and the bulldozer disappeared in the blast of the high explosive. Dirt and smoke billowed into the air. In the area surrounding the place where the bulldozer had been, prone figures were jumping up from the ground and running in all directions. A few didn't move from where they were, but it was a fair assumption that they would move soon.

The Chief piled back into his seat and said, "Remind me not to do that unless we absolutely have no other choice. That's a mess down there."

"Roger that," said Sim.

They all heard the message of thanks from the shelter, and the Chief told Sparks to resume course. He couldn't help asking the Chief one more question as he brought the plane around to its new heading.

"Still plan to do that to the people in Atlanta?"

"Much more," said the Chief.

* * *

******

The clouds closed in as the foothills steadily rose into mountains, and nerves began to become unraveled for those passengers who had been enjoying the view. The plane flew into a wall of gray that was so dark that it appeared to be solid. It was unnerving to see the black propellors cut into the clouds and the wings quietly slice something that the mind believed to be solid. Of course, everyone knew better, but knowing the clouds would part didn't help. It was still hard to watch.

There was also the question of what might be on the other side of the cloud. Was it a mountain, or was Sim navigating the passes accurately using his charts and a stopwatch? The Chief sat in the copilot seat quietly. His job was to watch Sim for hesitation or a break in his concentration.

As crazy as it seemed, when they passed an exact spot on his map, going an exact speed, he knew how long it would be until they reached the next spot where Sparks would need to make a course change. He would call it out with the Chief watching over his shoulder and restart his stopwatch. Sparks would make the course change while calling out that it was done. Sim would put an X on the last checkpoint and circle the next one. Even if the clouds broke, restoring visibility for a few seconds, no one took the opportunity to look out through the windshields because it would break their concentration.

They had planned for this to happen, and Sim had a list of times written along the flight path between the checkpoints. Even if they experienced a period of time where visibility allowed them to see beyond the next checkpoint, breaking from the routine would cause Sim the need to furiously recalculate if another cloud rolled into their path.

The three men on the flight deck were calmer about the maneuvers than the passengers because they could concentrate on their jobs, and as tough as the others were, they all felt like it was insane. On the plus side, if there were any military observation posts on the mountains, they would hear the plane, but they wouldn't know where it was.

Kathy decided to face the worst of it by standing in the open area above the 25mm cannon on the port side and quickly regretted the decision when she saw just how close they came to the trees. The pass was narrow, but more importantly, the next turn was going to be hard to the right, and Sparks needed to set up for the turn by getting closer to the mountain. Kathy went back to her seat. She gave Tom an evil stare when he asked if she had seen anything interesting.

Iris was squeezed into a back corner of the flight deck with a pair of headphones over her ears. She kept her eyes away from the front of the cabin and just focused on the radio in front of her. If they crashed into a mountain wall, it would all be over before she knew what happened, so she didn't want to see it coming.

Her job was to cycle through the broadcast bands the military would most likely be using to see if they had been detected. The static in her ears was a welcome distraction, and it drowned out Sim's voice when he called out for course corrections. It helped that she heard broadcasts from time to time and was distracted from the swaying of the plane and the changes in light.

It was also disturbing to hear unknown voices call out frantically in the hope that the plane was some form of rescue. In the space of minutes, she heard several such broadcasts. None were military, and each rapidly gave their positions and begged for aid. It was no surprise that radios were operating. What struck her was the desperation. There were a lot of people on the edge of losing their battle to survive.

One message was in a language she didn't recognize, and that one bothered her the most because she had spent enough time working on a cruise ship to meet people of many cultures. She remembered that she was recording the broadcasts and made a note of the time so she could play it for the Chief later.

The drone of the engine and the lack of swaying told everyone they were on a level flight path, and the Chief ducked through the door from the flight deck and gave everyone a thumbs up.

"We get to use visual flight for a while. Everyone okay back there?"

He tried not to grin at the sour expressions he got from everyone.

Colleen said, "Now I know what clothes feel like inside a tumble dryer."

There were some grumbled agreements from the rest of the group, and Tom said he didn't want to know how much longer until they would land because he didn't want to think about it.

Iris pulled off her headphones as the Chief came back in, and she gave him a half-smile that told him she wasn't happy about something. He pulled out a drop-seat next to her and sat down.

"Something tells me that there's something on your mind that doesn't have anything to do with the stunt flying."

"That's affirmative," she said.

Iris was strong-willed and had kept the shelter under Ambassadors Island functional for a long time. Not much got to her, so he knew better than to guess. She would tell him what she wanted him to know.

"We're doing a good thing," she said.

"You won't get any argument out of me."

"I know, but I feel like we should be doing more. There are a lot of people out there who need help. I heard them."

"We can't help everyone."

"I'm not so sure about that. I think that after we get Henry back home, we need to find a way to make contact with more people. I heard more cries for help than anything else. Most of them are probably just hanging on by a thread. People who survived this long deserve to live, but they can't put together anything sustainable. If they don't eventually get caught by the infected, they get consumed by some two-bit gang that takes everything from them."

"What you're saying is they need someone like the Sheriff, but not someone who's just in it for themselves?"

He met her gaze and saw she was trying to tell him that he should consider the job.

"You said it yourself more than once," she continued. "It isn't enough to just survive. You have to fight back."

"Let me think on it, and if you think it's safe to broadcast, see if you can touch base with anyone on your contact list that sounded real. You probably realize some are fake distress calls, right?"

"I know. Even the people we just blew away in Charlotte were just trying to survive, and if we didn't already know who they were trying to dig out of the ground, we would have gone right by. Being judge and jury could turn us into the bad guys."

He gave her a pat on the shoulder and let her know that he heard her loud and clear, and he added that he thought they were off to a good start, but maybe they could do more.

The Chief changed his mind about rejoining Sparks. Instead, he went back to see Jim Miller. He found him at the 40mm Bofors cannon. Bofors was the company that manufactured the gun, and they had been making cannons for over three centuries.

"See anything you like?" he asked.

The Army Captain was enjoying every minute of the trip. Liberating him from under Fort Sumter had been a priority for his sake, but it was also like getting a secret weapon back. He worked well with the rest of the group, was a brilliant strategist, and knew weapons even if he had never seen a particular model before. He had the guns on the AC-130 figured out in minutes.

"Hey, Chief. This thing is a work of art."

"Glad you like it. Between me, you, and Doc Bus, Sparks felt like someone was stealing his girlfriend. But that's not why I dropped by. You got any plans for after we get Henry back home?"

Jim eyed the Chief quizzically as if he could figure out what the Chief had on his mind by reading his face.

After getting out of Fort Sumter, Captain Miller had met with his troops. They had functioned under the command of the officers who had been promoted after his presumed death, and it wasn't a good idea to just yank the rug out from under them and take back the command. He could tell they had mixed feelings about it too. Some of them were all for it, but he wasn't. He told them to think of him as someone like they used to have before when they were happy to follow orders that came down from the Pentagon.

The new position gave him the freedom to make this trip to take Henry home, and he was surprised how much he was enjoying it. It was nice not to worry about his troops, and they felt like the people at the top of their command structure hadn't lost touch with them.

"You offering me a job, Chief? Already happy with the one I've got."

"Think of it as a contract extension. It was just brought to my attention that we need to do more to fight back against the infection. Iris wants us to take a bigger part."

"I'm listening," he said. "Did she tell you how?"

"She gave me a hint. We should go out looking for more people who need a hand, and we should take on a role like the Sheriff but as good guys."

"I hate to break it to you, Chief, but you pretty much do that already."

"I think she means with the plane. We should go out, listen for distress calls, and help when we can."

"Count me in. Are you still planning to wreak havoc on that group in Atlanta? That's a score for me to settle too."

The Chief nodded.

"We should have someone scout them while we're gone," he said. "Mind making the arrangements?"

"No problem. There were volunteers before we left Charleston. I'll see who I can get on the radio."

Light flooded the cabin, and they all knew the plane was out of the cloud cover. As harrowing as it was to be flying by instruments and some good navigating, the cloud cover was their protection from being seen by ground observers, and people on the ground sometimes had shoulder-mounted weapons.

The speakers came to life with Sparks announcing the obvious because before he finished, the plane was in its first sharp turn.

"Attention, all crew. Visibility has improved, so we're going to be hugging the treetops a bit. Descending now and entering the first of many valleys."

They felt the floor drop away from their feet as the plane leaned over on its left side for the turn, and no sooner did they get their feet adjusted when it leaned the other way. When it went into the next left turn, the Chief got a chance to position himself to see the terrain below through the open area above the 40mm.

Even after so many years, it was always a shock to see a horde following a road. Whether it was a big horde or just a few of the infected, it was something that always produced the gut reaction of wanting to see them eliminated. This time he saw something he knew was happening but hadn't witnessed for himself. A pack of large wolves was closing in on the last infected dead in line.

He didn't get to see the final results, but what bothered him was the fact that wolves preferred a fresh kill. Rats and carrion eaters like vultures didn't care if it was decaying meat, but if wolves were attacking the infected, it most likely meant that the horde had new members that hadn't been dead long. More living people who had survived for years were still dying.

The sight was left behind, but the Chief was more unsettled than ever. It didn't seem like they had made progress against the infected even though they had personally disposed of thousands. That's why it made him so mad that petty little dictators killed the living so senselessly.

Kathy caught the Chief and pulled him over to join their main group. She had a map spread across a table that folded down from the wall, and he could see that she had been tracking their progress. Judging by the red line she had drawn in a zigzag over the southern states, they had gone a lot further than he would have guessed.

He pointed at the line and asked, "Is that where we are, or is that where we're going?"

"We're making good time," said Tom.

The others all nodded in agreement, and Hampton said, "If we can get the fuel here, we should be able to make the crossing over the Atlantic without getting too close to the places where the military would likely be."

Tom had his finger on a spot that was in the middle of nowhere. It was actually a scenic little town in Newfoundland that had a small airport. To get to it, they had the added benefit of the nature preserves around Nova Scotia. It was far enough from the likely places for a military presence, with the exception of the Navy. There was no way to predict where they would be, but the Chief and Captain Miller were guessing that the joint forces of the United States and Canada would set up shop in Greenland. There were bigger airports with longer runways for the heavy bombers, and they were close to deepwater ports.

"How long before we reach our little airport?" he asked.

"Just under two hours," said Hampton. "By the way, Chief, we've all been under the assumption that the plan is to refuel and then fly a straight line to Ireland. Then we can make the last leg of the trip in a few hours, but we all have the same concerns."

The Chief could see that they were all waiting for him to tell them the plan that he had kept to himself so far, and he knew what was bothering them. There was no guarantee that there would be fuel at the airport in Newfoundland, but he had picked that airport because its remote location meant it was more likely to have fuel than the less remote airports.

Colleen asked, "Why can't we try Boston or Bangor? Both are in easy reach."

Captain Miller had drifted forward to join the conversation, and he said, "I can answer that. We were already using Boston as best as we could. The Navy brought in several small destroyers and worked the area over pretty well. Then we brought in the ground forces and set up a defensive perimeter around the airport. Everyone that could came in for fuel, supplies, and equipment, but what we didn't count on was the survivors."

"What happened?" asked Cassandra. "I wasn't in the States when it started. I would have imagined there was an evacuation of some kind. Greenland and Iceland are both close enough, and Canada even should have been safer."

Captain Miller shook his head.

"We eventually tried to regroup off the coast of Virginia and North

Carolina, but in the beginning, when the hospitals and the streets were overrun with the infected, every ship that could put to sea quickly was told to do so. We stuffed our gear into helicopters and got ferried out to the ships, and the whole operation moved toward Boston."

"Why did everyone go to Boston?" asked Hampton. "I remember watching the news reports of that mess in Charleston, and I imagine the port entrance was too narrow for the volume of big ships but was there a plan in place that designated Boston?"

Captain Miller continued, "Cassandra was right about one thing, and that was the possibility that the population density of Greenland and Iceland would allow for a military force to coordinate efforts more easily without a large civilian population to take care of. The problem was that resources needed to be collected before going there. Everyone needed to top off their fuel and their provisions first, plus Boston was on the way. Imagine what that looked like to the population of Boston."

Colleen said in a sad voice, "They thought they were being rescued."

"Right, and military forces that were sworn to protect its citizens from all enemies, foreign and domestic, were ordered to open fire on civilians in self-defense."

Kathy understood and added, "So there isn't likely to be any fuel, and even if there is, we wouldn't be able to get to it."

"People who did get fuel bypassed Newfoundland and went to Greenland," said the Chief.

"And after we got organized in Greenland," said Captain Miller, "the largest part of the fleet went down the coast to begin a coordinated attack on the infected. If not for someone getting the bright idea of bringing the infected to the ships for research, maybe we would have at least established a safe zone on the east coast."

"You think this little airport," Kathy put her finger on Springdale Airport, "will be the answer? You think they have fuel because everyone was too focused on Boston?"

"I do," said Captain Miller and the Chief at the same time.

The Chief continued for them both, "But we only need enough fuel for the trip back home. If we get fuel there and use it to make the crossing to Ireland, there's no guarantee we'll find fuel for the trip back. Besides, how do you think the Royal Air Force would react to an AC-130 gunship arriving on its borders?"

"How are we going to get from Springdale Airport to England?"

asked Kathy.

"Henry said he has that taken care of," said the Chief.

******

The last part of the flight was the worst because they felt so exposed. Sparks followed the course changes given to him by Sim and increased speed from Bathurst, New Brunswick, to Stephenville on the west coast of Newfoundland. Being out over the water meant they could be seen from a long distance, but if Sparks had flown close to the trees in the mountains, it was nothing compared to how close he flew to the water. Staying under the radar was imperative, but as the Chief described it, they were more likely to hit someone's radar mast than to be detected by it.

The terrain ahead was a striking color that seemed so incongruous with the cold climate. There were large stretches of trees with dense undergrowth, but there were also vast fields of open grass. Everything was in stark contrast with the cold water that surrounded it and sparkled in the sunlight. It was a startling view that would change rapidly when storms rolled in.

Sparks gained altitude as they reached Stephenville but not by much. Springdale Airport was only minutes away. The land was much flatter than he had expected, and he felt like he didn't need a runway, but the airport was where the fuel would be. Henry joined them on the flight deck and climbed into the copilot seat. Sparks pulled on a set of headphones and reached over to the radio. When he found the right frequency, he started broadcasting.

Henry had given him the information he needed, and it wasn't a long message. Hopefully, it would draw the attention of one person and not the military of any country, but if the military picked it up, they wouldn't know where it was coming from if they kept it short.

"Henry is looking for his friend Maggie. Contact information is in your logbook."

Sparks only said it once. If the message was received by the right person, she would know what it meant. The Chief had told him to broadcast the message on a schedule that matched the same times that the ISS had passed over this same location when Henry had made contact with the ocean-going tugboat, Maggie Mae. The skipper, Andi Hartford, would have logged the time, place, frequency, and duration of the contact in her ship's log. If she picked up the short broadcast by

Sparks, she seemed smart enough to understand that the message was intended to be heard only by her, but if it was intercepted by someone else, they wouldn't know what it meant.

The reason they had picked that particular time to make contact was also a deception. Henry had calculated the position of the ISS as it continued to circle the Earth. It was still up there, and if anyone on the ground or on an ocean tried to contact it, they would be able to tell that their message had been received, but they could only make assumptions about why they weren't getting an answer.

It was highly likely that the military forces of many countries had tracked the return of the Soyuz when Henry, Adam, and Natalia had decided it was time to come back to Earth, but for all they knew, the capsule had come back empty, and the crew was still up there. Regardless of what anyone thought, the ISS was still in orbit, and if Henry was able to establish contact with Maggie Mae, he could keep the conversation cryptic, and anyone listening might believe Andi Hartford was talking to the ISS.

It was a ruse that wouldn't last long, and to keep it convincing, the conversation would have to be kept short. Once the ISS was out of range, they would end the transmission until it passed overhead again. They would also have to work out precise language for Andi to understand that they were hoping she would rendezvous with them and give Henry a ride home.

The Chief was practically famous for saying that he had a plan. Typically, he had a "Plan A" and a "Plan B." In this case, he had a "Plan A" with a lot of holes in it, and when they pressed him on it, he had a "Plan B" ready to fill the holes. Everyone suspected this time he would need a plan C because there were too many things they didn't know, such as the conditions at the airport. There were plenty of things they would just have to guess at and hope they went well.

Because they were flying so low, the small airport appeared under them and whisked by quickly. Sparks threw the plane into a hard bank to the right to line up on a runway that crossed the main runway that had been intended for larger planes.

Sim had logged plenty of time behind pilots, and he was impressed by the quick decision. The Chief had just returned to the cabin and was climbing back into the copilot seat that had been vacated by Henry as they made the turn.

"What did I miss?" he asked.

"Sparks is banking for the backup runway. I think there was a problem on the main runway."

The Chief buckled his seatbelt out of reflex and turned to Sparks for confirmation of Sim's reports.

Sparks was busy with landing procedures, but he was also concentrating on whether or not he could sit the wheels down where he wanted to.

"We have to land for fuel, right?"

Sparks knew the answer to his question, and "Plan A" didn't include a backup plan for another fuel source, but the last thing they had expected was the number of infected dead that they would find on such a remote airstrip.

Kathy squeezed into the cabin behind Sim and asked, "What kind of crisis are we looking at this time?"

"Main runway is populated," said the Chief.

The two runways crossed each other at a sharp angle like an off-center letter X, with one slanted stroke being longer than the other. The airport terminal was much bigger than they had expected, and it was situated on the left side of the main runway and almost to the place where the runways crossed each other. The first leg of the main runway was covered with dozens of infected dead.

"There's only one thing I know of that will draw that many infected into the same place," said Kathy. "Why is there a terminal that size in a place like this?"

"That's what I miss the most about the Internet," said Sim. "I wish we could just do a search for this place. It's nice here. I'll bet this was not only a hopping tourist attraction in its day, but it was the stopping point on the way to a bunch more."

The Chief put a palm to his forehead and said, "I'm losing my edge on plans. When the infection started, this was the first place people from the mainland would've gone. They had the right idea to head north into the wilderness, but they didn't count on how many people were already here and how many had the same idea."

"And someone brought the infection with them," said Kathy.

"We can land on the short runway and avoid the heaviest part of the crowd," said Sparks, "but what we need is at the terminal, and if there's someone inside to rescue, we should do something about the infected."

"This is a no-brainer," said the Chief as he scrambled out of his seat again. "Can you bring us to a stop in the middle of the crossing?"

Sparks nodded, "Roger that."

"Good, but after you do, roll far enough to let me shoot down the length of the runaway without having the terminal behind the infected."

The Chief towed Kathy with him and signaled for Captain Miller, Hampton, and Tom to join him at the 25mm rotary cannon. He called out their stations and instructions, and everyone else did what he said.

"We don't want to waste ammunition, so we won't open fire until we're stopped. We won't be trying for headshots. We're just going to shoot down the middle of the crowd."

The AC-130 touched down, and Sparks cut back the engines and braked in time to put the guns where the Chief needed. From the port side viewing areas above the gun ports, everyone on board could see that their arrival had drawn even more attention. Infected dead that had been behind the terminal streamed in large numbers out to the runway. If there was someone trapped inside, they wouldn't be able to leave any time soon.

Sparks cut off the engines to conserve fuel, and the silence seemed loud until the Chief opened fire with the General Dynamics 25mm Equalizer. If the crowd of infected weren't dead already, the people in the plane would have believed themselves to be cruel and inhuman because the gun could fire over four thousand rounds per minute. The effect was stunning as it literally cut limbs and torsos like a hot knife through butter. Hundreds of the infected dead went down in seconds, and then the gun was silent.

As everyone's hearing returned, the roar of the rotary cannon was replaced by moaning. Even to a group as experienced as this one, it was unnerving to hear the sound of the horde coming from the pieces that were scattered across the runway. A few were closer to the terminal where they couldn't be shot, and they were unable to navigate through the killing field between the terminal and the plane. They fell down, crawled, stood up, and fell again.

"Are we going out there to finish them?" asked Hampton.

Kathy eyed the distance to the terminal.

"There are moving parts everywhere," she said.

Before they could decide and before the Chief gave the order, they felt the engines rumble to life, and the plane rotated to the left. It lurched forward, and in less than a minute, they felt the first bump as the big wheels rolled over the infected.

"That kid's a mindreader," said the Chief. "I was just about to tell him to drive us closer to the terminal."

5

BBC

Southern England - The Beginning

Symone turned her small TV set away from the children. She spent a few minutes explaining to them how important it was that they stay quiet, and she had hugs for both of them for making it so much easier for her to get them into the safety of the cellar. This was also the first time she had the chance to properly thank Emily for being so brave outside. She still couldn't believe her little girl had stepped up so well and maybe even saved her life.

"I don't know when you got so smart, but you chose a really good time to show it to me."

Emily beamed and returned the hug.

"Mummy, what's happening? Who are those bad people, and can Daddy come home now?"

Symone knew that Emily couldn't possibly understand everything that was going on. Neither did she. As a matter of fact, there was very little that she understood better than Emily. Part of what she did understand was that people were dead, and people were killing and eating each other. She understood it was happening, but she didn't have a clue why.

"Emily, you just proved to me that you can be a big girl who deserves answers, but I don't know what's happening, and all I can say is that we might be down here in the cellar for a very long time."

Emily's facial expression betrayed her true feelings a little. Despite the fact that she had been brave earlier, her lack of understanding had been bolstered by the fact that there would be an explanation later. She didn't need to know the details before. She just knew her mother needed help. Now that her mother admitted that grown-ups don't know everything, it frightened her a bit more.

Symone was grateful as she struggled to think of how to help Emily past this critical moment in time, and she realized her gratitude was toward their American friend who had convinced Henry that he needed something he had called a "man-cave." She remembered the conversation like it was yesterday, and she recalled asking Adam Calloway in a very serious tone why her husband needed a place where he could hide from his wife. Now she understood it had all been a fun way to say that Henry could get some solitude, but as it turned out, it was a place where she could hide safely with her children.

Henry and Adam had made it into a spectacular project. In a country where few homes had finished basements, there were a few that had cellars, and those were usually damp, dark places for storing fresh vegetables or bottles of wine and beer. Symone surveyed the small rooms around her and thought about how much more comfortable she and her children were because Adam felt like Henry should have a little space for himself.

The toilet was located in a corner away from the living area. Adam had joked that it was a particularly good idea to ensure the comfort of guests. They had compromised on a few things, but she understood the need for privacy and didn't balk at the added construction of the wall and door that separated it from the rest of the cellar. She was beginning to understand even better as she thought about how long they might need to hide in the cellar.

Henry and Adam were both good engineers, so they had worked hard to insulate the walls and to install proper drainage should groundwater manage to seep into the walls. Adam had told her if they were going to add electricity for something other than lights, then the cellar needed to be as dry as possible. She was glad she went along with the idea because now she could plug in both TV sets, and the cellar wouldn't get too cold. They would also be able to use the electric hotplate to warm up their meals.

"Emily, I'll promise you this much. I'll tell you what I can. I don't want you to be afraid, but there will likely be times when we have to be very quiet. So, I need for you to keep Adam company while I watch the news. If I learn something important, I'll tell you about it. Now, go watch TV with Adam so I can watch the news and find out what's happening."

Emily seemed content for the time being, but Symone knew the danger would be when the children got bored. She was glad they had so much food and other things to keep them busy, but the man-cave would feel like a prison shortly. She turned on her TV and tuned it to the BBC. It wasn't long before she saw it was far worse than she had imagined.

Symone had a flashback as soon as they showed the first report from the field. She remembered where she had been when there were the first reports from America on that day when terrorists had hijacked planes and flown them into the World Trade Center towers. She was standing when she saw it, and she had stayed on her feet. This time she was already sitting on her sleeping bag, but she felt a physical sensation similar to the one that had shocked her into remaining standing before. This time she felt herself sink lower into the floor, almost like her body had lost its bones. She was glad she was sitting because this time, she might have fallen down.

Unlike the terrorist attack that was thousands of miles away, this was almost in her own backyard.

"What are you thinking?" she asked herself quietly. "This is literally close enough to be the backyard."

It was video footage from a drone somewhere between her home and London, and as it panned across the countryside, she saw familiar places from nearby. The fields between homes were dotted with people who walked slowly as if they were injured. Some of them obviously were, and the reporter was saying something about the graphic nature of the images and how some viewers might find them disturbing.

"Well, you're the grandmaster of understatement, aren't you?"

The camera view switched to the reporter, a middle-aged man with thin hair that kept blowing into a peak above his head. He kept reaching up and pushing it down again so his viewers wouldn't see the bald scalp underneath.

Henry had asked her once if she realized she talked to the television when something got on her nerves. She had managed to tone it down a bit, but this was like smoking cigarettes. It would be a bad time to try to quit.

"Leave your bloody hair alone and tell us what's happening, you fool. Better yet, tell us what the authorities are doing about it."

"Mummy, you're talking to the TV again, and we can't hear our show," said Emily.

She saw Emily give Adam a sideways glance that was far more mature than the little six-year-old had been only a day ago, and she realized Emily was telling her she had gotten louder and might be upsetting Adam. She gave them a weak smile to hopefully convey that she understood, but she saw the worry on her daughter's face. She turned the volume lower on her own TV and leaned in closer to listen to what the reporter was saying.

"As the sun sets here on the crossroads, we see that the police have closed the roads to all traffic except emergency services. As a matter of fact, here comes an ambulance now."

The camera swung around in the direction of the oncoming vehicle. Symone recognized the crossroads as being only minutes from her house. The camera jerked around as if someone ran into it but then became steady. It was just in time for the audience to see the driver make a sharp turn and bounce over a ditch into a cornfield. The ambulance came to a stop and just sat there for a few minutes. The reporter seemed incapable of speaking in complete sentences and babbled something about the events being unexplainable.

The rear doors opened first, and the occupants of the ambulance tumbled out in a heap. It appeared that they were wrestling with each other, but then it became more apparent that some were biting the others, and the others were just trying to untangle themselves from the pile of bodies. Symone wasn't sure at first if there were four people or six. What she was sure of was that all of them were covered in blood.

Something bumped into the camera again. Since the microphone was on, Symone heard the reporter and the cameraman both expressing their displeasure about having their broadcast interrupted. Another voice, likely that of the anchorman in the studio, was heard in the background calling out to the reporter. He wanted the man with the thin hair to tell them what was happening, but if he had shut up like Symone was telling him to, he would have been able to hear that the reporter was asking a group of people what they were doing. It also sounded like he was in pain. He was shocked by what they were doing, and then he was screaming his question.

His voice was cut off for a moment as he and the camera both fell over. When she heard it again, it was the sound of sheer terror followed by pain. For a few minutes, it was a duet because the cameraman joined in with the reporter, then it was a chorus as the anchorman yelled in the background. This time he was yelling for them to get out of there, but he was far too late.

The camera continued to broadcast and was aimed at one of the four corners of the crossroads. It was kicked again and was pointed more toward one of the roads, and the audience got its fill of disturbing video. The reporter was face down on the ground with his thinning hair in the middle of the picture. A teenage girl had her mouth buried in the back of his neck and was pulling at the muscle as hard as she could. When it came loose, it tore away a large swath of his scalp along with the hair.

Symone turned away from the TV and was sure she would be sick. The only thing keeping her together was the worried face of her daughter. Fortunately, Adam had his back to her at the moment, and she managed to suppress the sound of her gag reflex. She unscrewed the cap from a bottle of water and drank freely for a few moments.

When it sank in that she had just drunk half a bottle of water as if there was an unlimited supply, it occurred to her that water wasn't going to be a problem for them, but it would be for everyone else they knew. All of their neighbors for miles around, everyone she knew, and everyone she didn't know would be trying to survive off of the limited resources in their homes. If they ventured out for more, they were likely to end up like the reporter, the police officers, and the ambulance crew.

She turned off her TV and said to the children in a firm but calm voice, "Keep the sound on your TV no louder than it is right now, and if you must say something either to me or even each other, it must be in a whisper."

They both nodded their heads, but she saw the quivering lips that meant she was scaring them. As if on cue, there was the first of what would become many visits to their kitchen. They could only imagine what it was they heard, but things fell, and some things broke. Slow, dragging sounds and thumps made them all face the stairs that led to the kitchen, and even though Symone didn't need to warn them, she placed a finger over her lips.

A glass shattered, followed by the sound of glass being crushed underfoot. Sounds receded outside, and some traveled across the dining room to the front door. Symone was seated closer to the stairs than the children, and she thought she could hear a sobbing sound, but then she heard it more clearly, and it was more like a moan than a sob.

She was glad the children were not likely to have heard it.

When the visitors left, Symone went back to her TV and turned it on. She hoped she would find some international news and possibly something that would tell her what the space program planned to do about the crew at the International Space Station, but before she could change channels, she realized that the BBC was getting as much mileage out of the camera at the crossroads as they could.

The anchorman in the studio was eulogizing his colleague even as the sun was going down in the background. The teenage girl had moved on, and there was no movement other than the swaying grass and trees. At least there was none until the scalped reporter twitched. Symone stifled the involuntary whimper that tried to escape from her mouth by covering it with both hands.

The crown of the dead man's head was pointed at the camera, now a dark purple stain that resembled a large eggplant. He was still face down, but he slid nose first across the asphalt road. The result was that he tore away his nose and left it hanging by loose skin as he pushed himself into a sitting position. He seemed to be just sitting and thinking about what he was going to do next, but when his head turned and faced the camera, Symone wondered how many other viewers were watching and knew he wasn't thinking. Those were dead eyes.

With great effort, the man somehow managed to push himself up from the ground. He walked straight at the camera and delivered one final act as a reporter when he fell on it, exhaled a loud moan, and then went on his way to wherever it was he needed to go.

Thanks to her husband and his American friend, Symone kept her TV and Internet connections longer than most people. It wasn't hard to become addicted to the graphic videos and descriptions that came from every country and every major city around the world. Being locked up in a cellar didn't help. It was very natural to have a desire to know what was happening outside, but a part of her made her remember that children were perceptive about their parents' emotions. After what she had already seen, she was frightfully aware of the danger she and her children were in and even more aware of the fact that it was going to get worse.

It was like the difference between a tornado and a hurricane. Tornadoes came and went. They happened fast, they did great damage, and they moved on. Hurricanes had a lot of advance notice, and they tended to hang around for a while. This had arrived like a tornado and was giving no indication of how long it would last, but it was looking more and more like it was going to be around for a long time.

Symone switched off her TV for a second time and remembered that she had intended to do a precise plan for the long haul. As part of a compromise with Henry about the need for the cellar renovation, a portion of the space had been allocated for the expansion of her pantry. It wasn't that grocery stores were too far away or that she minded shopping, but it was nice to have an emergency supply of canned food already in the cellar. When she added what she had carried down from the kitchen, there was a lot of food, and if this hurricane hung around for as long as she thought it would, there would be a need for all of it.

The second round of visitors upstairs arrived just as Symone had begun an inventory, but this time there were voices as cabinets were opened and closed, and their contents crashed to the floor. Her good dishes and her pots and pans were being flung angrily around the room. It was loud enough for her to hear the cursing from the intruders when they didn't find what they were looking for. Symone prayed that they didn't question the location of the refrigerator, and she crept carefully up the steps to the winch. She had clamped it to the steps, but she added her weight to it to reinforce her handiwork. If they didn't see the strap around the bottom of the refrigerator, they wouldn't realize it was on wheels.

She recognized the sound of the refrigerator door opening and held her breath. A satisfied shout was what she wanted to hear, and that's what she got. The male voice called out to someone else that there was beer. She begrudgingly admitted to herself that she had hoped the forager was happy about the food she had left inside the refrigerator. She had meant to bring the beer and forgotten. It seemed to satisfy the man, though, and a minute later, the door slammed shut, and the voices retreated from the kitchen.

"Please tell me Henry stocked his man-cave bar," she whispered.

"Mummy?"

Emily's voice was hardly above a whisper, but in the silence of the cellar, it almost sounded like a shout.

"It's all right, Emily. They're gone now."

She realized the cellar was dark, and the children's TV was off too. Emily must've done it, and Symone could see Emily was going to be a big help.

"Thanks for turning off the TV, baby, but I don't think we need to worry about the light. No one can see it under the door."

She tiptoed down the stairs and groped around in the dark until she found the lamp she had in the corner on a small table. She felt better when its warm glow filled the room. She saw that Adam was sitting on the floor in front of his blank TV. He had his head hanging downward, but she could see that tears had already run down his cheeks.

Symone crossed over to him and scooped him up into a hug.

"I know that frightened you, Adam, but both you and your sister were very good. You were especially quiet."

"I don't want to play this game anymore."

"So that was how Emily had gotten him to stay quiet," she thought. Adam was too young for the truth. It was one thing to teach your children about "stranger danger" and another thing altogether to tell them they would all be eaten if the bad people heard them in the cellar. Symone didn't think the last group would have hurt them, but they would have taken their supplies. If they were the kind of people who ransacked houses, then they weren't the kind of people who would be worried about whether or not their victims starved.

Her biggest worry was getting flushed out of hiding. If they were forced out into the open, she would have to find another place to hide, and she knew the cellar was likely to be the safest place for miles around. For the time being, she felt like all they had to do was stay safe until the authorities got things under control. That meant a day or two. If they rationed their food, she guessed they had enough to last at least a couple of weeks.

Speaking of food, it occurred to her that maybe a meal would help Adam get sleepy.

"Who would like to help Mummy make food? We have all of your favorites, and we get to cook it right here in front of the TV."

"Can we have anything we want?" asked Adam. The prospect of cooking food did seem to help.

"I know exactly what you would like," she said. She was hoping to distract him from whatever it was he had thought of and quickly snatched something from the wall of canned goods. It was a can of spaghetti shaped like little stars.

Adam's eyes lit up, and she was relieved to have guessed right. The rationing had to start now, and it was helpful that she didn't particularly care for the over-sauced, over-priced can of carbohydrates, but it would be the best thing for a kid right now.

"Here, let's find something for you to watch while it cooks."

Once she got them on a channel that didn't have anything about what was happening outside, she got the can of food into a pot and set it on the hotplate where they could keep an eye on it. As strange as it seemed, there were channels that made everything appear normal.

"Emily, would you be a good big sister and show Adam how to stir your supper when it needs it?"

Emily took over for her, and it was only a few minutes before the aroma of the contents of the steaming pot filled the cellar. Symone had to admit, the smell gave her a sense of well-being. They had survived the day and were actually doing better than she would have predicted earlier that morning.

By the time the food was ready, Symone had done a complete inventory of the shelves, cabinets, and boxes of supplies. She had expressed some silent gratitude when she found her husband and Adam Calloway had stocked the bar. She told herself she knew what she would be doing after the children were asleep, although moderation would be necessary.

There had also been an ample supply of snack foods which she presumed they planned to enjoy when they got together to watch sports. Henry had gotten Adam to watch football. Adam called it soccer, and Adam had gotten Henry to watch American football. It had been funny listening to them explain the rules to each other.

Thinking of her husband and his friend made Symone miss him even more than she had already, and she wondered if he was okay. She imagined he was very worried himself, and it was odd to believe he was safer in outer space than they were on Earth. That made her also wonder why she hadn't checked for international news to see what had happened at the Russian launch sites. It also occurred to her that she had already lost track of time.

As she searched her memories to recall the events of the last day or so, she rapidly changed channels. She wasn't entirely sure, but she thought it was possible that they had been in the cellar for two days.

"Or has it been three?" she asked herself.

She checked the time on her phone and saw that it said seven PM. Once again, she asked herself if that meant they had been in the cellar for another full day, then she remembered she could check her call history. She was surprised to find that it had been three days ago, and she tried to remember what she had cooked for the children on the previous day. The wrappers near her children answered that question for her, and she knew she had to do better. Maybe it was the shock of everything that had happened, but she had apparently just pumped her children full of snack foods up until the pot of canned spaghetti. It also meant whatever happened at Baikonur was over by now. She searched the channels hoping to see the view of the empty gantries that would have sent the rest of the supplies and crew members into space.

It took over a half-hour, but she finally noticed there were fewer channels broadcasting than before, and some were just playing loops of videos. One eventually did a rebroadcast of the tragedy at the Russian spaceport. The video showed the smoking remains of what had been the two launch sites as well as the destruction of the rest of the Cosmodrome. No one would be coming or going from there for a long time.

Her first thought was as irrational as everything she had seen since this madness had started. She picked up her phone and dialed her husband's number. She felt like she had to speak with him, and it didn't connect in her mind until it connected her call with his voicemail.

"I'm losing it," she whispered.

She saw Emily glance at her, and she was quick to give her a weak smile. She waggled the phone at her daughter and said, "I just tried to call your father in outer space."

Emily got a hopeful look for a moment and asked, "Did it work?" Then she gave her mother the same weak smile as if to say she was just humoring her.

Symone made a mental promise to herself that she was going to do better. She thought she had been doing fine, but she had to admit she had just put so much energy into their escape to the cellar that she had been running on adrenaline. She didn't even remember putting the kids to sleep in their camping gear the night before. She vaguely remembered the collapsible tent they had erected as an adventure in the far corner, but somehow she had passed the time without paying real attention to what was happening around her.

What she had been paying attention to were the memories of the front porch. The memories played in a loop, just like the videos on the TV stations. She saw the strange people coming toward them, the police officer who had been eaten before her eyes, and then the bravery of the female officer followed by her total retreat from sanity by committing suicide. Even as she watched that loop in her mind, she had gone through the motions of taking care of her children without even noticing.

Symone suddenly felt more tired than she had in her entire life. Even the time when Emily had been sick with a fever while she was pregnant with Adam. Henry had been away in training for his mission, and Symone had stayed awake around the clock caring for her daughter. She had been so exhausted, but she never got as mentally tired as she was now. She saw that Adam had fallen asleep next to a bowl and realized that Emily had done it again. She had finished heating his food and fed him while she had somehow retreated into her own thoughts.

That was the moment when she also felt warm, and she pressed the back of her hand against her own forehead. She had a fever. She knew it without using a thermometer because she had plenty of practice with the children.

Symone dug around in the big pile of camping gear that still remained to be sorted and extracted the first aid kit. She found the thermometer and slipped it under her tongue. She saw that Emily was watching her, so she tried her best to be nonchalant.

Around the thermometer, she asked her daughter, "When did you get so grown up? You're only six, you know."

Emily beamed with pride, but Symone also saw that the child was scared. She motioned for her to come over to her and give her a hug. Adam stirred but didn't wake up.

"Are you sick, Mummy?"

Symone pulled the thermometer out of her mouth and saw that the red line had crept up to one hundred and one degrees.

"I guess so, sweetie, but even Mummy gets sick, so I'm lucky you're such a big girl for me. I'll take some aspirin to get the fever down, but I'll need help with your brother for a day or two. Do you think you can help me a bit longer?"

Emily nodded and gave her another hug. Then she went over to her brother and cleared the debris of the last few days away from him. She got his pillow and put it under his head, and carried the things that needed to be washed over to the sink.

******

If anyone had told Symone she would stay feverish for four days, she might have become suicidal herself. How Emily had distracted Adam

70

and kept him fed was beyond Symone's belief, but apparently, it had something to do with Henry. He had told Emily there would be times when Mummy would need her more than she needed Mummy, and the little girl had taken him seriously. When the fever broke, Symone knew it was time to let Emily be a little girl again. She was determined to take over her role as mother of the children.

Symone boiled some water and sipped at a cup of coffee, another influence from Adam Calloway, who was determined to Americanize their family, although he had taken a liking to Earl Grey. There were only a handful of TV stations that were still broadcasting, and only one of them had a live person describing the events around the world. What any of it meant for Symone and her children was anyone's guess, but the future was growing bleaker every day.

During the time she had been overcome by her fever, Emily stayed with what she knew, and Adam was just as happy to keep eating canned spaghetti. As for her, she was ravenous and felt like she could eat everything they had, but she knew better. Maybe the fever had kept her occupied long enough for her to recognize that four days' worth of meals might become important. She listed what she probably would have eaten if she hadn't gotten sick, and then she split up the portion sizes to make a list covering sixteen days. When she added up the calories those meals represented, she was only concerned with whether or not the children got enough to eat.

"I guess I can afford to lose a few of those stubborn pounds that stayed around after Adam was born."

She patted her hips, and Emily giggled.

"While I was sick, did you hear anyone upstairs?"

Emily appeared to withdraw a bit, and she even shifted away from the direction of the stairs. She didn't say anything, but her nod said it all.

"Did they speak?"

Symone obviously wanted to know if the next round of visitors were like the first ones or the second ones. Emily shook her head from side to side, and Symone didn't know if that was a good or bad thing. At this point, she didn't know which ones would be more dangerous to them.

She didn't know why she had relied so much on the TV stations for news, but she finally remembered to check her Internet browser on her phone. Maybe it was because their WiFi had always been insufferably bad, but any new piece of information she could get would be welcome.

The websites loaded so slowly that she imitated one of the old modems that she barely remembered herself. Adam laughed the way he always did when she made that sound, and she saw that he was busy with his own TV but watching her. It was great that little kids learned technology so fast by watching their siblings. He could load a new DVD as soon as he got tired of the old one.

The page finally loaded, and Symone saw that it wasn't much better than the news channels. The major news sites had old news on them because no one was refreshing the stories. When she finally saw something new, it wasn't what she had wanted to see. A headline said all roads were still closed and that the majority of the government sources were saying to evacuate to the south or shelter in place. The military was attempting to regroup on Portsmouth and the Isle of Wight, but they could not provide protection for anyone who was trying to evacuate. The article on the headline went on to say that London was lost and that there would be no further attempts to rescue people who were trapped there.

Symone pulled her eyes away from the phone, realizing that Emily was still quiet. She saw that the little girl could use good news or encouragement just as much as she could. If they were going to be stuck in the cellar for a long time, she needed to remember that good news would carry them for more days than bad news. She wasn't going to lie to them, but she had to spin it for their sake.

"Emily, it says here that the military is concentrating their forces not far from here."

"Concentrating?" Emily wasn't quite sure what that meant, but her mother's expression told her it was a good thing.

"Yes, that means there are far more of them near here than usual. Maybe that means we will get help from them soon."

That felt like a lie, and when she gave it more thought, it was a lie, and she felt bad for saying it.

"Emily, listen to me. I think what would be best for us is to stay here for as long as we can, even if that means a long time. It won't be fun, and we may be tempted to leave, but we need to stay here at least until we run out of food. If that happens, then we will have to try to reach the military."

Symone could see that Emily was trying to understand. The little girl's brow furrowed as she studied the shelves of food, and she turned her attention to the cabinets and boxes of supplies.

"We have a bunch of food, Mummy."

Symone opened her mouth to answer, but an interruption from the kitchen startled all three of them. Tears poured down Adam's face immediately, and Emily moved from where she was sitting over to her brother even before Symone could. Symone didn't even think about what she was doing when she scooped up her semi-automatic pistol and checked the chamber to be sure it was loaded.

This time it wasn't a scavenger, it was someone who was doing their best to escape death, and death was already in the kitchen with them. It was a man and a woman who were defending themselves, and it was impossible to tell what their odds were of survival, but they sounded poor. Their screaming was loud when it began. Then the moaning was loud, but then the moaning drowned out the screaming. The screaming also changed. There was a difference between the screams of fear and the screams of pain.

After what seemed like forever but was only minutes, the screaming stopped altogether, and there was only the moaning. Shuffling feet and moaning covered the sound of what was happening after the screaming stopped, and Symone was grateful for that.

She sat with her back to the children and her gun aimed at the stairs until she heard them sniffling behind her. She knew those strange, sick people wouldn't figure out that the refrigerator was hiding a door, so she turned around and wrapped her arms around Adam and Emily. The three of them sat holding each other until the last of the shuffling sounds were gone from the kitchen. There was a long period of silence from above before they heard a new sound. It was more shuffling. It increased slowly, and Symone imagined people whose faces she never knew. They were pushing themselves, or what remained of themselves, up from the floor and beginning their slow journey toward the open door. Then there was finally silence in the kitchen again.

6

Outside

Southern England - The Beginning

Going into the cellar was a choice Symone would never forget, nor would she regret choosing that option over making a run for the coast along the south. She got to see what happened to people who made that choice. The remaining TV stations on the air had enough video from locations on every coast of England, and it was the same story no matter which side of the country people fled toward.

The Royal Navy had rescued people from overcrowded boats of all sizes. People were paying huge sums of money for standing-room with no baggage allowed, and many of the boats cast away from shore with passengers clinging to ropes as they stood along the tops and narrow sides of the cabins. Symone watched in horror as boats without proper keels would tip from side to side until they finally laid over too far and flipped upside down. The passengers were thrown into the water, and those who could swim tried to board other boats, but the helping hands were more often the hands of people pushing them away. Some of the unfortunate people disappeared under the surface and did not return. She saw it happen to countless men, women, and children.

That was when she learned someone in the news service had named the strange people who attacked those who were fleeing for their lives. They called them the "infected dead." All along the crowded docks, there were surges of people fighting to get away from the sluggish people who seemed to want only one thing...to bite the terrified people trapped between them and the water.

When the first overloaded boat rolled too far to one side, it dumped dozens of passengers into the water. The loss of ballast on one side caused the other side to become far too heavy, and the boat leaned so far back in the other direction that it just kept going.

No one in the water, on the docks, or on the other boats expected what would become of the passengers who drowned and sank to the bottom. There hadn't been time for most people to learn that they would come back after they died.

The knowledge came later when another boat flipped and dumped its passengers into the water. To Symone, it appeared that there were more people in the water than there had been on the boat, but there was so much chaos it was too hard to tell. Someone on a boat reached a helping hand to a woman in the water, and it was no small miracle that their hands met and grasped together. Another passenger on the boat leaned out at his own risk and caught the woman by her jacket and pulled her closer, but as the two passengers pulled her onto their boat, she opened her mouth wide and locked her teeth into the arm of one of her rescuers. She was immediately pushed overboard, but the bitten rescuer was seriously bleeding.

The reporter who was describing the scene sobbed audibly when she described what had happened next. The boat reached safety alongside a Royal Navy warship that was aiding the rescue, and as passengers were pulled aboard and wrapped in blankets, the man who had been bitten was shot in the head and dropped into the water.

It had been a hard choice to make, but watching people die in the water convinced her that she had done what Henry would have done. A few days into the events that had left so many people dead, Symone had managed to keep herself and her children alive. They were alive, but she wondered how damaged they were. Still, being damaged was better than being dead. Damage could be fixed...dead couldn't.

Adam had taken to watching the same TV show over and over again. It was something she knew about from a Developmental Psychology class she had taken years ago. He was doing his part to keep things from changing, and the ability to start the same DVD over again was his way to make something permanent. Unfortunately, he was able to escape too far into the permanence of that show, and he talked less and less as each day wore on.

The days never felt like they went by fast, but as each one began and ended, it felt like there were more hours in between. When Symone tried to engage Adam in a new project like a jigsaw puzzle or a toy, he responded emotionally and fought to stay in front of his TV. At least he was eating, and when he needed to use the toilet, he would hit the pause button and run off to the bathroom.

Symone only tried once to see if he could be distracted away from the TV by turning it off while he was gone, but it met with such a loud tantrum that she wondered what she would have been forced to do if it had happened while the strange people, the "infected dead" were in the house.

Symone kept her small TV turned away from the children. She spent a few minutes explaining to them how important it was that they stay quiet, and she had hugs for both of them whenever she passed near them, but she saw the curiosity on her daughter's face. Emily was getting more and more bored as she tried her best to let Adam have his way. She didn't know how much more a six-year-old could take, and she didn't think she could sacrifice her only source of outside information just to keep her daughter entertained with her favorite shows, so she decided it might be better to give her the facts...or at least the few facts that might help her daughter understand how dangerous the world had become. The facts might not come with an explanation that would've been acceptable under most circumstances, but at least the facts might keep her children alive. She also didn't know how long she could keep it from her.

She motioned for Emily to come over beside her, and it was obvious how much her daughter wanted to, as was demonstrated by how quickly she responded. It was faster than Symone wanted, and she hit the off button on her TV just in time. Emily's expression showed her disappointment, but Symone quickly explained.

"I'll turn it back on, but I wanted to talk with you first. How much do you know about what's happening?"

Emily appeared to gather her thoughts before she answered, and the explanation surprised Symone a little.

"You know that TV show you wouldn't let us watch about zombies? It's like that."

Symone hid her irritation and asked, "Did you see the show?"

"A little bit. That babysitter you got to stay with us the last time you and Daddy went somewhere was watching it."

If her memory was accurate, they had used the same sitter three times on Sunday nights while that show was on.

"We used her several times. Did she watch it each time?"

Emily nodded, but Symone experienced a weird epiphany. Now she didn't have to explain as much. She just needed to find out how well her daughter was processing it, and even more importantly, how well she would integrate it into what was happening to them in real life...or unreal life, whichever it was they were living.

"Okay, so remind me to find a new babysitter."

Emily giggled, but she checked to see if it was loud enough for Adam to hear. In the long run, it wasn't a good thing for him to be tuning out everything else, but for the moment, it was a blessing.

Symone turned on her small TV and rotated the screen a little so Emily could see it. The video was being shot from a drone camera over the cliffs at Dover. Rescue workers and soldiers were attempting to get as many people as they could down to the water, where ships waited to carry them to safety. Symone was a bit fuzzy on where they thought safety could be found because she had seen a similar broadcast from a station on the coast of Germany near Bremerhaven. There were no cliffs, but people flocked by the thousands for a spot on any boat that would take them away to safety.

Along the top of the Dover cliffs, there was a buffer zone where a fence of barbed wire had been hurriedly strung in a crooked line across hundreds of yards of green fields. It kept the crowd back from the cliffs by a mere fifty yards, which seemed perilously close considering the size of the gathering. If the crowd broke through, their forward motion would make them stream over the cliffs like lemmings.

Pressed too closely along the wire were thousands of people waiting for their turn to be allowed through gates that were spaced about twenty to thirty yards apart. When the gates opened for a few brief moments, there was a current of people that moved forward at the middle and along the wire. Those who were between gates fought to reposition themselves closer to the openings, frustrated by the fact that they were in front but not getting through.

Fights broke out, and even without sound, Symone could tell there were victims in the crowd who were severely injured. The gates opened, frantic people forced their way forward, and it was a struggle to close them again. Soldiers pushed back against the human wall, most of whom were waving their arms in the air. She could only imagine the deafening screams of the people who knew death was right behind them.

At the edge of the cliffs, dozens of chain ladders were strung over the sides, and for the really brave and determined few who needed less, there were ropes. Every ladder and rope was overloaded with downward climbers, and the soldiers were doing their best to hold back the next refugee in line to keep them all from falling. They were doing their best, but it was obvious that their best wasn't going to be good enough.

When the cleats that held one chain ladder in place pulled free, it was like watching a string slide along a floor as something pulled it away. At least forty people were on that ladder, and the cleats were not intended for nearly that many. As the ladder snaked toward the cliff, soldiers dove on top of it in a vain attempt to keep it from being lost over the edge, but they only succeeded in slowing the inevitable. Some didn't give up soon enough and were dragged over the cliff with it.

The loss of soldiers at the wire caused the crowds to push forward along a large section between the gates. On the other side of the wire, the distance between the barbs and the crowd decreased. Fast thinking people in that section threw their luggage and backpacks in front of their own bodies to keep from being pressed against the barbs, but there was an unintended result. The wire was quickly buried under an avalanche of personal belongings that formed a bridge. Thousands of people surged forward, literally pushing people over the bridge to the other side, trampling those who didn't move out of the way.

The breach caused a long collapse of the barrier that even took down several of the gates, and a swarm of humanity rushed to be the next in line at the ladders and ropes. The weight of the sudden increase on the ladders pulled the cleats from the soil, and the human waterfall began as all of the ladders pulled free. What the soldiers couldn't do, the civilians could…at first. Because there were so many more of them, the people piled on top of the ladders as they slid toward the cliffs, and their forward progress was stopped.

If the mobs of fugitives from death had been able to hold themselves back from the ladders long enough for the cleats to have been hammered back into the soil, maybe they would have been saved, but they didn't wait. Fearful of losing their places in line, people continued to climb downward, and they took the ladders with them.

Emily watched with her mother, and Symone saw that her daughter's face was expressionless. How she was able to suppress the horror, she didn't know. Emily saw that her mother was watching her.

"I know, Mummy. You're worried about me."

Then her daughter said the most amazing thing for a child her age.

"That's why you decided that we should stay here."

Symone didn't tell her she hadn't thought that far ahead when she made the decision to stay. It was enough that her daughter knew they had done the right thing. If Emily thought her mother had made the right decision, that was good enough for her.

Someone in charge of the rescue operation must have communicated a difficult decision because the armada of boats at the beach all pulled away at the same moment. People who were scrambling to follow were crushed under a torrent of falling bodies and chain ladders, and the human cascade continued to fall even as the distance between the boats and the beaches increased. Piles of unfortunate refugees of all ages grew along the beaches, and Symone had to wonder how many people on boats watched as their loved ones were buried under that human avalanche. Some even abandoned their own chance to survive by diving into the water and swimming back to the beach.

The network reporter continued to cry as she narrated the events to the viewers. Symone was surprised that she wasn't joining her, but when she considered her six-year-old was watching with her, she knew it was far better that she should demonstrate the kind of resolve that would help them survive. It broke her heart that she couldn't show compassion to be a more appropriate response, but she made a mental note to remember this day with her daughter in the future.

"Emily? When this is over, would you like to visit that place with me so we can place some flowers on the beach?"

She had hoped to help her daughter remember those were people, and what they were watching wasn't a piece of fiction that could be created by a little makeup and a lot of computer-generated graphics, but it backfired.

"Will the zombies be gone?"

It was too soon to think about fixing the trauma or the emotional damage that this might be causing her children. It was obvious that it would be a long time before the infected dead would be gone, and Symone was dismayed to see that the brutality of the tragedy at Dover wasn't over yet.

Those weren't living people who crawled on hands and knees from the water. Where the boats had been beached, there was now a long, narrow stretch of sand between the water and the piles of people.

Many were killed by the fall, crushed under tons of flesh that had pounded on them from above, but judging by the arms and legs that waved from the tangled bodies, too many would pay the price for being alive.

All along that narrow stretch of sand, the infected dead crawled from the water. Some pushed themselves to a standing position and staggered forward, but most simply made steady progress and didn't rise up until they were met by the squirming mass of humanity. Symone was glad there was no audio as the infected feasted on the injured, who were unable to free themselves from the people stacked on top of them.

"We'll wait for the zombies to be gone before we go there," said Symone. "We'll take Daddy with us and tell him all about what happened there."

Symone wanted to paint a picture in Emily's mind that included her father and a world free of those infected dead, zombies, or whatever they were. It might be too soon to fix the damage, but it wasn't too soon to plant a seed of hope. It would be hard for that seed to grow as long as the news broadcasts were so violent and tragic, but the only other choice would be to allow the seeds of despair to choke out their hope like weeds.

As if someone in the studio had the same thoughts, the picture changed to a military complex that was a beehive of activity. A tent city had been erected across a vast area, and truckloads of civilians were being delivered to orientation sites. The caption across the bottom of the screen said it was the Isle of Wight Evacuation Zone. A male reporter explained that the refugees were all receiving an orientation and medical examinations before being assigned to living quarters. It was rumored but not confirmed that members of the Royal family were already somewhere in the huge complex.

Symone was thrilled to see a broadcast about something positive even though they hadn't been able to make it to the evacuation zone themselves. Any small show of resistance to this terrible event was a welcome change, and it made her feel like there was a reason to hope.

The camera view switched from an overhead aerial shot to the inside of a massive tent where rows of tables served long lines of people. It wasn't food that was being dished out. It was an organized distribution of items the people were forced to leave behind. The reporter walked along the aisles while the cameraman got close-up shots of the uniformed men and women who handed out personal hygiene packages that held toothbrushes, toothpaste, soap, and tissues. He explained, with a small amount of humor, that the limited water supply would be enough to cover their basic needs, but men would have to forego the pleasure of shaving for a while.

It was all very orderly and civil, and it did a lot to lift the spirits of everyone in the processing center, but in the dim light of the cellar, Symone felt a chill. Something was wrong. She leaned in toward the TV, and Emily sensed that her mother was upset.

"Mummy?"

"It's all right, Emily. I'm just looking for something."

The camera was aimed at a woman who was smiling broadly at a soldier who had just handed her a package. He returned her smile, undoubtedly responding to her gratitude, and then extended a package to the next person in line.

Symone suddenly knew what it was that had her unsettled. It was the number of people who wore clean bandages. The smiling woman who had just thanked the soldier was wearing a bandage wrapped around her right hand, and the soldier had a bandage patch on his neck. When Symone scanned the others in line, there were more.

From the supply tent, the reporter made his way into an adjacent tent where hundreds of people were eating. The clamor was much louder than in the previous tent as people responded to the opportunity to sit and enjoy a hot meal with their fellow refugees. There were pockets of people who ate with their heads down, and Symone supposed they had less reason to celebrate, having lost loved ones or left behind their homes and other things of value. Overall, the mood was festive, and Emily felt the effects. It was good to see her smile, so Symone wiped the worried expression from her own face and forced a smile in its place.

That disappeared when the broadcast moved to the medical tent. There were no cots or beds with patients connected to IV poles. Symone supposed that was somewhere else, but this tent was an open ward filled with individual treatment teams who were primarily cutting off shirt sleeves with scissors and dumping disinfectant into various wounds, most of which were curved in shape. They were obviously shaped like bite wounds. It was natural to put out an arm or a hand to ward off an attack, so it seemed like most of the patients were receiving injections in one arm while being stitched and bandaged on the other. A few had suffered injuries to their backs, necks, and legs.

When the reporter finished praising the medical care that was being administered to the evacuees, they moved to the next large tent, but at the entrance, they were met by four armed guards who politely directed them away. The reporter had been attempting to put a positive spin on everything, and he even managed to keep a smile on his face when the soldier declined to give an explanation for denying their entry. The studio anchor team tried to pass along suggested questions, but the four guards efficiently kept them from getting a glimpse inside. Symone felt like she knew where the hospital beds were.

The studio took control with the announcement that they were going to go live to images coming out of America and other countries abroad. Amazingly, they cut away to a commercial. It was inconceivable to her that any product would want to be associated with what was happening, but then she wondered if she wasn't too hard on the sponsors or the network. They could be just trying to give their viewers a sense of normalcy. That was followed by another random thought about the military evacuation site and the way she had been bothered by the number of people wearing bandages.

"Why did that bother me so much? Was it because they were hurt, and I felt sorry for them? Was it because there were so many of them? Was it because I knew there were people who were hurt worse and even died?"

"What, Mummy? Are you talking to me?"

Emily brought her back to reality, and Symone saw it clearly. Bites were bad. She had a flashback of the front porch. Every single one of the sick people had been bitten. She ran the memories like a photo album on fast forward, and in every picture, there were bite marks. There were people dying, and then they got back up. The people who died in the water came back onto land and bit the first living person they could reach.

The commercial ended, and Symone was left with something other than what the sponsor might have intended. If they thought she, as a viewer, might feel a little more normal after an advertisement, they would be disappointed to learn she felt a cold dread. The world was so far from normal that it wouldn't be back for a long time.

The scene on TV was a montage of different cities in America. The editors had made sure to select scenes that had famous landmarks as backdrops so the viewers would recognize the locations. A few were a bit fuzzy to her, but she recognized Boston by the frigate docked in the harbor, New York with the Statue of Liberty, Washington DC because of the many historical sites, and Charleston because of Fort Sumter. The scenes were devastating. People were fighting for their lives, and most of them were losing.

As she watched, she wondered if the person who decided to run a commercial would run another one. If they were watching their own broadcast, she seriously doubted it. When they returned the broadcast to the studio, one of the anchors had left. The woman that remained seemed unprepared and searched for something to say. Lacking new direction, she launched into an explanation about why her co-anchor had left. She said he was worried about his family and had gone to be with them. Apparently, a number of the stagehands and the director had left as well.

"We're going to stay with you through the night, bringing you updates as they come in," said the news anchor.

She was a pretty young blonde, and Symone felt sorry for her. She had undoubtedly thought this breaking story would be a real career-maker for her, but as the story developed, she became more and more sure it was the end, not the beginning. Three hours later, she said she would return after a short break, but she never did.

******

Rationing became an obvious need by the end of the first week. As she went over her lists of different foods, Symone knew she had done a good job stocking the cellar with enough food for her to keep their calories high enough for at least six months. The irony wasn't lost on her that her husband was originally scheduled to be at the International Space Station for six months. She had seen a broadcast that mentioned the astronauts briefly and learned that they had at least received their shipment of supplies before the infected dead had come along.

So many astronauts had died on the ground in those disastrous launches that would have carried a full crew to the ISS, but their lost lives meant the others could stay at the station longer. That shipment gave them enough food to last six years if they rationed from the beginning. Symone silently prayed that Henry would stay up there. If there wasn't anything he could do for her and the children, it would be good if he could just stay alive with his best friends. She hoped he knew that, but she wondered what they would do when their food supplies were gone, just as she wondered what she was going to do.

Something told her they would be forced to make a run for it sooner or later. Where they would go was a good question because it seemed like everywhere they could go was just as bad as where they were coming from. Islands seemed to be the best option, but when she thought it through, islands could only hold so many people before they became too crowded. She pictured in her mind the sight of the flotilla of small boats drifting away from the coast.

"Where did they go? What did they do when they got there?" she wondered.

The power flickered off and on, and it made her more afraid. She couldn't keep the children calm and quiet in a dark cellar. Adam's TV didn't come back on by itself, and she panicked when he started to cry in loud sobs. Just because they hadn't heard anyone upstairs, it didn't mean the house wasn't overrun with the dead.

That brought her to another worrisome thought. If the power did fail, she wouldn't be able to warm up any of the food that she had been heating on the small hot plate. It wouldn't be pleasant, but Symone decided they would stay in the cellar for as long as they could, and if they had to make a run for it, they would try for Portsmouth. One simple reason seemed to make sense to her. The Isle of Wight was just too crowded. Everyone and his brother had gone to that evacuation center.

The news channels had been devoid of real information for days when suddenly the channel she had watched the most came back with absolutely dreadful news. As if things weren't bad enough, the middle-aged man who delivered the bad news said information from the military was leaked out that morning. The soldiers at the Isle of Wight who had been providing excellent care to the refugees were executing the civilians, and they were doing it systematically.

Symone's worst suspicions were realized when the man said the bites from the infected were fatal, no matter how minor. Once bitten, a victim would become sick, and within days they would die. There seemed to be no rhyme or reason to how long they would stay dead. Some would turn cold and stiff and stay dead for a day or more, but others waited no longer than a few minutes before they opened their eyes. There was some speculation about the severity of the bite that had led to their deaths, but the rules just didn't always hold true.

The hundreds of bite victims housed at the Isle of Wight evacuation facility became sick within the first few days, and as they died, they became dangerous. Eventually, the soldiers were told to gather all bite victims in one area away from the camp, and when the numbers grew too quickly, they had no choice but to dispose of them. They tried to do it discreetly by taking them away in trucks, but as the problem dissolved into chaos, the civilians were executed and then loaded into the trucks.

Symone considered what she would do if she had gone to the evacuation center. If she had noticed a bandaged hand on a member of the nice family next to them, she would have moved her children away from them. She could imagine that frightened families weren't turning in their bitten relatives. Without realizing what they were doing, unbitten people were exposing the soldiers to danger, and the military was determined to stop the spread of the infection.

In the dim light of the cellar, Symone studied the faces of her children and wondered how far she would go to protect them. She knew she would do whatever it took to keep them safe, and she could easily imagine herself using her gun to shoot a soldier who was after Adam or Emily because they had been bitten.

That reminded her of the gun, and for a few panicky moments, she couldn't remember where she had seen it last. The stairs...she had left it there days ago when she had gone to the bottom step and prayed that the sounds she heard upstairs would stop. She silently crossed the cellar to be sure she had left it out of reach of the children and that the safety was still on.

It was on a brick ledge high enough that Emily would only have been able to reach it using a chair. The metal felt cold in her hand, but she was reassured by its weight. It was their first and last line of defense.

If she hadn't been standing at the bottom of the stairs, she wouldn't have seen the very small shaft of light near the bottom of the door interrupted by something that must be standing right next to the refrigerator. Whatever it was, it came and went, blocking the light for split seconds at a time. Then it stopped where it was. Symone could picture the spot where someone or something was standing. It was exactly in the middle of a six-foot section between the window of the back door and the refrigerator.

A man's voice caught her by surprise, and she was forced to clamp a hand over her own mouth to stifle a cry.

"Did you hear that?" asked the man.

A second man answered, "Hear what?"

"Outside…when's the last time you heard a plane? There ain't been any planes in or out of Bournemouth in days, and I swear I just heard one."

The man's words were clipped, and by his accent, she guessed he was from somewhere around London.

It was quiet as the two men listened together.

"There it is again," said the first man. "We better get over there."

Symone heard the second man mutter something that must have been an agreement because she could hear him retreating from the kitchen as he spoke. The shadow at the bottom of the door disappeared as the first man yelled at him to wait because they needed to check outside first. It wasn't until they were gone that Symone realized she had the gun pointed at the door, and the safety was off.

As they made their hasty exit from her kitchen, Symone was dumbfounded to realize she hadn't thought about the airport. It had been an RAF base when it was built, but when it was returned to civilian use, it had served as a backup to Heathrow when the airlines needed to ground planes. It had long runways and could accommodate planes of all sizes. They had Boeing 747s and the Concord pay visits from time to time until they had been retired.

The countryside around the airport was flat and wide open, and somehow Symone had missed any news broadcasts about what had happened over there. If they were to attempt to travel south toward the coast, they would have a clear view of it from the road. She expected to see something drastic had happened there given the reports from other cities, but it was quiet now…way too quiet. When she thought about it, she hadn't seen a plane fly over toward Bournemouth or Heathrow even on the day before they had escaped to the cellar.

According to the men who had been in her kitchen, a plane had passed over the house. If someone was still in the air, she couldn't imagine why they would want to land anywhere near a major city. If the military couldn't keep it together at the Isle of Wight, she couldn't believe they would do any better at an airport. Sure, there were fences around most of it, but she didn't imagine those would keep out the crowds of people that had undoubtedly fled to the airport in the hope of getting a seat on a plane whenever they could.

The answer to Symone's puzzled thoughts came almost immediately. She could hear the high-pitched engines of the transport planes as their numbers grew. The vibrations shook the walls as more and more passed over the house lower than ever. Emily anticipated her next move by turning on her TV and locating the news channel that still had people working, but before she did, she made sure Adam was distracted by slipping in a movie that always grabbed his attention. The noise and vibrations had caused him to lift worried eyes to the exposed beams in the ceiling above him.

"We have just learned that the military is evacuating from the Isle of Wight," said the breathless man who had red-rimmed eyes from too little sleep.

It didn't surprise Symone, but she wasn't sure why the military thought they could do any better on the mainland.

"It may be the last time we are able to get live images from the Isle of Wight, and we have to warn you that some of our viewers may find these scenes disturbing, but it's important for you to know how dire the situation has become."

The camera view was from a drone, and even after everything Symone had seen in her own driveway, she wasn't prepared for what she saw on her TV. A soldier with a flamethrower was shooting great gouts of fire into tents. Even as he did, people engulfed in flames emerged from the tents and walked straight toward him. He was backing away from them as they approached, and he even targeted them again as if he could do more to them than he already had. Behind him, on the opposite side of the path that had served as the main street through the camp, the tents had already been set ablaze, and a crowd of roasting human flesh was gathering.

The soldier took an opportunity to see what was behind him as he retreated, and he found himself cut off from any escape route. He aimed his flamethrower again and turned in a circle as he scorched everything that was coming toward him. It worked for a few moments as burning bodies collapsed around him, but when their burned legs could no longer support them, they crawled. The circle around him grew smaller and smaller, and Symone saw that the final act of desperation committed by the female police officer in her driveway was no longer uncommon. The soldier dropped his flamethrower and pulled his service pistol from his hip. His act was just as rapid and decisive as Symone had witnessed before. The drone moved away, mercifully not showing what happened as the dead reached the man's body.

7

Springdale

Off the Coast of Nova Scotia - The Beginning

Across the Atlantic Ocean near the coast of Canada, a small airport had seen the same loss of life that was brought about by the lack of information that was too slow to be recognized. If people had been told not to treat the wounded, some would have had the strength to focus their efforts on saving the rest. It was the human nature of most good people not to leave the wounded behind. In most cultures, the dead aren't even left behind, and it was no different at the remote wilderness vacation spot.

It was a small town with a seasonal business built around the airport, and the locals got most of their news from the Internet. For that reason, the information was often unreliable at best. Over morning coffee before sunrise, there was already plenty of disagreement over how accurate the reports were.

The headlines said there were zombies terrorizing cities everywhere, but the hardy folks of the northeast joked that it wasn't anything new. There had been drugs, crime, and zombies in big cities for years, and people were just beginning to notice. The fact that the problems had been ignored for years made it almost a surprise that it was getting real attention now.

Some of the tourists were canceling their reservations and going home. There were plenty who were angry because they couldn't get their deposits back, and there were even more of them who were angry because they couldn't get a flight out for at least a couple of days. They were the ones who believed something crazy was happening, and they had to get back home to protect their belongings.

An equal number of new arrivals poured into the small airport and were happy to find they could book cabins on short notice. The first thing they did on arrival was to purchase large amounts of supplies and every bit of hunting gear they could get their hands on. The people of Springdale had every reason to believe they would have their best tourist season ever. Double bookings, inventory flying off the shelves, and even more people hiring the bush pilots to fly them north and drop them off. All because of some rumors about zombies.

Within four days, the owners of the small restaurants and stores went from happy disbelief to a slowly building, uneasy dread. After hours at a town council meeting, they were talking about a new problem. They were going to have an abundance of cash, and they never thought that could be a bad thing until they realized they weren't going to have their usual leftovers. After the tourists would leave at the end of the season, they wouldn't have enough supplies for themselves. The bad news was compounded when they tried to place orders with their wholesale distributors on the mainland. No one was taking orders unless they were giving shipment dates six months to a year away, and even those weren't guaranteed.

The main concern wasn't how to resupply, though. If they couldn't get supplies for six months, they would just stop making sales. If the tourists didn't like it, they could leave. The real concern was why so many of the tourists were sporting fresh bandages. Some were sick already, and some got sick shortly after they arrived. The town's little clinic was overrun with a demand for Tetanus shots and antibiotics. It didn't take long for the locals to find out the stories on the Internet were true after all.

Five days after the first mass arrival of tourists, the town's only police officer was faced with the first assault involving a bite wound. The airport had a few security guards, and they joined with the officer to maintain control, but armed tourists weren't about to take orders from a local constable when their family members were getting sick. The bite victim was the town doctor, and the person who bit her was being held in a single cell security room at the airport. It was a nine-year-old girl, and the distraught parents couldn't understand why she was handcuffed to a chair with both hands behind her back.

That was only the beginning of the end for a town that would have survived the outbreak of the infection if it had cut itself off from the outside, but there was no way for them to have known.

******

Present Day

Sparks got Plain Jane as close to the small terminal as he could, but there were still plenty of bodies between the plane and the building. The Chief didn't need to tell any of the experienced crew that the infected were almost as dangerous in pieces as they were whole, but he did it anyway. Even though it was a gruesome idea, he suggested that they should locate one of the small tractors he suspected the airport would have on hand to plow snow from the runway. He didn't have the usual half-grin on his face when he said it, so they knew he wasn't thinking of anything except keeping them safe.

The Chief, Tom, and Hampton all had tractor experience, so they set out in the direction of the maintenance hangar. It didn't take long for them to find exactly what they were looking for, but the battery was dead from seven years of cold weather and no use. They had to find the generator-powered battery charger and get some juice on the tractor's battery before they could get it to start. An hour later, they were driving between the terminal and the plane, creating a safety lane.

Whether it was for additional safety or strictly humanitarian reasons, they also walked the edge of the piles of remains and used their long blades and poles to permanently end the threats offered by the heads that still moved. With the bright sun shining down on the blood-stained tarmac, they finally walked in single file toward the terminal. The air was cool and crisp, but the smell of decay was still overwhelming. In the trees that lined the runways, hungry eyes watched as feral dogs and native wildlife were drawn to the scent.

It was almost completely silent around the small terminal where no more than a hundred or so people must have waited for the planes to come and go. Kathy was the first to make the observation that there were far more infected than that when they had arrived.

"Tourist season," said the Chief.

Hampton added, "We saw the same thing every year in Georgetown. We were a sort of pit stop between Charleston and

Myrtle Beach, so traffic always increased during the summer months. When a hurricane would come close, the tourists all waited until the last minute to leave, so it always got congested on the roads going out of town."

"Is that what happened here?" asked Colleen.

Hampton nodded.

"This would have been the central point of departure, and by the looks of it, I would guess that their main problem was a shortage of planes."

There were a couple of airplanes nearby that had suffered damage, and the evidence of gunfire was obvious. They were also stripped of parts that undoubtedly went to the winners of the shootout. One twin-engine plane was missing the propeller.

"I need two volunteers to keep watch while the rest of us check out the terminal," said the Chief.

Cassandra raised her hand, but the Chief shook his head.

"I need you inside. Your experience in close urban combat might be needed."

Sim and Tom took the hint and signaled that they would stay outside. They each moved to positions where they could see the full length of the terminal and the corners. They had already checked the maintenance hangars when they fixed the tractor, but they were more concerned with the woods beyond the runways. The wildlife had most likely found the infected dead to be both prey and predator, so these warmblooded newcomers were putting out an enticing scent of their own. With Sparks still in the plane watching the group from a distance, they had the area covered from three angles.

The rest of the group moved closer to the terminal doors and windows to see what they could through the grime that coated every inch of the glass. It was dirty on both sides, and the gloom inside offered no light that would reveal whatever threat might be waiting for them.

The Chief rapped the barrel of his pistol against the glass and waited. They expected the usual rush of bodies to the door, but it stayed quiet. He took in the expressions on the faces of the rest of the group, and they all gave slight shrugs of their shoulders. The quiet inside could mean plenty of different things, one of which was that the place was empty. Ten other reasons for the quiet could be bad.

He tugged on the handle next, and the door resisted opening. The rattle of a chain answered the reason why nothing had pushed the door open from inside. Everyone knew what had to be done next, so they all backed away from the door. The Chief fired several rounds at the corners, and the entire pane collapsed downward. When the noise of the falling glass stopped, there was nothing but silence.

"Someone locked everyone else outside," said Captain Miller. "If there's a survivor inside, they might be staying quiet because there have been others to come along since the beginning."

"They would be dangerous," said Kathy, "but this place smells like no one has been alive here for a long time."

"If someone had gotten inside Fort Sumter, they would never have guessed I was in there," he answered.

"Point taken," said Kathy. "We should go in with the assumption that someone might be alive."

Sim called out to the group as Kathy extended one foot through the shattered door.

"You can survive a long time inside an airport. Take it from me."

Each of them had survived desperate situations, but Sim had survived in a big airport. Although there were similarities, this one wasn't likely to have the amount of food and other essentials Sim had at his disposal in the major airport near Columbus, Ohio. There was one thing it did have in common that they were especially worried about. There had been no shortage of guns at this vacation spot.

Kathy had a keen sense of hearing. Added to her hearing, she had years of experience since the beginning of the infection. There was a certainty to a sound that told her whether or not it had been made by an infected dead or a living person, and she felt that certainty now. It was more like a "snick" than a "click" in her mind, and she told herself someone had just flipped off the safety on a weapon, or she had triggered a trap. She paused with her weight on the foot she had extended through the door, and she could feel through the sole of her shoe that it hadn't been the sound of glass being crushed. She shifted her weight back to the foot that was still outside, and then she fell backward to the ground.

The Chief had seen the shift, and in one smooth motion, he grabbed the back of Kathy's shirt and pulled. As he pulled, he let his own weight drop to the ground, and Kathy came with him. The bullet that would have hit Kathy missed by several feet. Years of practice had taught them both that falling down didn't give you the right to stay where you landed. They both rolled away from the spot as soon as they hit the ground, and a second bullet left a divot in the asphalt as it screamed by. It also gave them both an idea of where the shooter was...straight inside but at a high location. It was maybe a balcony or office that looked down on the terminal, or it could be the stairs that went up to that office.

Everyone moved to the left and right of the doorway and then spread out along the front of the building. They also had to stay low because there were too many windows. Being in the open seemed like the best way to approach the airport because the display they had put on when they cleared the infected dead would have made anyone inside welcome their arrival, or so they had thought.

"Over here," yelled Captain Miller.

He had found a place where the glass was gone from a smaller window, and he had a clear view of the balcony inside where the shot had come from. Everyone kept low as they crossed the front of the terminal to the right and grouped up around him. He pulled a small laser pointer from his utility belt and aimed it at the spot so the others could see. There was a barrel of a hunting rifle aimed downward in the direction of the front door, but it wasn't moving. It was just keeping steady aim on the opening.

"What's she waiting for, someone else to come through the door? Does she think we're going to rush her?" asked the Chief.

"Why would you assume it's a woman?" asked Kathy.

"A man wouldn't shoot a woman with that much blonde hair," he answered.

"You should think about having kids, Chief. You've already got the dad jokes mastered. You do realize someone just tried to put a bullet in me, right?"

Captain Miller gave them a stern look and said, "When you two get done with your routine, or whatever it is, we need to figure out how to get to that shooter."

Something caught the Chief's eye, and he held out his hand to Captain Miller.

"Let me see that laser pointer for a minute."

Captain Miller passed it over to him, and the Chief played the tiny red light across the ceiling above the shooter's position. Something seemed to glint brighter red when he passed over it, and the Chief came back to it again. As he moved the dot from the ceiling toward the door, he saw the brightness change a few times, but it mostly stayed bright in a straight line if he kept his hand steady.

Iris watched over his shoulder, and she squinted her eyes to block out the light everywhere except where the red dot traveled.

"It's reflecting back off of something," she said.

"Ever seen light travel through fiber optic cables?" asked Cassandra.

The Chief was glad to have such quick thinkers around him. He had already guessed by how still the rifle barrel was that it was a booby trap, but the laser pointer was the perfect tool for locating the string because it was most likely a monofilament line. The light from the laser pointer seemed to spread out when it hit the line.

The Chief deferred to Kathy's marksmanship and also considered it to be her right to be the one to take the shot. He suggested that she should just aim for the barrel. If it turned out they were wrong, and the gun was actually in someone's hands, it wasn't necessary to kill them. It would sting a bit, but having a rifle shot out of their hands wasn't likely to kill them.

Kathy made it look easy. Most people couldn't hit a target that small and that far away, but she got it on the first try. The rifle bucked upward and away, but it didn't fall. It was now pointed at a spot near the ceiling and to the right of the front door.

"Jim, you and Cassandra keep your guns aimed at that spot while the rest of us go back to the front door. If it moves, open fire and pin them down. We'll be inside fast if it doesn't move."

"Got it," said Captain Miller. He and Cassandra took aim on the rifle and waited.

Less than a minute later, the Chief led the others through the front door and quickly to the wall below the rifle. From close range, they could see the fishing line better, and they knew there wasn't a shooter in the balcony, but they didn't assume there wasn't one somewhere because there had been two shots. They spread out as they entered, but they kept moving forward. Hampton was the first one to find the stairs that went up to the balcony, and he took the steps two at a time. The carpet under his feet was damp and mildewed, so there was hardly a sound as he reached the top. He found the badly splintered rifle that Kathy had shot and one other that was set back further from the opening. Both had a monofilament fishing line attached to their triggers.

"All clear," he called out.

The others did the same from different places throughout the small terminal. The glass on the large windows was grimy, but there was more than enough light for them to do a quick sweep of the main room of the terminal and determine there were no more booby traps, infected dead, or living people. They were able to relax a bit, but the place was a mess.

In its glory days, the terminal had probably been a quaint but modern welcome station for tourists coming and going to the wilderness island. From here, they could set out in all directions to camp, hunt, and fish. In the distant forests, there were cabins and campgrounds, and along the coasts on the other side of the island, there were docks and a variety of fishing boats. Where the water was deeper, there were places where larger boats could dock, but to the west, there was a small marina where anglers could go after a variety of game fish without having to get seasick over deeper water. It was a paradise for people who wanted to get away from civilization, but it came with plenty of amenities and comforts.

Now the terminal resembled a battlefield fort. The way every piece of furniture was stacked across the windows, it was obvious that someone had been trapped inside, and something was trying to get in. It didn't take much imagination to guess what that "something" was. Since the booby traps were focused on the front door, they checked the other exits and found two more.

Hampton had grown up hunting deer, and he admired the Marlin 336 aimed at a side door. The lever-action rifle was popular with hunters, and he guessed it was new on the day it had been rigged as a booby trap. Picturing someone setting the loop of fishing line over the trigger gave him goosebumps because it felt like someone was watching him.

He called out loud enough for everyone to hear, but he kept his voice soft.

"Whoever set these traps has to be inside somewhere."

Iris and Colleen were at a door that entered a separate wing, and they waved at him to indicate there was something he should see. The others moved their way, carefully weaving through stacks of simple barricades that were obviously intended to be difficult for the infected dead to navigate. There was debris everywhere, and the stench that had been trapped inside the building was difficult to tolerate.

Kathy pulled a scarf over her face and, in a muffled voice said, "No one alive has used this terminal in a long time."

She added, "I think the survivors here, whoever they were, abandoned this part of the terminal after using it as their first line of defense. On a smaller scale, it resembles the cruise terminal in Charleston. After everyone boarded the ship, the infected swarmed through the place."

Colleen said, "We've seen these things dozens of times. There were probably over a hundred people in this little terminal. Most of them didn't know each other. Some had their kids with them. They didn't know what was happening or what they were going to do, but there were only two or three cops. They had their handguns, but they didn't just shoot people in the head. They tried to protect everyone."

Captain Miller added, "Some of them had already been bitten, but no one knew what was going to happen, so the people trapped inside instinctively tried to treat the wounded. They barricaded the doors and windows against the infected outside even though there were likely to be people inside who were screaming to let them in. Their husbands, wives, children, parents, and relatives were out there."

"The booby traps came later," said the Chief. "After they retreated."

The door where Iris and Colleen stood guard led to a large restaurant. It was decorated like the lodge in a ski resort, and during better days, it had probably felt warm and exciting. Everything was made of richly marbled wood with huge beams supporting an impossibly heavy ceiling that towered above the room. Up in the rafters, there were sleeping bags tied to the beams with ropes, and the long dining room tables had been hoisted upward and nailed into place as platforms. The new arrivals from the South gazed up with wonder at the evidence of the last stand made years ago.

"It worked for a while," said the Chief. "I would guess that there were at least fifty people up there at one time."

The Mud Island family and the others who had joined them later were all veterans of the apocalypse. They could all imagine everything that happened in the once beautiful restaurant. They knew they wouldn't be far from the truth if they guessed that the people had gathered inside the restaurant because there were smaller windows than those in the airport terminal. They could also be shuttered from the inside because the restaurant wasn't open the whole year. No one was experienced with anything like the infected dead, but there were plenty of locals in the crowd, and they knew about climbing trees to survive. They also knew that it was easier to shoot from higher places like deer blinds.

For a while, they kept the wounded and the weakest of the survivors up in the rafters, but then they learned what they had inside with them. Unfortunately, they learned too late. As the wounded died and turned their teeth toward the people tending to them, the number of survivors dwindled. Some fell from the rafters, but if the fall didn't kill them, there was a fate worse than death waiting for them. Judging by the number of black stains on the floor, that was how most of them died.

Cassandra remembered the nightmare she lived through on the hospital ship, and her eyes were drawn toward the swinging door that could only lead to the kitchen.

"Guys, if things went down the same way they did on the ship, the last of the survivors went that way."

They followed where her hand was pointed, and since there were no signs of living people inside the restaurant, they felt like there was no choice but to check for survivors beyond the door. Kathy took the lead because she was the closest one to it. She put a hand on it and just pressed hard enough for it to open half an inch.

She whispered, "There's not much light."

"Someone remind me why we're doing this," said Colleen.

"We have to be sure there aren't any survivors," said Hampton.

Colleen didn't say it in a mean way, but she said what most of them already thought.

"I don't think there are any."

Kathy let her eyes adjust to the low light and slipped quietly through the door. Before it could shut, the others followed. They all kept themselves low, bent over at the waist, and fanned out among stainless steel tables and appliances. Hampton was the first to make a sound that made everyone else stop moving. It was hardly more than a hiss through his clenched teeth, but they knew it was deliberate.

In the low light, they saw him point two fingers at his eyes and then the same two fingers at the floor. They all silently converged on his spot. The Chief, Kathy, Iris, Colleen, Cassandra, Henry, and Captain Miller all came together in the narrow space behind Hampton to see what he had found. Before Cassandra even saw what was there, she knew what the place was. Hampton was only a few feet away from the handle of a large stainless steel door, and she broke the silence in the room much louder than she intended.

"Don't open that door."

Everyone jumped as if the threat was real, and more than one of them collided with pots and pans as well as other debris from long ago. Empty cans and utensils of all kinds clattered in the dim light. It took a while for their hearts to stop pounding in their chests and for their nerves to allow the goosebumps to loosen on their arms and necks.

Hampton said in a much lower voice, "I wasn't going to." He gestured toward the floor.

The dark shape in front of the door had been a man before he had shot himself in the head. There was a sign around his neck that said, "Don't open the door. If you've survived long enough to read this, then you know why."

Despite the thickness of the door to the walk-in refrigerator, they could hear the sounds from the other side. The racket they had made when Cassandra made them all jump out of their skin had been enough to draw the interest of the dead inside. They were moaning and thudding against the door expressing that interest.

"I don't think there's a reason to expect anyone to be alive in there," said Kathy. "They must've started in the terminal, retreated to the restaurant, and finally wound up here."

The Chief pulled a piece of paper from the hand of the man who had closed the door on the dead. He had to pry the stiffened fingers apart to keep from tearing it in half. There was writing on it, and he guessed right that it was a message left behind for whoever found him. The note had one sentence on it that wasn't news to anyone who had lived as long as they had.

"Kill the wounded before they kill you."

Hampton said, "I remember when it all started that we felt like all we had to do was stay isolated in our little town, and we would be fine. They were so isolated out here that they probably thought they would be rescued any day. They didn't know that the rest of the world would have been glad to have a place in the wilderness like this, but the flip side of that coin was that they also didn't learn how to deal with it as quickly. If they had followed the advice on this piece of paper, at least some of them would have lived."

Henry had followed the others, but he had stayed unusually silent. One thought had crossed his mind, and he was having a hard time letting it go. His wife and children were somewhere, and the odds were high that they had been forced to hold out at home for as long as they could, but they would eventually be forced to run for a safer place. The only reason he had survived was that he was literally in the most remote location that existed. It could just as well be them inside that steel vault, and for the first time since his return to Earth, he felt his hope slipping away.

There was a commotion behind them at the door to the kitchen, and they all spun around thinking there was a new threat. Tom and Sim burst into the room. Neither of them was injured in any way, but the Chief read something in their expressions that made him say out loud what he was thinking.

"Why do I feel like one of you is going to say that we aren't going to believe you when you tell us what happened?"

Tom answered for both of them, "That's exactly what Sim said outside. You aren't going to believe this. Sparks left us here."

The news stunned them into silence, but the Chief was the first one to go past Tom and Sim. He had to see it for himself, even if there was nothing he could do about it. He crashed through the restaurant creating a new path where broken furniture was in the way. By the time he reached the front door and the tarmac outside, the plane was too far away for him to hear it. He could still see it climbing away into the clear sky, but the silence was complete.

The Chief looked at his friends as if someone could explain it differently or offer some sort of hope that Sparks was somehow forced into taking off, but he would be back.

Tom said, "When the plane rotated on the runway, we thought he was just getting into position for an easy take-off. We didn't think anything of it until he picked up speed."

"Even when he powered up," said Sim. "There wasn't anything we could do to stop him."

"Don't blame yourself," said Kathy. "We all got it wrong. Sparks must've played us all from the start and went along with everything until he got his chance to get his plane back."

"But why?" asked Iris.

Captain Miller suggested an explanation that made them all feel sick.

"Where did Sparks tell you he was from?" he asked.

The question was to the Chief, but everyone agreed he had said he spent a lot of time at the beach in California, but they thought he was from Houston. He had a bit of a drawl in his speech that made them all think he was a bit of a cowboy.

"There's a county in Georgia named Houston. They say its name a bit differently, but a part of me always thought that kid was from Georgia," said Captain Miller.

The implication wasn't lost on the Chief. If that plane belonged to the militia in Atlanta, then their settlement above Green Cavern in Guntersville was in big trouble. The worst part was that they were stranded, and they couldn't even warn them.

Defeat didn't come easy to the Chief, and the others could see the silent rage that was boiling inside him. There had to be a way to warn Doc Bus and Ed so they could evacuate the town. It wouldn't be the first time that everyone from above was brought inside the shelter, and there was nothing that militia could do to get inside the shelter once it was sealed.

"I may be able to help," said Henry.

Henry had been so quiet that the Chief was almost surprised he was there.

"Let's hear it. No idea is a bad idea right now," said the Chief.

"Well, as you Yanks like to say, the game isn't over until it's over. We still have Maggie Mae. If we can find a way to let her know we're here, we can see if she can get a message to the shelter by sending it through Gentry in Huntsville. The Maggie Mae has long-range satellite gear, and she should be able to bounce a signal that far. It's a race against time, but at least it's not that far from Huntsville to Guntersville."

The suggestion galvanized the Chief into action.

"Someone find the communications equipment in this place and get it working."

The rest of the group didn't hear what the Chief said, but they all saw the smile on Jim Miller's face when the Chief leaned in close and whispered something just to him. Whatever it was, they were sure they would know later because it didn't seem like a good time for the Chief to be telling his friend a joke. It had to be something the Chief normally referred to as "Plan B."

******

The radio equipment was still intact, and there was no shortage of generators. In the excitement of getting the equipment operational, they almost forgot about who else might be out there listening when they started to broadcast. If it was the United States Navy or another branch of the US military, there was always a chance that Captain Miller would be identified. It pained the man deeply not to be able to do his duty for his country, but he felt like the oath he took as an officer didn't include placing his people at risk by bringing the infected dead back to their ships at sea. That was why he had deserted with about one hundred people. For all he knew, the military had followed through with their plans and had all paid the price with their lives.

Henry offered a logical solution. He would make the distress call, and if the military arrived before they could contact his friend with the ocean-going tugboat, they would have to hide Captain Miller. The other thing to consider was how fast Sparks would get back to his friends and when they would launch a strike against the shelter at Green Cavern. One thing that they had on their side was the fact that Sparks would be forced to refuel before doing anything else. If they were lucky, he would have to go out of his way to refuel before flying to Atlanta. It would all depend on Henry and how fast his friend was able to reach Gentry Campbell in Huntsville.

Henry would probably have been happy to be a stage actor if he hadn't become an astronaut, and he gave a masterful performance on the radio. He even managed to clip his refined way of speaking by putting on a somewhat uncultured accent. He pronounced his name as if there was no "H" at the beginning and said "hello" the same way.

"Ello, ello, ello…is this bloody thing working? This is Enry Tisdal calling out to Maggie Mae. Can you 'ear me?"

The rest of the group stayed completely quiet, but Cassandra had to put her hand over the bullet wound she had gotten in Huntsville. Holding in her urge to laugh was making it hurt.

On his third try, the voice of Andi Hartford came from the speaker. She was amused by Henry's attempt to disguise his identity, but she went along with it. They didn't know it at the time, but she had been crossing the bay just north of their island when the AC-130 cleared the treetops and banked toward the mainland. It wasn't something she saw every day, and her educated guess was that it had been at the Springdale airport. The call from Henry made her feel like coincidences were piling up, and she only half believed in them anyway. The two had to be related events.

"This is Maggie Mae. Making good speed near the Scilly Isles. Coming up on Bryher now, so your signal is weak. I won't be able to make the morning stop at Springdale as planned."

After that brief message, every word was missing a syllable or two as if the signal was breaking up. Henry never lost his accent as he tried to get her to respond. When he finally gave up, everyone was surprised by his reaction. He even claimed it was a roaring success and gathered his gear together.

"Do you know something we don't know?" asked Kathy.

"Yes, my dear, and we have to hurry. What time is it?"

They all checked their watches and saw that it was getting close to midnight, which only seemed to make Henry move faster.

"I'll explain as we go, but we don't have time to waste. We're just about a mile from the deepwater docks where the Maggie Mae will be waiting. I assume this lot can do a mile by midnight."

They gathered their gear and were on the move in minutes. As they ran at a brisk pace, Henry explained that he had several conversations with Andi Hartford about the possibility of making a water landing with the Soyuz capsule, but without accurate telemetry, the landing zone would be anywhere from Nova Scotia to the Scilly Isles. Their calculations based on their orbit always put their optimal reentry time at midnight, and he assumed she meant midnight when she said early morning.

"But she said she was near the Scilly Isles," said Iris between running breaths.

"She knows that's near where I want to go," answered Henry, "and we never talked about Springdale. That was her way of letting me know that she knew where I was calling from. She might have even seen Sparks take off, but she couldn't say that with the risk someone else may have been listening."

There was some doubt among the group as they ran, but Henry's excitement was infectious, and they covered the mile between the airport and the docks by eleven-fifty.

8

Fear

Southern England - The Beginning

Symone remembered a little game Henry had started with Adam Calloway one evening when he had come over to cook supper with them in the yard behind their house. He was always introducing them to American things, and on that particular night, it was something they already knew quite well, and that was the value of a good measure of Jack Daniels with no ice or water. It was just for sipping and savoring. He was disappointed because he wanted credit for their discovery of the pleasure, but they upstaged him by suggesting he should try an equal measure of their favorite scotch, Royal Salute. He said he didn't like scotch, and Henry had replied that Adam had apparently never tasted Royal Salute.

"What if you like Royal Salute better than Jack Daniels?" asked Henry.

"Not gonna happen," answered Adam in his quaint American accent.

"I'm just asking, what if you do?" Henry persisted.

Adam appeared to be thinking it over and then said, "Then I guess I'll have to drink both of them."

They had laughed hard at the answer, in part because they had already each sipped their way through two glasses of Jack, but also because Henry should have known the answer without even asking the question. It wasn't really that funny, but the "what if" part of it stuck. It was followed by several more questions just like it, but it had stuck with the Tisdal children as well.

They adored Adam Callaway, so the next morning, when Symone asked her son and daughter if they would like cereal or pancakes for breakfast, they asked in unison, "What if we want both?"

Emily and Adam had laughed hysterically at the breakfast table, and Symone made a mental note to tell the men to either watch what they say in front of the children or wait with the whiskey until after bedtime for the little ones with big ears. It was harmless, but it had shown her they were paying close attention to what the grownups said.

Now they were in a dark, damp cellar, and it was a painful reminder of better days...much better days. The little TV was illuminating Adam's angelic face, and Emily was reading a book using a small LED lamp she had found in a box of junk that had been stuffed away in a corner. At least exploring the recesses of the cellar had kept them busy from time to time. Symone had exhausted their supply of perishables, so pancakes made from a box of powder mixed with water would be the only choice. When she had asked the children if they wanted breakfast, Adam had asked for eggs, and Emily said pancakes.

It made Symone think, "What if we could have both?"

The simple question made her remember that evening and the following morning, and it hurt.

"How long have we been hiding down here?" she asked herself.

She didn't remember, and it would have surprised her to know it had been over two weeks already. It might also have surprised her that it wasn't two months because she found herself to be experiencing mood swings. One moment she felt strong and capable because she had kept her children alive longer than so many others, but she would suddenly realize it was a lifetime battle that would go on until she couldn't do it anymore.

Her question to herself changed to, "How long will we have to stay in hiding down here?"

"There it is again," she thought. "Another mood swing...glass half-full or half-empty? Who cares?"

The smell of pancakes beginning to get a little too well done snapped her out of her thoughts, and she told Adam there were no more eggs, but she would let him put extra maple syrup on his pancakes. That brightened him up, but Symone was glad because it would also hide the burnt flavor on one side of the pancakes.

It had been quiet upstairs for almost a week, and if there were more airplanes, she didn't hear them. All of the television stations had gone off the air, and there was nothing but static on the radio. The only thing that they had to pass the time was the little TV and video player that Adam used, and she was willing to let him watch it as much as he liked if it helped him deal with the cellar, but she knew better than to think it would last. She didn't want it to go on permanently. She just wanted it to go on long enough for her to figure out the next move.

"Speaking of which," she thought, "you know what it has to be."

She sat back against a pillow on top of her sleeping bag and studied the children. She wondered if she could do what she had to do, but the more she thought about it, the more she realized she only had one choice.

"No, that's not correct. I have lots of choices, but none of them are good. Some are only not as bad as others."

"What, Mummy?" asked Emily.

She didn't realize she had said her last thought out loud.

"I'm sorry, baby. I was just thinking out loud. Come over here and let me tell you something."

Emily understood by now that the invitation meant Mummy wanted to tell her something without Adam getting upset, so she hurried over and sat down with her back to him. That way, Symone could lean closer and talk without Adam seeing her face and the conspiratorial way they whispered.

When Emily was situated, Symone said softly, "I think I have to go out and see what's happening. It's the only way we'll know if this thing is over and if help has arrived."

Emily had been stronger than Symone could have hoped for, but the fear on her face was obvious. Big puddles of tears collected on her lower eyelids and didn't fall until she blinked. She pinched her lips together to keep her mother from seeing that she was fighting back the crying, and Symone knew she couldn't put any more on the little girl's shoulders. She wrapped her arms around her and pulled her close, whispering that she would be fine and not to worry. That was when Adam exploded.

Whatever defense mechanism had been allowing him to keep everything inside, it broke down when he saw his sister's back heaving in great big sobs. His own sobs burst loudly into their dim prison, and as strong as Emily had been, she wasn't able to contain her own fear enough to help him. Symone held her arms wider for Adam to join them, and he didn't hesitate. His little body slammed hard into his mother and sister, hard enough to hurt, but Symone didn't show it. Instead, she just cried along with them.

The three of them held each other and cried themselves out. Symone tried not to worry that someone or something upstairs would choose now to come into the kitchen. If they did, it would only end one way, or she would die trying.

When the sobs came to an end, Adam said what Symone was already thinking.

"Mummy, I don't want to be here anymore. I want Daddy, and I want to play in my room."

Emily was still processing what her mother had said that had caused the dam of emotion to burst, but she couldn't bring herself to say anything to help this time. She wanted to say something that would help to calm her little brother, but her strength was gone. Symone could see the hopeful look Emily gave her. She hoped her mother could come up with the answer.

Symone put her face in front of theirs and said, "Remember when you asked Daddy why he has to go into outer space? Do you remember what he told you?"

They both said yes, and Emily said, "To explore space and learn things we don't know."

Adam was nodding his head as Emily quoted their father.

"That's right, Emily, and now I have to be an explorer, but not in outer space. I only need to explore outside the house. I won't be gone long. I'll only be gone long enough to see if it's safe for us to leave the cellar."

"I want to go with you," said Adam. He was on the verge of crying again, and Symone didn't want to push her luck, but she knew how he was. If he cried hard enough and long enough, he would get tired and fall asleep. She could use that right now, and she could be back before he woke up.

Symone stood up and lifted him with her. She carried him over to where the little TV still shined its light on the place where Adam's sleeping bag was spread out. Emily sniffled a few times, but she didn't say anything. She had an idea of what her mother was doing, but she hoped she was wrong. She did her best to contain her own emotions and felt a little sleepy herself. Emotions could drain kids the same way they drain adults.

After Symone tucked Adam into his sleeping bag, she returned to Emily at her own spot and put her hands on her shoulders. She tried to convey strength through her hands to the little girl as she looked into her eyes.

"While Adam is asleep would be the best time for me to give this a try. I won't stay gone long. You know I have to do this, Emily. What if I go up there and find that this thing is all over?"

"What if something happens to you?"

"Nothing will happen to me. I promise. Now, let me get this done before Adam wakes up."

Symone used the pressure she had on Emily's shoulders to gently lay her back onto the pillow where Symone had leaned against the wall. She hoped it would make Emily feel like she was the one in charge of her brother if she sat where her mother had been.

She moved quickly from her daughter so the moment wouldn't be stretched out for too long. If she was going to do this, it was best that she did it in daylight. She had lied about one thing, so she needed daylight to be able to do what she wanted. She had lied about how far she would go once outside. She doubted she would learn much by checking around the yard, and she wasn't sure she would learn much more by going only as far as the neighboring houses. She hoped to go outside and find the military had restored order. At the very least, they would have posted notices in prominent places, and Emily assumed the crossroads would be considered an appropriate place. If she could, she would go at least that far, and if she didn't find anything, she decided that would be enough for one day.

Symone packed a few essentials into a camping backpack. She needed the gun and some spare ammunition, a bottle of water, and a couple of protein bars from their supplies. She would definitely drink the water, but she would save the protein bars for the children unless she needed them to keep herself going. The gun wouldn't get used if she could help it.

The stairs threatened to spoil her plans by creaking and groaning as she went up to the winch. She gave Emily a thumbs up and was rewarded with a smile, even if it wasn't exactly enthusiastic. She released the straps that held the refrigerator against the door and pulled them in. Then she unlocked the door and leaned against it, slowly increasing the amount of pressure until the refrigerator rolled forward. It stopped after moving only two or three inches. Symone tried to remember if there was anything that could have been placed on the other side of the refrigerator that could possibly keep it from moving, and she realized that the gap between the refrigerator and the big island that served as their informal gathering place was about the same as the width of the dining room table. She wondered if someone could have dragged it or something that size into the kitchen and left it there.

She searched for a place where she could plant her foot for support and found that the clamp that held the winch to the steps was perfect. She put one foot against it and leaned into the door with all of her weight. There was the sound of something heavy dragging across the kitchen floor, but the refrigerator moved slowly under her pressure. By the time it was wide enough for her to fit through the gap, she was practically lying on the stairs, but it was open.

The sunlight coming through the gap was almost painful to see, but she welcomed it after weeks in the gloomy cellar. It was blindingly bright, but she preferred that over trying this at night. She didn't want to waste a moment of that precious light, so she pushed herself into the gap and squeezed through into the open area between the back door and dining room. The table was still where it should be, so she took two steps around the refrigerator to see what was wedged between the appliance and the island. She had to cover her mouth with both hands to keep from screaming.

The bodies of two large men were in the gap. That explained the dragging sound, and their size explained why it was so hard to get the refrigerator to budge. Both of the men were abnormally large, and Symone's first impression was that their clothes were several sizes too small. Then the smell hit her despite having put her hands over her mouth, and she turned away and gagged. If she had been eating more in the last two weeks, her shrunken stomach would have forced out what little bit of food she had inside her. The same wasn't true for one of the two men, and the movement of the refrigerator had compressed his bloated body against the island enough to cause gas to be expelled. The sound and the smell were the last straw for her stomach, and she got sick.

Symone was on her knees and doubled over when she heard Emily call out softly, "Mummy, are you okay? Something really stinks."

Since the door had been shut and she had wedged a blanket into the crack at the bottom to block sound or light, the smell had stayed in the kitchen. Symone managed to push herself up so she could close the door, and as she did, she retrieved her backpack and instructed her daughter to put the blanket back over the gap. She could hear Emily's feet on the stairs and hoped Adam slept through this part.

The refrigerator rolled easily back into place, hiding the door, but as its pressure was taken from the two bodies, one rolled off of the other loudly, forcing more gas to escape. The sound alone was enough to get Emily moving. She didn't want to be there for the arrival of the smell.

She hadn't really felt the need to go upstairs because there wasn't anything she had forgotten to take to the cellar. She was wearing a pair of jeans, a sweatshirt with a hoodie, and running shoes. The temperature was mild outside, so she wouldn't freeze or get too warm. The disappointment came in the air. She had involuntarily held her breath in the kitchen, and once she got outside, she let it out and replaced it with a deep inhale. She anticipated the fresh, clean smell outside, but she got something just a little less concentrated than the odor in the kitchen. The whole place smelled like rot. She wondered if it was just due to the massacre in front of the house, but her senses told her it was going to be like this everywhere.

Emily was going to have her hands full with Adam if she wasn't back before he woke up, so she checked the front of the house first by running across the garden from the kitchen door. She didn't know if she accurately remembered how bad it had been, but all it took was one second to confirm that it had been bad. Everyone was right where she had last seen them, and a few more had joined the crowd since. Two of them were still moving despite injuries that should have left them incapable of anything more than rotting like the others.

The plan was to reach the neighbor's house where she had heard the gunshots. Part of her was afraid they would see her coming, and the shooting would start again, but another part of her said they would know the difference between the astronaut's wife and whatever it was those other people had become. Either way, if she was going to make contact with them, it couldn't be by sneaking around outside their house. She set out at a fast pace in that direction.

It took just over thirty minutes to cross the fields and pick her way through the dense stretches of trees that separated them from their neighbors. She thought it would take less time, but while she didn't want to sneak up on her neighbors, she realized she had to sneak around those other people.

"What did the news call them? The infected dead? Infected with what?"

Saying it out loud made it real when she heard a growling sound somewhere nearby. She had drawn the attention of one that was pinned under the wheel of a farm tractor that belonged to a neighbor who still insisted on growing his own crops. It was a small farm, and Symone could see the path the tractor had taken from the barn to its present location. It had been driven straight through a field of tall corn, and in the middle of the path were several bodies.

From a safe distance, she studied the man under the wheel. At least it looked like a man to her. It seemed intent on reaching her and was pulling against the ground with both hands. All the while, it made a sound like it was choking on something.

"Infected with what?" she asked for a second time.

She said it out loud, almost as a question to him. She knew he couldn't answer her, but if she was out here for answers, she was beginning to doubt there would be anyone who could give her any. If they were infected, could she catch what they have by breathing the same air? She hoped not because she had gotten a nose full in her kitchen, and Emily could smell it down in the cellar. Before she had lost the news channels, she had heard that they spread the infection by biting people, and she remembered the scenes from the Isle of Wight. She knew she wasn't going to trust anyone who was wearing a bandage.

The home where the tractor had come from wasn't the one where she could hear the gunshots, and she wondered if she should check there too, but something told her she would at least have some idea of what to do next after her visit to the other neighbor. She imagined that the noises being made by the man under the tractor wheel were angry protests when she set off again in the other direction.

The last stand of trees that separated her from the neighbors was the perfect fence. There were thick brambles that grew to her height, and she couldn't see through them. She had to move along the thick, thorny bushes sideways until she found an opening, and it was a narrow one. Judging by the shreds of clothing, the opening had been made by something oblivious to the pain inflicted by the sharp thorns. She carefully picked her way through the opening, but she paid the price but getting stuck by thorns on both hands. She had no doubt that the path was created by one and then followed by many more of the infected.

When she reached the yard behind the house, she saw a swing set, a sandbox, a sliding board, and an assortment of other yard toys. She didn't know her neighbors, other than that one time at the market and the phone call that was less than a minute long, but she knew they were elderly. It occurred to her that they had created this little haven for their grandchildren.

A curtain blew outward at an open window on the second floor, and she stood still expecting to feel the pain at the same time that she would hear the gunshot. She suddenly felt like she needed to go to the bathroom, and she didn't know what to do with her hands. Should she put them in the air or just stand still? She chose in between. She reasoned to herself that she didn't want someone to think she was reaching for them the way the infected dead tended to do, and she wanted to demonstrate physical control rather than to just have her arms dangling by her side. She slowly extended both arms at the same time until they were straight out at her sides.

"Smart move."

The voice wasn't rough or deep. It just didn't project well, but she could tell it was a man, and it came from somewhere nearby but not in the upstairs window. Symone didn't know what to do next, so she just waited. If the owner of the voice hadn't shot her yet, he wasn't going to shoot her if she stood still.

"Have you been bitten?"

The question surprised her, but after only a brief moment of thought, she understood that was most likely the first question she would ask a stranger she was holding at gunpoint.

"No, I haven't been bitten," she answered, and then because she wanted to break the tension or maybe because she was married to Henry Tisdal, she added, "Have you?"

"Lady, I didn't think I would ever have a reason to smile again, but I think I may actually laugh. The last person I asked that question didn't have a sense of humor anymore. That is if he ever had one."

Symone risked a glance in the direction of the voice. An elderly man with broad shoulders and long, gray hair had a shotgun aimed at her, but he was smiling. It was the man she had met at the market…Helen's husband.

"I'm sorry about Helen. My arms are getting tired," she said, "and I have two small children hiding in my cellar at home. Are we good?"

It was the right thing to say because he responded immediately.

"Is anyone with the children?"

"No, I had to leave my six-year-old to watch my four-year-old, but I had to know what's happening. We've been hiding down there for weeks."

"You've been down there since it started? That was a month ago."

Her mouth dropped open, and then she remembered the fever. More time must have passed while she was sick than she had thought, and her children were even better about it all. The man came toward her and lowered the shotgun as he did.

"That was you on the phone warning me about the gunshots?"

She nodded and lowered her arms. Her shoulders really were starting to burn, and they weren't quite as straight out from her sides as she thought.

"Yes, that was me. What happened to all of the bodies, or did you miss?"

"They were smelling up the place pretty bad, so I moved them. I used old George Morton's tractor to haul them away. He won't be needing it anymore because he was one of the ones that got inside the house at the start and got to Helen. I left it parked over there somewhere on top of Morton's son-in-law."

Symone had to admit that the man had a sense of irony that bordered on sarcasm, but it was also poetic justice, and she didn't feel alone anymore.

"I'm sorry, Mr. Clark. I'm sorry about Helen, and I'm sorry I don't remember your first name. I'm Symone."

She held out her hand, which felt like such an empty yet necessary gesture.

"Helen was a good woman, and I miss her, but I'm not done living yet."

He took her hand in his oversized hand and shook.

"I'm Arthur, and no, not the famous one. Just lucky enough to have the same name."

Symone liked him and was glad he had survived. She suddenly felt exposed out in the open and asked if they should go inside.

Arthur shook his head and said, "I'll feel better about going inside when I know your children are safe."

******

Emily heard the refrigerator roll away from the door, and she was so excited that her mother had come back so soon that she ran up the stairs to meet her.

"Mummy, Adam has been asleep the whole time you were gone."

Emily had never been afraid of monsters, and she had only made her father check under the bed and in her closet because she knew he enjoyed their little game. She never woke her parents up at night, even the time when she thought there was someone standing in the corner of her room. She had gotten calmly from her bed and walked to the place on the wall by the door where she knew the light switch was. When she turned on the light, she saw that the monster standing in the corner was the coat rack that used to stand by the front door. She had insisted on putting it in her room when her parents talked about getting rid of it. Because she didn't believe in monsters, she didn't scream, and when she saw it wasn't her mother standing at the top of the stairs, her voice seemed to freeze in her throat. She just stopped talking, and then everything went black. She had never fainted before, and she probably wouldn't have if she was capable of screaming.

Adam was still sound asleep, and he didn't resist as he was scooped up into arms that made him feel warm and comfortable. A firm hand was on the middle of his back as his head lay on a shoulder, and he was allowed to sleep. He was carried up the stairs and out the door, but as they passed the refrigerator, the man took magnets from the front of the appliance that had held pictures drawn by the children. He repositioned them on the side of the refrigerator facing the open cellar door and placed a card under them.

******

Arthur only took a few minutes to get his "bug-out" kit, as he liked to call it. He saw that Symone was carrying her own, and he asked about the contents as they got ready to leave. When he found out that was where she carried her gun, he said that wouldn't do.

"How do you plan to defend yourself with a gun that you carry inside a backpack? You can't ask these things to hold on for a minute while you fumble around with zippers and straps. Good God, it isn't even loaded."

Symone explained what had happened in her driveway and that guns hadn't helped the police officers much. She corrected herself and said that the only thing one of them succeeded in doing was when she decided to shoot herself in the head. Otherwise, guns didn't mean you were safe.

Arthur agreed with her and said it would be a good idea if she didn't have the gun at all and tucked it into his own backpack. As soon as he did it, she felt vulnerable, and that was exactly why he did it.

"Can I have my gun back, please?"

"Why, did you remember why you brought it in the first place? What did you plan to do, load it if I needed help?"

"Yes," she answered sheepishly.

"Good thing I didn't need help. Let's see if we can't improve this situation."

Arthur pulled something out of a closet that bore an odd resemblance to a harness, and she didn't realize what it was until he draped it around her and had her put her arms through the loops. She didn't even mind him doing it because it was kind of like her father getting her ready for school. She felt safe around him.

When he was finished adjusting the shoulder holster, he said, "This holster was made for a model Smith & Wesson like yours, so once you get comfortable with the weight, you'll almost forget it's there. But when you need it, it's a lot closer to your hand than it would be inside a backpack."

She had to agree to everything he said. The holster was comfortable, and after a few minutes, it felt almost like carrying her pocketbook. She also felt the reassurance of having it where she could reach it. He had her pull the gun out then put it back several times. At first, she had to look at it to do it, then he had her do it while keeping her eyes straight ahead. She felt like her first time away from the cellar in a month was a big success.

Symone followed Arthur closely through the bushes surrounding the backyard. His broad size caused the thorns to be spread away from her as they passed through, and Arthur wore a pair of heavy gloves until they were in the open. He took a moment to tuck them away afterward, and he pointed out that a bug-out kit wasn't complete if it couldn't fix any problem and still be something you could carry. She made a mental note to add gloves to her backpack.

When they passed the tractor, she said, "You didn't care much for George Morton before this, did you." It was more of a statement than a question.

"He bought that tractor from me five years ago."

She was a little confused, so all she could think of to say was, "And?" This time it was a question.

"Never gave me the money."

She tried not to laugh, and the only reason she didn't was probably the sight of the big tire parked firmly on the back of George Morton's son-in-law.

They were halfway back to Symone's house when they saw their first horde. Two dozen or more of the infected were directly in their path and traveling from left to right. They had to duck down behind large tree stumps and wait for over thirty minutes for the last of them to pass by.

"They walk like they're together," said Symone.

"If you're asking me why they do that, I don't have any answers. We assume birds flock together because they know they're with other birds. We even have a saying about birds of a feather flocking together, but then we have other birds that don't want any other birds like them coming around except when they mate. Hell, we don't even know if these things think, and they seem to recognize their own kind, but I highly doubt that they mate."

They walked in silence for a few minutes until Arthur started to say something, stopped, and then tried again. He seemed to want to ask her about something but couldn't get the words to come out the way he wanted. He finally just said one word as a question.

"Henry?"

"Same thing you just said to me. I don't have any answers. In a way, I feel like he was in the safest place anyone could be. He was with his best friend in the Space Station. If anyone could keep Henry alive, it would be Adam Calloway. We named our son after him."

"So, he's still up there?"

"As far as I know. I heard one reporter say they would have a hard time coming down without someone giving them ground telemetry, in which case there were two likely outcomes and one highly unlikely outcome."

"Which would be what?" asked Arthur.

"Well, the likely outcomes are that they would come in at too steep of an angle and burn up in the atmosphere. If they didn't burn up, they would hit the Earth like a bullet squashing itself against a steel wall. The other likely outcome would be that the entry angle would be too shallow. They would bounce off the Earth's atmosphere like skipping a stone on water, except the water is curved, so they wouldn't lose momentum and sink. They would just keep right on going out into space."

"You said there was an unlikely outcome."

"Yes, that would be they somehow get the angle exactly right, and they have a good landing in a perfectly safe place."

All he could say was, "Oh, I see."

They were close enough to the Tisdal home for them to see the roof over the trees, so Symone explained what she knew about the terrain around the house. Arthur assured her that he knew the layout because he had known the previous owners. He had been inside the home, and he admired her ingenuity using the refrigerator to hide the cellar door. He told her he regretted that he hadn't thought to come over and find out if she and the children had survived. In all honesty, he didn't want to come over and find them the way he had expected them to be.

When she tried to express the same sentiment about why she didn't check on him sooner, he stopped her and said she had two children to worry about, and an apology would be ridiculous. He did, however, appreciate the thought.

She felt like things were looking up, and before entering the clear area around the house, they scanned the area for unwanted guests. Everything appeared normal, so they increased their pace across the open area and hurried for the kitchen door.

Just before reaching the porch, Arthur put his hand on her arm and said, "Let me lead."

With the barrel of the shotgun ahead of him, he eased the kitchen door open and peered inside. If Symone could read his mind, she would have known that his first thought was just confusion. It just wasn't the way it was supposed to be because Symone had told him she put the refrigerator back in front of the door before leaving the house. She saw his hesitation, if not his confusion, and hesitation meant something wasn't right. A wave of fear swept up the middle of her spine, and she felt the fine hairs on the back of her neck move.

Arthur couldn't stop her from pushing past him even though he tried. In her mind, the only way to protect her babies was to assault whatever it was that was threatening them. In his mind, he knew the danger could still be down there in the cellar with them.

Symone charged into the kitchen so fast that she collided with the refrigerator and literally bounced into the open door. She ignored the foul smelling bodies but noticed they had been moved away from the refrigerator. Somehow she kept her feet under her and managed not to trip on the winch where it was clamped three steps down. She reached the bottom with Arthur close behind. For a man in his seventies, he was fairly agile, and he even considered stairs to be a likely place for him to demonstrate how to fall with style, but this time he was only concerned with confronting the threat, whatever it was.

Symone was screaming the children's names and searching every dark corner of the cellar. Arthur pulled out a flashlight and aimed it ahead of her rather than to search elsewhere. He kept the shotgun aimed into the light, but deep in his heart, he thought if the children were there in some dark corner, it was already too late. If they found them, they would already be like the others, and it would be better for Symone if he found them first.

It became obvious that the children were gone, and Symone ran up the stairs to search the house. She ran from room to room, calling for them. As much as he wanted to, Arthur couldn't keep up, and he returned to the kitchen hoping to find a clue. He met Symone as she was coming back down the stairs from the bedrooms and handed her a white piece of paper the size of a business card. Handwritten on one side were two sets of numbers that she thought might be coordinates. On the other side was an embossed symbol that Arthur recognized immediately.

Symone had tears streaming down her cheeks as she begged Arthur, "What does it mean?"

"It's a cap badge from World War I. The symbol is a grenade with seventeen flames. It means *a grenade fired proper*."

9

Maggie Mae

The Atlantic Ocean - The Beginning

Every day seemed like the same thing to Andi Hartford. Dodging contact with military ships from more countries than she could believe, she navigated close to shore and then ran to deeper water when she had to. The advantage of her pride and joy, the Maggie Mae, was its ability to do the heavy lifting of a sea-going tug while still being able to maneuver like a sport-fishing boat. Then there was her high-tech array. When the boat was built, Andi wasn't content with the original gear that was installed at the shipyard. She inspected the purchase of the tug by the worldwide shipping company that employed her, and she told the builder they needed to do better. The result was the most advanced sonar, radar, and communication system in a civilian boat.

It didn't hurt that Andi was good at her job. She was one of only a handful of women who could be called Captain, in part because a woman was CEO of the maritime giant that hired her, but she was also very qualified. She was a graduate of the Merchant Marine Academy and had actually wanted to captain a supertanker, but a short stint on one of the modern ocean-going tugboats was all she needed. She fell in love with the hard work of a captain who often worked alongside the deck crew. Most of her time might have been spent on the bridge, but on a tugboat, she could take a hands-on approach to her job. She knew every inch of the Maggie Mae because she had to be its captain and crew when needed.

There had been a crew of sixteen before the infection. Twelve crew, the captain, two cooks, and a full-time doctor. Now it was just her and the three men who had helped her push away from the dock before the crowds overwhelmed the police barricades in Boston. She didn't even know them before then, and it broke her heart that her crew wasn't on board, but if they hadn't cast off their lines and pushed away when they did, she doubted she would be alive today.

Andi thought about that night every day. The crew was on shore leave, and she needed at least three hours to get them back to the tug. Some of them had families, mostly parents and brothers or sisters, but a couple members of the crew were married with children. When she put the call out to them to get back to the tug as fast as possible, every member of the crew asked if they could bring their families, girlfriends, and even neighbors. She didn't have time to debate the issue with them, so she said yes to all requests. She didn't care who came back with them as long as they got there before she had to shove off.

She remembered the waiting part well. The Maggie Mae was tied up at the last berth, farthest from all of the screaming and shooting that marked the frantic attempts of a large population converging on the only logical way to escape death. She stood on the dock behind a row of supply containers with an AR-15 resting on top. The crew knew where the boat was berthed, so she had killed all the lights. They would run to the berth, not to the lights. From what she had seen on the other boats nearby, people ran for what they could see, and desperate people overwhelmed boats of all sizes. They didn't care who was in their way, and very few of the boats pulled away from the docks with their original crews. Judging by the way they collided with each other, it was doubtful they were escaping with their captains or first mates at the helm.

Andi was prepared to shove off by herself if necessary, but she was fond of her crew, and she at least had to give them a chance. As time passed, though, she became more and more afraid that she wouldn't see any of them again. She was so intent on the battle underway in the city that she couldn't tear her eyes away. The blazing fires, the sirens, the gunshots, and the screaming all rose together into one chorus of total chaos. She never even heard the men approaching from behind her.

They must have come from the water because they were wet. All four were likely ejected from other boats for various reasons, but they fell on her like rabid animals. One of them hit her hard enough to drive her through the barricade of supply crates. The thought always made her reach to the back of her head, where she now owned a tender scar a few inches long.

The last thing she remembered before hitting the rough dock with her face was hearing one of them say to get the gun and to bring her along for entertainment. When she regained consciousness, someone else was holding her with her back against a bulkhead and a compress against her head. Through bleary eyes, she saw the Maggie Mae was about three feet from the dock and drifting further away. On the dock were the bodies of the four men. Beyond them and moving fast were hundreds of people…a wall of humanity running ahead of something she couldn't see. The man holding the compress had helped her to her feet, and her legs weren't half as steady as she liked, but he had been different from the others. In an urgent but shy voice, he told her that he and his brothers would be her loyal crew if she would save them.

Andi had to smile when she remembered his choice of words. She couldn't remember ever hearing a crewman swear his allegiance or loyalty that way anywhere except in a movie, and she would learn later that Jessie Allen had been raised that way.

She had accepted his pledge with little more than a nod of her aching head and a whispered yes, and he had helped her up the steep ladders to the bridge. She was only partially aware of the other two men, but she heard them shout words of thanks as they busied themselves with the difficult task of getting the tug far enough from the dock before the wall of people arrived. Unlike the four wet men who arrived before them, they appreciated what she was doing for them. Andi started the big engines and immediately put everything she had into getting the distance they needed.

Jessie appeared with a new compress for her to hold against her head. She knew he had found the galley because this one had ice in it.

"After we're clear of the area, I'll come back and take care of that wound for you real proper, Ma'am."

"Don't call me Ma'am. I'm not old enough to be your mother yet."

She tried to say it in a friendly way, but the shy young man had that expression that gives away when someone feels like they messed up.

Despite her head throbbing like someone was still hitting it with a hammer, she managed to say in a much nicer tone, "Captain will do, and thank you for taking care of my head. Oh, and for saving me from those other guys."

His smile told her she had succeeded in smoothing over his feelings, and as she would learn later, Jessie, Donny, and Ivan were the real deal. They were three young men who had been raised well and were everybody's best friends in their neighborhood. Everyone knew and loved the Allen brothers, according to them. They worked together on the docks and signed on with local tugs when they could. Each of them wanted to be a harbormaster, but as she also learned, they had a real aptitude for everything they did. Jessie had been toying with the idea of becoming a nurse, but so far, he had only taken a few classes at a tech school. Donny knew his way around a kitchen, and Ivan had x-ray vision when it came to finding problems inside engines.

Andi would learn all of those things and recognize her good fortune over the next day, but the immediate appreciation of the men came when the people charging full speed toward their berth saw the inevitable. They weren't going to make it to the tug that had gone from three feet to twenty yards away, so their hope turned to anger. While many still ran ahead, others paused to take aim at the big target. They shot blindly at the Maggie Mae, and all Andi could do was hope a bullet didn't hit anything important.

Jessie appeared again, but this time his brothers were with him. They didn't dwell on introductions, but Jessie had apparently schooled them a bit. Each one addressed her as Captain as they efficiently took over her bridge duties. Ivan took the helm as Donny eased her away and into a tall Captain's chair. Jessie immediately went to work on her head injury, first cleaning and inspecting it.

"I don't know how you feel about drinking on duty, Captain, but this is gonna hurt. You need a few stitches, and we found this in the galley."

He handed her a bottle of cooking sherry, and she didn't feel like she was setting a bad example by using it to dull the pain. When Jessie applied a disinfectant to the wound, she stopped him long enough to take a bigger swallow than the first one.

"How's the boat?" she asked. She hoped she covered the pain a bit by acting tough, but she didn't know the young men well enough to know they all admired her grit.

Ivan said over his shoulder from the helm. "She's fine, Captain. We'll inspect her for damage, but other than a few windows on the starboard side, the bullets didn't do anything obvious."

Andi studied them one at a time and saw the similarities. They all had dark hair and handsome features. They were lean and strong. Before she could stop herself from thinking it, she realized if she was a few years younger, she would be after all three of them. She winced and took another swallow of the sherry.

"Did I hurt you, Captain?" asked Jessie.

"No, you're doing fine. Are you guys brothers?"

Donny answered for the three of them because Ivan had his hands full navigating out of the harbor at a higher speed than allowed, and Jessie was concentrating on the stitches.

"Yes, Captain. All three bred to be Red Sox fans, but I was the only one to get the good looks. They've learned to live with being ugly."

Despite being busy, Ivan and Jessie both chimed in with good-natured banter, and Andi could see they were inseparable from the start.

******

Thinking back on that day, she always felt like the brothers were the reason she had survived, not just because of the people on the dock, but the way they had taken care of her since. There had been plenty of scrapes since then. Besides the military, there were the infected dead, and then there were the bad actors, as Donny liked to call them. He had called the people on the dock bad actors, and he said they were the people who never seemed to understand that taking care of someone else was the best way to take care of yourself.

Over seven years later, the wound on the back of her head was a scar that she was constantly feeling with her fingertips, and the young men who had saved her were older and more mature. They were still the same in a lot of ways, but they were grown-up versions of the three guys who showed up at the right time in Boston. She didn't think they would disagree for one moment with her plan to make a little trip across the Atlantic for a friend in need.

The Maggie Mae cruised just above idle speed into the bay to the north of the island. The moon was almost invisible behind thick clouds, so they had the blessing of darkness and just enough wind to cause a small chop to the seas. Noise from the lapping waves covered the sound of their engines just enough to keep her from worrying about being heard. She didn't think Henry would risk a signal light, so she planned to give him all the time he needed to get where they could see each other. By going into the bay, she could turn around and come back out while hugging the coastline until she was at the back of the marina. The water was deep enough right up to the banks, and during tourist season, it hadn't been uncommon to see anglers camped along the coast all the way back to the lodges near the airport.

The docks came into view along the starboard side just as Ivan came into the wheelhouse, and she could see in the glow of the red instrument panels that the man was surprised to see the darkness on the bridge. He also eyed the coastline that was close to starboard and gave her a questioning look by lifting his eyebrows.

Andi had assumed Jessie was the youngest of the Allen brothers because of his almost boyishly handsome features. Ivan was a bit more rugged and stocky in build, so she had thought he was the oldest. It was the other way around, but she had always deferred to him as the oldest. Along with his more mature appearance, he had also displayed a thoughtful and calculating behavior. As a matter of fact, Jessie and Donny seemed to listen to him when he gave his opinion.

"I felt your turn to port, and then I felt the turn again back toward open water. What's happening? We're close to the banks?"

"I was about to call you and your brothers to have a talk. Any of you happen to catch the aerial activity just before sunset?"

"Yeah, Captain. Donny said he heard a prop job increasing power somewhere. We laughed at him until we saw an AC-130 banking toward the mainland. You see where it came from?"

"It came from Springdale, and I don't know what's happening, but I have a feeling it was something that went wrong. I heard from a buddy of mine afterward."

Ivan had that incredulous expression anyone would get if they heard from a friend after an apocalypse, let alone seven years later.

Andi had to admit she was enjoying it.

"Do you remember the astronauts who were at the space station when the world ended? Well, one of them is making his way from Springdale to the marina. With any luck, we're going to help that man get home."

Ivan couldn't be accused of being dumb. He was putting two and two together fast and said, "The Brit? Henry Tisdale is meeting us at the docks?"

Andi chuckled, "I'm impressed. Yes, it's Henry Tisdal. He's undoubtedly found his way this far, and we can get him the rest of the way. Would you do me a solid and tell your brothers for me?"

"We're going to England? Is England okay with that?" He was

making a bad attempt at looking worried as he asked.

She loved the way each of the Allen brothers could take the tension out of whatever was happening.

"I have a feeling that we would get an escort from the Royal British Navy if they learned we were bringing Henry Tisdal home."

Ivan disappeared below decks to tell his brothers what was happening. Andi thought about how much they had grown but how much they had stayed the same. She knew that he would first tell them to cut off any lights and go to red without her having to give the order. There was enough light for her to bring the Maggie Mae alongside the last dock, but they didn't need to advertise their arrival. Henry would see the red lights because he would be watching for her.

******

Andi had been to plenty of small ports and private docks since the apocalypse began, and it was never safe. Pockets of the infected popped up out of nowhere. She reasoned that as long as there were living people, there would be a fresh supply of dead people. Living people got stupid and either got themselves killed or killed someone else.

A month earlier, she had coasted up to a private dock in the middle of the night. It was quiet and seemingly deserted, but as the sun came up, a US Navy destroyer was anchored only a quarter of a mile astern. She didn't know if it had been there all along or if it had arrived after her, but with the sun behind it, it was not the first thing she wanted to see that morning.

Expecting to be hailed and boarded, Andi had called her crew out on deck to await their fate, but after thirty minutes, it became obvious that something was wrong. The deck of the warship should have been teeming with activity, but there was no sign that anyone on the craft had taken an interest in them. She got her binoculars and used them to scan the ship, but there was nothing to see. The same wasn't true for the dock.

Jessie sounded the alarm in time for them to back away and put enough distance between themselves and the dock, but they were still close enough to learn the fate of the crew from the destroyer. Over half of the infected that fell from the dock into the water were wearing Navy uniforms. That was the problem for ships at sea. Sooner or later, they had to resupply, and the bigger the crew, the more supplies they needed, so they had sent a large portion of their crew ashore.

Ivan yelled out, "Did you see that, Captain? Some of them were wearing bandages on their arms."

The implication of his question was obvious. Crewmen were bitten, and their wounds had been treated. Even after all these years, they couldn't bring themselves to do what they should have done. The bitten eventually turned on their shipmates, and if some of them were still on the destroyer, it would explain why nothing was moving over there.

"Correction," she said half out loud. "No one is moving above decks, but below decks is probably a whole different story."

Ivan knew the answer before he asked, but he wanted to be sure. "Are we going to try for any salvage, Captain?"

She gave him a solemn shake of her head. It saddened her to see that a representative of humanity's best line of defense could be eliminated by carelessness, and even though there were things on board the destroyer she wanted, she didn't want them bad enough to take the risk.

That was last month, but over the years, they had seen worse and had closer brushes with death. They had been attacked by swarms of seagulls too many times to count, and if they anchored in one spot long enough, it was no longer a surprise to find crabs clinging to the hull. As a matter of fact, they had swarmed over the aft deck one afternoon in numbers straight out of a horror movie. Donny wanted to cook them, but the others felt like crabs that try to get caught should be avoided. Plus, they all knew what crabs liked to eat, and those didn't look like they had been going without food.

Approaching a dark pier in a remote location wasn't at the top of Andi's bucket list, but it had to be done to help Henry. She just hoped she was making the right decision.

A splash up ahead was all the warning she needed. She knew they were close to the docks even though she couldn't see them yet, but the infected seemed to have the hearing of hunting dogs. One of them probably heard the tug approaching and walked off the end of the dock toward the sound. Either that or Henry had reached the rendezvous spot already and was clearing out the stragglers in the area.

Andi settled on the first explanation for the splash when the docks appeared out of the darkness, and she saw through the dim light a group of people running up a ramp toward the last dock. She was glad they chose that one so she wouldn't have to use her engines to maneuver. She gave a slight turn to port and let the big tug coast sideways. The three Allen brothers spread out along the railing and tossed bumpers over the side.

"As soon as the last one is aboard, push us away. We're staying just long enough for the last foot to hit the deck."

They gave her a wave to indicate they understood, and Ivan turned on a flashlight to give their passengers a path to follow. The first infected dead to come from the dock onto the boat fell past Ivan and landed face first in front of Jessie and Donny, and the second one came so close behind that Ivan neatly sidestepped to keep it from grabbing him. Henry's group was coming at a run, but the infected must have been sitting on the dock in total darkness until the boat bumped against them.

Andi was alarmed to have the infected on her boat, but Jessie and Donny amazed her again. With one of them on each side, they grabbed the filthy creature that had landed on top of the first one by the wrists and ankles and carried it between them to the opposite side of the deck. Their forward momentum was all they needed to launch it over the rail, where it sailed out into the water. They went back to the other one and grabbed it before it could push itself up from the deck, and in seconds it was joining the first one. When they returned, Ivan was helping a large group of heavily armed people over the rail. They all hoped it was Henry Tisdal's group because they appeared to be seriously ready for anything.

******

The Chief was taking point when they reached the abandoned docks, and no one said a word. They all knew that the darkness could be hiding anything, and the Chief, in particular, remembered the night he had rushed too quickly ahead of Allison. Tom's wife had been fatally bitten by an infected because he had rushed. He still blamed himself for her death.

When he ran up the ramp that led from the solid ground out onto a series of docks, he caught a glimpse of red light to his left and changed directions to go that way. He was betting that Henry Tisdal's friend was a savvy sailor if she had survived over seven years, and a smart sailor would be running with only red lights.

The wooden planks under his feet protested when his weight

passed over them, and he was a bit worried about how much they could take. The white paint on the railings was chipped and peeling, but at the height of its glory days, the docks must have been an attractive sight to tourists. Time, the weather, and neglect had taken their toll on the wooden structure, though, and the boards felt soft in places. Dark spots meant people had bled on the docks, and there had been enough blood to ruin the wood in some places.

When the tugboat loomed out of the darkness and slid sideways toward its berth, the Chief saw the two infected dead step into his path. He couldn't shoot them because he would hit the boat if he missed. He also saw that he would get there too late, but that didn't stop him from trying. He broke into a sprint, and the rest of his friends did their best to keep up.

From the bridge of the tugboat, Andi had the advantage of being high enough above the action to see what was about to happen in the dim light. She knew that Jessie and Donny were clearing away the infected that fell into the boat, but she wasn't sure the people on the dock would be able to see well enough to tell her crew from the infected. She had to risk being detected but decided that was better than a confrontation between allies. She flipped a switch and bathed the deck and the dock in white light.

Jessie and Donny cleared away the second infected dead only a brief moment before the Chief landed where it had been. They kept going toward the other side, but they cast glances back toward the Chief as they moved. He had to be the biggest man either of them had ever seen, and he hit the deck of the tugboat like a linebacker.

Behind the big man came at least eight or nine people, but Andi couldn't tell for sure, and she wanted to cut off the white lights as soon as possible. The Chief was glad to be able to see well enough to make the jump, but he also didn't care for the feeling of exposure the white lights gave him.

The deck felt good under his feet. There was something about being on the water that made him feel better. Maybe it was the sea where he felt most at home, but it was also knowing that the darkness around the boat was water and not hiding places for the infected. The lights snapped off just as he was about to tell the men who stood to one side of him to signal the bridge to go back to red. They were all temporarily blinded by the change, but they didn't have time to think about it because Andi poured on a surge of power to get away from that location. If anyone had seen that flash of brilliant light from a distance, they would already be heading for the docks.

Everyone behind the Chief had just landed on their feet when they felt the deck rise slightly in the direction of the bow. They grabbed at the side rails and had to keep from falling by going to their knees. It all happened so quickly that the Chief and Kathy both turned to do a headcount. For one horrible moment, they thought someone was missing, but as their eyes adjusted to the darkness, they saw everyone had made it.

The powerful engines drove the tug out to sea and away from the docks, but even Andi wished she could at least aim her bow lights into the black night ahead. The Atlantic was big, but it could get pretty crowded along the coast when desperate survivors spotted a golden opportunity. Those who had fast enough boats had turned to piracy and were always ready to make a move on unsuspecting travelers.

The Chief appeared alongside her in the bridge, and she wondered how he had gotten there without her noticing. She also wondered how he didn't hit his head on the low ceiling.

"Chief Barnes," he said. "How can I help?"

The sense of urgency in his voice was enough for her to know that he understood they were in danger.

"Visibility is too low for this speed, and I can't use lights yet. You'd be surprised by how crowded this place probably became just because we advertised our location a few minutes ago. Someone's likely to be moving into position ahead of us already. Tell your people to get down because I'm expecting a firefight any moment."

"We can do better than that," he answered. "This isn't our first rodeo. If someone blocks our course and starts shooting, they won't be aiming at the bow. You're going to be their target, and we aren't going to let that happen."

He disappeared just as quickly as he had arrived, and she would have been impressed by how easily he descended from the bridge to the main deck. His sea legs carried him to his friends, who were lined up along the starboard rail still crouching out of sight. The three crewmen who had helped them aboard had gone to their duties, and as far as he knew, they weren't armed. What he needed at the moment was firepower.

Over the sound of the engines, the Chief called out his instructions, and everyone moved forward along the bow. Andi saw their dark shapes moving into the curve of the bow, and she had some idea of what they were doing, but she never expected what she saw.

Less than sixty seconds after they were in position, she was practically blinded by the spotlights that flooded the bridge, and over the sounds of the engines and the waves hitting the bow, she heard someone shout over a bullhorn.

"Heave to and prepare to be boarded."

She knew the pirates would only give one warning, and the Chief had been right when he said the bridge would be their target. If she didn't pull back on the throttle immediately, they would open fire.

What the pirates didn't count on was the kind of resistance they met. They had their spotlights aimed high toward the bridge and left her bow rails in the darkness. That gave ten expert shooters the chance to get their weapons braced on the bow. Andi's hand reached for the throttle but never made it that far. The bow of the tugboat lit up with a frightening ferocity. It was unlike anything she had ever seen.

There was never any return fire from the other vessel. They had been hit by such a barrage of bullets that it only lasted a few seconds, and it caught them unprepared to respond. The spotlights winked out, but the light was replaced by several fiery explosions. Fuel vapors were ignited by hot bullets, and the would-be pirates were killed before they had a chance to even question what hit them.

Andi's hand finally reached the throttle, but instead of slowing, she gave the Maggie Mae just a little more speed. The tug easily brushed aside the burning wreckage of the boat in their path. As they raced through the debris, she saw it had been a small fishing boat that had probably been used to carry tourists from Springdale out for a day of deep-sea fishing. The pirates had undoubtedly liberated it from the original owners. She had very little sympathy for the people who were still diving into the water to douse the flames on their clothing. Some of them were actually screaming in her direction for help, but she knew if they had boarded the Maggie Mae, they would have tossed her and her crew into the water without so much as a life vest.

No one assumed it was over. For the next thirty minutes, everyone stayed in their positions and waited for the next unsuspecting pirates, but if there had been others, they were deterred by the fate of the first attackers. There were plenty of ships hijacked by stronger survivors, but there were very few that went up into flames on either side. Boats and ships were precious commodities in the new world. The infected weren't a threat as long as the crew was uninfected, so they were at least a safe haven where survivors could get a good night's sleep, but too often, they were a threat to each other.

"Does that happen a lot?"

Andi was startled by the Chief's second arrival.

"Do you always sneak up on people like that? Wait, don't bother. I know the answer, but do me a favor and make some noise or something. I'm not used to it out here on the ocean."

He flashed her his famous smile, and she couldn't help but relax. He had always known he had the power to do that, and it seldom failed.

"Yes, Ma'am...Captain."

"Your people took care of that little problem fast."

He nodded grimly.

"I think we all have some pent-up anger right now. That was our first chance to let it out."

"Did you save some for whoever it is you're mad at?"

"Oh, yeah. They deserve far worse than what you just saw."

"It wouldn't have anything to do with that plane I saw take off from Springdale, would it?"

"Good guess. We learned the hard way not to trust the pilot."

"Have you given any thoughts to how you plan to get home after we get Henry back to his family in England?"

Andi knew they had to be good people, or they wouldn't be helping Henry, but she didn't really know them. From the moment she had seen the plane lift off above the trees, she had wondered how they planned to get home. She didn't know if they were stranded or if they planned to take her boat when they were done.

"I hadn't given it much thought," said the Chief. "I guess I've been a bit busy with the idea of getting Henry home in one piece."

Andi decided she needed to lay her cards on the table and see what this new stranger would say. She already knew his people could take the Maggie Mae if they wanted to, but the Chief didn't give so much as hint that it had crossed his mind. She made a pretense of checking their heading and making a course correction as she asked. That way, she wouldn't have to make eye contact.

"What if you can't find a way home?"

The Chief rubbed the stiff growth of hair on his cheeks with a big hand and furrowed his brow.

"I guess I'll have to learn to like scones for breakfast, but I'll never get used to tea over coffee."

Andi couldn't stop herself from making eye contact after that answer. She thought to herself, "Could this guy be more charming?"

Before she could stop herself, she said, "I don't know how it happened, but somehow I've become the Atlantic passenger service. I'll give you a ride home if you can help me locate fuel."

"I'm sure we can manage that," said the Chief. "Would you mind if I ask for one other favor?"

"Anything," she said, and for some reason her own answer made her feel embarrassed.

She thought to herself, "This guy has really gotten under my skin fast."

In a more professional tone, she said, "What else can we help with?"

"I see that your communications array is about the best there is. Mind if I make a couple of long distance calls?"

Andi pointed at the communications console and said, "Make yourself at home."

She didn't try to listen to the Chief as he made several connections, but she heard enough. The last two were warnings of attacks on Huntsville and Guntersville, and she could see the weight of the world lifting from his shoulders with each call he made.

More people came into the bridge, and Andi suddenly became aware that she had been so engrossed in the Chief that she had forgotten about the others. She wondered if he had that effect on other people or just women. A tall woman with shiny silver hair slipped an arm around his waist from behind, and Andi felt a pang of disappointment. Despite their age difference, she found herself attracted to this older man she had met only moments ago.

Another man slipped past the Chief and Iris to extend a hand to Andi. She recognized Henry Tisdal from news clips and took his hand.

"At last, we meet," he said. "Let me introduce you to my friends."

There were introductions all around in the bridge, and it was a bit crowded, but the Maggie Mae was made for a big crew, and Andi couldn't remember the last time it felt so full of life. They all thanked her for picking them up from the docks so quickly as if she had done the heavy lifting.

"It was your fast response to the pirates that saved us," she said. "That was a piece of work. With any luck, we won't have to repeat the performance, and we'll have you back with your wife and children in a few days."

Henry should have smiled more at the comment, but in the back of his mind, he couldn't help but wonder what seven years had been like for his family, and his smile faded.

"Have you been able to make contact with them at all?" she asked.

10

Frantic

Southern England - The Beginning

Symone was beyond frantic. All she could think was that they couldn't be gone. Despite the evidence, she would turn around, and they would be there. She had simply missed them when she had searched the first time. They were hiding, and they didn't know it would be safe for them to come out.

Arthur was patient with her and even stood guard while she searched the house for a second and third time, but he was only letting her vent her fears. The children being gone wasn't something she was just going to accept, and he was waiting for her to wear herself out because he was too old to handle a physically fit woman of her age.

Eventually, the exhaustion took over, and she collapsed into a kitchen chair, oblivious to the dead bodies and the smell. She put her head down on the surface of the table and sobbed uncontrollably. Arthur kept one eye on her and one on the garden outside the kitchen. During Symone's meltdown, he watched six of the infected go through the yard. They appeared to be going in the direction of the airport, so he assumed there had been some random noise from there.

He also studied the ground. From his angle, the sun cast its light across the yard in a way that it appeared to reflect back from the grass that had been flattened by something heavy. In his experience, he had only seen grass flattened that way by treads on tanks or personnel carriers. He supposed it could have been a bulldozer, but adding that evidence to the card with the symbol of a grenade gave him the hope that the military had passed through and that they had somehow found the children. As soon as Symone was capable of hearing his conclusion, he could tell her, but he didn't want her to go charging after them. The tracks led in the same direction he had seen the infected follow.

Arthur believed in his heart that the children would be safe with the military. Maybe they were safer now than they had been before, but that didn't stop him from believing their place was with their mother. Safer or not, until they knew for certain where they were, there was at least a chance they had been flushed out of hiding and were either dead or infected. The lack of blood in the cellar was encouraging, but right now, the only encouragement that would work with Symone was to see the children standing in front of her.

Dusk was on them when Symone suddenly got her second wind. She bolted from her chair and lunged across the kitchen toward the door. Arthur barely held his ground, but his success was the difference between life and death for them because another group of infected had appeared from the front of the house. If Symone got by him into the garden, they would be on her fast. He somehow managed to get his arms around her and grab his own wrist with his free hand, dropping his weight to the floor. They were too close to the window on the door and would be seen at any moment.

In a low voice, he pleaded with her to stop fighting him until she finally quit struggling. They had bumped against the door at least twice, and the dull thumps on the wood sounded ten times louder than it really did, but they were enough to make the infected curious. He could hear them at the bottom step of the porch. He locked his eyes on hers and put a finger across his lips.

They were far more exposed than Arthur wanted them to be, but it was too late to move from where they were. Symone finally understood, and she pushed herself closer against the old man as the two of them tried to make themselves small against the bottom of the door. If the first infected creature managed to see their dark shapes by looking downward through the glass, they would know soon enough. Its shadowy form blocked out what little bit of light was left to the day. If it had been in the morning or during full daylight, they would have been easy to see.

There was a scrum of the infected dead on the porch within seconds as more joined the first one. They all jostled for position at the window, and that was likely to be the reason why the first one didn't spot them. It got pushed away before it had the chance to search for more than a few seconds. The same thing happened to each of them until the pushing became aggressive enough to cause one to fall down the steps. The ruckus it made was enough to draw the attention of the others, and they were distracted away from the door. Another tripped and fell over the legs of the first, and it was the chance Arthur and Symone needed to be able to crawl into the dining room.

"Go," he whispered, and he followed closely on her heels.

Once they were around the corner, Arthur was able to put one eye safely to the doorsill for a quick peek. He could see their shadows on the glass, but they were once again moving as a group away from the door. Whatever it was that had gotten their attention before, they could hear it again, and they stumbled with renewed determination across the garden.

With a bit more authority, he said to Symone, "We won't find your children if those things find us first. Get yourself together, and we'll figure out where to go from here."

Symone's eyes were still wet with tears, but there was sanity behind the tears that hadn't been there before. She nodded her head in understanding and waited for him to go on.

"It's getting dark outside, and those things don't sleep. I know you don't want to wait, but we can't go stumbling around out there hoping to get lucky. I can feel it in my bones that your children are safe."

"Where?"

Her voice sounded raspy and dry from crying so hard.

"I can't answer that yet, but that embossed card wasn't there before, was it?"

"No, it wasn't mine or Henry's. I feel like I've seen the symbol before, but I don't remember where."

Arthur appeared to be considering what to say next as carefully as he could. He didn't want to make a promise to her that he knew for sure what the card meant, but he had a suspicion.

"I think we have to follow the infected to the airport. There are tracks outside that you probably couldn't see now, but I think a military unit passed through your yard. It might even be a special unit assigned to the Royal Family."

Symone's eyes widened, and he saw hope in them, maybe more than he wanted, but then he saw her gain control, and she nodded in understanding again.

"Whoever they were," he continued, "they will have a full day head start on us, and they travel differently than we can. They are out in the open, and we must take a detour."

"To where?" she asked.

"We may be forced to circle around the airport and then approach from London. There is far too little for us to hide behind to the south."

The thought of getting close to a populated area was terrifying. The news reports all said to avoid metropolitan areas, and the early stories of the attacks by the infected made it impossible to believe they could survive such a journey.

"Why can't we go northeast and approach from the nature preserve?" she asked.

The nature preserve was hundreds of acres of protected forests, meadows, and hiking trails. In her mind, it would provide perfect cover for them.

"Because that's where most of the people in London already went," said Arthur. "Some were attempting to cross the preserve to reach the coast while others just felt like it was safer there. Unfortunately, the infection traveled with them and caused it to become scattered from London all the way to here and beyond. There are probably thousands of them in those trees."

She saw what he was getting at. To the west, there were plenty of the infected, but the smaller towns and ample cover meant they could travel undetected if they were at all lucky. Once they were north of the airport, they would be close to London, but there would be relatively less infected…in theory.

"We can leave at first light," said Arthur. "It might take us a day or two, but if we went in a straight line following those tracks, we would have the infected in front of us and at our backs the whole time. We wouldn't be able to find safe shelter at the end of the day."

Resigned to the inevitable, Symone did her best to put on a good face and a show of strength. She wiped at her cheeks and said she was going to go to the cellar to prepare their travel packs. Arthur stopped her and gave her a gentle reminder that they were in more danger than the children if they were indeed in the company of the military. They needed to secure themselves in the cellar as they had before.

Together they moved quietly to put things back in place. They sealed themselves inside the cellar with the refrigerator once again drawn up against the door. Afterward, they spent about an hour sorting through the essentials they should take with them and settled on the basic survival needs. When that was done, Arthur encouraged Symone to rest. He was asleep in minutes, but Symone stared into the darkness for hours. Her children were out there somewhere, hopefully alive.

******

She didn't know if she had slept or not. It seemed like she could hear her own blood pumping in her ears, and her body felt like she had been in a fight. Odd aches and pains seemed to sting her joints. Symone felt her forehead and found it was covered in sweat. She saw that Arthur was awake and watching her.

"I'm not sick," she said defensively.

"I know, but it wouldn't hurt to check your temperature. I imagine you have a thermometer down here for the children."

He gestured toward her supplies, and yes, she had planned for the children's needs, so there was a thermometer in the first aid kit. As a matter of fact, she had used it when she was worried about Adam's long period of silence. She had worried about his health but not her own. She saw by Arthur's face that there was no sense in arguing about it, so she reached for the blue and white box and fished out the old-style mercury thermometer. She glared at him as she shook it down and placed it under her tongue.

The three to five minutes she waited for it to do its job was enough time for her to realize she had nothing to be angry with Arthur about. If anything, it was the other way around, but she could see he wasn't angry, just concerned, and he had a right to be.

"I wasn't bitten," she said around the thermometer.

"I didn't say you were, but there have been plenty of other bugs throughout history. If you have one, we should figure out what to do."

"We already know what we're going to do. We're going after my children…or at least I am. You can stay here or go home."

She sounded a bit ungrateful, and it came out more harshly than she had intended. She was just thinking ahead to the moment when she would read the thermometer and get bad news that might mean a delay in leaving.

Arthur didn't answer. If anything, she saw his expression soften a bit. He knew what it would mean to her if they couldn't leave.

Symone slipped the thermometer out of her mouth and focused her eyes on the tiny red line inside. It was half a notch past one hundred and one. She had some idea why her joints hurt so much, and the headache didn't seem to be there a few minutes earlier. She held it out to Arthur rather than to say the results. He took a quick look for himself, already guessing it would be high.

"I have a nasty feeling that's on its way up instead of down," he said. "Where are your strongest antibiotics?"

"Shouldn't we try aspirin first? If it's bad enough for antibiotics, we're going to be stuck here for days."

"You've been hiding in this damp cellar since it all started. It could be pneumonia. If it is, we have to get antibiotics into you and move you upstairs into dryer air. The sooner we get moving on that, the sooner we can leave."

******

The last thing she remembered when she woke up was taking a big dose of penicillin. She was in her bed and self-consciously aware that she was wearing pajamas. Arthur was sitting in a rocking chair with a rifle across his lap, and judging by the assortment of items on her nightstand, she had been there awhile. The remnants in the bottom of a bowl still smelled like chicken noodle soup, but she was hungry. Arthur sat the rifle within easy reach and unwrapped a sandwich he had ready for her.

"Tuna salad," he said. "I figured you would wake up soon and be hungry. Your fever broke about an hour ago."

"How long?"

Her voice was hardly a whisper, and her throat was sore. He held her head for her while he helped her drink from a cup.

"I had a hard time keeping you hydrated. You're going to need to drink a lot of water the rest of today if we're going to be able to leave soon. There's been a steady parade of those monsters for the last week."

"A week?" she asked.

"Yes, a week. I know what you're thinking but listen carefully. We would've been up to our necks in those things. A good many of them have been soldiers. I think when they evacuated the Isle of Wight, some came back infected, and the ones who flew out went to the airport at Bournemouth. My worry is that some of them may be infected too."

Symone was confused. She understood what he meant when he said there were too many of them. Even if she hadn't been sick, it was better that they had stayed in the relative safety of the house. What she didn't understand was why he thought the soldiers were sick. Then she remembered the bandages. If they carried their wounded with them, then they brought more infected back to the mainland.

"Maybe they only flew out the healthy ones," she said hopefully.

"Maybe. Maybe that's why there's still activity there a week later. That's why the infected are all going that way. I heard a lot of automatic weapons fire last night, so the military could be making a stand there."

She had a horrifying thought, and Arthur must have been able to see it in her face because he became worried again.

"What's wrong? Are you feeling sick again?"

"What if someone from the military took Adam and Emily to Bournemouth airport, and what if the infected are there with them? Even worse, what if the infected are able to beat the military?"

Arthur could see that Symone had come out of one nightmare only to remember that she was living in one. He eased her back onto the pillow behind her and suggested that they would cross that bridge when they came to it. She got sleepy as soon as she finished her sandwich, and her eyes closed again.

******

It took two days for Symone to feel strong enough to travel. During that time, she ate and drank, but mostly she worked on ways to pack their gear so they could carry more without it being too heavy. She also spent a lot of time counting her blessings for finding Arthur. If she had returned home without him and found her children gone, she would be dead by now. She would have been easy prey for the infected because she would have run out the door into their waiting arms.

On the morning of the third day, she was finally strong enough to travel and was satisfied that the gear was manageable. They were ready to go, but the moment they stepped outside the house, they felt exposed. No infected dead were within sight, but for all they knew, there could be an army of them just beyond the field at the front of the house. Their goal was to reach Arthur's house, which was more to the northwest of her own home. They could gather a few of his things, mostly ammunition, and from there, they planned to travel as fast as they could along a country road to the west, away from the most populated areas. If all went well, they felt like they could circle to the airport near Bournemouth in two days before going northeast toward London.

One thing they noticed within minutes was that there was no sound of weapons firing. Then again, there were no other sounds. There were no birds, no dogs barking, and certainly none of the familiar sounds of civilization. By the time they reached Arthur's house, the silence had gotten on their nerves. They didn't dare speak even in whispers. Everything they tried to say and every step they took seemed to be amplified. Even the light breeze that moved bushes and leaves sounded loud enough to make them stop and warily study the shadows. It wore them out, and Symone felt her hands shaking when they closed the door to Arthur's house behind them.

They could tell immediately that someone had been inside since he had gone home with Symone. Someone had nailed broken furniture across the inside of the front door and some of the windows, but the barriers had already been breached. Blood on the wood and on the floor was evidence that the dead had gotten into the house, or there had been a battle between groups of living people. Shell casings scattered around the rooms told them at least some of the combatants were alive at the time. Arthur was glad to have missed whatever it was that had transpired in his absence.

"I only need a few minutes," he whispered.

Symone couldn't bring herself to answer, so she just nodded. Both of them felt like they were standing in the middle of a death trap that was simply waiting for the right time to close. She felt like she was frozen to the spot where she stood, and she didn't have to be told twice to stay where she was. Arthur disappeared to the second floor, and Symone pressed her back against a wall to wait.

He came back only five minutes later with a gym bag that bulged with the weight of ammunition boxes. Arthur was leaning to one side.

"How are you going to carry that?" she asked. "It has to weigh a ton."

"I imagine it will get lighter over time, but when it comes to being able to run fast or to be able to shoot my pursuer, I'll choose the second one for now and run faster when the ammo is gone."

Symone reached into the bag and retrieved a box of 9mm bullets. It said fifty rounds under the brand name, but she was amazed by how heavy it was. She was impressed that the old man could carry a gym bag full of the boxes. It wouldn't help him much, but she transferred a dozen of the boxes to her backpack.

Arthur replaced the boxes with a small photo album.

"It won't help us as much as ammunition," he said sadly, "but it's what my wife would have brought along."

"You didn't say anything when I packed mine," she answered.

A thump somewhere in the house reminded them of how dangerous it was to forget for a moment where they were, and they quickly gathered their gear and went back outside. By the time Arthur shut the door behind them, there were more thumps as something moved closer to where they had been.

They ran stooped over under the weight of their heavy packs, and followed the gravel driveway for a hundred yards before they came to a paved road. There were still plenty of trees to hide them from being spotted from a distance, but there was always that feeling that something was watching from the trees. Arthur pointed to the wire fence along one side of the road and moved closer to it as he ran parallel to the road.

"If we run into any of the dead, throw your backpack over the fence and then climb over. The fence will at least slow their progress while we get away."

"What if the dead are on the other side of the fence?" she asked.

"Don't throw your gear over it."

Arthur said it with such a straight face that she felt like laughing for the first time in weeks. As it turned out, his theory of how to elude the infected dead was put to the test only a few minutes later when they saw that they were drawing closer to a small group of them as the infected walked on damaged legs down the center of the road. He took Symone's backpack from her and used his greater height to place it on the other side of the fence. Then he did the same with his before helping Symone by pulling the wire upward as she squeezed through.

Once on the other side, they took stock of their surroundings and saw rooftops in the distance. They had traveled farther than they had guessed and were close to one of the many small towns that dotted the countryside. They knew it would be their first test in their journey, and they used the cover of tall grass and trees to get closer. Symone lagged behind Arthur as he followed a crooked course toward the buildings, and he wasn't aware that she wasn't behind him until she had actually lost sight of him. When he suddenly realized he was alone, he dropped his heavy gear and retraced his steps. He found her lying prone on the ground with her face buried in her hands, sobbing violently.

He didn't know what else to do because he had no idea what had happened, so he dropped to his knees and pulled her into his arms.

"What happened? Did you see something?"

He furtively turned as he held onto her, trying to see beyond the tall grass that hid them from prying eyes.

"Were you bitten, are you hurt?"

Arthur held her out away from himself to check for bloodstains, but there weren't any.

Symone weakly said between gasps for air, "What if we see them? What if we see Emily and Adam in that town? What if we see my children, and they're *them*?"

She said the last word with disgust, and Arthur understood. It had never totally left his mind that the children were missing, but it wasn't always at the front of his thoughts the way it was for Symone. Arthur mentally told himself that he had to do better, remembering that it would always be her hope that she would find her children. The next face she wanted to see was one of theirs, but she was more likely to see the face of one of the infected.

Arthur felt like they would be discovered at any moment, but he knew Symone had to come to terms with her loss. She shouldn't give up hope, but she had to find a way to keep the agony under control. If she couldn't, no matter what fate had found the children, theirs would most likely involve teeth.

Symone became so still in his arms that Arthur thought she had fallen asleep from exhaustion. When he lowered his face to hers, he saw that she was somewhere far away in her mind, but she wasn't gone.

"I'm sorry," she said just above a whisper. "That's the last time that will happen. I promise."

"You don't have to be sorry," he answered. He kept his voice no louder than hers.

"Yes, I do. We're going to die out here. I'm going to get you killed if I can't keep it together. I won't give up hope, but I'll stop expecting to see them around the next corner."

He couldn't begin to imagine the hell she was in, but he marveled at the determination in her voice. It was the breakthrough she needed in order to have a chance at survival.

"Arthur? Is it too much for me to keep hoping that Henry will find us too?"

Arthur had given it some thought since meeting Symone, and he had actually come to the conclusion that lots of other things were more likely than Henry surviving in space, surviving the return to Earth, and finding a way home. Hell freezing over was one of those things, but right now, Symone needed to hear that was possible. After all, there were dead people walking around everywhere. If that was possible, then so were the things they hoped for.

He said in a gentle voice, "You should keep hoping that Henry will be back too. Hope is what we need if we want to stay alive."

They stood up together and cautiously took in their surroundings. There were infected moving on the road, and if Arthur was correct, they were the group of infected they had already passed. He could be mistaken, but it appeared that there were more now than before. He supposed it was possible that others had joined them from the woods on the opposite side of the road.

"So that's how hordes get started," he whispered to Symone.

It seemed to startle her, and he realized she couldn't see them over the tall grass. It also occurred to him that the group of infected would reach the town ahead of them unless they moved more quickly.

"We should go, but stay low, and just to be safe, let's angle away from the road. I don't want to be too close to that intersection where the town begins."

Like many of the small towns in the area, the storefronts faced the main road that happened to pass their way. The main intersection didn't get enough traffic for it to warrant anything more than a small round-about. On one corner, there was a convenience store with a gas station, and across from it was where people went if they had more serious shopping to do. On their present course, Symone and Arthur would exit the cover of the tall grass at the side of the gas station. They had to do it before the small horde of infected reached the round-about, or they would be out in the open.

Arthur scooped up his heavy bags where he had left them, and the two survivors began their race with the dead. It only took a few minutes to reach the fence along the street that separated the field from the town, and because they increased their angle of approach, there was no way to know if the horde would enter the round-about and see them before they reached cover. It was a choice they had to make. They could stay hidden where they were until the dead were beyond the first few buildings, or they could climb the fence and run for the buildings on the other side. They decided that sitting still was more of a risk.

Symone handed her backpack to Arthur to lift over the fence and then climbed through the wire as he held it apart. For an old man, he did a pretty good job of getting himself over the fence, and he didn't waste a second getting to the street. They were on the pavement and running as best they could with so much weight. When they reached the cover of the gas station, Arthur dropped his gear again and changed directions. He pressed himself against the wall and eased back toward the corner until he could see the round-about. His skin crawled when he saw that the horde had changed directions toward them instead of going straight through town. If they had yelled at the dead as they ran, they couldn't have drawn more attention than they had.

"Run."

His face probably told her enough without even saying to run, so he didn't need to say more. This time running would mean not stopping to rest when they got tired. It meant not stopping until they knew they had outrun their pursuers.

"We need to change directions every block or so," he said through gasps for air. "This is a small town, but there's a community on one side. We might be able to lose them there."

Symone knew the town, too, so she knew which community he was talking about. It was filled with middle-class people who commuted to London for work. Endless rows of houses would give them plenty of cover through the neighborhood, and back yards would give them places to stop and rest.

They ran past a school, then a post office, and finally a police station. It seemed so odd not to go to the police for help, but she already had. That didn't work out so well. Every building they passed had some evidence of what had happened. Vehicles stood in the roads where they had been abandoned, and nothing had prepared them for the sight of so many victims. Human remains were identifiable only by the torn clothing.

The town ended abruptly at a park, and they hurried across to the entrance of the suburban neighborhood. It was immediately obvious that they had guessed wrong about finding cover. What they found were crowds of wandering dead that hadn't been drawn away from the area by the sounds coming from the airport at Bournemouth.

There was one home with a walled garden that offered them their best chance to hide and rest for a few minutes, so they pushed their gear into some hedges and crawled in on top of the bags.

"We're in trouble, aren't we," said Symone. It was more of a statement of fact than a question.

"Yes, but I have an idea," said Arthur. "You stay here, and I'll see if I can find a way inside this house. If I can get in, we can stay here until tomorrow morning and then try to go around the neighborhood. At least that horde won't know where we went."

"Why can't we stay in these hedges? What if you can't get inside or if the house is full of infected?"

"They could find us by accident out here. At least if we're inside, they can't stumble over us."

She could see that he had his mind made up, so she resigned herself to waiting alone in the thick hedges as she watched him crawl out. She had a bad feeling, but it seemed like she had never stopped having bad feelings once they had begun on that first day. She thought to herself that if she ever stopped getting a bad feeling, it would probably be the day she made the mistake that would kill her.

Symone almost crawled out after Arthur. Instead, she grabbed their gear and crawled further into the dense hedges. If she got low enough to the ground, she could still see his feet almost to his ankles. She watched as he cautiously moved across the yard until his feet passed behind some lawn furniture and out of sight. She never felt more alone until that moment.

******

Arthur liked the way the backyard was shielded from the street in front of the home, and from what he could tell, there were no windows on neighboring homes that intruded on the privacy of the property. He would have no difficulty reaching the windows or the back door. There were so many that the odds were good that one would be unlocked. He supposed the second floor would be the most likely possibility, but even if he could find a ladder, it wouldn't be too smart to be that exposed.

He had just stepped between the lawn furniture and an outdoor cooking pit when the single crack of a gunshot broke the silence. He didn't feel any pain, but it knocked him onto his back, and he couldn't move. He felt warmth spreading across his chest, and there was a smell like hot copper.

* * *

******

Symone heard the dreadful sound from her hiding place, and she lowered herself down until her head was resting on her backpack. At the spot where she had last seen Arthur's feet, she could see something else. It took her a few moments to understand what she was looking at. Arthur had been wearing a dark-colored shirt like the one she could see now, but this one almost seemed to become darker as she studied it. Then it became shiny as if it had gotten wet. The full reality sank in, and with it came a sense of total defeat. Her only choice was to lay where she was and wait.

It probably felt like it took longer than it actually did, but her eyes never left the thing that she knew was Arthur's body. She was grateful that she couldn't see the rest of him. If she had been forced to see his face, she felt like she might have used the next bullet in her gun on herself the way the police officer had.

There was the slightest twitch followed by a massive convulsion. Then the movements became steady as she watched the thing that used to be Arthur turn over onto its stomach. With tremendous effort, the thing pushed itself into a standing position, and Symone stared at the same pair of feet she had seen when Arthur was still himself. She cried softly and waited, wondering if the feet would move toward her or away from her. They shuffled left, then right, turned in a complete circle, and eventually disappeared behind the lawn furniture for a second time.

It was with a momentary thought of vivid regret that Symone decided it would be best to sleep in the hedges for a night. She had a distant thought that she had suggested the same thing to Arthur, but she didn't know if she had actually said it to him. It didn't matter now. Arthur was dead, and saying I told you so was not going to change a thing. If she had been able to see further out into the yard, she would have seen Arthur crash through the hedges at the opposite end of the house and stumble to the street where others of his kind were gathering.

11

Road to London

Southern England - The Beginning

The idea of going anywhere near London was a mistake. Symone had underestimated the number of things that could go wrong. It wasn't like the suburban neighborhood where she had lost Arthur. That had been a bad idea too, but she had learned to deal with a few things just by being there. For one thing, there were many homes that were still occupied by their owners. People who stayed put in the vain hope that help would arrive at any moment. Many homes were occupied by new residents who had simply needed places to be safe while they figured out what to do next, and they had moved in whether they were invited or not.

When food ran out in any given home, the occupants ventured out to loot the homes next door. It was as if every neighbor believed the family one or two houses away had somehow squirreled away enough supplies to support themselves and their neighbors. People who were down to their last can of beans found themselves killing the people who had recently been over for cookouts and birthday celebrations. It was all done in the name of protecting their own families.

Some neighbors banded together after sharing rumors of stockpiles of food. They stormed the homes of the people included in those rumors and ransacked the cupboards and refrigerators, all the while killing the infected that roamed their streets and the neighbors who wouldn't share their food. Many of the looters made it no further than the front yards with armloads of canned or boxed food when they were shot by other new arrivals. They were relieved of their burdens as they lay dying on the untended lawns, and quite often, they witnessed the deaths of their assailants before their own eyes went blank. The violence didn't show mankind at its best.

By the time Symone and Arthur had arrived, the only living residents of the neighborhood were hungry and desperate. Their sunken and crazed eyes were at every window where they watched for the infected...they watched for rescuers...and they watched for unwary travelers who might just happen to have one more can of food.

Luckily for Symone, no one had seen her and Arthur when they had crawled deep into the hedges. It wasn't until Arthur had ventured across the back yard to the house that he had been spotted by the man inside. Since Arthur didn't have a backpack, he had nothing to share. That meant he was only there to steal from the man, and that also meant he had to die. He didn't shoot Arthur in the head because he was angry at Arthur for coming to his home without food, so a bullet through the heart was all he deserved. Besides, the man inside the house knew that the intruder in his yard would get a bullet in the head as soon as he showed his dead face outside of the yard.

Less than five minutes after Arthur crashed through the hedges on the other side of the house, there were three more gunshots. Neighbors who had heard the shot that killed Arthur were drawn to their windows closest to where they had heard the single pop. They readied themselves and were rewarded by the appearance of an infected dead, and like deer hunters who had just seen a twelve-point buck walk out of the woods, they raced to be the first to claim the prize.

Symone stayed under the dense cover of the hedges and silently cried for over an hour. She wondered where civilization had gone, and she thought about what she had done so far to be able to survive. While she still grieved the loss of the old man who had already claimed so much of her heart by his kindness, she questioned how she was any different from whoever it was who had just pulled the trigger. She remembered that she had also sat at the bottom of the stairs in her own cellar, praying that the people in her kitchen would go away, and as she prayed, she kept the pressure on the trigger. She would have shot people to protect her children, and she wondered if someone inside the house was just doing the same.

It got darker as the hours went by, and the crying became a heavy feeling. It sapped what little energy she had. She went to sleep despite the eerie stillness that was occasionally punctuated by distant screams. There were shuffling noises accompanied by growls. She knew what made those sounds, but her exhaustion was total, and she resigned herself to either sleeping or being killed. She didn't care anymore. Her husband was in outer space, her children were missing, and the only friend she had was killed only a few yards from where she hid.

"Come and get me," she thought.

For a moment, she was afraid she had said it out loud because the dark shapes only a few feet from her head moved. She laid perfectly still and watched as the shapes turned in a circle. She wasn't sure the shapes were boots until they moved away, this time with deliberate steps. Symone instinctively knew they were not the feet of an infected dead. They moved too quietly and coordinated, and there was no stumbling or shuffling. She also knew not to give away her position. Another pair of feet passed by the same spot, and she made a guess that they belonged to people who were attempting to get close to the house without being detected.

Fifteen minutes after the boots went by, she heard a window break. There were shouts followed by gunshots, and then there was screaming. There was silence again, but it was broken by the growling and shuffling noises she knew would come later. She thought she would go mad when she heard the last terrified scream because it meant an infected had found a survivor. It was brutal to hear, and it tugged at her heart to be so close and unable to help.

Sleep finally got a firm grip on her, and she blocked out the sounds of the night. If anything passed by her as she slept, it didn't disturb her. It was a combination of fatigue and resignation. If she died in her sleep, it just wouldn't matter to her.

She slept well past sunrise, and she was thirsty. For a moment, she didn't know where she was, and there was a familiar smell. The breeze carried gray smoke in a swirl through her hiding place, and she recognized it. Something was burning, and she could hear the cracking of glass that was about to explode from the heat. She had inhaled some of the smoke, and there was a bitter taste to it.

Several pairs of legs brushed past the bushes, and she knew it was time to move. She stuck her head out where she could see the back of the house, and a quick look told her everything she needed to know. The acrid smell mixed in with other odors was the smell of burning plastics. Siding, wires, and all the trimmings that made a modern-day home were the recipe for a nasty smell, but the smell was rivaled by the sound. It roared out into the morning and called for every infected dead to come to it. They were drawn to it like moths from every direction, and she was too close for comfort.

Symone was shocked to see that the infected walk directly into the flames, but as mesmerized as she was by the spectacle, it was going to get much more crowded, and it would only be a distraction that would help her as long as it grew in size. She pushed her backpack ahead of her and dragged Arthur's heavier bag of supplies behind her until she reached a privacy fence that met with the dense hedges. It meant she was being forced out of her hiding spot, but she had to get around to the other side of the fence. She couldn't see past it, so she didn't know if there was even any cover beyond it, but the side she was on was exposed to the back of the burning house. In a few minutes, there would be enough of the infected dead in the yard for them to see her. She had no choice, so she drew on every ounce of strength she had gained from a good night of sleep and forced herself to move quickly. She lifted her backpack and pulled on the straps of the large bag as she burst into the open and climbed over the fence. The weight of her baggage kept her from having any chance of stopping her momentum as she fell from the top. The privacy fence sat on the rim of a steep drainage culvert, and she went over the edge head first.

If she were counting her blessings, there would have been a trade-off between tumbling down a hill into a ditch and getting out of the open in a hurry. Not to mention the arrival of her heavy baggage on top of her. She was once again on the ground in relatively good cover. The bottom of the culvert had not been maintained for some time even before the infected dead had come along, and small bushes had sprung up down the middle. She managed to see far enough in both directions to tell that she was on the perimeter of the neighborhood, and she could circle around it without being seen. Her only concern was that the infected dead could just as easily roll down the slopes of the culvert from either direction. If the sides were too steep for them to get back out, they might walk down the middle just as she was doing.

She made up her mind quickly. The fire was making enough noise for her to move as fast as she could under all the gear she carried. She could abandon a large part of it, but she wanted to find a safe place where she could sort through it for the most important stuff. A cluster of small buildings on the other side of the road had just what she was looking for. A pub with an old-fashioned sign hanging over its door was far enough from the road without making her be exposed for too long. If it was uninhabited, it appeared to be a sturdy place to hide.

It was a struggle getting up the side of the culvert, and she was sure she would be seen by the infected, but the billowing smoke from the fire appeared to still be increasing. Every infected she saw down the road was moving toward it with a singular goal, and Symone found herself between the pub and the building next to it much sooner than she had hoped. She was gasping, but somehow she had managed to stay invisible…or so she had assumed.

Arthur had died because he never considered the possibility that normal people would shoot an old man who wasn't infected. All he wanted to do was see if the house was empty so they would have a safe place to sleep. They could have fed the person inside in return for shelter. Instead, the person inside had considered Arthur to be a threat and had made the decision to shoot first and ask questions later.

Standing with her back against a wall only a few feet from the windows of the pub, Symone felt totally stupid and totally exposed. If there was someone inside watching her, she knew they were sizing up the cargo she was dragging behind her. Even worse, they were sizing her up. Still attractive despite everything, she might have just run headfirst into something worse than getting shot, and it only added to her feelings of dread for her to not see any infected dead pressed up against the other side of the glass. That could mean one of two things. The place was either empty, or it was occupied by someone who was just waiting for her to come inside.

She never intended to just run to the front door and open it, but she didn't have another plan. She hadn't given it any thought because she had to move fast. Faced with the need to make a decision, she put down her backpack and the large bag Arthur had carried. As she did, she slipped the Smith & Wesson from its holster without being conspicuous. In one swift move, she crossed the gap between the two buildings and pinned herself against the wall between two of the windows.

The last thing she expected was the crash that came from the building where she had been standing. She hadn't paid that building much attention because it was some kind of curiosity shop. It was a place where tourists could pick up a few souvenirs on their way to Stonehenge or maybe on their way back to London.

The infected dead inside crashed through another display case, but she had mistakenly thought the first crash was because it had seen her.

From her new vantage point, she could see it falling into things inside the store, but it wasn't at the window trying to reach her.

"It hasn't seen me yet," she said in a low voice. "Okay, Symone, time to make a decision. Are we staying or going?"

Hearing her own voice seemed to galvanize her and make everything a bit more real. She suddenly understood she had to make the decisions again. Arthur had made it easier because in their brief time together, she wasn't making all the decisions. She found herself moving toward the front door, and she was surprised to realize why she had chosen it over the back door. It was a conscious decision. The infected dead didn't know the front of a building from the back of it, and if there were any infected coming from that direction on their way to the fire, they would see her as soon as she got there.

At that moment, she didn't know how right she was, and as she reached the front door of the pub, six of the infected on their way to the fire entered the gap between the pub and the curiosity shop from the back. She pulled on the handle, and she was surprised for a second time within seconds that the door opened easily. She stepped into the cool darkness of a foyer where coats still hung on hooks, and she held her breath. As she patiently listened for any telltale sound inside the pub, she saw the row of infected dead walk by the window where she had been standing. They passed right by her backpack.

She got the kind of chills you could only get if you were walking through a graveyard at midnight. That had been way too close for comfort. She found herself to be more aware of everything at that moment. She was aware that she couldn't hear the infected as they stumbled past outside. She was aware of the rough grip on the Smith & Wesson as she squeezed it too hard. She was aware that there was no smell of death inside the pub, and most of all, she was aware that she could hear a clock ticking somewhere. If there was someone inside with her, they were quieter than she was.

She held the gun across her chest with her right hand, and she used her left hand to feel for the doorknob. She was grateful to find it had an old-fashioned lock to go with the old-fashioned sign outside. There was a key in the lock, and she gently turned it. The click it made was much louder than she wanted it to be, but she was satisfied that nothing could follow her inside.

Her eyes adjusted to the gloom, and she saw that the place hadn't been completely ignored since the start of the infection. As a matter of fact, while some people had looted the pharmacies, there were others who considered alcohol to be more valuable. That was the case here, and from what she could tell, every bottle that had been on the shelves was gone. There were broken beer glasses on the floor, and all of the beer taps were in the open position. Someone had built a pyramid of shot glasses on the bar. If they did it as they drank the shots, her guess was that they didn't make it home that night because the base was an impressive row of twelve glasses. She felt a pang of regret because a cocktail would be a fine way to end the day.

The thought of a stiff drink made her think of food, and she remembered what she had to do. There was still plenty of time left in the day, but she might not be as lucky down the road if she decided to press on for a few hours. She had food in her bags outside, and she had to expose herself again to get to it, but she doubted there was anything in the pub that was edible. It would just be a matter of timing and a little good luck, but she thought she could get the backpack and the big bag of gear inside. She decided she would check out her surroundings first.

Stepping carefully around the broken beer glasses and other debris, Symone made her way from the front door to the opposite end of the pub. It would be a good idea to be sure she didn't have any undetected company in any of the rooms used by the operators of the pub. The small office where the owner did the paperwork was ransacked just like the bar itself. Bloodstains across the desk and chair were a clue that the owner was present when the place was looted. Whether the blood belonged to the owner or the looters didn't matter anymore.

The bathrooms were across the hall, and Symone wasn't ready for the sounds she heard coming from the other side of both doors. Since the doors opened outward, she was terrified that something would burst into the hallway with her at any moment. Faced with the certain knowledge that she couldn't go back outside and the chance she may be caught inside with whatever was inside both bathrooms, she acted quickly.

The barstools were made of heavy wood with high backs, and she hoped she guessed right that they would be tall enough. She hurried into the bar and grabbed the nearest stool, dragging it by the heavy top until she got it into place outside one of the bathrooms. Once she had it in place, she tipped it over onto its side. With satisfaction, she succeeded in getting its legs against the wall on one side of the hall and the high back against the door on the other side. She didn't wait to see if it would work and rushed back for a second chair. The thumping sound of it falling into place caused a chorus of groans from both bathrooms, but from what she could tell, nothing tried to come out. She tested her handiwork by tugging on both doors, and they didn't budge.

Satisfied that she was safe from the infected dead in the bathrooms, she finally moved on to the last door. She knew it would be the kitchen, and somewhere would be a storeroom. There was no doubt in her mind that both were ransacked, but she needed to be sure they weren't harboring something else.

What little food the kitchen had before was most likely taken on the first day because there wasn't even a smell from something that might have spoiled. It made sense to her that the neighborhood a short distance away had plenty of people who were patrons of the pub. People who crowded the place for football parties crowded it again for their share of the food and beer when both became scarce.

There were two storerooms at the back of the kitchen. One storeroom had been for the liquor, and one had been for the food. Both had been emptied, but to her amazement, the cap of a solitary bottle stuck out from the top of a cardboard box, and when she pulled it out, she found it to be an unopened bottle of single malt scotch. She stared at the familiar label and fought back the temptation to crack the seal. If there was one thing she couldn't afford, it was not to have her wits about her. As much as she would enjoy it, there would be trading value to it down the road.

Her last item to check off her list was the back door. She found it to be locked with a heavy bar across it. That satisfied her but gave her one disadvantage. She couldn't see out the back of the building to tell if there were more infected dead coming from that direction. Still, it was better than she had hoped for.

With the knowledge that she was safe and secure for the time being, Symone made her way back to the front door. There were several infected dead crossing the road, but they all had their backs to her. Beyond them, the smoke was still thick from the fire. She could only imagine how bad it was at the source, and she wondered if maybe enough of the infected would walk into the fire for it to make a difference.

A little courage was what she told herself she needed. Just a little courage. She went before she would have the chance to change her mind. When she made a mad dash for the gear sitting between the buildings, her mind revised her choice of words. It changed courage to stupidity, and there would be nothing she could do if there were more of the infected coming her way. She didn't even look. She just grabbed both bags and ran. Her mind filled in those seconds of exposure by counting as she ran, almost as if counting would replace what was happening.

Her feet found the wooden steps, and she heard the pounding they made under the extra weight she carried, but the pounding of her heart was almost louder in her ears. Inside with her back against the door, it sounded like her heart was beating so loud that someone else would be able to hear it too. From where she was, she could see out through the side window where the bags had been, and there weren't any infected dead swarming after her.

She spent the next hour on the floor at the spot the farthest she could get from the front door and the restrooms. All she wanted to do was listen and be safe for a bit. She felt like she had wasted an entire day to travel only a few hundred yards, but when she managed to get herself under mental control, she compared it to climbing out of a deep hole. She was in a big trouble hiding in those bushes, and there was no way she would be able to travel far in daylight with the infected being drawn toward the fire from all directions.

After an hour to calm herself, she saw that it was getting dark outside. She decided to eat a can of spaghetti without trying to find a way to heat it up. There were probably cans of Sterno somewhere in the bar, and she even had a few cans left, but she didn't have enough drive left in her. All she wanted to do was eat and then get to sleep. Tomorrow would be a better day.

******

Symone woke up only an hour later. She didn't know if it had been a random noise or if it had been the dream she was having. In the dream, she saw her children inside the window of the house where she had been hiding under the bushes. She saw it catch fire, and she wanted to go to them, but someone else inside shot at her every time she tried to get closer. When she sat up too quickly, she knocked over the bottle of scotch she had found, and the noise was loud enough to make her hold her breath. It didn't draw any unwanted attention, but it was enough to stretch her nerves to the limit.

She knew she wouldn't be able to go back to sleep until she got the dream out of her mind, so she decided it would be a good time to sort through the bags. She couldn't continue to carry her backpack and the bag Arthur had carried, and it appeared to be a decision between food and ammunition. She made a pile of each, and it was obvious that the ammunition weighed more, but she couldn't see herself leaving it behind for that reason alone. She got a mental image of throwing a can of spaghetti at a group of the infected. Then she thought about what it would be like to have plenty of bullets but no food.

The piles got shuffled around with some of each in different types until she saw her solution. The rifle that had belonged to Arthur was the biggest thing in his bag, but she wasn't even sure she could shoot it. She set it aside and then stacked all of the ammunition for it beside the gun. The weight change made the difference she needed, but there was something else she could do. All of the canned food joined the bullets and rifle. What she had left to carry were plenty of power bars and dried fruits. Arthur had four bags of beef jerky and trail mix in his bag. The rest of the weight would be water, the first aid kit, and her ammunition for the Smith & Wesson, which she knew she could shoot well.

Symone ventured out from her hiding place and carefully made her way to the office without using her flashlight. She found a piece of paper and a pen and wrote a note that she addressed to whoever found the rifle and food. She explained that the supplies had been too heavy to carry, but she hoped someone who really needed to have a better day found them. She put it all up on the bar where it would be easily found and tucked the note under the heavy box of ammunition at the top of the pile.

There was something vaguely satisfying about leaving supplies for a stranger to find. She didn't let herself give in to the thought that it might be a scavenger who wouldn't do the same thing for someone else. Instead, she thought about the possibility that it might be a family that was just trying to hold on for one more day. This stuff would be enough to give them that day. Symone hoped it would buy her the same thing from whatever force was in charge of fate.

Once she had finished the job of sorting the gear, she found that she was able to rest again. She allowed herself one small sip from the scotch, eyed the bottle as the sip burned past her tongue and throat, and gave in to one large swallow. It hit her hard, and she fell into a deep sleep.

******

* * *

This time she slept until sunrise, and it was the light shining across her hiding place that woke her up, but there was something else. A familiar humming sound she hadn't heard since the day the police came to her house. The humming got louder as she listened, and that confirmed for her what it was.

Symone bolted from her hiding place in a mad rush to reach the door. The sound of an automobile engine sounded out of place in the new world, but for some reason, she felt like she had to see it. It had to have something to do with her missing children. She could feel it in her bones.

It turned out to be two vehicles, and they weren't cars. They were already passing the pub at high speed by the time she made it to the door, and even though she didn't know what she would have done if she had gotten there before them, she was disappointed to be too late. She wasn't too late to see their brake lights become brighter, though.

Both motorcycles came to a stop and then made a tight turn in the center of the road. It wasn't clear to her why they turned around, but it could have been because of the number of infected that were walking on the centerline of the road in their direction. The bikes had stopped only a few yards from the infected, and Symone saw one of the riders raise his arm. He was holding a handgun and was obviously going to shoot one of them, but the other man waved an empty hand in the air. The armed man put the gun back into its holster, so her guess was that the other guy had stopped him.

The motorcycles gained speed quickly and traveled the short distance back to the pub in seconds. She found herself to be backing away from the door because this time, they didn't keep going. They pulled up to the front of the pub just as if they were just two bikers out for a ride and a pint of beer. In the old days, they would have walked up the steps to the front door, but today they were in a hurry. They grabbed at the handle outside and shook it violently.

Symone didn't back away quickly enough. Her legs felt like rubber the moment she realized they were coming to her door, and even though she backed away, her fight versus flight instincts failed her. Fright made her slow and indecisive. She had a flashback of the moment when she ran out onto her own front porch and saw her little boy at the top of the steps and the infected dead coming toward him. She had reacted then, but this time she froze. One of them saw her.

"Open up, lady!"

He shook the door harder and slammed a flat palm against the wood.

"Don't make me break down the door! If I do, then those things will get in too!"

From where she stood, she could see that one of the men was older than the other. The younger guy was behind the man pounding on the door, and she could see he was watching the road. It didn't appear that he was too comfortable with what he saw. When he turned his face toward the glass on the door, she saw real fear.

That made her move. Part of her was screaming in her ear that she was about to let two bikers into her safe place, while another part of her was screaming that she would want someone to open the door if she was on the other side of it. The part of her that had reasoned Arthur didn't need to die won the screaming match, and she rushed toward the door. She fumbled with the key, and the shaking and pushing from outside was making it harder to turn.

"Stop pushing on the door," she yelled.

She was surprised that he listened, but as soon as he stopped putting his weight against it, the key turned in the lock, and the door flew open. Symone got out of their way, and it was a good thing she did because they were much bigger now than when they were outside. She backed into a corner and watched as they hurriedly pushed the door shut again. Faces were already appearing on the other side of the glass. They were grotesque, and they worked their mouths against the glass as if they were trying to eat it.

The two men backed away from the door, seeming to forget all about her for a moment. All she could see were two large backs. Both were wearing sweat-stained tee shirts and smelled like they hadn't showered in a month...or maybe a year. Symone did her best to suppress a gag, but it escaped anyway. Both turned toward her and stared at Symone like they hadn't seen her through the glass, and there was something else she couldn't put her finger on, but she didn't know if she was supposed to be afraid or happy they had arrived.

The growling and bumping against the door intensified, and whatever it was she had seen in their faces, it had to wait a few minutes because that many infected could test the ability of that door to stay closed.

"We have to cover the glass to make them forget about us," said the older man. "What can we use?"

He turned to Symone as if she would know something he didn't, and the part of her mind that had protected her children at the beginning made an appearance.

"Tablecloths," she said.

"This place has tablecloths?" said the younger of the two men. Now that he was inside, she could tell he was in his mid-twenties.

Symone had thought it strange that a pub would bother with table cloths too, but she had found them in the storeroom along with some things that had been used at a wedding celebration.

"Special occasions," she said. "I think they kept them for weddings and birthdays."

Fortunately, the box of wedding decorations also contained tape and tacks for when they decorated the bar. After retrieving it from the storeroom, the three of them worked together to cover the door and the windows of the entrance. Either the situation was making her able to deal with their smell, or she got used to it, but once they stepped back to admire their handiwork, their close proximity elicited another gag. She found herself to be standing between them, and both of them were close to a foot taller than her, so she was uncomfortably close to their armpits. She tried to discreetly put one hand over her mouth and nose.

The older man said, "Lassie, if you're finding our lack of proper hygiene to be offensive, you would probably like to know that you don't exactly smell like a rose yourself."

Until that moment, Symone didn't know if she would be safe with the men, but she also didn't know she smelled like dirt, smoke and possibly had crawled through dog droppings when she escaped from the yard behind the house. The way the older man wrinkled his nose at her wiped away her indecision about being safe with them. She decided if he could muster up a sense of humor in their situation, he would be someone she liked.

"Symone Tisdal," she said as she held out a dirty hand.

He eyed her hand as if she might be holding some of those dog droppings, then grinned and took her hand in his big, equally grimy hand.

"I'm Joseph Porter, and this young man is my son, William. Now that we've been properly introduced, if you will kindly point me toward the washroom, I will attempt to make myself more pleasant to be in the company of a lady."

"Uh, I'm sorry, Mr. Porter, but I believe it's occupied."

12

Atlantic Crossing

Aboard the Maggie Mae - Year Eight

The Chief was so at home on the water that he convinced Andi and her crew to let him take the helm for the first watch. The seas were calm, and the moon was too small for it to give him much light, but he wanted the serene feeling he always got from a few hours of steering through the ink-black water. Andi gave in and said she would take everyone else below and show them to their quarters. Iris gave the Chief a kiss and told him to have fun, and being as astute as she was, she was a bit amused by the glance of regret she saw on Andi's face.

Everyone followed behind Andi except Jessie, who made himself comfortable in one of the tall chairs on the bridge. He was a little protective of Andi and the Maggie Mae, and he had expected his shift at the helm, so he wasn't sleepy. He decided he would stay at his post and get to know this big man who seemed so at home that Andi had left her boat in his hands.

The Chief was glad for his company, and although he guessed Jessie had a motive for staying behind, he had a motive of his own. He was curious and wanted to get to know the crew of the Maggie Mae and hear their stories about survival since the beginning of the apocalypse. Jessie was hesitant at first, but the Chief's likable personality soon had the younger man talking nonstop.

Jessie started at the beginning and how they had met Andi. It sounded familiar to the Chief because he had been in the Charleston harbor when it started. One thing he had thought about from the first day was what it must have been like after the sun went down on the chaos and carnage they had left behind. They had sailed out of the harbor with their own problems on the cruise ship, and to tell the truth, he would have preferred to have been on a tugboat like the Maggie Mae. Still, if he had been at the helm of a tug, he might have done something stupid like try to rescue people, and that hadn't worked out so well for most rescuers.

In the light of day, it had been a terrifying sight, but at least they could see what was happening around them. As Jessie described it, the darkness only blocked out what they could see, but there was still the sound of it and the smell. He said he didn't realize it until later when they were out on the open sea where there was only the salt air, but as Boston went up in flames, there was another smell besides the burning buildings, cars, and boats. There was the smell that came from thousands of people dying, whether they were burned or murdered by the hordes of infected. He said he didn't think he would ever forget that smell.

"I figure that's what fear smells like," said Jessie.

The Chief could see Jessie's face in the glow from the instruments, and he could tell Jessie was looking out over the open water, but he saw a memory. He didn't interrupt and waited for him to continue.

"We headed straight out to sea that night...full speed, ignoring distress calls. We'll never know how many we could have saved."

The rule of the sea is to answer a Mayday call at all costs, and the Chief had to wonder how many calls had been ignored. Around the world, ships of all sizes had pulled away from ports as people begged over their radios for someone to help. Jessie's conscience was still bothering him over seven years later.

"We had a big family. The Allen family goes back generations, and if we had gotten a Mayday call from someone named Allen, I think we would probably be dead by now. We would have answered the call and never made it out of Boston harbor. We heard Mayday calls for a day and a half."

"Did you see any Navy or Coast Guard ships? Were they responding?"

Jessie's head lowered, and the Chief knew instinctively that he had touched on a sore spot.

"We saw a US Navy cruiser sink a Coast Guard ship."

Being former Navy, the Chief felt like he had to say something to defend the actions of the cruiser, but Jessie beat him to it.

"It was just after dawn on the first day out of Boston, and the Coast Guard ship had so many survivors on board that they were almost hanging onto the side of it. They also had plenty of the infected with them because they had been doing what came naturally to them. They were answering Mayday calls. You could see the dead moving around on the decks attacking people who didn't let go of the railings soon enough. There were people in the water with their children on one arm and an infected dead on the other. The Navy did what they had to do."

"How long did you stay away from land?" asked the Chief.

As bad as it was, Jessie was visibly relieved to move on from that first day.

"We stayed away from land and from other ships for a month," said Jessie. "Every time we got too close to a Navy ship, they warned us to stay away, but they sort of conducted a survey. They always asked if we were carrying anyone who was bitten. A week or so into it, they asked more questions like who was on board and who had we lost since leaving port."

The Chief said, "They probably shared the information with other vessels, and they cross-checked your answers with each other."

"We figured as much," said Jessie. "We were surprised that they never drafted us and put us to work for them."

"Don't count that out just yet," said the Chief. "Even all these years later, you can bet that they know you're out here, and they know you've survived this long by not bringing the infection on board."

Jessie moved his eyes from the water ahead and seemed almost to be studying the Chief. The Chief was aware of the lapse in conversation but not totally surprised by the unspoken question written on Jessie's face.

"You want to know if any of our group is infected," said the Chief.

Jessie nodded, "The thought had crossed my mind. Andi was expecting Henry Tisdal, not a large group of people."

"I can only answer you one way, and that's because I've asked the same question more times than I can count. People will lie to protect an infected loved one, or maybe their own lives. They'll tell you the bandage on their arm isn't covering a bite wound. It's actually a bandage to protect themselves from being bitten. I don't expect you to believe me just because I say so, but we're all clean, and you can tell Andi we're fine with being inspected for wounds."

That seemed to satisfy Jessie for the moment, so he let it drop. In his experience, he had learned to spot the hesitance when people had something to hide.

"What about the pirates?" asked the Chief.

"All the time. They hide along shorelines mostly, but they'll follow your wake for hours and try to come up your tail at night. Donny is on stern watch right now. As a matter of fact, he's due to report in about now."

As if on cue, Donny's voice came over the radio, but it wasn't to give the routine all-clear message.

"Hey, Jessie, we've got something on the hook back here. I think they've been there since we made the pick-up, and they're gaining."

"Let me see if Andi wants to waste fuel trying to outrun them, or maybe she'll want to let them catch up. With the extra firepower we have on board, maybe we can rid the Atlantic of a pirate."

Jessie gave the Chief a grin that the Chief interpreted as hope that he would volunteer, which was something the Chief couldn't enjoy more.

"I think we can earn our keep by providing a little pest control," said the Chief.

"Can your people shoot?" asked Jessie.

The Chief didn't answer, but Jessie saw the grin.

Thirty minutes later, they were gathered at the stern, and it was obvious that the other craft was gaining on them. It was far too dark to tell what kind of ship it was, and they wouldn't be able to tell until it was really close. According to Andi, the Navy never pursued them the way this boat was, and it wasn't likely to be another ocean-going tugboat.

"Definitely unfriendly," she said, "and I'd rather not let them get close enough to take a shot at us. Bullets have a way of hitting things that can't be fixed in the middle of the ocean."

Kathy was using a pair of binoculars to see what she could tell about the boat. Her guess was that they were overconfident. They were running under full power with plenty of lights on, so they weren't afraid to be seen.

"You sure the military doesn't pursue like this?" she asked Andi. "If we shoot first and they're Navy, you can bet we're going to lose that fight."

"Positive. The Navy wouldn't light themselves up like that, and they would be broadcasting to us. These guys are probably part of a gang, and they're sending a message to anyone else out here to mind their own business."

The Chief said, "I have a suggestion if you don't mind."

Andi didn't mind at all. It was the first time she had felt really safe in years, and she told the Chief he was more than welcome to take command.

"In the days of tall ships," he said, "the Captain would give orders to a squadron of marines. The modern military still does it, so you keep command but let me earn my pay."

The Chief gathered his group around him and explained what they were going to do, and they all saw the logic in his plan. They also saw the humor. They spread out along the straight railing of the wide stern, each with a rifle balanced and aimed at the approaching boat. Everyone was down on one knee and did the best they could to stay on target despite the bouncing tugboat.

Kathy, Tom, Iris, Hampton, Colleen, Sim, Cassandra, Jim, and Henry all waited for the Chief to count it down. When he yelled the command to shoot, they all pulled the trigger just once, sending a volley of nine shots at the boat. He counted down from ten, and they sent a second round of bullets.

The effects were obvious. The goal was to cause more confusion than damage because only lucky shots would cause damage at such a distance. Having nine bullets arrive at the same time had to be a shock to the pirates. If they didn't hit anything, they were at least heard, and the lights from the high-speed boat seemed to wobble. When the second volley was fired, they changed direction and rapidly faded away.

Andi was impressed, and she couldn't hide her admiration of the Chief's simple solution to a big problem.

"I can't believe it," she said. "You accomplished more with eighteen bullets than we would have if we had just shot it out with them. We couldn't have done more with a big deck gun."

"They had no way to tell if it was nine shots per volley or fifty," said the Chief. "All they knew was bullets whistled past them on all sides."

Kathy said, "I beg your pardon. I hit my target both times."

The others all chimed in, claiming to have hit their targets, and Andi could see why this group had survived for so many years. They trusted each other, but their camaraderie allowed them to overcome obstacles with a little humor thrown in.

The laughter and joking settled down, and everyone waited for the next order, which was simply to get some rest. Everyone filed through the main deck hatch that led toward the crew's mess and quarters, leaving Andi alone with Henry Tisdal for the first time since they had made their rendezvous. It was a bitter-sweet moment given the last question she had asked him when they came aboard. She had seen by his expression that he hadn't been able to contact his wife.

He held his hand out to her again and said, "I can't thank you enough for your generosity. You're taking a great risk to get me home."

Andi shook his hand, but she shook her head as well.

"It's risky just being alive right now whether you're on the land or the sea. Why wouldn't I help you?"

"You know what I mean, Captain. There are enough risks right now without taking on the extra burden of helping people."

Andi pointed at the hatch that had just closed behind the group of newcomers and asked, "Why are they helping you? Could it be because there's something left of the human race? Not everyone chose to survive by killing fellow survivors or stealing what meager supplies they were able to scrounge up."

"They are remarkable people, aren't they?" he said.

Andi put her arm around Henry's shoulders and guided him toward the hatch.

"What do you say we go below and join them? I have a feeling they didn't take my advice to get some rest. I'll bet they're all in the crew's mess enjoying some safe time together."

Andi wasn't wrong. Everyone was taking the opportunity to sit and enjoy each other's company in a safe environment. The gentle swaying of the Maggie Mae through the calm swells only served to remind them that there couldn't be a horde of infected dead for miles, and relaxation was just as important as sleep. Ivan had gone to the bridge to take the helm, and his two brothers had stayed behind to get to know their passengers. It had been a long time since they had been around such an amiable group, and by the time Andi and Henry arrived, they were already laughing uncontrollably at their stories.

It also appeared that all of them had good sea legs, and at the mention of food, they had manned the galley and were in the middle of throwing together a midnight meal. The Chief was quick to reassure her that they would help to resupply the food, and she was equally quick to let them know that she was willing to share whatever they wanted.

Over scrambled eggs, bacon, and hash brown potatoes, they

exchanged stories about the years since the arrival of the infected dead. They told her about where they each were when it started, and it didn't take long before the topic of the shelters came up. Andi was stunned to learn they existed but wasn't totally surprised, and she had her own bombshell that she dropped on them. She had heard a rumor that other countries had protected their leaders by building bunkers and safe rooms in their capitols.

"How many leaders actually made it to their shelters?" asked Kathy.

"We haven't heard any information that would indicate one way or the other," answered Andi.

Hampton said, "It didn't seem to work out so well for the leaders in our country. Sim can give you the details about what happened to our President because he was there, and we know what happened to one Senator. For the most part, it was a good idea, but it didn't work because no one planned for zombies."

The Chief could have corrected Hampton, but he chose to ignore the fact that Hampton was trying to provoke the usual debate about whether or not they were zombies. He wanted to hear more about what Andi knew. He started to ask, but Henry beat him to it.

"What about England? It's hard for me to believe that your country had such a monumental undertaking without including England."

Andi's thoughts went back to what her source had told her to see if there were any clues about which countries had been so farsighted that they had done as the Americans had.

"We were stopped by a military vessel that was flying a German flag. I remember we were all afraid that they were going to take us prisoner, but all they wanted was the same thing we did. Information...all they wanted was information. As a matter of fact, they gave us some fuel, supplies, and even a few weapons. They said they had attempted to make port at several European cities but had found the same thing everywhere. As soon as they docked, they were forced to leave. They were making their way to the United States in the hope of finding a safe port."

"Ever see them again?" asked the Chief. "Hopefully, they'll find their way to Charleston."

"No, we've seen other flagged ships, but mostly they keep their distance. We know a few have gotten closer so they could check us out, but as time has gone by, I think everyone has worried about the same thing."

The Chief finished for Andi, "Getting the infection on board."

Captain Miller had just been listening because he was sure Andi would say she had spotted the carrier group that had set up its base of operations in the Atlantic not far from their present position. It wasn't a secret he planned to keep from her indefinitely, but he was at least a little concerned that they would run into the US Navy and he would be identified as the traitor who had separated from them along with about one hundred soldiers. The questions from the others eventually got her around to the part about a destroyer that had tried to resupply and had met with disaster. That told him what he needed to know. The Navy had bigger problems to deal with than one deserter.

Andi and the Allen brothers had plenty of sea stories to share, but despite the urgings of the others for her to go on, she insisted that it was their turn. She was particularly curious about the oil platform in the Gulf of Mexico and whether or not it had ever been reopened. She could imagine that someone with access to a seaworthy ocean-going tugboat was in a position to use it as a base of operations, and the Chief didn't disagree.

"Before we spend the whole night telling you about Sim winding up in the shelter with the President of the United States and Iris being stuck inside Ambassadors Island for years, answer one question for us," said the Chief. "Did any of the rumors you heard indicate that England might have built a shelter? I can't imagine that they would pass up on a contingency plan for the Royal family."

"Oh, I'm sorry. I got sidetracked. The Germans wanted to know the same thing. They had suspected the British military had a shelter on the Isle of Wight because all of the news reports indicated that was where they had set up a massive refugee camp. The German ship was out of Bremerhaven, so they were attempting to use the English Channel to reach port, but the Channel was so congested with boats that they returned to the open sea. They said every boat was loaded with people needing medical attention, and they had already received a warning from the French Navy that they had lost several ships when they rendered aid."

"So the rumors about the Isle of Wight weren't true?" asked Henry.

"Well, not entirely. The German Captain mentioned the Grenadier Guards."

Henry perked up at the name of the elite unit, and the Chief did as well. They both recognized the name of the historically distinguished regiment that supplied the guards at Buckingham Palace.

"What did he say about them?" asked Henry.

"He said he saw an airplane take off from the Isle of Wight. It was heading north which could mean anything, but he saw the insignia of the Grenadier Guards on the tail."

Kathy shook her head and said, "Doesn't sound so promising to me. As a matter of fact, it sounds like they evacuated the Royal family to the Isle of Wight and then had to move them again."

"I can tell you this much for certain," said Andi. "The Royal Navy is concentrated around that area. Every contact I've had with friendly ships has confirmed that the Isle of Wight has a blockade around it. That's why we're going to make a high-speed run for the Isles of Scilly. There are one hundred and forty-five islands, but only five are inhabited. We can duck into them and get you close enough to the coast of England for you to travel the rest of the way by land."

"How far would that be from where we need to go?" asked Kathy.

Andi didn't appear to be comfortable with the answer, and her hesitation caught the eyes of everyone watching.

"Why do I get the feeling I'm not going to like the answer?" said Tom.

The rest of the group went silent, waiting for the answer.

"A little over two hundred miles," said Andi. "It's possibly about two hundred and twenty-five."

Cassandra got Andi's attention and asked why they couldn't just hand Henry off to the Royal Navy. After all, he was a national hero. Everyone else had been thinking the same thing, and they were all nodding their heads.

"They obviously think Henry's dead. I mean, we can try, but I don't think they'll buy it. Put yourself in their shoes. They've had their fair share of celebrities showing up wanting protection from the military, and as far as I know, the Britons are the only people who've managed to keep a foothold on land. That is, aside from groups such as yourselves. No government has publicly come forth to claim success in fighting back the infected."

The Chief was perplexed, and his forehead was furrowed. He held up a hand to interrupt the others when they all started to speak, but he was fairly sure they all had the same question. He was thinking back to the first time they came across Captain Miller and his men. They were in need of rescue themselves, and the Chief had sacrificed valuable fuel from their plane to give them the opportunity they needed to make a retreat. If the US Army had failed to establish a foothold at an existing base, how had the Britons done it, especially when they were so close to London?

Andi anticipated his question and answered before he could ask it.

"I didn't know anything about the Americans building shelters when I spoke with other ships," said Andi. "If I had, I would have assumed the Britons had done the same thing, and I would have known what to ask, but there's one thing that doesn't make sense. Why would they put it so close to the most populated part of England?"

Everyone had to laugh when Andi finished her question because the Americans had challenged public awareness by building some of its shelters right under the noses of large populations. The shelter under Columbus, Ohio was the biggest in terms of who it would protect. The escape system was miles long and extended all the way to the airport, while the shelter itself was directly under the downtown area. Some of the shelters were in rural areas, but even Fort Sumter had been built close to a large population.

The Chief didn't want Andi to think they were laughing at her and was quick to intervene.

"There's a man back in Alabama who was part of the original builders club, and he could probably explain this better, but from what I know, locations near populated areas were easily built under the noses of the residents of the area because they had other projects going on at the same time."

"The tunnel," said Andi. "When they built the tunnel, they were far enough away from the construction, but they had to transport large amounts of earth from the sea bed, and they used the airport at Bournemouth as a staging area. Maybe they were working on something else at the same time."

******

The gentle swaying of the Maggie Mae and the big meal eventually lulled the tired passengers into a restful mood, and people slipped away to their bunks. The Chief returned to the bridge to resume the disrupted shift at the helm. This time it was Andi who followed him up the ladder. Jessie took his cue and said goodnight, leaving the two of them alone. Andi hadn't been so strongly drawn to a man in years, and she had to find out if it was really a long shot for her to think things weren't that solid between him and Iris. He let her down more gently than the swaying under their feet.

"Andi, you should know something upfront. I didn't fall from grace with the sea," said the Chief. "The sea has been my first love, but Iris is part of the sea. She was also a sailor when we met, and as long as we're together, we feel like the sea is nearby."

"Wow," she answered.

She couldn't think of anything else to say. His one simple comment made it clear to her, and it made her respect him all that much more. If he was beyond her reach, at least it was because he was an honorable man who had found his soul mate.

"Okay. I get the message but thank you for leaving my self-esteem intact. I don't have to worry that it's because you don't find me attractive."

"We don't have a problem there. You're plenty attractive, and I wasn't the only man aware of that at the table in the galley."

Andi wondered what she had missed, and when she thought about it for a moment, there was a pair of pale blue eyes that had caught her attention earlier. Captain Miller had been quick to smile when she spoke directly to him. She had been taken with the Chief, but when she analyzed herself, she realized it was because of his adventurous nature. Just as she was drawn to the challenges of the ocean, the Chief was drawn to the challenges of seemingly everything. He stood out in a crowd, and that made her miss the handsome Captain's quiet mysteries. Picturing him in her mind, she saw that his quiet presence was also a story that she would love to hear. Maybe that was what she saw in the Chief. There was a wealth of things to talk about, but Captain Miller would be worth getting to know better. She laughed quietly.

"What did I say?"

Andi didn't realize he had kept watching her after he had spoken, and her laugh could have been taken the wrong way.

"Oh, I'm sorry, I was just deep in thought for a moment. That was a very skillful parry. You let me down and put me off on the scent of someone else at the same time, but don't worry. You were right. Captain Miller was very attentive, and I could have been more responsive. You don't think he was put off so much that he won't try again, do you?"

"Not a chance. He knows that Iris and I are permanent."

Andi was satisfied by his answer, but she thought to herself again, "Why does he have to possess the most magnetic smile even as he holds me at a distance?"

Bob Howard

* * *

******

The sun was just making its appearance on the horizon, and the Chief was finally ready for a short nap, but there was a blemish in the middle of the bright glow of the sun. It was too soon to tell what it was, but it was definitely something man-made, and it was growing in size by the minute. The Chief keyed the shipboard intercom.

"This is the Chief. Captain to the bridge."

He didn't have to give instructions to everyone else. They would know something was happening just by his short request for Andi to join him. The Allen brothers followed her up the ladder. All the Chief had to do was point toward the sun.

"What is that?" asked Jessie.

Donny was behind him and said over his shoulder, "It looks like an island with a lighthouse on it, but there aren't any islands out here, are there?"

Andi and the Chief both answered, "No."

The details began to take shape more quickly as they closed the distance between themselves and whatever was floating on the ocean. The lighthouse gradually became a tall mast that had been reinforced to give it more bulk, but it was big enough for them to be unable to detect any swaying or movement as the swells pushed by it.

As the sun rose higher behind the structure, they were able to see that there was a large container ship behind it, and the reason they hadn't seen it sooner was that the stern was facing directly toward them. It also grew in size as the distance narrowed. The tower appeared to be fastened to the stern, and as details emerged, they were able to see the people at the top. They appeared to have spotted the Maggie Mae because of their height. A crowd was visible on a catwalk.

"I should have expected this," said the Chief. "There would naturally be people who would have found a way to survive out here rather than to ever enter a port again."

Hampton was taking his turn with a pair of binoculars, and he couldn't resist voicing the arguments about why it wouldn't be such a good idea to get close to the colony.

"Mankind evolved on land and returned to the sea for some of its resources, but there's no way people could survive without a clean water source, crops, and medical services. Everything would be short-term at best. We're hundreds of miles from land, so there's likely to be

170

a crisis or shortage every day."

The Chief nodded, "I agree, so they return to land for necessities and bring them back, which means the people living out here run a tight ship. We're not likely to be welcome, but they sure are going to want everything we've got."

Andi was the first to see what the others were missing.

"Does anyone notice anything peculiar about the people on the tower?"

The bridge was quiet as everyone with binoculars took a moment to study the people more closely. They were still a few miles away from the floating settlement, but the movements of the people in the tower were familiar.

"Are they infected dead?" asked Kathy.

"There's a fence around the top of the tower," said Andi. "I can just make it out. It was probably erected to keep people from going over the rails in rough seas. There's no way people could've lived out here without safety features to protect them during bad weather."

The Chief added, "My thoughts exactly. Anyone who's spent time on the water knows what heavy seas can do to something that wasn't designed to take it. Strapping together boats and barges may work in science fiction movies, but they would take a beating in real life."

"Speaking of barges," said Henry. He had managed to get his turn with the binoculars and had spotted something he recognized.

"Do you see that large, flat area next to the tower? I think it's one of the platforms used by those private space companies to land their rockets. Do you remember them? They had them landing at sea until they were sure they could safely bring them back over land."

They all redirected their attention to that spot and saw Henry was right. Most of them had seen the landings on TV, so they knew what they were looking at.

"It's been repurposed as a dock," said the Chief. "Can anyone think of a good reason for us to stop there?"

Judging by the way everyone lowered their binoculars and the silence on the bridge, the crew of the Maggie Mae and her passengers were all either too stunned by the question to answer, or they were giving it serious thought. Either way, they were all waiting for the Chief to say if he already had a reason for them to dock at the platform.

When no one answered, he knew they were all waiting for him to say how the benefits of exploring the odd structure could possibly outweigh the risks. Every single one of them could give a list of reasons why they should change course and make a wide circle around it, but unless they were missing something, there were no obvious benefits. Just as he was about to answer their unspoken questions, Henry broke the silence.

"I can read the name of the container ship on the stern. It's been painted over and has a new name painted on it, or maybe they started to name it but stopped."

The Chief focused on the place where the name was painted in big white letters. He lowered his binoculars and said, "Henry, you just gave us all the reasons we needed not to dock there. It says Wari. That's the name of a cannibal tribe in the Amazon."

13

Fellow Survivors

Southern England - The Beginning

In a world where people were killing each other over food and water, Symone didn't know what the men would do to her. Aside from a good sense of humor, she didn't know if they would kill her or take what she had and leave her for dead. All she knew for sure was that she was feeling the last of her willpower ebbing away. She felt weak and helpless, and whatever the Porters did to her, she wasn't going to be able to stop them. After the introductions, she saw the father, Joseph Porter, had noticed the few items she had stacked on the bar with the note under the box of ammunition. In a slack-jawed sort of way, he ran one hand across the stumble of his gray beard as he did a mental inventory.

Symone didn't know what to say, and she didn't realize she was breathing so shallowly that she might as well have been holding her breath. She became increasingly aware that she had her back to William, and she didn't know what he was doing behind her. In her already stretched imagination, she saw the young man sizing her up, and her shoulders stiffened. She wanted to turn around and confront him, but just as she wasn't breathing, the rest of her body felt frozen in place. They had seemed so normal when they were all facing the same danger, but now that they were alone, she wondered if she had made the mistake that would cost her everything.

"They seem to be losing interest," said William. His voice was so far away that the fear that had gripped Symone slipped just enough for her to turn and locate him. He wasn't even behind her. Instead, he was at the door peeking out through a small gap in the covering they had put over the glass windows. She let out a deep breath.

"Are you alright?" asked Joseph. "Maybe you should sit down. William, get away from the door and help me with the lady."

With one on each side of her, the men guided Symone to a chair at the bar. Joseph hooked a thumb in the direction of the rifle and asked, "Yours?"

"Sort of."

He reached for the note and read it and said, "It's a good thing you did, Mrs. Tisdal. If you had left before we came along, we would have found the note and supplies, and we would have remembered there are still good people left in the world."

"I guess you qualify as someone who needs those things," she said. "I just couldn't carry it all anymore."

"And you qualify as someone who needs a little help. Would you care to travel with us for a bit? Riding a motorcycle with those biters everywhere isn't the best way to go undetected, but it beats walking. Those things never sleep, but they're slow. On a bike, you can outrun them."

"I'm going to London. My children are missing, and I thought the authorities there could help me find them. Can you take me there?"

"Your children are missing?"

There were several unspoken questions there. They had been on the road since everything started, and they had met many frantic parents who were searching for their children. From what they had seen so far, the children weren't likely to be found, and it was best that they were never found because it would be better for their parents not to see what their little ones had become.

"This is a picture of them," said Symone. "It was taken six months ago, but it's close."

She shoved it close to Joseph Porter's face the same way so many parents had, and he did his best to keep his eyes on it long enough to make her feel like he was being attentive.

"I'm sorry, Ma'am. Maybe we'll stumble upon them as we get closer to London. There are rumors that the military has things under control. I'll bet they're in a camp eating a hot meal and getting tucked in for the night by social workers."

Symone relaxed a bit, not because she believed what he said but because he said it. It was obvious that he was attempting to reassure her, and once again, she had allies. So far, things hadn't worked out for her allies, but maybe this time would be different.

William stepped past her, going in the direction of the hallway, and asked, "Why are you traveling alone, Ma'am?"

"I haven't been alone until today. My neighbor was with me, but someone shot him in that neighborhood across the highway. I just got here myself."

William disappeared for a few minutes, but it didn't take long for him to get back.

"We can take care of those things in the bathroom, but you did a good job making sure they stayed where they were. You should see it, Dad. Locked 'em both up with barstools."

The father and son gave Symone a parting grin and went back to the hallway together. They were confident enough, but Symone still felt the need to cradle her pistol in her lap. If anything came from that darkened hallway other than the Porters, she would end them.

By the sounds that followed, she could tell they had entered the first restroom. It was followed by a short period of quiet before a ruckus began on the other side of the hall. The Porters emerged from the darkness wiping long blades with rags. She hadn't seen the blades before. Neither man was smiling as much as they had been before.

"That was close," said William. Joseph Porter was nodding.

He said, "You had a wee bit more of a party going on in those restrooms than you thought. How many were there?" he asked his son.

"I counted four in one and five in the other. I thought it was going to be one in each room because they were so quiet, but they almost got out of the first room because I wasn't ready."

The father added, "They're mighty slow, but they just keep coming. It's easy to get pushed to the ground by the weight of 'em. We were going to each take a restroom at the same time. Good thing we didn't."

Symone couldn't help wondering why they were still inside the restrooms if the doors opened outward and asked the men how she could have been so lucky.

"Your luck was someone else's bad luck," said Joseph. "There were blokes piled up inside both doors, blocking the others from pushing on them."

"They must've gone in there to hide," said William. "Thought they could wait it out, but someone inside was already bitten."

175

"Or maybe all of them were," said Symone. "When I called the police, one of them was wearing a bandage when they arrived. They didn't know yet."

"Whatever happened," said William, "We moved all of them into the Men's room, so the other one is empty, and we can use it if we have to."

After a short period when no one spoke, Joseph took it upon himself to suggest what they should do to get a good evening and night of rest before setting out in the morning. Symone was glad to have him take charge, but she couldn't shake that nagging feeling that anyone who teamed up with her was signing their own death certificate.

They settled in under a make-shift tent made from tablecloths stretched over two rows of chairs. With their window coverings and the tent, they were able to light a can of Sterno and warm up some canned food. The Porters continually expressed their gratitude to Symone, and she finally relaxed enough to talk openly. When the conversation got around to her being the wife of the famous astronaut, the Porters couldn't hold back their astonishment. They wanted to hear all about her husband, and they even had something to add of their own. They had heard a radio broadcast in which the reporter had remembered there were still people up at the International Space Station who couldn't come home without help.

The thought of Henry and Adam being unable to come home to help her find the children was disheartening, but as she said to the Porters, he was safer there in space.

"I don't disagree," said Joseph, "but from what I've heard about Henry Tisdal, if he knew his children were missing, he would jump from the space station to get here."

They went to sleep in the early hours of the morning after each taking turns with the bottle Symone had found. She had to admit the sweet burning sensation of the liquor sliding down her throat brought moments of clarity before the alcohol dulled her thinking. Moments of optimism were followed by moments of pessimism laced with reality. Unless the children were with someone powerful, there wasn't much chance that they were alive.

She awoke with a fuzzy taste in her mouth and was grateful when Joseph passed a cup of coffee in front of her face.

"Where'd you find that?" she croaked.

"Bartenders have a way of hiding things under a bar. There's a stash behind the tab ledgers that must've been there for those times when someone needed to be sobered up before they were sent home."

"I wish I could thank them," she mumbled as she sipped. It seemed to clear her eyes and her thinking as it soothed her throat.

"The eggs and bacon came from my backpack," said William.

Symone couldn't believe her eyes, and she almost forgot to thank them as she greedily dove into the food.

The much-needed rest followed by a breakfast that was almost unfamiliar to her made the optimism return. Maybe she wouldn't find her children today, but she felt like they were safe. Part of her felt there was no way she could feel this good if her children weren't also feeling good. A parent would understand that feeling.

Joseph came inside carrying a case of something, and she was startled to find he had gone outside. He sat the case down next to their supplies, and she saw it was a twenty-four-can package of Ensure. It wasn't what she would call a satisfying meal, but that's what a survivalist would call it.

"Look what I found," he beamed. "Along with the power bars and beef jerky, we can eat without drawing attention to ourselves by lighting a campfire."

"Where'd you find that?" asked Symone.

"In that neighborhood across the highway. Those people are so busy shooting anything that moves that it's easy to tell which houses are safe. I just watched for a bit and then circled around to the quiet ones. There was lots of stuff. I also got these."

He emptied cargo pockets on his pants with boxes of ammunition. Each was fifty rounds that fit her Smith & Wesson. He offered her a box, and she didn't hesitate to accept. She slid it her way, checked its contents, then put it safely in her own backpack. She made a mental note to get a pair of cargo pants like his so she could reach the pockets quicker. Her own blue jeans were too tight to make the pockets better for nothing more than her cell phone, and that wasn't exactly useful.

"How long are we staying here, Dad?"

Joseph mulled over the question for a moment as he regarded Symone.

"If I had to guess, I'd say our new friend here had been sick recently. I remember when your mom looked like she was just getting her color back."

Symone was impressed by Joseph's powers of observation, but she hoped he saw she was far enough into recovery to be back on her feet.

He made his decision but added a caveat.

"We can go today because the weather is good, but if you start getting sick again, I'll know. I won't hesitate to find us another place to hole up."

Symone didn't want to talk her way out of it, so she just gave Joseph a weak smile and nodded her acceptance of his terms. She energetically finished the scraps of food on her plate and got up to gather together her backpack.

Fifteen minutes later, they were easing the front door of the pub open and checking around the corners of the pub. Smoke still drifted above several houses across the highway, but there were no infected to be seen. She climbed onto the back of Joseph's motorcycle after she saw William mount the other. Joseph handed her a helmet that he kept as a spare tied to the sissy bar behind the seat, and she quickly pulled it on and strapped it in place. When the motorcycle engines came to life, she was sure they would be swarmed, but the two men didn't wait around to see how many would be drawn to the sound. Before she knew it, they were moving at a crisp fifty miles per hour, and she felt exhilarated.

Symone wasn't high enough in her perch behind Joseph to see what was up ahead, so she shifted left and right to see around his big arms. She had to admit, it made her feel more secure to be behind the man, and it gave her a pang of guilt because she thought of her husband. It was short-lived, though. Her next shift to the left revealed a moderately sized horde of the infected blocking the road.

William slowed to a stop alongside them and then gestured to the left. A side road about fifty feet from the horde disappeared behind tall grass and trees. They couldn't see what was further down the road, but there were no infected. They took the left turn and found themselves on a dirt road that snaked between trees and sent up plumes of dust behind them.

It sounded louder under the canopy of trees, and as they watched them go by where they interlaced overhead, it became obvious to them that they were following a private road to a residence of some sort. Their suspicions were confirmed when they saw the facade of a great country home at the end of a circular driveway. They circled until they were in front of a pair of huge double doors and came to a stop. The silence seemed to close in on them.

"What do you think, Dad?"

Even though the question wasn't directed at her, Symone answered for all of them.

"We're not alone."

The trees had ended with the dirt road, and it was easy to see the surrounding fields to the side of the house. The tall grass in all directions didn't hide the heads that bobbed into view as if the fields were lakes, and as they watched, more heads bobbed above the surface as they responded to the sounds that had emanated from the approaching motorcycles.

A quick look back down the dirt road dashed any hope of escape the way they had come in. Infected dead were emerging onto the road from both sides, and as they did, they turned in the direction of the three survivors.

"Our only choice is to get inside and hole up for a while," said Joseph.

The trio was off of the bikes and onto the stairs by the door as fast as possible, but just as they suspected, it was locked. William produced a crowbar and shoved it into the gap by the lock.

"Try not to destroy it, Son. Maybe we can lock it behind us."

William did a good job prying the door open with minimal damage, and they scrambled inside just as the first of the infected were reaching their bikes. They quickly dragged and pushed a large bureau that dominated a wall of the foyer over to the door, then stepped back and listened as the creatures arrived.

Satisfied that they wouldn't get in, they turned their attention to the rooms behind them. It was dark and quiet, and the sheets draped over the furniture told them the home had been empty when the infected had become part of daily life.

"This is a big place," said William.

The others murmured their agreement in low voices, and Symone added, "There's most likely a caretaker nearby. Probably lives in a cottage behind the main house."

"One way to find out," said Joseph. He pulled a flashlight from his backpack and slowly walked up a staircase that curved upward. "You two check out the downstairs. If there's a basement, wait for me to get there before you go in."

When he got to the landing at the top of the stairs, he could see the caretaker's cottage behind the house, and it didn't look so good for the caretaker. The front door of the cottage stood open, and the infected dead near the door weren't showing it any interest. For all he knew, one of them was the caretaker, but he was sure no one was alive inside the small home.

There were eight bedrooms upstairs, so Joseph didn't finish going through all of them before the others came looking for him. He motioned which ones were clear by giving a thumbs up, and they began sweeping the rooms together.

"There's a caretaker's house out back," said William.

His father nodded and said he had noticed it.

"Find any supplies worth keeping?"

Symone and William nodded together and motioned for him to follow them. They went down the stairs two at a time. When they reached the bottom, they curled back below the stairs into a small door that led to sparse rooms that were undoubtedly servant's quarters. One of them wasn't like the others, and it resembled an armory.

"Heavens," whispered Joseph. "What were these people, part of a drug cartel?"

William said, "We can't take it all, but there's plenty we need. There's a box of Claymore mines over here."

Joseph examined the contents, and the obvious value of Claymores was that they could be placed around them if they got caught out in the open. They exploded outward, so they could clear a path if surrounded. Each of them loaded as much as they could carry, including a few more 9mm handguns and gun cleaning kits for good measure.

"Any food?" asked Joseph.

"The pantry has a lot of canned goods. Someone either had a fondness for sardines, or they knew the value of fish oil. Either way, they're small tins that won't weigh us down."

"Now we just have to find a way out of here," said Joseph. "How bad is it outside?"

Symone tried her best not to move a heavy curtain too much. The windows weren't boarded, and she didn't want to stir up the infected on the other side of the glass.

"Bad enough," she said. "These windows are strong, but they aren't boarded up, so we can't stay here."

Joseph unwrapped one of the Claymore mines and read a small information tag on the wrapper.

"If I can open the back door and put this outside, we can cause a distraction. We got what we needed from this place. William, you watch the front door. Symone, you come with me and get the door closed fast when I duck back inside."

The plan was simple enough to work. Joseph reached outside and placed the explosive device in the proper direction, then trailed a thin tripwire back under the door as Symone closed it. They thought they were ready for it, but the concussion from the explosion almost took down the whole porch. For a moment, they were afraid the door would be gone too, but once they recovered from the shock of it being more powerful than they expected, they could tell it would work to draw the infected to the back of the house.

It wasn't until they began a mad scramble to reach the front door that Symone saw the card on the refrigerator door. It was under a magnet just as it had been on her refrigerator at home. It was that same symbol that Arthur said he recognized as a 'grenade fired proper.' She grabbed the card and checked the back of it. There was a row of numbers that matched those on the back of her first card. She shoved it in her pocket, and for some reason, it made her feel hope.

William was waiting for them at the front door, and he held up one hand palm outward as a signal to wait.

"Now," he said.

He yanked the door open and didn't wait for them. They followed close on his heels, and they saw the last of the infected had gone around the corner of the house. A swirl of black smoke blew around the corner in their direction, and when they got to the motorcycles, they saw a large cloud above the house. The mine had been more efficient than expected, setting fire to the old wood-frame house.

"Too bad," said Joseph. "I didn't think we would ever come back this way again, but someone could've used the rest of those weapons and ammo. When the fire reaches that lot, it's going to put on quite a show. I expect the infected will show up to watch."

Even though they wanted to get as far from the house as they could before the fire reached the room that would explode, there was at least a short piece of road that wasn't currently occupied by the infected, and they were able to push the bikes before starting the engines. Further down the road, more infected dead were being drawn in by the initial explosion, but they could maneuver past them for now. The big explosion was likely to cause a population increase that would make the road too congested, and a small part of them wished they could stay to see it.

When they reached the main road where they had been blocked by the horde, they saw it was clear for the most part. Two of the infected were crawling in the road, both attempting to follow the horde that had left when they set off the Claymore on the back porch of the house.

A massive boom rolled across the fields, and they knew the small armory had ignited. Both men also knew that every infected dead for miles would be converging on the house, so they increased their speed to be gone from the area. They passed stragglers as they crossed the road, but they eventually came to a long stretch that helped them to relax a bit. They could see London in the distance, and the road intersected with a four-lane highway headed for the city.

There had been abandoned cars on the country road they had used, but it was nothing like what they found on the wide highway. Every lane was jammed. Some cars were firmly tangled with others. Bent metal and broken doors stuck out in jagged traps everywhere, and many of those traps held their prey hopelessly squirming to get free. If there was a clear path through the hundreds or thousands of cars, they couldn't see it.

"It seems we're going off the main road," said Joseph. "It'll be bumpy, but we can use that."

He pointed toward a railway line that was at least going in the right direction, and he didn't wait for William to agree before rolling down an embankment in the direction of the railroad tracks. He built up some speed and easily cut a path up to the tracks despite having Symone on the bike with him. If she thought her teeth were getting banged together on the ride to the tracks, it was nothing compared to bouncing over the cross ties. She wasn't going to complain, though. From what she could see of the highway, they wouldn't make it ten yards over there before feeling hands or teeth tearing at their skin.

Over the sound of the motorcycles and the bouncing that made her voice go up and down, Symone yelled in Joseph's ear, "Remind me why we're going to London."

William laughed as he answered, "You don't think they gave up the Palace, do you?"

Symone knew Joseph saw themselves cruising up to the gates of Buckingham Palace in time to see them swing open. Guards would wave them through to safety, and she could show someone the cards with the grenade on them. Her children would be waiting for her in safety. She thought that would be great, but London had been a city of almost nine million people before the end of the world, and she wondered how many of those people had done exactly what the suburbs had done. Too many had probably said, "I'm not going anywhere, and you can't make me." Those who tried to leave were in the cars that choked the roads out of the city, and those who went to London seeking help choked the roads into the city.

"Pull over."

Even she was surprised by her demand, but Joseph kept bouncing along the railroad tracks, not totally sure he had understood her.

"I said pull over. Do it now, or I'll jump."

Joseph heard that well enough, and even though he didn't think she would really jump, he couldn't understand why she would want to stop now. He let the bike slow on its own, the bumps becoming a bit more pronounced, but he didn't want William to hit them from behind. He had been matching his father's speed and decreased with him. As soon as they were stopped, Symone got off and took a few steps away from the tracks.

"What's wrong?" Joseph asked Symone as if it was something she saw up ahead. In a sense, that was exactly what was wrong, but she wasn't seeing it. She just knew it was there.

"This is a mistake. We'll be dead long before we reach Buckingham Palace, even if the military managed to keep the infected dead from getting inside, and I doubt they did."

As soon as she said it, Symone realized what it was that had been nagging at the back of her mind. It was the same scenario that had played out on the Isle of Wight, and it had most likely happened at the Kremlin, the White House, and Buckingham Palace. Soldiers who weren't bitten were quick to go to the aid of their comrades, dragging their bloodied bodies to safety. The creed of soldiers around the world was not a single man left behind, and there was no amount of screaming or threats from superiors that would change the desire to bring in a wounded comrade in arms. That would come later when it was too late. That would come when comrades begged for a mercy death...when they begged not to become one of the infected. Even then, there would be that one soldier who didn't want to die, and he or she would keep their wound secret.

"A mistake?"

"The infection gets inside everywhere. Even if they stop the initial attacks on the Palace, it has gotten in by now because they would treat their wounded," she said forcefully.

Joseph hadn't seen the broadcasts from the refugee camps at the Isle of Wight, but before he could protest further, Symone stopped him with one question.

"If William gets bitten, will you be able to do the right thing? Will you shoot him in the head before he becomes one of those things?"

Joseph turned off the ignition on his motorcycle, and when William did the same, the silence closed in. Confusion furrowed his young brow as he wondered what he had missed.

"Have you gone mad?" asked Joseph.

Symone had only known the two men for days, but the kindness she had become accustomed to was nowhere to be found in his face. It wasn't hatred or even anger she saw. It was more like disgust, and she would have preferred hatred.

"Would you shoot one of your children if they were turned?"

The question was like a fierce slap across her face, and she suddenly understood the cruelty of her own question. She felt ashamed for thinking it would hurt Joseph any less. She covered her face with both hands, and the despair she had controlled so well took hold of her. Standing in the tall grass by the tracks, she felt her legs grow weak, and she didn't resist the urge to sit. Her muscles and bones failed her like never before, and for the first time since her children disappeared, she faced the reality of her own question to Joseph.

William wasn't naive, but he still hadn't understood the drastic emotions displayed by both Symone and his father. He didn't know why his father didn't go to Symone and comfort her the way he had seen him do for total strangers, so he dismounted from his motorcycle and did it for him. He knelt beside her and gave her the support her own body couldn't summon.

Joseph softened a bit when he saw his son display the compassion he had taught him, and he grudgingly swung his leg over the seat of his own bike and walked slowly to them. He put his arms around both of them and waited while Symone cried herself out.

They would have stayed there for as long as it took to reconcile their feelings, but the new world had other plans for them. A low growl somewhere in the tall grass below them was the unmistakable groan of an infected dead as it crawled on broken limbs toward them. William abruptly stood up and took long strides toward the growl and silenced it with a long knife he carried on his hip. Joseph and Symone both watched him, and they felt a new sadness for the anger on his face. The infected had interrupted something important to him, and it wasn't something he could get back.

"I'm sorry, Joseph."

"No, you don't have to be. It was a reality check. You're right, you know. Even if one-tenth of the population of London went to

Buckingham Palace for help, they would've been overwhelmed, and short of strip-searching everyone, they could never have prevented a bite victim from getting inside."

"What of the Royal Family then?" asked William.

"Evacuated to somewhere safe," said his father.

Symone was wiping tears from her cheeks and managed to say in a low voice, "They went to Wight first, then they disappeared. None of the news broadcasts knew where they went."

Joseph turned in the direction of the city. His eyes took in the tracks, the distant buildings, and then the closer trees off to the east.

"We need to know, and it would be easier if you stay here."

The thought made Symone's eyes grow wide, and her mouth opened in shock. Before she could object, Joseph turned close to her face and said, "We need to know, and that's final."

******

The old railway platform was little more than a concrete block building that served as a restroom and sitting place for people who enjoyed watching the trains come and go. It stood beside the tracks at least a mile from the main station and had been left to become weather-worn and gray. The roof was low enough for them to lift Symone up with the bulk of their supplies, and billboards advertising everything from beer to laundry detergent stood high enough on top to hide her from the dead eyes that might pass by. She could also remain undetected as she watched the progress of Joseph and William as they rode into the city.

She wiped at wet eyes again as they waved and renewed their ride on the tracks, going at a faster pace now. She put the binoculars to her eyes when they became too small to watch without them, and she scanned left and right of the tracks for movement. She saw none, and yet she expected so much more.

She finally lost sight of her friends when they reached the end of the tracks. They didn't enter the train station, instead choosing to veer onto a side road that took them away from the main entrance. Tall buildings quickly blocked them from her sight even though she could hear the distant hum of their engines.

******

* * *

William followed as closely to his father as he could, and it enabled him to keep pace with him, but it took away his ability to watch their flanks. If he had been able to spend more time watching their left and right sides, he would have seen that the sound of their motorcycles was waking the quiet city. When he finally saw the infected on his right as they made a turn in a curve to the left, the sudden realization was that they couldn't just be on one side. He stopped with his front wheel turned too far and lost control. William went over the handlebars.

Joseph saw it in his rearview mirror and smoothly turned on the asphalt in one spot. They could both smell the smoke from his tires, and years of riding gave them every reason to believe William would be up and riding again in seconds. He was back to his son's side in seconds and helping to lift the heavy motorcycle to an upright position.

It was only seconds, just as they knew it would be. That was why they were so surprised to find the infected dead were already filling the streets on all sides. They decided the safest route was the way they had come into the city, and they accelerated down the last street where Symone had seen them.

She heard the high-pitched RPMs when William had gone down. She didn't know what that meant, but it sounded wrong to her. Then she heard the scream of both engines as they once again came her way. This time she understood they were the sound of a life and death escape. She put the binoculars to her eyes and found the place where she had last seen the motorcycles and was just in time to see them erupt into the intersection. As they made the turn toward the train station, they seemed to leap into the air as they collided with infected that were pouring into the road from all sides.

Symone watched helplessly as the bikes landed badly, wobbled as their riders fought for control, then disappeared under a writhing crowd of the infected. There were two gunshots...only two, and Symone wondered if the first one was for William and the second was for Joseph.

14

Wari & Scilly

Aboard the Maggie Mae - Year Eight

Seven or more years at sea had taken its toll on the hull of the big ship. Without routine visits to a shipyard, the weather had caused it to take on a brownish hue that no longer reflected light. It just looked dirty and uninviting. Several small boats were pulling away from the big concrete platform at the stern. They hardly seemed bigger than fishing boats meant for recreational purposes, but everyone on board the Maggie Mae knew the dangers of underestimating the ability of pirates in small boats. There were enough of them before the apocalypse, but now there were no safe coastlines.

"We should see if they have radios," said the Chief. "If they have any shoulder-held rocket launchers, we want them to be at maximum range."

Andi ordered Donny to hail the boats over the radio and warn them off. She didn't have to tell him that he should imply they were armed and prepared to defend themselves. The truth was that she had tried several times to locate the same weapons for the defense of the Maggie Mae but had never been able to find a cache that hadn't already been raided.

"I've got someone," said Donny. He switched on the speaker so everyone could hear the incoming broadcast.

"You've entered the territorial waters claimed by the Independent

Atlantic Union. Your boat is now the property of the IAU. Heave to and prepare to be boarded."

"Not exactly my plan," said the Chief. "Captain?"

His one-word question to Andi was his request for permission to handle the situation. Andi had no doubt that the Chief would always defer to her as the captain, but when it came to a battle at sea, she couldn't think of anyone who she would want to be in charge more than him. A simple nod in his direction was all he needed.

The Chief keyed the microphone and answered the hail.

"Approaching vessel, these are international waters. Any attempt to board this vessel will be met with a swift and decisive response. You are already within range of our defensive capabilities, and we would advise that you maintain your present distance."

It was a bluff, but the Chief's tone of voice was enough. He had mastered the art of projecting the cold confidence of someone who knew they had the upper hand, and the effect usually gave the enemy reason to be uncertain. They could see the bows of the approaching boats drop lower when they reduced their speed.

The voice came back over the radio just as he expected.

"That's not a very friendly answer," said the man. He couldn't have sounded more sarcastic.

"It was no more unfriendly than your message," answered the Chief. He pushed home his point by adding, "I suggest you remain at that distance while we proceed on our way. We won't be stopping to visit. We plan to pass your port side, but we'll be monitoring your position."

The Chief gave Kathy the order for everyone to take up firing positions along the starboard side, and he told everyone to watch for anything that resembled a stove pipe. He also suggested to Andi that they should adjust their course away to the northeast as they passed the ship.

With the sun higher and a clear sky, they were able to see more of what the people had become without civilization. There were a few sailboats tied up at the platform, and they could only imagine what had happened to the survivors who had obeyed the order to heave to and prepare to be boarded. Above the platform loomed the tower, and the closer distance allowed them to see the cages on the landings that circled it. They were crowded with the infected dead. The infected reached through the wires of the cages in all directions for unknown reasons. Their arms waved randomly as if blown by the wind as they reached for something only they could see. The crew of the Maggie Mae couldn't hear them, but they could guess what they sounded like.

There was a group of people below the lowest landing that was caged, and they were moving with a purpose that gave away the fact that they were living people. As the survivors watched from their stations along the starboard rails, they saw the people open a trap door in the landing and reach up with hooked poles. It was easy to get the infected to drop down through the open door, but they were harpooned and roped as they fell. The trap door was pushed shut, and the people and freed infected disappeared from view below the rail along the deck.

"That tower is like an upside-down Pez dispenser," said Tom. "What're they doing?"

Everyone else groaned at the analogy.

The answer to his question came only a moment later when the people reappeared at the stern above the platform. They lifted the squirming body of the infected over the side and lowered it quickly to the back of a fishing boat that had idled into a position to retrieve it. The morning sun reflected off the big shining hooks that were tied to the body. As soon as it was aboard, it was tossed over the stern, and the boat moved away at a moderate speed, trolling out a line tied to the big hooks while the body surfed behind it.

"We've seen this before," said Kathy, "but never on this scale. They're deep sea fishing using the infected as bait. If we had a ship-to-ship missile, this would be a good time to use it."

To the relief of everyone, they didn't stay around long enough to see if the fishing boat caught anything. Andi kept the Maggie Mae at a steady speed but not so fast that they appeared to be afraid of the small armada of fishing boats that followed them for a few miles, but as the distance increased, so did their speed. Just like the first pirates, she planned to keep the speed on well into the day so they wouldn't have to worry about anyone catching up with them that night.

After supper that evening, there was finally an opportunity to discuss the events of the morning. Andi had been at sea for so long that she and her crew weren't really in touch with how bad it had gotten on land. Even though there had been times when the Mud Island group had been able to tell them about some of their adventures, there was no way to do justice to how bad it was. Most of them were gathered around the dining area when Andi asked them to tell her more. She wondered if she would even be able to survive on land now.

Kathy told her about the way it was in the beginning and described the exodus from Charleston. She tried to convey to Andi how desperate everyone was, but there was no way to do it justice. The massive, roaming hordes were something that couldn't be imagined, and the only way to really grasp it was to see it.

They took turns describing what they had seen. Hampton and Colleen told their story of the little army they were part of that tried to push back against a horde near Charlotte. They made good progress at first, but there was no way to beat a horde of the infected because they didn't care about dying. No matter how many of them they shot, they just kept coming.

Sim was the one who gave the best description of the power of a horde. Despite the fact that they had all seen the horde that marched toward Charleston and nearly died when their helicopter had crashed, it was his description of the airport runways in Columbus that held everyone in awe. The runways were packed with the infected, and the planes that held terrified passengers sat motionless, waiting for a rescue that wouldn't come. They were like sardines in cans, and they knew what was waiting for them outside.

When he finished, Kathy took over again and told Andi about the first year and their trip up the Stono River at night. It was there that they got their first look at how far survivors would go when they ran out of food. It didn't start out that way, but the people who lived safely at a marina eventually discovered they could use the infected dead as bait to catch blue crabs. The crabs were already in plentiful supply, but the immeasurable number of infected dead in the river would present them with a food source that guaranteed a population explosion below the surface of the water.

"Wasn't the crab meat contaminated?" asked Andi. "I mean, we've been eating seafood for years, but we've stayed away from bottom-feeders because we know what they eat. We've even seen crabs and lobsters become aggressive toward people."

They all confirmed for her that the settlements that ate crabs had disappeared, probably from eating poisoned meat. They also described the crabs that had grown in size and tried to climb into the boat with them. What they were all leading up to was the fact that the people using the infected dead as bait were probably going down that same road, and it wasn't a stretch to suspect they had already given in to the temptation to sample what they had in the cages if they got tired of their seafood diet. They would eventually pay for that mistake.

******

The weather cooperated with their journey to England until they were only a day away from the closest of the islands. The choppy waves and cold spray made everyone stay below decks, but it was almost restful compared with flat water and watching for other ships to appear on the horizon. It served as a cloak for them to get closer to their goal without being noticed. They were well aware that being detected most often meant trouble. If the other craft was manned by people who meant them no harm, they would at least be suspicious of the Maggie Mae. It used to be that the people on ships at sea were somewhat of a family. They were brothers and sisters who faced the same perils, but now they were jealous neighbors at best. Everyone wanted what someone else had. While the crew of the Maggie Mae thought of themselves as the exception to the rule, others wouldn't see them that way. The well-crewed tugboat would appear formidable to most people.

A contact on the radar display to port stayed on a parallel course going away from the mainland, but it reappeared an hour later, going in the same direction as them. It was making better headway than the Maggie Mae, and the Chief suspected it was a British warship.

"If we can see them, they can see us," said the Chief.

Andi was on the bridge with him, and they had discussed what they would do if approached by the Royal Navy. Playing it straight was their best option. Get Henry out in front as fast as they could and hope his name meant something.

The contact sped on ahead until it was out of radar range, but no sooner had it disappeared when a new contact appeared to starboard. It was on a course to intercept them just before they would arrive in the area of the Scilly Islands. Located at the end of the westernmost tip of the English mainland, it was referred to as Land's End on maps, and it was close to the entrance of the English Channel.

"I guess this is it," said the Chief.

Andi nodded, "No avoiding this one. Looks to be doing close to twenty knots and has us square in his sights."

Through the gray weather, they both tried to spot it with their binoculars so they would have some idea what they were up against. The best-case scenario would be the Royal Navy, but there were plenty of other things it could be.

"I can't see anything," said the Chief. "It should be visible by now."

Just as he said it, he saw something slender dip below the surface. One second it was there, and the next second it was gone.

"Wait a minute," said Andi. "Radar isn't getting anything now."

"Switch to sonar."

The thought of a submarine stalking them gave them both chills, and Andi switched to sonar without saying anything.

"There it is," she said. "Bearing 075. Slowing speed to about fourteen knots."

"Ever wonder what the troop ships during World War II ever felt like?" asked the Chief. "We need to go hard left rudder and pour on as much speed as we can. Where does it get shallow near Scilly?"

Andi put her finger on the chart that was spread out on the navigation table. "There are two small islands here, and the first of the larger islands spread across the spot right here." She traced her finger across the row of islands and said, "Right here is a narrow channel between the first two islands and larger ones. No submarine would try to go through there. After almost eight years, the charts would be too outdated to give reliable depths."

It was an all-out race for the next fifteen minutes, but they saw they had just enough of a head start to get into the channel. If they were calculating the speed of the submarine correctly, it was slowing its forward speed as they coasted over a quickly rising seabed. Working together, with Andi calling out course changes, they made a sweeping curve to the north of the largest island. It was little more than a desolate piece of rock with no habitable areas, but it was big enough for them to hide behind. The next islands were larger with some vegetation, but they didn't think they would come to an inhabited island until they reached St Agnes.

The radar showed they had given the submarine the slip, but the Chief could see there was deeper water ahead, and he didn't doubt that the crew of the submarine knew the waters of the area better than they did.

He asked Andi, "Is there a chance the sub can cut us off up ahead if he realized what we were doing?"

"I'm afraid so," she answered. "If he broke off the chase soon enough, and I think he did, then he might be running up the southern coast of St Agnes as we pass to the north. This gap between St Agnes and Garrison Walls is deep enough for him to get ahead of us and just lay in wait for us to pass by."

"What's this spot?"

The Chief put his finger on a small harbor that cut into the northern coast of St Agnes.

"That's not a deep harbor, but it's deep enough where the dock reaches the water. There are usually a half dozen or so sailboats at anchor to avoid bad weather, but nothing is likely to be near the dock. The sub wouldn't be able to see us in there because the water is too shallow for them to get close. If I'm thinking the same thing that you are, we can tie up there and wait a day or so for them to give up."

"A day should be long enough for them to think we went north into the Celtic Sea," said the Chief.

This was the kind of cat and mouse game the Chief liked to play on the water. He sometimes said he was born before his time and would have been at home on a tall ship with nothing but sails and the wind.

"Where's the nearest place to refuel?"

"In this harbor right here."

Andi traced a line from St Agnes across the channel where the submarine was likely to be going, and then she looped around the island into a larger harbor.

"What about people?" asked the Chief. "Are we going to run into any problems?"

"At St Agnes, probably not. The St Mary's Isles of Scilly Terminal where we'll get fuel originally had a population of close to two thousand people, but it probably had a lot of tourists there when the infection started. Heaven knows how many people went there to get away from the mainland."

******

About an hour later, the Maggie Mae coasted toward the dock in the tiny harbor. Low visibility beyond the island helped to make them feel like they were able to go in undetected by anyone at sea. As for the likelihood they were spotted from land, they could only hope they were as lucky because there were plenty of places where watchers could be hiding. With a population of less than one hundred, it was doubtful that any of the locals had survived the infection, but if they had, no one could blame them if they weren't as welcoming as they had been when tourists found their isolated town.

There was a scattering of small boats anchored in the cove. It was too small to call a bay and not deep enough to call a harbor, but there was enough room for them to be spread out away from each other. Kathy had taken up a position on the bow of the tugboat and was using binoculars to get an idea of what kinds of threats might be hiding in the early morning mist that hung over the water. There were no signs of movement on any of the decks, but they were too experienced at survival to believe there weren't any surprises waiting inside them.

"How many do you see?" called the Chief through an open window on the bridge. His voice seemed unnaturally loud in the stillness. As an experienced seaman, he knew how sound carried over the water, but he had no illusions that they were still undetected if anyone was out there.

"Twelve," answered Kathy. "Biggest one is that twenty-five footer off the port bow. It's also the only one with the sails properly stowed. If any boats are occupied, it would be that one."

The sound of water lapping against the shore drew his attention back to the dock, and he watched as the crew of the Maggie Mae, including his friends, went about the business of getting them safely tied alongside the concrete structure. He imagined that a wooden dock wouldn't have survived as well as a more permanent, concrete dock. It also made him wonder if there weren't more resources on the island than he originally thought.

He called out to Kathy again, "We're going ashore as soon as the sun is high enough to burn off this fog. I'll send someone to relieve you at the bow. We need to have eyes on the water the whole time we're here."

Andi was watching the only building that could be seen from the dock. It had a big sign on the front that was obviously intended to bring travelers ashore. It was damaged, but she could see enough lettering to tell it said, "End of the World Tavern."

"I wonder if it was named that before the infected came along, or if it was made after it started," she said without lowering her binoculars.

The Chief lifted a pair to his own eyes and said, "I guess we'll find out."

"Why do we need to go ashore?" she asked.

"Call it a hunch," he said.

"Care to fill in the details of that hunch?"

"I think someone might be here. If so, they might be able to give us some insight into what to expect on the mainland."

"Forgive me for stating the obvious, Chief, but I think we can guess what happened on the mainland. This place is just like Springdale without an airport. It must've been jammed with small boats that escaped from the mainland. Everyone pictured the little cove as their own personal safety net until they got here and found out they weren't the first to arrive."

"Those people are all long gone. The people we're likely to encounter now are the ones who got here after everyone killed each other off."

Andi lowered her binoculars and studied the Chief. He clearly had something on his mind, and she could see that his brow was furrowed. Whatever it was he had picked up on, there was a clue out there on the island she had missed. She put the binoculars back to her face and concentrated on the landscape. She felt like she was trying to find Waldo in one of those colorful kids' books, but she didn't think it would be as easy as a dude wearing a red and white hat and glasses. She saw it faster than she expected.

There was a car sitting in front of the tavern. She couldn't see all of it, but she could see enough to know it was clean. It hadn't been parked in one spot for the last seven or eight years. Most cars had been neglected for so long that they had become dull from exposure to constant sunshine and weather. This one should have been covered with the brown layer of fine dirt that was blown over it along with the moist, salty air that carried the dirt. The windows should be the same color as the body, but they were clear lenses set into the dark blue body of the car.

"What do you think of the car?" she asked the Chief.

"I think that keeping a car clean is a sign that someone cleared the infected off of the island first."

Sim took over the bow watch from Kathy so she could organize a small group to go into the interior of the island. There was something that resembled a small town further inland than they could see, and the more he thought about it, the more the Chief wanted to talk with survivors. He wanted to find out how they had made it this far. He was met on deck by Kathy, Captain Miller, and Cassandra. It was their best-trained squad, and he knew they could be a lethal group if they had to be. Armed with rifles and sidearms, they climbed onto the dock and set off on the only road that led away from the boat. It was a hard-packed dirt surface that had been maintained despite attempts by vegetation to take over.

The road followed the shoreline to the left for about a hundred yards before it turned hard right in the direction of the tavern. It was slightly higher than the dunes and marsh grass on both sides, and they felt exposed out in the open, but cutting across the grass that got deep in places would be an invitation to a bite on the leg. In the early days of the infection, there were probably a few thousand people who had made it this far and plenty who didn't make it further. The Chief thought to himself that it would be a good idea to set the tall grass on fire to clear up any doubt that there were no infected on the island.

The first evidence that there was more happening on the island than newcomers would expect was the pair of signs, one on each side of the road. They read MINEFIELD. In smaller print under the one-word warning, there was a handwritten message.

"If you're alive, uninfected, and mean no harm to people here, walk in single file on the right side of the road to avoid the mines."

"It's not true about the road," said the Chief. "Someone has driven on this road recently. I expect there are mines on the sides, though. Most likely means there were military survivors here. If someone is watching, we want them to know we mean no harm, so let's line up."

With Cassandra in the lead, they continued to follow the road toward the tavern. It grew in size as they got closer, and they saw it had been impressive during tourist days. When the road opened up into the parking lot outside the building, Cassandra moved to cover behind the car while Kathy and Captain Miller went to the sides of the building to see what was on the other side. The Chief stood facing the front door in a non-threatening stance, hoping that anyone watching wasn't increasing the pressure on a trigger. He knew the M4 on his back would be a cause for concern, but he figured it would be logical to survivors that visitors would be armed.

There was only a faint sound as a window near the front door slid open, but the voice was clear.

"Good morning. You might want to take cover behind the car. Sometimes when they step on a mine, the body parts fly pretty far. Imagine getting hit in the head with a three-pound roast."

The warning had no sooner been given when the ear-shattering explosion ripped through the silence of the island. It was loud enough to make the Chief's ears ring, so he wasn't surprised that it knocked him forward onto the ground. His first thought was to wonder if he would find a piece of shrapnel in his back. He laid still for a few moments trying to sense a wound. He knew that pain would come later because shock tended to make people scream in fear rather than from the wound. Some would scream only to find they hadn't been hit, while others who were hit might just stare in disbelief at the place where their arm used to be.

Not finding the wound with his mind, he reached around to the back of his head, his arms, his legs, and his lower back. There was a piece of meat a few feet away, and something about it didn't seem right. It had mottled skin on one side and something like hair, but it didn't look like it had been blown off of an infected dead.

Boots crunched on the dirt near him as an elderly woman walked up and lifted the meat from the ground.

"Well, that's not the best way to hunt wild boar, but this will do after I clean it up. It should feed the lot of us. Help me look around for more."

The gray-haired woman tossed the meat to the Chief, where he still sat on the ground. He couldn't be accused of being squeamish, but he would have preferred not having to catch it and would have dodged it if he had been standing. He watched as she worked her way back and forth at the place where the grass met the parking lot.

"There's a six-foot buffer zone into the grass. If you don't go further, you can use it to hide in, but there hasn't been much use for it lately. At least I can check it for more flying meat. Ah! Found another one."

Kathy and the others rushed up to him. Kathy saw the bloody mess in his lap and was already opening a first aid kit in search of sterile gauze.

"Take it easy, Chief. We've got you. We'll have you fixed up in no time."

The expression on her face when he handed her the meat was something he would treasure. He could only wish he had a camera so he could preserve the moment, and he kept a straight face so she wouldn't catch on too quickly.

Cassandra and Captain Miller each took one of the Chief's arms and helped the big man to his feet. They were doing their best not to laugh at Kathy. She was still trying to figure out what the Chief had handed her and where it came from. The woman came back and handed her a second piece.

"Be a dear and carry this one since you're bringing the first one," she said. "Come along. The explosions sometimes cause the dead to show up if there are any nearby."

She walked ahead of them as if strangers dropped by every day, and they fell in line behind her to go through the front door. She pointed at the lock as they entered.

"Last one in, please be sure to latch the door. Wouldn't want to get a surprise visitor."

Kathy was the last one, and she had to juggle the two blood-soaked pieces of meat to get a free hand. When she latched the door, she saw that the lock was surrounded by steel and would probably keep out anything that wasn't carrying a sledgehammer or explosives.

The inside of the tavern was straight out of a movie set. Everything was made from rich, polished wood, and the other side of the bar was lined with mirrors behind rows of liquor bottles. The woman walked behind the bar and grabbed five glasses. Without asking their preferences, she grabbed a bottle of bourbon and poured each of them a generous glass.

"You being Yanks, I suppose you could use a taste of home. Cheers."

She upended her glass and exhaled a contented sigh after she swallowed. Everyone else took a swallow, but even the Chief had a slight shiver as the brown liquid burned its way down his throat. The woman was already pouring herself another glass.

"I don't usually hit the hard stuff this early in the day, but I don't get to celebrate visitors very often. My name is Beatrice Smythe, and what brings you to St Agnes?"

Her forward way of treating them as if they weren't a squad of well-armed survivors was charming in its own way, and they felt like children who had been herded into the school principal's office and told to explain themselves.

The Chief opened his mouth to speak, but she cut him off one more time.

"If you're wondering why I can so cavalierly invite strangers in, I'll just ask you, what choice would I have? If it turns out you are to be my end or bring me to harm, I couldn't stop you."

That brought out the Chief's best smile, and she said, "Oh, my. Let me have another sip before that smile goes away."

The bourbon relaxed all of them, and the Chief gave introductions amid handshakes and even a few hugs. Beatrice couldn't wait to share her experiences, and there was plenty to tell. Because they were curious about the mines and the exploding pigs, she started with them. The mines were placed around the populated parts of the island, and someone brought the wild pigs from St Mary's because they would attack the infected on sight and eat them.

"It was a marvel to see," she said. "They even ate the bones. There was nothing for us to clean up after the boars got done. Unfortunately, they also escaped captivity, and occasionally they step on one of the mines."

Needless to say, the four newcomers to St Agnes were already thinking ahead to supper, and none of them wanted to eat pork. Bacon would have been nice, but not if the bacon came from a pig that had been living on an infected dead diet. They didn't have the heart to tell Beatrice how risky it was to eat the meat, and they had seen instances where the meat didn't seem to be contaminated. It just wasn't something they were willing to test.

"So there are more people here?" asked Cassandra.

"Not anymore," said Beatrice. "The last of them died off over a year ago. A few of them left for supplies but never came back. The last of them was killed by an infected that washed ashore. They still wash up once or twice a week. Most of them are like beached whales. They can't do any harm, and they just lay there and bake in the sun. The animals and crabs get to them eventually, but sometimes they come out of the water, and you had best see them before they see you."

"Would you know if there were others on the island? You know, other survivors?" asked Captain Miller.

"Certainly…as a matter of fact, there's someone on one of the boats near yours. I'm sure you noticed."

"Anything we should know about them?" asked the Chief.

"I don't know much about them myself, but I think they go somewhere once a month to resupply. They use an inboard engine to leave the cove, and they stow their sails before they come back. They have to be refueling somewhere."

The Chief nodded with appreciation, "Thank you, Beatrice. That's something we needed to know. It sounds like they can tell us where the fuel station is at St Mary's."

They had expected to find a hardcore survivor if they found anyone at all. They didn't expect the sweet old lady who anyone would love to have as their grandmother or great aunt. Beatrice had plenty of guns and knew how to use them, but she said she had given up on the idea of defending the island a long time ago. If someone came along and wanted to stay, they were welcome to do so. That meant they could have their share of whatever supplies she had. That philosophy had worked well for her, and it even helped her to replenish her supplies when a group made regular supply runs to St Mary's. She said when they didn't return, the rest of their friends went searching for them. They didn't make it back either.

She guessed that over the years, there had been at least fifty people who came along who stayed, but they met with the same fate sooner or later. The last group had turned the restoration of the tavern to its former beauty into a project, and it had been their place of sanity away from the real world.

Kathy asked, "You were here at the beginning?"

Beatrice seemed to focus on a spot behind Kathy as she thought back to those days.

"It was a long time ago, wasn't it. I think seven years because I marked the turning of the seasons, but I don't know if I forgot to do it one year or if I did it twice."

She poured another glass of bourbon before she went on.

"We knew about the infection because of the Internet, and people began arriving with only the clothes on their backs and lots of money. Everyone wanted to buy necessities, and they didn't understand that we didn't have any to sell. I shared my food, toothpaste, and toilet paper with strangers and their children, but it wasn't long before I didn't have any to share. Then they turned on each other like one of them had more right to that roll of toilet paper than someone else. I saw people getting shot over toilet paper. Then they got back up off the ground and bit the nearest person."

"We've seen it," said the Chief in a compassionate, soft voice. He gave her hand a squeeze.

"It got worse," she continued. "It spread across the island and turned them all into those things. As they turned on each other, more people arrived seeking shelter. I'm sure some left immediately if they saw what was happening here before they came ashore. I don't know for sure because I hid in the tavern cellar for over a month. When I came upstairs, I was surprised to find they hadn't even gotten inside."

"Where did they all go?" asked Cassandra.

"Into the water, I suppose. I ventured out one day and went to the dock. I saw some walking into the water all the while reaching toward one of the sailboats."

The Chief said, "You must have a guardian angel. You're lucky to be alive, and I don't think anyone would object if you came with us when we leave for the mainland."

Beatrice seemed startled by the offer and said, "Heavens, no...why would I want to do that? No one ever comes back from there."

The sound of a mine exploding caused all of them to run for the front door.

"There goes the neighborhood," said Beatrice.

As they crowded through the door into the parking lot, they spotted the plume of smoke rising about a hundred yards away. The grass and dunes rose slightly and then dropped lower near the site of the explosion, so their view was partially blocked. From where they were, they couldn't see what had stepped on the mine.

"How many mines are out there?" asked the Chief.

Beatrice shook her head.

"I don't know. I think I heard one of the men say there were over a hundred. I haven't heard two explode in the same day in a long time."

She had no sooner finished when another exploded in the same general direction. This time they saw dark chunks flying upward, but the clothing attached to the chunks told them it wasn't another wild boar.

"Mind if we go upstairs to those front windows?"

"Follow me," she replied.

Beatrice led them back inside and went to a set of stairs hidden behind a door just past the bar. She said the stairs were out of view to keep patrons from knowing how to get to her home upstairs.

It was the master bedroom that had windows facing the front. They saw that Beatrice made her bed in the mornings, and they could understand why she might not want to leave. Despite feeling lonely at times, you couldn't beat the safety she enjoyed.

From the window, it was easy to see what had tripped the mines, and if they guessed right, there were going to be more explosions any minute. They could count at least twelve infected dead dragging their wet bodies on a slow walk across a sea of brown and green grass. The terrain was too sandy for much more to grow across that stretch, and as they made their slow march inland, the sand clung to their wet clothes and made them move even slower.

Captain Miller chuckled and said, "By the time they get here, they're going to weigh a ton."

As he finished his comment, another stepped on a mine. It was a bit spectacular, and they could deny it all they wanted, but it was almost fun to watch. It was easy to forget that the infected used to be people.

"Why now?" asked Cassandra.

Beatrice said, "I suspect your arrival may have stirred up the ones sitting on the bottom of the cove. They wash in with the tide and sit out there until something causes them to take notice. I saw a dingy out there one day, and before I could warn the people in it, they were capsized and dragged under. It isn't too deep in places, so the nasty things don't have to do more than stand up."

The sound of gunfire drew them away from the infected that were making their way ashore. The next explosion came from somewhere closer to the docks, and even though they couldn't make out all of the details, they could see the Maggie Mae well enough to see someone go overboard. The long silver hair left no doubt who it was.

15

Alone

Southern England - Seven Years Later

When Symone thought back on those days when it all began, she could remember Arthur's face. For some reason, it had stayed with her. She remembered what happened on the first day, but the police officers who came to her house were just as faceless as Joseph and William had become. As hard as she tried, the closest she got to remembering Joseph was the look he had given her before she had collapsed on the railroad tracks, and she didn't want to remember him that way. So, she did her best to block him out. He had passed through her life, and they were teammates for a brief time. That was all. William was a total blur to her. He was Joseph's son, and he was too innocent to die, but he was also too innocent to survive. That was something Symone learned in the years that followed her departure from the flat roof of the train platform.

Her children's faces were the same as the last time she saw them. Too much had happened in between the day they disappeared and now for Symone to even imagine how they must've grown. Her belief that they were alive never wavered. The fact that Emily would be thirteen years old and Adam would be eleven were nothing more than facts to her, and they were facts that didn't change the way they appeared in her mind when she thought of them. She still only saw their angelic faces...the faces of a four and six-year-old.

The face of her husband was hidden behind the face shield of his spacesuit. She had watched him do a spacewalk on the news once, and the golden shield hid his face. At night she felt like he was still up there in the darkness. During the daytime, she didn't think about him at all.

The search for her children began the day she left her home with Arthur, but the real search seemed to begin when she saw Joseph and William die. That was the day she decided the only way she would ever see Adam and Emily again was by relying solely upon her own decisions. The first one she made was to go in an entirely new direction. She decided to go southeast, away from London and toward Folkestone. She somehow knew the Channel Tunnel was important. She didn't know why, but she became obsessed with the idea of going there.

In the old days, it was less than a two-hour drive from London to Folkestone, the city where the tunnel reaches English soil. In between on the M20 highway, there were only two large cities, but they were big enough to cause larger populations to grow in the smaller towns between London and the coast. Commuters to all four cities, London, Maidstone, Ashford, and Folkestone, caused the bedroom communities to flourish, and the population between London and the coast grew to over a million people. Add to that the exodus from London toward the Channel Tunnel, and there was a guarantee that Symone would not be alone on her journey. The normal two-hour drive took closer to a year.

There were days when remarkable weather and few of the infected crossed her path, and it seemed that she would be able to finish her trip by the end of the day, but then she would find herself nearly surrounded by hordes moving north that would push her back further than she had been the day before. Twice she found herself closer to London than she had been when she was in the company of Joseph and William. Despite being pushed back, despite having to hide for days or even weeks, despite close brushes with death, Symone arrived nearly a year later, not far from the entrance to the Channel Tunnel. Seeing the dark mouth of the entrance through her binoculars, she was disappointed. There was no movement anywhere.

Symone had always been resourceful and creative, but she had never set out to be a survivalist. Her unique skills were always motivated by the needs of her children. If one of them had a project, she studied what she needed to in order to be part of it. She taught herself to draw with them, play the piano with them, and cook the best desserts with them. Since they disappeared, everything she did was based on her desire to see them again, so she continued to learn just as if she was learning with them. Almost as if she had practiced with them, every time she notched an arrow and took aim with her bow, she imagined her children beaming with pride.

The bow had been a thing of wonder to her. Still hanging on a rack in a sporting goods store, she had stared at it with the thought that it had to be a trap. It was left there to draw in the unsuspecting survivors who had felt like they had just gotten lucky. She waited for almost half a day before venturing into the store to claim the prize. An unopened box of arrows sat on a shelf below the bow, and there was a note taped to it. Reading it made her think of the note she had left on the bar in the pub.

The note said so many of the same things she had written that night. Her anonymous benefactor felt like someone might survive if they found the bow and arrows and that no one needed two of them. They were departing from the store with everything they needed, and best of luck to the survivor who found the bow. She was grateful, and she was determined to make good use of it.

She practiced for hours at a time, seeking out the infected that traveled alone. Sometimes she would go after pairs or groups of three, but it was important that each arrow was retrieved. Just like bullets, there wasn't a resupply store around every corner, but because they were silent killers, arrows were even more valuable than bullets.

From her vantage point to the west of the tunnel entrance, Symone watched for any movement that would indicate there were living people in the area, but all she saw were the uncoordinated infected dead that staggered and fell. Some got back up and struggled onward until she lost sight of them, but it seemed like more and more of them crawled or stopped moving altogether. It made her wonder if they hadn't reached a point when the population had been reduced so far that there were fewer of the living to become victims...no victims, no newly infected.

Then her bubble was burst when she saw a fresh, new parade of the monsters come from out of nowhere, and she realized there was no hope other than to keep herself alive and to keep searching for her children. She watched this new group march steadily toward the entrance of the Channel Tunnel, and she knew if the tunnel was important, there was still no way that she could go into that gaping darkness alone.

The spot she had chosen where she could watch the tunnel entrance was on a hill about a mile away. Besides being able to see the tunnel, it was close to a small airport that had been used for small, single-engine planes and helicopters. There were a couple of planes that had probably belonged to rich people who needed to get to the tunnel on business, but for the most part, there appeared to be an abundance of planes that belonged to people who just enjoyed flying along the coast. Since she couldn't fly a plane and wasn't crazy enough to think she could try, it wasn't the airplanes she was interested in. It was the small tower that sat at the side of the runway. Even from that distance, she could watch the entrance of the tunnel without worrying about what might be coming up behind her. She knew she could easily get trapped in the tower, but the last year had made her increasingly wary of hiding in less than savory places.

She had been awakened one night by a crawling sensation on the back of her neck. It wasn't the same sensation she seemed to get when her skin crawled because she had heard a sound close by…a moan, or a leg being dragged on the asphalt. This was really something crawling, and she had done what anyone would have done. She recoiled as if she could see behind herself if she turned far enough, and she clutched a cupped hand to the back of her neck. A warm, sticky sensation filled her hand, and she recoiled a second time when she saw the size of the spider she had flattened at the base of her scalp. Another spider fell from her arm when she wiped the wet mess from the palm of her hand. That would be the last time she chose to sleep under a wooden porch.

The tower had a single ladder that rose almost fifty feet to the small room at the top, but it could be retracted half that distance, and it was clean with no signs of spider webs. Her first thought was it wouldn't be so bad getting trapped in the tower if she had enough supplies to last a week or two at a time, so she set to work on her new home.

Plastic jugs of water were her first priority, and she spent an entire day scavenging them and getting them up the ladder. Tired but satisfied with her first day of stocking the water, she watched the sunset in the distance and wondered what her husband would think about her strong arms and legs. She doubted she could have climbed that ladder a dozen times with empty jugs a year earlier.

The next day was spent in search of food supplies that hadn't been picked clean. Most of the stores had shelves that were totally bare, but as distasteful as it was, the best sources of power bars were in the backpacks still strapped to the infected dead...so Symone went hunting.

A few random infected provided her with a half dozen power bars, but that wasn't going to be enough. She felt like there had to be a way to improve her odds of finding food, but everything she thought of seemed to increase the risks. In the end, Symone decided there was no choice, and she went to a local store where someone had destroyed the glass door in front. That meant two things...the shelves would be empty, but the aisles wouldn't be. There would be infected dead walking around inside the store, mostly because they had stumbled inside and couldn't find their way back to the door. The ones she would be hunting for would be the ones that had been alive when they went inside.

The only light inside the store was what came from the big glass windows along the front. They were coated with dirt, but the gloom would give her some of the cover she needed. She crouched at the shattered door and listened for several minutes.

"They're in there all right," she whispered to herself.

Before taking the first step over the aluminum frame of the broken door, Symone studied the floor on the other side. She saw that she would need to be careful not to make noises by stepping on broken glass or accidentally kicking something that had been knocked from a shelf. She gathered her nerve and took a deep breath before going inside, remembering that grocery stores smelled pretty bad even after so much time had gone by. The copper smell of blood was familiar, and there was no escaping something so inevitable, but it seemed that the smell of rotten meat combined with rotten dairy products made the smell of old blood almost bearable...almost. The irony of the contents on the first shelf made her cover her mouth because it had caused her to open it to laugh. There were several neat rows of canned air freshener spray. She took one and tucked it into a cloth sack because it would be nice to spray her clothes later.

She lowered herself to the floor and kept her eyes focused on the deepest shadows at the other end of the aisle. She had to resist even glancing toward the front of the store once her eyes became adjusted to the gloom. Once she was sure there was nothing waiting for her at the end of the aisle, she ventured deeper inside. Keeping low, she swiveled her head from side to side, always stopping for a moment with her eyes on the darkness ahead. She saw a roll of Lifesavers on the floor to her right. She retrieved them and had to resist the urge to open them immediately. The blue wrapper made her mouth water at the thought of peppermint, but she instinctively knew the few moments she would take to open the wrapper could be her last moments alive.

At the end of the aisle, she did her best to make out the details to her left and right, but one direction was just as bad as the other.

"There should be a rule," she thought. "All stores should be arranged the same way so it would be easier to find something."

She chose to go to the right and made a mental note that there was a box of dishwasher detergent still sitting on the shelf. She turned it outward to make it easier to see if she had to navigate out of the store quickly, then she was faced with a new dilemma. If she went back up the next aisle, her eyes would be facing the daylight that filtered in through the dirty windows. She wondered if she could walk back up the next aisle using just enough of her peripheral vision to be sure it was safe.

Symone crouched so low to the floor that she was almost sitting on the dirty tile. She listened as she tried to work up the nerve to back into the next aisle, and her decision was made for her when she heard the distinctive sound of glass being crushed under moving feet. She reached back and found the feathered tip of an arrow and silently notched it on the bow. She heard the crunch again and sensed that it was further away than the first time.

The shadows on her left seemed a bit darker, and something made her feel like it was an alcove of some kind.

"Restrooms?" she wondered.

With one hand keeping the pressure on the arrow to keep it ready, she reached with her other hand and felt a familiar shape. It was a drinking fountain positioned in the center of the alcove between the two restroom doors. Above the fountain, where customers would see it more easily, someone had hung a cork bulletin board. Tattered remains of old store sales, babysitting services, and things for sale still littered the board, and even though the corner had seemed dark when she had first found it, her eyes could see well enough to recognize that familiar shape she had seen for the first time when her children disappeared and then later in the country home. This time was different, though. Pinned behind the card with the gold embossed exploding grenade was a photograph she had forgotten. It was a message left for her to find. It had been on her refrigerator, and in the dim light, she could see her own smiling face as she wrapped her arms around her children and leaned into her husband. It filled her with grief and hope in a split second. In that instant, she knew she was close. She had made the right choices. Her children were nearby, and someone wanted her to find them.

******

The discovery was enough to make Symone forget where she was, and she knew the next few minutes were going to mean the difference between life and death. It wasn't that she made more noise than the other random sounds inside the store. It was the type of sound she made. The sound of a human voice in the darkness seemed to ring like a bell.

"Oh, my God."

The responses came back to her from all directions as if they were focused on her spot.

Symone grabbed the picture and the business card from the bulletin board, but she was careful to retrieve the thumbtack that had held it in place and put it between her lips so she wouldn't drop it in the dimly lit corner of the alcove. She shoved the card and photo into her sack and retrieved the can of air freshener in one smooth motion, and carefully pulled the thumbtack from her mouth. She didn't know if it would work, but it was her only chance if she was right about the number of infected dead that were closing in on her position.

She leaned against the door of the ladies' restroom to keep it open a few inches and, with her free hands, wedged the thumbtack into the top of the can of air freshener. Once it was loudly exhausting its lavender-scented contents into the air, Symone placed the can into the gap at the bottom of the door. Then she went as flat to the floor as she could and crawled into the closest row of shelves. She pinned her body against the back wall and prayed that she was far enough out of sight.

In the gloom, there was a rush of bodies. The infected collided with each other as they tried to get as close as they could to the noise that had disrupted their domain, and the collision caused them to stumble into the open restroom door. Their feet repeatedly brushed into the can of air freshener, sending it spinning noisily across the tiled floor inside the ladies' room. The clattering of the aluminum can only served to agitate them more, while only a few feet away on the bottom row of shelves, Symone didn't dare to move.

The door to the ladies' restroom swung shut, and the only sounds inside the store appeared to be coming from the other side of the door. Since it only swung inward, she had managed to trap them all inside. Their constant collisions on the other side were practically a guarantee that the door would stay shut.

"How dumb can these things be? Even a cat can pull open a door," she mumbled.

Symone eased herself from her hiding place and listened intently to the store. There was a fair amount of noise from the other side of the restroom door, but the rest of the store was quiet. She decided she didn't have much time before more infected outside the store would drift through the opening, so she took her chances and moved faster. She also decided to risk using the small LED flashlight she had for just such an emergency.

One thing that had always amazed Symone was the wastefulness of grocery stores. If something fell from a shelf and went under the bottom shelves, employees didn't seem motivated to go after it. Things fell through gaps in shelves or were kicked by customers, but no matter how it happened, there were always things under the bottom shelves. Covering most of the end of her flashlight, she began her search for those forgotten items.

The biggest discovery of the day was the plastic bag full of beef jerky. As far as she knew, that stuff never went bad, and you couldn't beat it when you wanted something to chew. Besides the jerky, she found a variety of items that were well beyond safe to eat, and she put them on a shelf so she wouldn't discover them again. She was disappointed to find that the Twinkies were open on one end. She was perfectly willing to test the theory that they lasted forever. A brick of ground coffee was the next major find. She decided she would eat it with a spoon if she couldn't find a way to heat water, but when she discovered an entire case of Ramen noodles, she knew that she would find a way to heat water even if it meant setting fire to her tower. After she ran out of Sterno, she ate the noodles after soaking them in cold water, and she learned to like ground coffee on a spoon.

******

That wasn't the last time she went to that store. She carefully fashioned a door from shelves to replace the one that was broken because she continued to find supplies hidden in the strangest places. It was almost as if someone was planting the food and other necessities for her to find, but she knew that wasn't true because nothing was ever in a place where she had found something before.

Once she even went there as a sort of anniversary celebration. She had lost track of time and didn't know the exact date, but she was fairly sure it had been about five years since she moved into the little tower. The inside of the tower showed it just by the amount of junk she had carried up the ladder. The blankets and cardboard she had used to insulate the walls used up a lot of her space, but they had kept out some of the cold. She had watched seasons come and go, and she could tell how many had gone by when she remembered the worst snowstorms.

There was the first winter when she had seen a horde crossing the runway in the snow. Several had stopped moving long enough to freeze, and she remembered how some of them had gotten up and staggered away after the thaw. She hoped she could thaw out too.

That was when she finally discovered there was still electrical power in the tower. She was already worried about freezing along with the infected dead on the runway and had ventured to a maintenance hangar in search of warmth after an unbearably cold night. She found a portable heater buried behind a massive amount of junk in a locker and couldn't stop herself from having a daydream about sitting in front of the heater in the tower. In her daydream, there were electrical outlets for the heater. She cursed herself for not searching the maintenance building before.

"Well, at least I can come down here and thaw out every morning," she said out loud.

The heater wasn't heavy, so she carried it over to a workbench and plugged it in. She turned it on and vigorously rubbed her numb fingers in front of the glowing coils inside. She felt like an idiot when it suddenly dawned on her that she had never investigated the lack of electricity to the tower, a place where it must've been needed before the infection.

She was reluctant to leave the heater, but it didn't take her more than five minutes to locate the breaker box, and when she opened it, she saw that one of the big double switches was in the OFF position.

"Could it be that simple?" she asked herself.

Symone got a firm grip on the switch and pushed it to the right, where it would line up with all of the others. She didn't know what she expected, but it wasn't the wailing siren that split the stillness of the morning. If there were any infected out there that weren't frozen, they would already be moving in her direction.

She flipped the switch off again, and the siren wound down to silence. Symone didn't hesitate. She was determined to have heat in her little home, so she flipped open the big toolbox that had been used to work on planes and quickly found one tool she knew she needed. She unplugged her new heater and ran into the cold morning air with it tucked under her arm and the tool in her back pocket. It wasn't easy climbing the cold ladder with one free hand. Ice had formed on the rungs, and she lost her grip several times, but in the distance, she could see the dark shapes that were answering the call of the siren. She knew she had to move fast if she wanted heat today.

As soon as she pushed open the hatch above her, she shoved the heater inside and then turned in a circle on the ladder. She was searching for the siren and hoping it wasn't on top of the hut that she called home. She spotted it immediately, and it would be a long reach from the ladder. Then she did something she would never have believed possible for her. She pulled the tool from her back pocket, a pair of long-handled wire cutters, and made sure she kept her grip on them as she hooked her legs through the rungs of the ladder. She felt the cold biting into her legs through her jeans, and her fingers were losing their feeling, but she forced herself to let go of the ladder with her other hand. Stretching farther than she thought she could, she cut the wires on the siren.

It was a race against a slowly moving horde of the infected, but they didn't feel the pain of the cold, and they weren't gasping for every breath of air. Symone almost wanted to stay inside the hangar because it felt so good compared to being outside, but for a second time, she was pushing the breaker to the ON position. She didn't realize she was holding her breath until she let it out. There was no wailing sound this time.

There were three of the infected between her and the tower when she burst into the open outside the hangar. She slammed the door shut and then ran at an angle to the tower before changing directions and going straight for the ladder. The infected were slow to react, and it was good that they gave her those precious seconds she needed because her hands felt like they couldn't take more of the cold from the metal rungs. She knew if she made it to the top, she would have to retract the ladder, but it would have to wait. She would risk it for however long it took to get the feeling back in her hands.

It felt like it took an hour to reach safety. She never would have believed she had climbed the ladder in only ten minutes, but once she crawled through the hatch, she found the cord on the heater and shoved it into an outlet. She was rewarded with the faint smell of metal getting hot, and then the coils glowed red. She cried, but then she laughed while she cried a bit more, and she knew she would remember this morning for a long time.

The heater was still doing its job after the fifth winter had come and gone, and Symone had spent countless hours with her binoculars raised in the direction of the tunnel entrance. She watched the infected go into the darkness, and sometimes she saw them come out, but she never saw anything moving near the mouth of the tunnel as if there was any purpose. Still, she felt like the tunnel was the answer, and there was plenty of free time to figure out why it mattered so much to her. She thought it had something to do with a comment her husband had once made when Adam Calloway was visiting.

Symone recalled Henry had talked about how many tons of soil had been transported from the bottom of the English Channel and deposited inland, and he was sure it wasn't adding up. When she had asked what he meant, Adam had answered for him that it seemed like they had dug more soil and bedrock out of the Channel than needed to complete the tunnel. He also pointed out that there was far less being excavated from the French side of the tunnel. When she asked why it mattered, her husband had said he felt like they had been building more than a tunnel.

"What else could they be building?" she had asked, but neither Henry nor Adam had a reasonable guess.

She couldn't explain it, but a thought was growing inside her mind that had begun when she remembered that conversation...something that was telling her she would have to go into that tunnel to find out what she wanted to know.

******

Some nights felt longer than others because she couldn't sleep. On those nights, she wondered what her children were like. She wondered if they would remember her, and she wondered who had left the photograph on the bulletin board. She pulled it closer where she could see it in the moonlight, and for what had to be the millionth time, she asked herself why the cards never had a message on them besides those numbers...why they didn't tell her what to do.

It had to be that the person or persons who left the cards knew she would figure it out, and her next question was always why they had expected that of her. She was holding the picture up with the black sky and the stars behind it when the answer came to her. She had a random thought that Henry was up there somewhere, and if she held the picture high enough, he would be able to see it too.

That was when she realized he was meant to see it. He was meant to see the original card on the refrigerator, and he was meant to find the third card with their photograph behind it. It was a message to him that said he would know where the children were and that they were safe.

For one full minute, she felt that flush of hope anyone would feel when they thought they had the winning numbers to the lottery. She felt that thrill a sports fan felt when it looked like the ball couldn't possibly miss the net. Symone felt that overwhelming relief she knew was possible once she knew for certain that her children were still alive. Then it ended. It crashed down around her like she had gotten the lottery numbers wrong, or the ball hit the edge of the goal post and careened away toward the side of the field. A moment of joy was followed by a moment of sadness as she remembered her husband wasn't there to tell her what the secretive cards had meant. How could she know the meaning without Henry?

It was also the first time she had a new feeling about her husband. Somehow she knew he wasn't up there anymore, and it didn't make her afraid. It didn't make her worry that something had gone wrong on the Space Station. Instead, it was a feeling that he wasn't too far away if he was back on Earth again.

Symone spent the rest of that night watching the sky instead of the tunnel entrance. There had been many times before the infection when she had known the location of the International Space Station, and she had delighted in finding that one bright dot of light and tracking its path across the sky. She had no way of knowing its path now, but she almost felt as if she would know Henry was no longer at the station if she could find it in the night sky.

She fell asleep just as the sun was rising the next morning, and she still had the binoculars in her hands. When she saw the movement at the tunnel entrance, her binoculars were at her eyes in a split second. She had to blink to focus, but she could see clearly enough that there was a group of people entering the tunnel in single file. The infected didn't do that. They appeared to be wearing military uniforms, and as they approached the entrance, she could see them raising weapons aimed ahead of them. They also carried flashlights that were powerful enough to pierce the darkness of the tunnel, and they didn't hesitate. Symone instinctively knew this was what she had been waiting for, but now that the moment had arrived, there was nothing she could do about it. The column of soldiers disappeared as if the darkness had swallowed them.

Frustration grew inside Symone like a tumor. She was angry at herself for not considering what she would do when she finally saw something happen at the tunnel. It was noon before she finally realized she had never thought about what she would do because she had never really considered whether she would see a friend or foe. It wasn't that she was afraid of who she would see, but the reason she retracted the ladder on the tower certainly wasn't because she was worried that the infected could climb. She just knew she couldn't trust everyone she met. Still, if they were going into that tunnel, she would prefer to be with them rather than to try to go in by herself, and the fact that they were military meant something to her. She trusted the military, and she felt like they would protect her.

When the idea came to her, she didn't hesitate for one moment. A quick scan of the area revealed a clear path to the hangar, and the nearest infected dead was at least a mile away. She lowered the ladder, and by the time she reached the ground below, she had a mental list of the things she needed from the maintenance supplies.

Being married to an astronaut had its advantages. Henry had always been tinkering with something, and sometimes she actually paid attention when he insisted on explaining whatever contraption it was that he was building. Because she had listened, she at least had the basics mastered.

Once inside the maintenance hangar, Symone found a tool belt and strapped it around her waist. She filled the pockets with a variety of tools and odds and ends she had seen Henry use. Electrician's tape was practically everywhere, so she took two rolls, and at every workstation, there was a portable lamp that had a big clip at one end so it could be mounted wherever it was needed. She unplugged one and tucked it into the belt. The last thing was a coil of super-strong line that she guessed was used to tow planes but was extremely lightweight. She put it over her head and under one shoulder and headed back to the tower.

Less than thirty minutes after the idea had come to her, Symone had her pile of supplies inside the hatch and spread out on the floor.

"Now comes the hard part," she said out loud.

With one end of the tow line tied firmly to a metal pole inside the tower and the other fastened around her as a safety line, she thought she must've understood how Henry had felt when he had stepped out into space with his tether line being the only thing that kept him from drifting away into the blackness. Of course, she knew she wouldn't drift away…she would plummet to the ground, and Henry wouldn't have an audience waiting outside to eat him. One glance through the open hatch was enough to see that her audience was there. Three infected dead were milling around below her, but their aimless wandering stopped as soon as she appeared above them.

Symone lowered herself through the hatch and knew what she was going to do was actually very simple to anyone who had ever taken the time to work on a car or an electrical appliance, but it was new to her, and she would be doing it fifty feet above the ground. Still, it went much better than she had expected and much faster. She located the wires she had cut on the siren and then carefully used an odd tool Henry had shown her. It had holes in it that were used to strip away the plastic on each wire. She carefully pulled a roll of white wire from her tool belt and fastened one end to the first wire, and wrapped them with black tape. She pulled the second roll of wire from a pocket, but this one was black. She attached it to the other wire the same way, and after inspecting her work, she climbed back inside the tower.

The next part was easy because she could do it sitting on the floor without her audience moaning below her. She removed the bulb from the lamp and then the protective cover over the place where the wires were attached inside. She attached and taped the black and white wires where they connected inside the switch and then reassembled the cover. When she was finished, she held her breath again the same way she had when she had turned on the breaker the first time. Symone carefully plugged in the lamp and turned the lamp switch to the ON position. The siren wailed below her feet.

She turned it off quickly and leaned back against a wall to let her satisfaction sink in and to enjoy her small measure of success.

"Okay," she said, "the next time I see you guys, I'll have a way to say hello."

******

* * *

The opportunity to say hello came far sooner than she expected. Only one day after finishing her handiwork, she was watching the tunnel entrance when the soldiers emerged from the darkness. They were wearing tan camouflage uniforms that appeared to have reinforced padding along the arms. They were once again walking cautiously in single file, and their rifles were extended outward in different directions. They paused for a moment but then moved forward in the center of the road. Symone switched on the lamp.

The wail of the siren split the still morning air, and she watched through her binoculars as the column of soldiers appeared to freeze in their tracks. The one in front raised his hand in a fist as some sort of signal, but it was clear by the way the others had stopped that they had anticipated his command.

She saw with satisfaction that even though some of them continued to sweep their weapons to the sides of the column, the three in front had closed up in a group and were clearly using their binoculars to locate the source of the siren. When she saw them stop with their eyes aimed squarely at her, she switched off the lamp, and the world went silent.

"Hello," she said.

16

St Agnes

Isles of Scilly - Year Eight

Iris had been watching the sailboats that were anchored in the cove. She was particularly curious about the sailboat with the properly stowed sails. The rest of the boats didn't appear to be sea-worthy because of broken masts, dangling lines, and tattered sails that hung loosely over the decks. She suspected that they had coasted into the cove with crews that were only alive long enough to drop anchors. After that, the hidden dangers of the island claimed their lives.

Something had caught her eye that made a swirling motion in the water near the sailboat, and she was shocked when a dark shape rose out of the water. It was clearly a man, and he was only waist-deep in the water. One step forward toward the sailboat was all he needed to disappear underwater again.

Donny was the nearest of the three brothers as they went about their tasks maintaining the Maggie Mae, and she called to him that she had seen something. He took the binoculars from her and surveyed the area while she explained the appearance of the man. There was no doubt that he was an infected dead, but the immediate concern was how shallow the cove really was.

"We figured they were out here," said Donny, "but we should be okay as long as we don't get in the water."

The booming explosions from the island caused them all to come on deck and watch with concern for any sign that they should send a rescue party ashore to help the others. There was a long period of silence between the explosions that had them frustrated and anxious about what to do, and they had also neglected to pay as much attention to the cove as they had been. They almost missed the fact that the explosions had also gotten the attention of the infected and surprisingly caused the people on the sailboat to expose themselves.

Across the cove, there were infected standing up in shallow places. Some disappeared immediately, but some took several steps toward land before once again falling into deeper water. It took on the appearance of one of those carnival games where the mole would pop up and then disappear if you didn't hit it fast enough. They appeared and disappeared too fast to count, but there had to be dozens of them. The infected faced the island for the most part, so they had their backs to the sailboat when two people and a small dog emerged from the cabin. To the horror of the crew of the Maggie Mae, they jumped over the side rail and swam desperately in their direction. The small dog barked before jumping.

If the barking dog wasn't enough to draw the attention of the infected, the frantic thrashing of the pair that swam toward them was. Everyone could see one was a man, and one was a woman, but neither was a good swimmer, and they were further hindered by the appearance of the shallow bottom rising in front of them. One moment they were flailing their arms to gain forward speed in the water, and the next moment they were attempting to gain purchase with their feet in the soft bottom sand. The effect was a lot of falling and a lot of noise.

Iris and the others were all shouting at the top of their lungs to go back. If they had known for sure there were survivors on the sailboat, they would have found a way to reach them, but swimming the distance between the two boats was not an option. Ivan and Jessie appeared on both sides of her with rifles and began the process of eliminating the infected that stood up long enough for them to get off a clear shot. They concentrated their fire on the heads that appeared between them and the sailboat, but there was always a need to delay before pulling the trigger because the next head to appear was too often one of the swimmers.

That delay was finally too long, and the man screamed as he stood up practically in a hugging embrace with an infected. Even as Jessie pulled the trigger that sent a bullet smashing into the head of the infected, he hoped the bullet would kill both of them because he could see it had its teeth buried in the man's face. He wasn't that lucky. The infected fell away, pulling a large piece of the man's cheek with it, but leaving the man standing with his hands pressed to the wound and screaming at the top of his lungs.

His screaming would have been the opportunity the woman needed to make it the rest of the way because the infected nearby had all been drawn to him, but she did what so many people had done since the beginning of time…she tried to help him. She made it to the place where the bottom rose under her feet and pulled herself up to his height, but she was only there for a few seconds before she screamed with him. Jessie gave them both the only thing that could really have helped them, and he made sure he didn't miss. Two shots rang out, and the screaming stopped. The splashing that followed was a feeding frenzy he had only seen with sharks.

Iris was the first to spot the small head that had its ears pinned back and left a small wake in the shape of a V behind it. The dog was keeping its nose above the water and paddling in a straight line for her, and she leaned as far as she could toward it to offer encouragement.

"Come on, puppy! You can make it. I've got you."

It happened fast. Iris had the dog by the scruff of the neck and swung her arm with the frightened animal around for Colleen to receive it in her cupped arms. As Colleen cradled the dog and Iris let go, she fell backward. An infected had reached up from below and grabbed the collar of her jacket. When it fell into deeper water, it took Iris with it.

Without the Chief aboard the Maggie Mae to protect his wife, the responsibility fell to everyone else. At least that was what raced through each of their minds in the seconds that followed. Without a pause, everyone went over the side except Colleen, Andi, and Henry. Colleen rushed inside the cabin and wrapped the shivering dog in a blanket. She quickly checked for bites, and finding none, she closed the cabin door to keep it secure inside and ran back out to help the others. Henry and Andi had thrown a variety of rescue items over the side, including ropes and life preservers, but they weren't done yet. They were lifting a heavy cargo net that was stowed in a locker for just this sort of occasion. With it hanging over the side, more than one person could climb aboard at the same time.

Colleen helped them to lift the heavy net into place and attach it to the side rails. They gave it a shove, and it unrolled to its full length into the water. Then all they could do was wait. Although the water wasn't very deep along the dock, the visibility was poor, and all they could see were shadows moving.

Donny was the first to reappear, and he burst to the surface with Iris over his shoulder. She was conscious, but she was gasping for air because she had taken in a big mouthful of water when she had been pulled in. Andi and Colleen pulled Iris to safety while Henry grasped Donny's extended arm. With the help of the cargo net, they pulled them aboard, and with fear in their eyes began the awful task of checking for bite wounds. Iris had a scratch on the back of her neck near where the infected had grabbed her. It wasn't a bite, but it would need to be watched for infection. Donny had been wearing a work jacket, and they all saw the tear in the material on his right forearm. He pulled back the sleeve and revealed the purple bruise left by the jaws of his attacker, but the skin wasn't broken.

Iris was still unable to catch her breath, but Donny was quick to return to the side rail to help Hampton and then his brothers. One by one, they were retrieved from the water, and one by one, given a clean bill of health. Several of them had bruises like Donny's, and they knew how lucky they were that no one had an open wound.

Groaning came from the other side where the cargo net still hung, and they found three of the infected grasping the net as they attempted to pull themselves from the water. They were easily removed by blows to their ugly heads.

"I couldn't see a thing down there," said Hampton.

"So that was probably you that hit me in the head," said Ivan.

The fear and tension of those few minutes in the water had caused each of them to pump massive amounts of adrenaline through their bodies. The result was exhaustion, followed by relief. When Ivan touched his hand to the side of his head in mock pain, there was a small, general laugh from everyone, but it wasn't like they had done in the past. This one had been too close. This group had been through a helicopter crash, fights with hordes of the infected, venomous spiders, and more close calls than they could count, but this time they knew they should have lost someone...not could have, but should have. Instead of laughing, several of them quietly cried while the rest wiped at the corners of their eyes. Time had taken its toll on their usual resilience.

Colleen went inside the cabin then came back out with the dog wrapped in a blanket. It was still shivering a bit, but most of the shivering was the excitement of seeing so many friendly faces at once. It wanted each of them to keep petting its head and scratching behind its ears, but the best part was the plate of food scraps Hampton sat in front of it.

"We could have saved those people if they hadn't gone into the water," said Iris.

Andi nodded at her and said, "And we would have, but they were clearly desperate. Who knows how long they had been without supplies?"

The sound of a car driving down the road toward the dock shouldn't have surprised them, but the once-familiar sound had become foreign to them, and it felt like trouble. They rushed to defensive positions, but before they could all reach safety, the car slid to a stop, and their four friends dove from the open doors. They didn't know what they would find, so the Chief made the leap from the dock, over the side rail, and onto the deck in two long strides. He was to Iris before she could even tell him she wasn't hurt. He had to inspect the scratch on the back of her neck for himself, and she could see the uncertainty in his face.

"It's just a scratch," she said. "When it happened, the infected had a hold of me by the back of the neck, so its mouth couldn't have bitten me there."

The description of the attack was meant to make him feel better about it, but she could see it had the opposite effect. Iris reached for the young dog that was still licking at the plate Hampton had set in front of it. When she lifted it to her face, it resumed licking her nose and cheeks with excitement.

"You wouldn't have wanted me to let this adorable creature be caught in the water by those things, would you?"

The Chief visibly softened but then became serious in a split second. He was confused about where the dog had come from and didn't know about the couple that had tried in vain to swim to their boat. Everyone started talking at once, and it was hard to follow, but he eventually pieced it together. Then it was his turn to explain a few things. Beatrice had gone unnoticed until then.

The Chief introduced everyone to her and explained that she was the owner of the tavern. She also knew where the fuel depot was located on the next island, and even though she wouldn't make the trip with them, she could show them where it was on a map. The icing on the cake was that she had a personal account at the depot, and if they still had electricity to the pumps, her pin might still work. Beatrice literally blushed when she shook Henry's hand and said she would be helping her country by doing her part to get him home to his family.

They were interrupted by splashing somewhere toward the bow. Tom was the closest to the sound and the first to locate its source, but he had no sooner found it when there were several more similar splashes. The first one was a single infected that was making a poor attempt to pull itself up from the water. It was almost pathetic as it lost its grip and slipped back into the water, but the row of infected dead that slogged out of the water where it was close to the road was anything but pathetic. He could see six of them already on solid ground, and at least a dozen more had their heads above water. The exploding mines and the gunshots had attracted the attention of far more than expected. The couple jumping into the water had no idea how bad it could be under the surface.

The Chief did a headcount of the dead and asked Beatrice if she would reconsider their offer to take her along. She politely declined, saying she had given it a lot of thought over the years, and if it was as bad as they said it was, she didn't want any part of it.

"Well, I guess we can at least thin down their numbers for you," said the Chief. "We wouldn't want to see all of your mines used up in one day."

Kathy followed the Chief's lead when he picked up a rifle and selected his first target. They took out the infected on the road first to keep them from reaching the tall grass on the dunes. The infected made it easy for them by walking toward the sound of their gunfire. Once they were all eliminated, they moved on to the ones still in the water.

Hampton lifted a rifle and said, "Mind if I join you?"

By the time they were done, they had shot at least sixty of the infected. The three shooters swept their rifles back and forth over the water in search of new targets, but it appeared they had taken care of the problem for the time being.

Beatrice stood behind them, shaking her head in awe. "If I had known there were so many in the water, I might have reconsidered your offer."

"They'll be back if you want to change your mind," said the Chief.

"I know, but maybe I won't be around by then," she answered. "Besides, I would just be in your way. If you have the urge, you can check on me on your way home, but isn't it about time you got him home?"

Beatrice gestured toward Henry, where he had joined Colleen to give the puppy some affection.

"I guess you're right, but leave the light on for us. We'll check on you, and we'll bring back some supplies when we do."

On his signal, Andi gave him a nod, and the Allen brothers went to their assigned stations. Beatrice took a few minutes to talk with Henry and to wish him luck. By the time she was done, the Chief was ready to help her up onto the dock. She watched as the powerful engines of the tug came to life, and it backed away. It had been a long time since she had visitors, but she felt like she had met a real hero, and seeing him reach home made her feel like her country would survive. His return may have been a small thing, but it represented something much bigger. The efforts of an American team of friends to bring him home meant there was still a union that had survived and would overcome the impossible.

******

As the Chief entered the bridge, Andi asked without even taking her eyes off of her instruments, "You don't think it's a bit risky to make the run from St Agnes to St Mary's before dark?"

"If that sub is still out there, they expect us to cross between the islands at night."

"I don't think I would ever want to play poker with you," said Andi. "You know it's nothing more than the toss of a coin? Day or night... which one will the prey do?"

"I've never lost a coin toss," said the Chief.

Andi lifted her eyes to see his face in the hope that she would see what kind of expression he wore when he was bluffing. She had already seen the little grin he used when delivering a subtle joke, and she had seen the incredible smile that preceded his deepest laugh, but if this was the expression he wore when he was bluffing, she was sure she didn't want to play poker with him. It was totally unreadable... totally blank. One day she would test what he said about never losing a coin toss, but today she decided she would just go with his gut.

The weather cooperated. The fog that rolled in was as thick as anything she had ever seen, and she didn't have to ask the Chief if he had seen worse. Binoculars would be useless, and they would have to count on their instruments. Andi set the heading at fifteen degrees and calculated the time it would take for them to reach St Mary's. She estimated that it would only take fifteen to twenty minutes at maximum speed, but in the thick fog, she knew a slower speed would be safer, and she planned to change her course to forty-five degrees at twenty minutes. If her calculations were correct, five minutes after making the turn, they would be slightly north of St Mary's Isles of Scilly Terminal.

The highest compliment the Chief could give her was not to check her navigation chart, even though Kathy and Tom came into the bridge and asked how they could even see where they were going. He simply told them they were on a plotted course and a timer. Almost on cue, the timer chimed, and Andi eased the wheel to the right and set her new course and the timer at five minutes.

"Where are we?" asked Kathy.

The Chief put his finger on the chart at a spot north of St Mary's and said, "Five minutes from the fuel terminal, but if this fog doesn't lift in the next two minutes, we're going to drop anchor."

"What's your call?" asked Andi. "Heads or tails?"

The Chief gave her a smile he saved for the times when he wasn't going to laugh or answer a question.

"Whether or not fog will lift in five minutes isn't as predictable as day or night, but we'd better drop anchor if we don't want to pass the terminal. Besides, we could use the time to make a decision about our problem."

Tom asked, "What problem? We have a new problem?"

He turned to Kathy for a clue about what he had missed, but all she did was shrug her shoulders. He could see that she was waiting for the Chief to tell them all what he was thinking. Even Andi didn't know.

Andi announced over the intercom that they were stopping and to maintain a quiet status. Then she dialed the speed to ALL STOP and watched as they coasted to zero before dropping the anchor. The water was calm, and the tug bobbed gently as their wake caught up with them.

"We need everyone in on this," said the Chief. "Captain, if you could please leave someone on the bridge, I think everyone else should meet in the galley in ten minutes."

Andi knew the Chief had discovered a serious problem when he called her Captain, and she guessed that whatever the decision was that they had to make, it would at least be partially on her.

Ten minutes later, they were all squeezed into the galley except for

Ivan. Although they were at anchor, he had been given specific instructions to watch the radar closely.

"I won't keep everyone guessing," said the Chief. "We have two problems. First, this fog was a blessing because this is the only fuel terminal on the map before boats make the long trip to the mainland. I should have thought of it sooner, but I would expect survivors to be guarding it. We might have to fight for the fuel, but the only way to approach this would be by raft. We need to go before the fog lifts."

Even though no one had to raise their hand to be recognized, Hampton raised his. It caused everyone to chuckle, but Hampton wasn't smiling.

"You said two problems, and my guess is you saved the bigger one for last."

The Chief took a deep breath before beginning.

"It's something Andi said. She asked if the sub would be expecting us to cross between St Agnes and St Mary's in daylight or at night. I figured it would be at night, but I should have said it would be neither. They'll be waiting for us between St Mary's and the mainland. It's a much wider stretch of open water to cross, and it won't matter if it's day or night because they'll have plenty of time to detect us."

The galley was silent as everyone weighed the problems the Chief put in front of them. They knew the first problem was really not as bad as the second because he was a former SEAL. In some ways, they knew he was actually enjoying the thought of going ashore in a raft for a covert operation. The second problem had everyone stumped. There was no way they could outrun the sub if they were detected, and the likelihood of them going undetected was slim.

Captain Miller felt like he was back in the Army when he heard both problems, and his mind automatically prioritized solutions. In this case, it was easy because he knew the team that would go ashore would be the people with military experience. He knew that Cassandra had done covert operations, and anyone who could survive on a ship full of the infected as long as she had would be an asset for what the Chief had in mind. When he moved to the second problem, he thought back to how he felt when he saw Sparks leaving with the AC-130.

"These islands remind me of Springdale. There were more trees there, but that's not what I'm talking about. I was thinking along the lines of how much tourist business they would do if they had an airport."

Everyone turned toward Henry. He was the one person who was likely to know for sure if there was an airport on the island.

"Who's got the map?" he asked. "If I recall correctly, it's only a mile or so inland from the fuel terminal."

Andi opened a cabinet and shuffled through rolls of maps until she found the right one. She spread it out across the table where everyone else could see it, and the shape of the runway was too prominent to miss.

"It isn't a big airport," she said, "maybe even smaller than Springdale, but it would have serviced planes that carried at least a dozen people, so maybe we can get lucky and find something that got left behind."

It was fair to say that Henry had always hoped to reach home and be with his family, but the idea of reducing the time from days down to hours was staggering. If he hadn't already been sitting, he would have needed a chair.

"Are you okay?" asked Colleen. She had seen the way he had put one hand across his forehead and then both hands.

"I'm fine. It's just that the airport at Bournemouth is so close to my home. It's less than ten miles from my house. We can walk to it in a few hours."

"I hate to disappoint you," said Kathy, "but aside from a few open areas, the map shows that area is well populated. It might take a few days to get from the airport to your home."

"How big are those open areas?" asked the Chief. "Any of them big enough to land a plane?"

Henry thought for a moment and said, "Yes, but I imagine they've all become somewhat overgrown by now. They're mostly farms that went unplanted given the time of year the infection began."

"We have to get lucky and find a plane first," said the Chief. "If we do, we can approach the airport from the north to see if any of the places are suitable. If not, Bournemouth will have to do."

******

To say that Chief Joshua Barnes was in his element would have been an understatement. From the first moment they lowered the inflatable raft into the water, followed by the gear they would need, they could all see he was focused. Cassandra and Captain Miller climbed in ahead of him and stowed the gear while the Chief went over the plans with everyone else.

Since the Chief didn't do anything without a plan and a backup plan, he was making sure everyone knew where they were supposed to be and what they needed to do. They needed the fuel, and judging by the map, that would be the easy part if it wasn't guarded by survivors. If there were infected dead in the area, they weren't likely to be in large numbers because it would be too easy for them to walk or fall into the water.

The infected dead in the water was their biggest concern. Charts showed the depth around the fuel pumps to be at least thirty feet. That would rule out most possible surprises from below, but it also meant they wouldn't be able to leave the raft and swim to the dock unless they stayed just under the surface, out of sight yet out of reach from any infected.

In their experience, if an infected dead went into the water, they would sink after all of the air escaped from their bodies. That's when they were still dangerous. If they detected living prey in the water with them, they did their best to walk or reach for it. Unsuspecting swimmers could be easily pulled lower just long enough to be bitten. If the infected had been on the bottom long enough, their decaying bodies would fill the closed cavities in their bodies with hydrogen sulfide, carbon dioxide, methane, and hydrogen. Their bodies would expand, and then they would float to the surface. They would be less mobile, but it was a disturbing thought to know one could float up like a beach ball as they were passing over it, and accidental bites were no less fatal than intentional bites.

Fortunately, Andi and the Allen brothers were avid SCUBA divers, and they had wetsuits in their storage lockers that had been designed to resist penetration by teeth. They were tested with sharks in mind, but the Chief was sure that anything that could withstand the razor-sharp teeth of a shark could be effective against bites from the infected dead.

He said, "When alive, humans only apply one hundred and sixty-two pounds of pressure per square inch, but sharks can bite about eight to ten times harder. There's one thing to remember if an infected manages to get its mouth around any part of your covered body. Do not try to pull free. That could cause a tear in the suit allowing the teeth to reach your skin. If you find yourself in that predicament, you should use your knife to kill the infected and then pry open its jaws."

With that in mind, they were all clad in black wetsuits without the breathing gear. They had snorkels, masks, fins, and gloves made from the same material as their wetsuits. Knives were sheathed against their calves on both legs and on one hip. On the other hip, they had short-range radios that also emitted a homing signal, so the crew of the Maggie Mae would be able to keep track of their progress.

Iris had to admit, the form-fitting wetsuit was appealing in the way it brought out the Chief's muscular features, and she could see that she wasn't the only woman who had noticed. Andi was pretty and much younger, but Iris knew her husband well. He just wasn't wired in a way that made it possible for him to be unfaithful, and at this moment in time, he was too focused on his mission to notice the admiring looks from Andi. She also didn't blame Andi for what she was thinking, and it made her appreciate the Chief even more. Instead, Iris took it as a compliment.

She gave him a quick hug and kiss as he was about to lower himself into the raft, but she didn't let it linger. She wanted her husband to be focused on one thing. Besides, the fog was being used to their advantage, and it would be smart not to delay.

When they drifted away from the side of the tugboat, Cassandra was in a prone position down the middle of the raft with her M4 aimed over the bow. The Chief and Captain Miller were also prone, but they were both straddling the sides of the raft. Both had small paddles and were working in unison to propel the raft forward as quietly as possible. It didn't take long for them to be swallowed up by the fog.

Once they were back inside the bridge, Andi reminded everyone that it was essential that they remain quiet, and any lights that were used should be inside a closed space.

"We're holding our position for one hour. We know we're safe right where we are, so we aren't going to risk moving until we hear from the team."

"What's Plan B?" asked Iris.

Andi said, "Right now, I have the Allen brothers watching for any other boats that may be approaching or leaving the fuel terminal. I also have Colleen and Sim on the first watch using headphones to listen in for the slightest sound from the hip radios. The team knows all they have to do is give it a couple of clicks, and we'll move to their location. I'm watching sonar and radar. If we receive a series of rapid clicks from more than one radio, it means they had to get away fast, but they can't get back to the Maggie Mae, and we shouldn't come to them. In that case, they'll cross the bay to the main beach and try for the airport on their own."

Henry had been listening to Andi's explanation, and the last part of the plan made him frown.

"I hate to rain on your parade, but if they find a plane, it would be a good thing for me to be on it. Should I have gone with them?"

Andi had to smile at the question because the Chief had actually told her Henry would say that.

"The Chief said to tell you they would probably need to get a plane in working order if they find one at all. Then they would do their best to hide it before returning for the rest of you."

Henry was still frowning and said, "But that doesn't take care of whatever the problem that would conceivably make them bug out fast."

"Let me guess," said Iris. "The Chief said going to the airport for a plane would give him the time he needed to figure out a plan for that."

"That sounds about right," said Andi.

******

The fuel pumps were heavily guarded, and the Chief realized there was a hole in his plan to cut and run for the airport. It might be heavily guarded too, and they didn't have the firepower to take the airport and the terminal.

"So much for having time to think about it," he said to Cassandra and Captain Miller. "We have to take the fuel pumps while we can and hope they don't have communications with the airport."

They had passed close enough to the fuel pumps for the Chief to slip into the water and swim closer. When he got back, he reported that the main pump was located at the end of the dock, and there was another further along on the inside of the dock where smaller boats could get fuel instead of waiting for larger boats to finish. The smaller boats were protected from the open sea because they were surrounded by a quay. He suggested they could beach close to the dock and deal with the guards at the small pumps first. There would be no support for the guards at the main pump, and that should give them more time to bring the Maggie Mae in for fuel.

"Any chance we could negotiate for fuel?" asked Captain Miller. "They might be friendly."

"You're an optimist, and yeah, we should consider that, but there was a warning sign by each of the pumps."

"What did the signs say?" asked Cassandra.

"There were people nailed onto them over the word FUEL, and their arms and legs made a big letter X."

Cassandra said, "Yeah, I think that means don't ask for fuel."

17

St Mary's

Isles of Scilly - Year Eight

The moon was barely a crescent above the horizon as they slid the raft quietly onto the sand below the big concrete pier that led to the pumps. No lights were lit on the pier where guards were posted. They were about twenty yards inland from the fuel pumps that serviced the smaller boats, so the water was just deep enough for the raft to travel the last few yards without scraping along the bottom. It gave them all a scare when something pushed upward under the raft. The Chief had rolled quickly over the side and grabbed an infected dead by the back of the neck. When he attempted to pull it from under the raft, he found that it had been anchored to the sand with a steel cable around its waist.

"That's a new spin on minefields," he thought.

He pushed the infected a little further away but not before sliding a knife from his leg holster and slipping it into the soft spot at the back of the infected's neck. He pushed it upward into the brain, and the creature quit struggling.

The Chief surfaced and pulled himself back to his usual position, then told the others to keep their arms and legs out of the water until they were ready to beach the raft. In the meantime, they should watch for movement in the water as they approach the shore. If he had planted the infected dead along the beach as a deterrent against intruders, he would have attached a sharp piece of metal to them that would have sliced a raft right down the middle. He was glad the people behind the trap didn't think the way he did, but maybe they had, and the next one would be the killer.

The two guards at the small boat service pumps were sitting next to each other. Obviously bored, they were smoking and talking as if there couldn't be anything nearby that threatened their lives. The years of seeing few people and fewer infected made them careless. The only problem was that they were facing inland.

"We can just shoot them," whispered Cassandra, "and we can't get close enough for knives. How do you want to do this?"

"They're drinking," answered Captain Miller. "Besides impaired reaction time, I'll bet one of them has to relieve himself before we run out of time."

All three of them knew that the scenario was likely to play out in a specific way. One would decide to relieve himself, and the other would be likely to either turn away or relieve himself too. They would most likely separate from each other and even face in opposite directions. That meant they would be on opposite sides of the dock. Now they just had to get in position and wait.

The Chief went back into the water and swam to the other side of the dock. The thickness of the concrete above him would muffle any noise he might make if he ran into more infected dead. He wasn't surprised to find they were tied to the pilings, but he had to silence each of them quickly before they sounded the alarm with their eerie groaning. When he got to the other side and was across from the two men, he checked his surroundings before settling in to wait.

Captain Miller gave the Chief a head start before slipping into the water and swimming to the spot directly below where the two men sat, while Cassandra went inland and took cover behind an abandoned car that sat near the entrance of the pier. It would be her job to radio the Chief and Captain Miller to tell them what their targets were doing and if it was possible to take them out.

A little more than a half-hour later, one of the men got up and walked to the other side of the pier and stopped directly above the Chief. The other man remained seated, but he turned his attention away toward the quay where small boats were at anchor. Cassandra radioed the Chief and Captain Miller just as the first guard stood up and walked away. She could tell that the Chief was going to be able to catch his target by surprise, but she wasn't so sure about Captain

Miller.

Her gut told her that waiting for luck to give them a hand wasn't an option, and any moment she would see the Chief pull his target over the side. If he did it too soon, the other target might have time to shout a warning. Cassandra picked up a piece of gravel that was just heavy enough for her to throw with accuracy and gave it a heave straight at the sitting target. She didn't want it to hit him, just make him turn his head. It landed on the pier about ten feet short of him and bounced to a stop. His head turned, and his eyes went downward.

Cassandra saw two large shadows rise from the sides of the pier. The target on the Chief's side was facing his killer, but his hands were occupied, and his brain didn't catch up to the facts fast enough. The Chief used one hand to clutch the man's shirt at the middle of his chest and pull forward. The other hand had a knife pointed upward at the man's chin. It slid in all the way to the hilt without a sound.

Captain Miller's target was a tougher kill, but Cassandra's timing had been good. As the rock came to a stop, and the man flexed his leg muscles to stand, there was a resistance that pulled him sideways as Captain Miller gripped his shirt collar. If it was a football game, he would have gotten a personal foul penalty because it was called a horse-collar tackle. The man didn't cry out because all he knew was that he was going in the wrong direction. Then he didn't know anything as the Captain's knife did the rest.

The pier was long enough that the main pumps were in total darkness in the distance. Neither of the guards had a radio, so the process of eliminating the others would be easier. Captain Miller was about the same size as the guards, so he stripped one out of his clothes and put them on over his wetsuit. This time they wouldn't wait for them to take a restroom break. They decided he would walk right up to them. They set their watches for ten minutes, which should be more than enough time for the Chief and Cassandra to use the raft to get to the end of the pier. Even though they had to circle outward far enough not to be seen, they were certain they could be where they needed to be in less time.

When the time was up, Captain Miller picked up the rifle belonging to the guard he had killed and slung it across his back in a relaxed manner, then he walked at a leisurely pace toward the end of the pier. He was careful to walk quietly but not so quietly that it would surprise the guards. He also didn't want to be so relaxed that his slouch would make him appear to be an infected dead. He apparently did a good job because he could tell when the guards glanced in his direction and watched him approach for a few seconds. Then they went back to whatever it was they had been doing on a small table between their chairs.

It turned out to be a card game that they could finish later because they didn't need to be killed. When they turned their attention back to their card game, Captain Miller unslung the rifle as he walked. By the time they realized it wasn't one of the guards from the other pump, he was close enough to order them to freeze. Any thought of resisting or reaching for their weapons was erased by the appearance of the Chief and Cassandra. Clad in their black wetsuits, they were shocking enough, but the size of the Chief made them both incapable of moving.

They made quick work of gagging the two men and tying them to their chairs. The less they could tell someone else about the encounter, the better. So burlap sacks were draped over their heads. They would be able to hear people moving, and they would hear the Maggie Mae, but they wouldn't be able to describe the boat or the crew.

The Chief keyed his radio and said in a low voice, "It's clear."

He could hear the tug idle up just a little, but the engine ran so smoothly that it seemed to glide in out of the dark. By the time it was in position by the dock, Cassandra had the fuel hoses ready to go. There were two, and they wanted as much as they could get.

Captain Miller climbed over the railing of the Maggie Mae and spread out a map. By the time the fuel had been topped off, he knew which direction they were going next. They had said their goodbyes earlier, but there was still time for quick handshakes and hugs. The plan was for Andi and the three brothers to go far enough from shore to avoid detection and possibly find a place where they could drop anchor. The charts showed an uninhabited island to the northwest named Samson, and southwest of there were some rocks that could provide a place to hide. They could drop their anchor and cut off the engines to save fuel. Andi said she could give them six to eight weeks to return, but they should keep in mind that she might have to make a run for it if detected.

The Chief had told her they would be back within radio range in less than twenty-four hours if they couldn't get a plane in the air, but if she didn't hear from them by then, she could assume they had gotten lucky. The main thing was to keep the Maggie Mae and her crew safe by not giving the sub a chance to find them. If they could find a plane, the sub would sit out there and wonder where they went until it finally gave up the hunt.

The Chief didn't surprise easily, but sometimes he was a bit naive about women. When he held out his hand to shake Andi's and to thank her for getting them this far, he was caught off guard by the way she pulled him closer and kissed him on the mouth. Iris had her back to them when it happened, but Kathy had a front-row seat to the show. Her eyes went wide, but she was mostly just amused by the big man's inability to avoid what was coming. He was like a deer caught in the headlights of an onrushing vehicle.

That was earlier when everyone had a chance to say goodbye, and Kathy wasn't surprised that the Chief didn't let it happen again. He stayed on the dock and gave a shy wave to Andi as she got ready to glide the Maggie Mae back out of the quay. Kathy thought if she was reading Andi right, she was enjoying making the Chief uncomfortable, but just like Iris, she was well aware of the attraction Andi had for the Chief.

Now that there was distance increasing between the boat and the dock, they formed up in single file with Cassandra in the lead, and the Chief's mind was able to go into a more comfortable place. This was combat, and he was at home as he hefted a canvas bag of gear onto his shoulders and fell in behind Hampton.

Kathy brought up the rear, but before taking her place in line, she leaned close to the right ear of one of the two guards.

"We know we can't just leave you tied up here on this dock," she whispered. "That would be inhumane. One of those infected could get lucky and find you before you got free, or you could blindly fall off the dock while trying to untie yourselves."

As he listened, the man undoubtedly thought she was going to kill him, so he was surprised when she slipped the handle of a knife between his fingers where they were tied behind his back.

"I want you to count to one thousand before you begin cutting at the rope. Can you do that for me?"

The head under the burlap sack was nodding before she finished the question.

Kathy caught up with the group and fell in behind Tom. He glanced back at her with a grin.

"How long did you tell him to wait?"

In a low laugh, Kathy said, "I told him to count to one thousand. I'm willing to bet he started cutting when he reached ten, but that was a pretty dull knife, so it'll take him until a thousand to cut the ropes."

* * *

******

Strung out ahead of Kathy and Tom, they could tell the members of the group by the way they moved. Cassandra was way up front, with Sim following a few paces behind her. Sim was followed by Captain Miller. He was the one who had mapped out the short distance they had to travel to reach the airport, so he could relay directions to Cassandra through Sim. Then came Iris, the Chief, Henry, Colleen, Hampton, Tom, and Kathy. Kathy watched with pride as the group moved from one piece of cover to the next and marveled at the difference between the way they did things now compared to seven years ago. The only member of the group with a gun pointed ahead of them was Cassandra, and she would only shoot if caught off guard.

Cassandra held up a fist to signal a stop, and she went to one knee. Captain Miller used only a few words but mostly hand signals to give her instructions. They had made good time without seeing people, whether alive or dead, and they had apparently left the populated part of the island behind because there were trees and fields ahead. If you asked any one of them, they preferred the part with buildings because it was easier to see movement on the roads.

A street sign said they had been following Telegraph Road, and Captain Miller directed Cassandra to turn to the east into a field. He let Iris know to pass the word that they had to go about a mile through the tall grass and trees, and Cassandra should have the Chief toward the front with her. His SEAL night combat training would be a big asset from this point on.

The Chief moved ahead of Sim and whispered to Cassandra that he was there. She didn't turn around, but she acknowledged him by tapping on her right ear. He saw her hesitation as her hand froze by the side of her head after the tap. It didn't turn into a fist immediately because she wasn't sure of what she was seeing, but then it closed shut, and she dropped to a knee. Everyone behind her did the same.

The Chief counted to ten before he eased up by Cassandra's right shoulder. His night vision had always been good, but there was something up ahead that was spoiling it. Someone was actually using a lantern to light up their campsite. That meant they were either stupid or very sure of themselves. If it was the latter, they could already be in a trap.

"Can you see anyone inside the light?" he whispered.

Cassandra shook her head from side to side as her eyes tried unsuccessfully to locate anything that resembled a person. The Chief rotated further to the right to be sure they weren't being flanked. The glow of a second lantern spread through a thick crop of trees about two hundred yards to their right, and there was a faint sound behind him that he knew was a signal from Kathy.

Captain Miller whispered, "There's a light behind us. It came from the last street we passed after we left the road. Someone was waiting there then fell in behind us."

"That doesn't make sense," answered the Chief. "Have Kathy slide off into the bushes and wait for the light to pass her."

The Chief got Cassandra's attention, pointed across the fields to the second light, and then told her about the light behind them.

"What do you make of it?" she asked.

"Not sure," he said, "but I thought someone was trying to herd us to go straight between the lights when I saw the second one. Might've worked if not for the one behind us."

"I agree. They either have the upper hand, and they know it, or maybe they want us to see them."

The Chief considered Cassandra's guess for a moment and then realized, if you wanted to get the attention of a group that moved like commandos, you wouldn't do it by making noise.

"Kathy is going to take cover and let the light pass her. We'll know in a few minutes what we've stepped in."

Cassandra and the Chief led the group at a slow pace in a direct line toward the midpoint between the two lanterns. They moved just fast enough to keep from arousing the suspicions of their follower so Kathy could get in position behind them. Less than ten minutes later, word came up the line that the light behind them had gone out.

The lanterns in the trees to their left and right made it harder for them to adjust to the dark places, but the Chief could see well enough to know Kathy was coming to the front in a hurry. Next to her was a woman in uniform. The uniform was less than complete after so many years, but just as Captain Miller and Cassandra still wore their old uniforms as if they were born in them, this appeared to be a soldier who had hung onto her training. She carried the now extinguished lantern in one hand by her side, but the only weapon he could see was a long knife on her hip. He guessed she must have been young when the infection started because she couldn't be a day over thirty.

It took a moment for everyone to realize they could see a little better because it was totally dark again. The lights to their left and right had gone out, and everyone went into a defensive posture as they unslung their M4 rifles. Each of them tried to locate the threat they were sure would come next.

"I signaled for them to go dark by turning off my lantern," said the woman. "They'll wait where they are until I signal them again, but it isn't safe here. You must be going to the airport, and we had to stop you somehow without getting shot."

"How many are there?" asked the Chief.

"There are just the three of us girls left now," answered the woman. "Are you the leader, Sir? May I summon them to come in?"

The Chief could see that the woman was almost holding her breath as she spoke, and he had to remind himself that not everyone was equipped to survive the way they had. They were long-term survivors who had become a force to be reckoned with, but they had their fair share of close calls and brushes with death. They had lost people, but somehow they had survived long enough to find themselves an ocean away from home. This young lady had her own story, but he couldn't imagine it was too great for her on this little island.

In a gentler voice that made Iris proud of her husband, he told the soldier to take Cassandra, Kathy, and Colleen with her to retrieve the others. It would be safer and would draw less attention.

"Collect the first one and drop her off with us, then get the second one. After you get back, you can give us whatever intel we need before going the rest of the way to the airport. We'll wait here in the tall grass where we can at least see in all directions. I'm not keen on the idea of going into the trees at night."

"Yes, Sir."

Being an enlisted man in the Navy, the Chief wasn't totally comfortable with the salute she gave him, but he could see the relief and something close to pure joy on her young features. He had a distinct feeling that they had just rescued someone else.

The foursome disappeared into the darkness and the tall grass. Within seconds there was no trace of them, and the remainder of the group spread out in the darkness and waited in silence. Fifteen minutes later, there was the faintest of signals from Cassandra that they were coming back. They quickly deposited another young woman who stared at the Chief with wide eyes, and then they disappeared again just as quickly. This one seemed too afraid to speak, and Iris put an arm around her as they crouched low in the grass. Whatever it was

Iris whispered to her, it appeared to help. The girl nodded and visibly relaxed.

It took longer for them to return a second time, and the Chief was just beginning to worry when he heard Cassandra again. The third member of their party was more self-assured and gave them all a cheerful smile, but for the same reason, the others had been relieved and amazed. She was glad to be rescued.

"We can do introductions later when we're in a safer place," said the Chief. "For now, I just need to know who the ranking soldier is."

"We're all the same rank, Sir. We're Privates, or at least that's what we were before," said the one who had followed behind them with the lantern. "I'm Private Ellie Bowles, that's Private Chloe Haddock, and that's Private Isabella Dixon."

"You can call me Izzy," said the one with who had come in last. "After this long, I don't think we're Privates anymore."

The Chief shook her hand when she offered it because he didn't want to make them worry that they had made a bad judgment call by getting their attention. As a matter of fact, he wondered what it was about his group that made the three women believe it was safe to intercept them. That could wait until later, but he filed it away in the back of his mind that maybe he was the one making a bad judgment call.

"Like I said, introductions can wait. We have a lot of names for you to remember, but we need to keep moving. What can you tell us about the airport? Are there any planes that still fly?"

Ellie said, "That's why we had to stop you. We could guess you were going to the airport. That's what we would be doing if we were trying to get off this island, but the airport is controlled by the same people who control the fuel pumps at the dock."

"How long have you been watching us?" asked Kathy.

None of them answered at first, but Izzy finally spoke up in a shy tone that gave the impression they were concerned about how the Chief and his people might take the answer. She said it more like a question than a statement of fact.

"Since you came ashore?"

Instead of becoming angry, the Chief asked, "How bad are the people on the dock and at the airport that they don't know we're here?"

The unspoken words that were exchanged through eye contact between the women were all he needed. He had turned it around to make it sound like he thought his group was brighter than the people running the island, and he read the insult in their faces.

The Chief whispered to Captain Miller but didn't try to hide what he was saying from anyone.

"Heard enough?"

Instead of answering the Chief directly, he took it as his cue to act, and he raised his M4 in their direction. In the darkness, they couldn't read the expression on his face, but they understood his meaning and raised their hands.

"If you make a sound, all three of you will be shot."

Captain Miller's voice was so calm and low that they didn't doubt his threat.

Colleen asked, "What's happening here? What did I miss?"

Kathy answered for the Chief by stepping behind Izzy and pulling a strip of cloth around her face to gag her. Cassandra joined her as they did the same for the other two and then tied their hands behind their backs.

Being stuck in the middle of an open field with nothing for cover except tall grass was not the best place to make a stand, but going into the trees to their left or right when they couldn't use flashlights would be worse. With the three young women secured, the Chief pulled everyone in close to explain what he had in mind and to see if anyone else had a better plan.

"They had time to set us up," he began, "or else they've used this trap before. They're young enough looking and harmless enough that anyone would fall for it."

"The guys on the dock," said Kathy. "We left them a way to cut themselves loose rather than to leave them to be eaten. You think they had a radio we didn't see?"

Hampton was like his wife and had been fooled by the trap, so he was still processing how he had missed it. It made him feel like they should be dead now, and that made him feel like he had failed to protect his wife.

He asked, "Are we ready to start killing everyone we meet because they might be bad guys?"

Kathy said, "If you're asking me if I think it was a mistake to give him a knife so they wouldn't get killed, we did what we thought was the right thing at the time. We couldn't take the dock without killing the first two guards, but there's no way that we're going to kill everyone that stands in our way. We don't know what we're up against yet, but we've been in worse situations."

Tom pulled a small rain cover out of his pack and unfolded it on the ground. The tall grass helped him make it like a small tent, and he was able to use a penlight to examine a map he had gotten from Andi's supply of charts. The Chief crawled under from the other side, and a moment later, Kathy appeared next to him.

"See anything useful?" asked the Chief.

Tom put his finger on a spot and said, "According to this map, we're protected only a few yards ahead by this small pond. If it's deep enough, no one can attack from that direction. That leaves three sides to protect."

Kathy said, "I don't think anyone will attack now that we have three of their people as hostages."

"Depends on how mad they are about the two we killed at the dock," answered the Chief, "and now that I think about it, if they could spare four people to guard the dock at night, they might be a sizable force. We couldn't have done it any different, though. The infected dead they used to mine the quay were probably people who had asked for fuel."

"What do you think they expect us to do?" asked Tom.

"Retreat," answered the Chief. "If they've used this trap before, my guess is that they've seen what people in the trap did. Left, right, or backward is where people had to go, so that's where they will be waiting. Let's see what they do if we cross the pond. If we do it fast enough, we might be able to reach the airport before they know where we went."

"One more thing," said Tom.

He moved his finger in a straight line across the pond to the small airport.

"If there are planes, where would they be, and wouldn't they be guarded?"

The Chief answered, "When you have no intel, assume the best and the worst. There will be planes, and they will be guarded."

"They'll also be fueled," said Kathy.

They found that the pond was surrounded by trees and low bushes, but they were sparse and didn't provide much cover. They decided to tie the hostages together on one tree and leave them at the edge of the pond because it would slow them down too much to drag them along. Blindfolds were added to the gags because it would give the group a few more seconds head start before the women were tempted to make noise. They moved silently using hand signals, and the only thing anyone said was what the Chief whispered to the three women.

"We're not leaving a knife to use to free yourselves like we did for your friends. If you make a sound, hope your friends hear you before any infected dead come along. You may think there aren't any out there, but I saw three less than twenty yards from here."

The last part was a bluff, and he could tell by the way their heads turned left and right that they had bought it. They couldn't see anything, and maybe that would keep them quiet long enough. The Chief circled the air with one finger over his head, and the group moved out fast.

In their usual order, they entered the pond and found the water to be deep enough for them to be forced to swim. To the Chief, it was just like SEAL training, but the water wasn't cold. Some of the others, Sim and Henry, in particular, weren't good swimmers, but with the help of the others, they stayed above water and kept moving forward. Fortunately, the bottom appeared suddenly, and although it was a bit soft, there were enough rocks for them to pick up the pace and walk the rest of the way.

Cassandra stayed with the plan and kept moving once they were out of the water, and there was no opposition waiting for them. In their minds, they could picture the people who ran things on the island. They had years to practice this trap, and right now, they were waiting for their prey to appear somewhere else, so time was on their side as long as they put some distance between themselves and where they left the three young women.

The airport appeared ahead, and Cassandra pointed toward the back of a low building. The windows had been covered with paper, but they could still see a faint light glowing inside. Next to the building, there was a row of three twin-engine planes facing away from them. One was missing a propeller, so they knew it wouldn't be guarded. The best the Chief was hoping for was that the guards would be inside the building because they had gotten sloppy, but that was too much to hope for.

Cassandra saw the infected dead first, and it reminded her what kind of people they were dealing with. There were two of them, and she signaled that she had eyes on something. The others all saw them too. Each of the infected was attached to a thirty-foot leash that allowed them to walk around the planes. There was just enough light for everyone to read the signs that hung around the necks of the infected. They said, "I ASKED FOR A PLANE."

"How do we know which plane to take?" asked Cassandra.

"The infected haven't seen us yet, or they would be making noise. Three groups...Cassandra and Kathy take out the infected before they have a chance to sound the alarm. Then get in position to shoot anyone who pops out of the building. Henry is behind the stick on the plane in the middle, and I'm flying the one on the left. Everyone else split evenly and follow the pilots."

Iris asked, "We're taking both planes?"

"These people don't need them," answered the Chief.

"Or deserve them," added Kathy.

The Mud Island survivor group had worked with each other as a team for so long that the Chief didn't need to assign everyone to specific teams. Everyone just naturally fell in behind Kathy and Cassandra as they rushed the two infected dead. They were fast, but the dead moaned a split second before they arrived, and that meant whoever was inside the low building had been warned. Both of the women took out their targets and immediately dropped to a knee, swirled their rifles to the front, and took aim on the door.

The door opened outward, shielding the men inside for a moment, but that worked more to the advantage of Kathy and Cassandra. They knew the men would have to come around the door to see the airplanes and whatever it was that had disturbed their warning system. They shifted their aim slightly to the right and pulled their triggers at the same time. The first man was punched by both bullets and knocked to the ground, but the second man had the sense to grab the doorknob and pull the door shut.

"Cover the window," said Kathy as she moved from where she was around to the front of the building. She put two more bullets into the door to give the man inside something to think about. Behind her, she heard Cassandra fire a short burst at the window.

"He's down, but there may be more," said Cassandra.

Kathy heard both planes roar to life behind her, but she didn't take her eyes off the door. Another man inside must have thought she was escaping because the door burst open for a second time. Going from a lit room to the darkness outside made him blind to the spot where Kathy was standing, and Kathy could see the mistake register on his face. For some reason, she had a mental image of him placing the signs around the necks of the infected dead, and she felt no remorse as she pulled the trigger.

Both planes were already rolling forward, and Cassandra accepted the hand extended from the open door of the first one to go by her. Hampton used his long reach to pull her inside as it turned and rolled past Kathy. The second plane was following close behind the first, and Kathy kept her eyes on the light from the doorway until the last second. She slung her rifle over her head and neck, whirled around, and threw out her hand all in one motion. She knew from the feel that it was Tom's strong hand that had hers in its grasp, and she let her momentum carry her through the open door.

Henry rapidly got into position at the end of the runway and didn't hesitate to apply full throttle. If he hadn't gone immediately, the Chief would have collided with him because his plane was moving forward as if there wasn't another in front of him. Both planes cleared the end of the runway just as some very angry people fired weapons in their direction. Then they watched in frustration as the planes banked toward the mainland.

******

The planes were what they had hoped for and more, and it wasn't lost on any of them that they might as well have been parked on that runway for the Chief. They could tell he was overjoyed to be flying it, and Henry even had some stick-time on one. They were former military aircraft named the Short C-23 Sherpa. Made in Northern Ireland, they were built to operate from unpaved runways, so it made sense that they were used for island hopping to the tourist attractions. They could carry up to thirty passengers and had been the primary means of transportation between the islands since being retired from military service.

Everyone had room to spread out, but it wasn't going to be a long trip. The Chief told them all to catch their breath and get something to eat because they would be landing at the airport north of Bournemouth in just about an hour. With daylight only about two hours away, they would be leaving for Henry's house shortly after landing. Henry could hardly breathe, and he wasn't hungry. He just wanted to get home.

The planes felt like they were racing toward their goal even though most of the world below was too dark to see, but they were flying low at over two hundred knots, and what they could see went by fast. Despite what the Chief had said, relaxing wasn't something they could do. They had traveled a continent away from home, and they were finally about to get their first look at what the infection had done to another country. Before they knew it, the Chief announced that he had a visual on the runways, and they were going to do a pass to decide whether or not it was safe to land.

Everyone was at a window when the two planes dipped lower and slowed their forward speed to a crawl compared to the cruise speed. There were no lights, but they were only trying to judge whether or not the runways were clear enough for them to land. The Sherpas could land with some debris on the runways but not if the debris was vehicles. There was just enough light for them to tell that one of the two main runways was choked with the burned-out hulks of airplanes and fuel trucks. The second runway wasn't as bad, but it was not going to be safe to land on it. The debris was more random and spread out in a way that would cause them to have to navigate the runway. It looked like their only choice was going to be one of the service roads along the side of the airport.

They brought the planes around for a second pass when Henry abruptly changed directions.

"I have a visual on a clean landing area," he said over the radio.

The Chief didn't see it, so he matched Henry's course. Sim was in the co-pilot seat, and he didn't see anything except the service road for the small, private planes.

"Henry, this is Sim. Are you talking about that service road? It's not straight."

"I don't plan to use that part of it," answered Henry. "It's more than enough room to land. What do you say, Chief? Is that about twelve hundred meters to you?"

"About twelve hundred and one meters," said Sim. "That will give us one meter to play with."

18

Hello

Southern England - Year Eight

Symone knew better than to be on the ground waiting for the soldiers, but it was everything she could do to make herself stay in the tower. She kept her binoculars trained on the last place she had seen the soldiers for a full minute after they had disappeared into the trees coming in her direction. It was a broad tract of heavy woods, and she knew it could take them over an hour before they would emerge on her side. Two hours later, she was switching back and forth between her side of the trees and the area near the tunnel.

Below the tower, there were at least a dozen of the infected wandering around in search of the siren, and she had no doubt there would be more. She knew she could stay in the tower for several days, but her dream of leaving the tower for the tunnel was fading just like a dream that faded right after waking up. She tried to cling to the memories of the dream, but by the time the sun reached the horizon, she wondered if that was what it had been...nothing more than a dream. She had imagined the soldiers because that was what she wanted to see.

"No, Symone...they were real. I saw them, and I made them see me. It wasn't my imagination."

After saying it out loud, she knew it had been real. She just didn't know where the soldiers had gone, but she was sure she had seen them. The sun dipped lower, and darkness spread over the runway. There were now dozens of the infected whose dark shadows dotted everywhere she could see. She had called together a horde, and if the soldiers were still out there, they couldn't possibly help her without putting their own lives at risk. What bothered her the most, though, was their total disappearance. She had to consider the possibility that they had encountered the infected in the forest, but she quickly put that idea aside because she would have heard the firefight over the groaning below.

"No, they must've gone somewhere else after I lost sight of them," she said aloud, "but where?"

Despair settled over Symone, and she sat her binoculars aside. She felt tired, so she lowered herself to the small cot she had made on the floor. Right now, sleeping was the only way she could deal with failure. She had gotten her hopes up so high that she had actually envisioned her children waiting for her inside the tunnel. She saw them the way they had been at first. They were just small children. Emily was still six, and Adam was still four. Then she saw them as the children they would be now. Adam would be close to twelve years old, and Emily would be about fourteen.

"All of those years have been lost," she said as she drifted off to sleep.

******

The two planes came in low with Henry in the lead, and he spotted his home easily. Before the infected dead had arrived and before he had flown to the International Space Station, he and Adam Callaway had made it a tradition to fly over the house and wag the wings of their jet aircraft. They knew Symone, Emily, and Adam would be outside waving at them.

Henry dipped lower with the plane into a tight arc so they could get a longer look at the house and its surroundings. The only movement they saw was a small horde on the highway that ran in a straight line to the south.

Kathy's voice came over the radio to tell both planes she had spotted a possible landing area.

"We can check the conditions at the airport first, but I think I've found something interesting. I don't know what it is, but it has a long stretch of pavement next to it."

She called out the coordinates, and Henry led the way to something that he had never given much attention. From the air, it had the appearance of being an abandoned airstrip, but it was most likely some form of an industrial park that had been under construction when the infection had arrived. Whatever it was, they could land and walk to his house in little more than an hour.

The Chief brought his Sherpa in closer to the paved area and said over the radio, "I don't know what it is, but it's less populated than the airport. Before we land, let's make a pass to the north and see what's happening there. Maybe we missed something at the airport."

Henry was glad to oblige, but the idea of landing and being home within the hour was much more appealing than landing at the Bournemouth airport.

"We already saw what's happened there," he said. "There's a tangle of wreckage on the runways and tall grass in between. There's an army of the infected walking among the planes that never made it off the ground or were crazy enough to land. What would make us want to land there?"

"We have plenty of fuel," said the Chief, "but we have to be sure the British military didn't at least hang on to something as important as an airfield. Wouldn't it be great to find someone who had survived? Besides, Henry, airfields have hangars, and I'd prefer to hide these planes rather than to leave them parked out in the open."

Henry was desperate to see his wife and children, but he was still a military man, and he had to remember they were in a war that demanded strategy. He begrudgingly agreed with the Chief's plan to at least take a look at the airport again, and the planes banked together in that direction.

It was only minutes later when they made a second pass over the runway, and with more light from the approaching dawn, they all had to admit it was worse than they had seen on the first pass. When Henry said there would be a tangle of wreckage, he had delivered an understatement. More than one plane must have tried to land at the same time, possibly because they didn't have enough fuel to stay in the air while others landed ahead of them. There appeared to have been a chain reaction on the runway, and the worst wreckage was where planes had tried unsuccessfully to land and then avoid other planes. So, the worst wreckage was practically everywhere.

Sim was reminded of the scene at the airport in Columbus when they first landed. The airport where they had landed with the

President of the United States on board was a chaotic mess. The runways were jammed with the infected, and planes had become mired in the soft patches of grass between the runways. Countless thousands of people had died ugly deaths, but it was compounded when desperate pilots had attempted to break free from the congestion by getting their planes back into the air. Collisions on the ground and in the air caused many people to die, but it was almost better than being consumed by the mobs of infected that roamed almost every square foot of the airport.

That had been a large airport compared to the one below them. In a way, this was worse because so many planes had attempted to land, and they had fewer places to do so. Blackened hulks of passenger planes were locked together like a jigsaw puzzle, and when one exploded and burned, the flames spread easily to the others.

"Unsafe to land," said Henry over the radio.

"Roger that," said the Chief. "Proceed to the second site."

Henry didn't waste any time getting back to the landing site Kathy had spotted, and the Chief was right behind him. Both planes touched down seconds apart and came to a stop two-thirds of the way down the straight stretch of pavement. A long, concrete building sat alongside the makeshift landing strip, and the Chief instructed Henry to stop across from the building. There was still well over a hundred yards of space between them and the building, but as they had agreed on the way, they wanted to land and shut down their engines as fast as possible. To the opposite side of them, there was nothing but a heavily forested area with farmland beyond. Hopefully, they wouldn't attract too much attention before going quiet.

Everyone got out of the planes and spread out to face all directions. First and foremost, they had to decide if it was safe to be on the ground, so everyone who had a pair of binoculars was using them to search for the activity they might have attracted.

"Along the tree line," said Cassandra. "I have three infected dead about fifty yards away and closing. I'll save my ammo and go get them. Someone cover me."

Cassandra shouldered her rifle and pulled out her machete. It would only take about three minutes for her to engage the infected, so Tom and Hampton spread out to her left and right to take aim at them. In the meantime, Kathy had spotted two more at the far end of the runway. The Chief suggested that it would be better to let them get closer before eliminating them. By the time Cassandra got back from disposing of the group by the trees, they were closer, so they used the same approach with the newcomers. Cassandra went with Kathy to help move the bodies off of their new runway.

They divided into two groups, with Hampton staying behind in charge of one group to guard the planes. They had plenty of daylight left, so they knew the other group could make it to Henry's house and return before it would get dark. Taking off from an unlit airstrip at night was not as easy as doing it in broad daylight. The Chief, Kathy, and Cassandra went with Henry in the direction of his home.

******

Henry had no illusions about what he would find, but he had to cling to his hope. He hoped he would burst into the house after being gone over seven years, and he would find by some miracle that his wife and children had endured. When they left the cover of the trees near the edge of the property, he broke into a run and sprinted toward the back door. It was open, and he knew that wasn't good.

The wooden porch in front of the door was stained black, and the smell was of old rot. The heap of moldy flesh wrapped in what had been a shirt and jeans was likely the cause of the smell. It lay half in and half out of the doorway, and Henry had to step over it.

Henry saw where the refrigerator was and knew instinctively that his wife must have been responsible for moving it. He went straight for the open cellar door, and the winch that was fastened to the steps reminded him of how smart Symone could be.

When the others came into the kitchen behind him, Henry was still standing in the open cellar doorway, one hand gripping the door and the other gripping the frame across from it. He stared down into the darkness below but gave no indication that he was aware of either them or something below.

"Henry? Are they here?" asked Kathy.

He didn't appear to have heard her, so she opened her mouth to ask again, but he cut her off.

"I don't want to be the one who finds them," he said. "I didn't think before. What if they're down there? What if I find them like that guy?" he gestured toward the long-dead man in the doorway.

"We've got this, Henry. You stay up here with the Chief. Cassandra and I will check for you."

Kathy placed a gentle hand on his arm and eased him away from the opening. Cassandra clicked on a flashlight and took the first few steps carefully, not wanting to trip or run into something that had been unable to get back up the stairs. She saw the winch and put two and two together just like Henry. Someone, probably Henry's wife, had used the winch to pull the refrigerator over in front of the door.

The beam of her flashlight cut through total darkness, so she took her time. Kathy's beam joined hers, and all they could see was a ransacked cellar. There weren't any bodies, and it had obviously been searched more than once by people desperate for supplies. It didn't take long for them to come to the conclusion that Henry's family wasn't in the cellar, so they rejoined Henry and the Chief to search the rest of the house.

They had a momentary scare when they discovered more bodies in the master bedroom, and Kathy moved to keep Henry from seeing them, but he couldn't stop himself and pushed past her. His relief was palpable, and then he felt sorry for the people who had died there. He was on such a rollercoaster of emotions that he couldn't stand it anymore, and he rushed to check his children's rooms. The doors were closed, but the rooms were empty of people, either dead or living. Henry sat down on his son's bed and put his head in his hands.

The Chief motioned to Kathy and Cassandra to follow him, and the trio descended the staircase to the first floor.

"We need to give him a few minutes by himself," he said.

"Where do we go from here?" asked Kathy. "I don't think any of us really expected to find her or the children still hiding in the house, but we've seen stranger things."

"I haven't the slightest idea," answered the Chief, "but I've been giving some thought to the discussion we had with Henry about his suspicion that more soil was removed from the tunnel than necessary. We might as well go have a look at the tunnel, but I don't expect to find someone outside with a sign that says welcome on it."

Henry emerged from the room and walked slowly down the stairs. All the others could do was wait for him to speak because there wasn't even a clue for them to follow.

"We've come a long way," he said in a clear but low voice. "You good people got me back to my home at the risk of your own lives. I won't ask you to take another step for me. You should make your way back to Andi and get back to your homes."

Three heads were shaking from side to side even before he finished speaking.

Even before he finished the last few words, Kathy was giving him an answer for the whole group.

"You misunderstood what we said we were going to do. If we just wanted to drop you off in England and send you on your merry way, we would have told you so a long time ago, but I seem to recall that we said we would get you back together with your family. So don't be in such a rush to push us out the door."

They could tell he wasn't going to argue with them, but he felt bound by honor to release them from any obligations they had placed upon themselves.

"Let's get back to the others," said the Chief. "We'll have a plan before nightfall."

******

By the time the Chief and the others got back to the planes and the rest of the group, they knew it wasn't going to be an easy decision about what to do next. While they had been gone, the others had gone to the perimeter three times to dispose of infected dead that were stumbling in their direction. That meant only one thing…there were still plenty of them in the surrounding areas, and the closer they got to London, the more they were likely to encounter hordes. The discussions and ideas dragged on long enough that nightfall was on them, and they didn't have a plan.

On a positive note, they could at least sleep comfortably inside the planes because they were each big enough for thirty people. Even though there were two planes, all of them except the two on watch were gathered inside one, so they could talk over their options. They were even able to cover the windows so no light could be seen from outside. Hampton and Colleen had drawn the short straws first, and the others were just tossing out ideas to see if anyone could come up with something new. By ten o'clock, they were repeating old ideas. By midnight everyone was too burned out to keep trying, but Henry lit a spark under the whole group with one comment.

"Did any of you know that Titus Rush met with the Queen on several occasions? I read all about him while we were in the Huntsville shelter. Quite an impressive man, from what I understand. He was somewhat of a hippy but brilliant in his own way."

Henry hadn't noticed the way everyone had gone silent and were just staring at him. He kept talking for another minute until Kathy held up her hand like a school girl wanting to be called on. It was apparently becoming a habit with their group. The gesture made him chuckle, but then the others followed Kathy's lead and raised their hands. He pointed at Kathy.

"Tell us everything you read about Titus Rush meeting with the Queen of England," she said.

"Well, I read that Her Majesty was so pleased with Mr. Rush that she offered him a knighthood. He declined the offer saying that it was an honor that was best reserved for subjects of the crown and that he was deeply moved by the offer. So, instead of being knighted and becoming Sir Rush, she made him an honorary officer in the Grenadier Guards. He apparently had done something of great importance for the Queen, but the text I was reading didn't disclose the nature of his service."

"Oh…my…God," said Kathy. "There's a shelter somewhere around here."

Iris said, "All we have to do is find it."

Everyone was suddenly energized, and Henry felt real hope for the first time since finding his home to be little more than a moldy burial vault.

The Chief said, "Okay, everyone. No idea is stupid unless you keep it to yourself. These are all maps of England. If you were Titus Rush, where would you put a shelter?"

"Something doesn't fit," said Henry. "I've always suspected that the Channel Tunnel was a cover for something else because there was so much soil dug out from under the English Channel, but the Treaty of Canterbury wasn't signed until 1986."

Colleen was curled up under a blanket and studying a map not far from the main group. She and Hampton had finished their turn on watch, and she felt like she would never get used to the cold, damp air outside.

She said, "Treaty of Canterbury…wasn't that the name they gave to the agreement to build the tunnel?"

"How did you know that?" asked Hampton.

She gave him a mock frown that made grooves appear across her little Irish nose and said, "I read."

Hampton knew enough about women to quickly add, "I'm impressed. I don't think any of the rest of us knew that."

"You may still be onto something though, Henry," said the Chief. "Remember, some of the shelters weren't built overnight. The one at

Fort Sumter took a decade, but the shelter at Mud Island was ready in just over a year. The hardest part of that one was the moat and the power plant, but it was a relatively simple operation compared to the big ones."

Iris added, "The shelter under Ambassadors Island took eight years to build."

Captain Miller said, "Maybe England only built one, so they began it around 1970 and then added to it after 1986."

That Chief got that intense expression on his face that meant someone had given him the answer. It was a cross between satisfaction, amusement, and determination.

He said, "Added to it or connected to it. What if they took the opportunity to build the back door in 1986 by connecting to the Channel Tunnel while it was being built? Henry, you said more soil was dug out of the Channel than necessary, but what does it translate to? Was it twice as much?"

Henry rubbed his chin and thought back to his discussions with Adam Callaway. It was so long ago, but he remembered it like it was yesterday.

"The Channel Tunnel is only thirty-one miles long," he began, "and of course, not all of the soil was brought out onto the English side. Roughly half would have been hauled to France, but long after they completed the connection under the Channel, they were still hauling truckloads of soil from the entrance near Folkestone."

"How long after?" asked Kathy.

"Months," said Henry.

Hampton was still engrossed in the map spread out in front of him. He had been proud of Colleen's knowledge of the Treaty of Canterbury, especially since no one else besides Henry had known about it, but it had drawn his eyes to one spot. Canterbury...the place where they signed the treaty, was only about twenty miles from Folkestone, but northwest of Canterbury was a vaguely familiar island.

"Hey, Chief, this island is shaped like a big version of Mud Island."

Hampton didn't have to say it twice because it was too much of a coincidence. Hampton had his finger sitting on an island roughly twenty miles northwest of Canterbury. It was large compared to Mud Island, and according to the scale on their map, the area of the Isle of Sheppey was around thirty-five to forty square miles. That was about right for the Queen of England and a few more people.

Henry launched into a fascinating history lesson about the island,

and the more he said, the more they fell in love with the idea that Titus Rush had worked his magic somewhere on the island. First of all, it was somewhat isolated from the mainland. Sitting at the mouth of the Thames River, it was surrounded by water on all sides, and it could only be accessed by one road or by boat. The main reason they thought it was a fitting place for a shelter was because of the irony in its history. It was apparently the site of many battles with Vikings and was occupied by invading forces many times. It was a very strong possibility that the last stand against the infection in England was on the island where they had defended their sovereignty many times.

"Thirty-five square miles is too much land to cover," said Tom. "How're we going to search the whole thing? I mean, even with the planes searching grids, we aren't likely to recognize it from the air."

The Chief shook his head and said, "I don't know, but we know enough about Titus Rush and the way he hid his shelters to know that searching for it isn't the best answer. We could search every square inch and still miss it. What we need to do is sit down and study the island for anything unusual."

"That's a tall order," said Iris. "The only person here who knows anything about the island is Henry."

Henry had a small grin on his lips. "I guess it's up to me then."

Iris said, "I like that look. I've seen the Chief do that when he knows something that no one else does. Spill it, Henry."

Henry really did know something, and the more he studied the map, the more the grin spread into a smile.

"Your Mr. Rush must have been quite a character. Tell me," said Henry, "did he have a knack for hiding things in plain sight?"

"Not always," answered Kathy, "but don't start celebrating too soon. You could be standing right in front of it, but if you don't know what the code or combination is, you could be standing there the rest of your life."

"What kinds of codes did he use?" asked Henry.

"Songs, coordinates, dates so obscure no one would think of them... things like that," said the Chief. "There's no way to know for sure. Like Kathy said, you could be standing in front of the entrance and never see it, but he did leave clues."

"But you did get inside them. You figured out the codes to how many shelters?"

Iris said, "We had help with some of them. We always seem to have the brightest people surrounding us. You, for instance. I would venture to guess that the riddle of this shelter would be in your lap, especially since you seem to have an idea of where it might be. By the way, do you ever plan to tell us where, or do we have to beat it out of you?"

"Well, if you had beaten me for any reason before the infected dead arrived, this is where they would have sent you...one of these three prisons. Would Mr. Rush have found it to be useful to place his shelter near three prisons on an island?"

Colleen said, "You had my hopes up at first, but why would you be so sure that the shelter is on the island?"

"Sim, is there a pencil and straight edge of some kind in the navigator cabinet?"

Sim produced them immediately. He had found everything he needed when they stole the planes at St Mary's.

Henry thanked him and then turned his map over. He laid the straight edge on the blank paper and drew several lines. When he was finished, he held it up to the others.

"Does this look familiar?" he asked.

"Of course," said Captain Miller. "I was stuck inside that place by myself for a year. That's Fort Sumter."

The rest of them nodded their agreement. The shape of Fort Sumter was distinctively the same as a home plate in baseball. The game of baseball was invented by Abner Doubleday, and he fashioned home plate in the shape of Fort Sumter. Whether it was a coincidence or on purpose was not known for sure, but the fact remained they were the same shape.

Henry turned the map back over and added three more lines on the long end opposite the pointed side. He held it up, and they could see it was still Fort Sumter, but now one side of it had a truncated pyramid sitting on it.

* * *

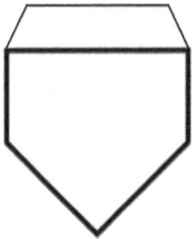

"Our countries have a few things in common," said Henry. "We put prisons on islands, and we love our sports. This is what Fort Sumter would look like with a football field added to the blunt side...or soccer, as you Yanks call it. This is the shape of Her Majesty's Prison Elmley. Elmley and Fort Sumter would be identical except for the soccer field."

The resemblance between the prison and Fort Sumter was obvious, and they all stared at it with open mouths, but their minds were at work on the rest of the puzzle. Where would the front door be, and what would be the code that opened it?

Sim was staring closely at his own map, and he surprised everyone when he almost shouted, "I've got it! I asked myself why anyone would put an aviation museum across the street from a prison, but then I remembered this place. Anyone really serious about their profession also knows its history. This is the British version of our Kitty Hawk, North Carolina. Look closely at the names of the streets near the prison."

It was like a "Where's Waldo" competition again as everyone poured over their maps in search of what Sim had found. It had to be obvious because Sim showed no sign that he was going to tell them.

Hampton saw it first, and Sim couldn't have been more pleased by his reaction.

"Holy...that can't be a coincidence. The museum is located on Wright's Way. As in Orville and Wilbur Wright?"

Henry said, "Would you believe the Wright brothers visited the Isle of Sheppey in 1909 to meet with the Short brothers, about six years after they were successful with their first powered flight at Kitty Hawk? Ironically, the Sherpa we're sitting inside at this very moment was manufactured by the same company that was founded by the Short brothers."

"I'm starting to feel the presence of Titus Rush," said the Chief. "Okay, let's put the clues together. We have a shelter under Fort Sumter, and the prison is almost the identical shape of Fort Sumter.

The prison is next to an aviation museum on the road named after the Wright brothers. So, we have an American connection, but sometimes coincidences just add up to nothing."

Iris said, "I know you're just trying to see if you can punch holes in the theory, but remember we already decided Sheppey Isle was the most likely place for the shelter. Going on the theory that we're right about that, the coincidence about the shape of the prison becomes smaller."

"I agree," said Kathy. "All we're trying to figure out now is where the entrance would be, and when you think about it, something like a museum would be an excellent place to put the main door. Can you imagine the clues inside a museum?"

"We're forgetting something," said Tom. "All of the shelters have fake places of safety outside. Mud Island had a houseboat, Fort Sumter had the actual fort above the shelter, and Green Cavern had a village above it. Some are big, and some are small. Where's the fake shelter? Is it the prison? That's the last place most people would go."

The Chief directed his comment to everyone, but his eyes were on Henry.

"Unless the prison was just a front."

Henry rubbed at his chin and the stubble that was growing on his cheeks. He was doing his best to remember what he had heard on the news before and after the infection had begun. He had never been to the aviation museum, but he liked the trail of bread crumbs they had followed to this point. He had the appearance of a man who was bothered by something despite their progress.

Iris asked, "Are you thinking about your wife and children?"

He didn't lift his head, but they still heard the barely audible answer.

"Are they in the shelter? I mean, even if we're right that the prison is actually a shelter, how would Symone have gotten there with Emily and Adam?"

There was a collective silence. In their exuberance over figuring out where the shelter was, they had ignored the original goal of finding Henry's family. Kathy broke the silence with the only thing that could be said.

"Remember, Henry, we went off on this idea to locate the shelter when we considered what Symone would have done...where she would have gone. You recalled that she had been there when you and Adam Callaway talked about the tunnel construction."

Captain Miller added, "That part is actually making more and more sense. Let's go on the assumption that the Channel Tunnel is a back door to the shelter, and the shelter is under the prison. Would the Royal family have been transported to the shelter by the back door? I don't think so."

"What are you getting at?" asked the Chief.

"The back door was for rapid transit of survivors after the initial collapse. The Royal family would have been evacuated by helicopters just like our President, but instead of taking them to a waiting airplane, they were most likely flown straight to the shelter. Once they were safe, the military did just as ours did. They attempted to fight back by establishing safe zones. When they got pushed out of their safe zones like the Isle of Wight, they opened the back door and began their retreat."

Henry felt hopeful as he listened to the conjecture by Captain Miller.

"You believe they were scooped up during that retreat?"

Captain Miller was glad to make the famous astronaut feel better, so he quickly continued.

"You said it yourself. You could tell from what you saw at your house that they had done the best thing when it started. They dug in and sat tight. The people who panicked and tried to find a way out were the ones who died first. Once the military saw they couldn't fight the infected, they began their evacuation. If they had tried to do an evacuation earlier, they would have just wound up carrying infected survivors into the shelter."

Iris continued the possible description of the evacuation for Captain Miller.

"There would have been too many people boarding the trains. The military would have been able to control the evacuation better if they sent out teams, located survivors, and then escorted them to the trains that were bound for the Channel Tunnel. I'm sure they knew where your home was and sent a team there."

Cassandra felt like it was time to make a suggestion that she had been mulling over in her mind.

"We have two planes, and we have two good objectives. Maybe we should split up. One plane can try for the front door, and one can try for the back door?"

No one answered immediately, but it was as if someone had turned on the lights.

The Chief said, "Let's check these maps for landing areas. I'm sure there's somewhere to land near an aviation museum. Henry, do you know of anything near Folkestone?"

"There's a small airport not far from the Channel Tunnel entrance. I landed there in a Cessna once. It's big enough for the Sherpas, and you can see the tunnel from there."

"Which objective is likely to require the most firepower?" asked Kathy.

Captain Miller said, "The Tunnel. I think the Chief should fly that route with me, Kathy, and Cassandra. Henry should fly the second group to the island with Sim, Hampton, Colleen, Tom, and Iris. That team would make up for combat skills by being a larger group."

"I agree," said the Chief. "We'll leave at dawn."

******

Symone waited several days in the hope that the horde of infected would diminish in size. The problem was that nothing was happening to draw them away. There were no loud sounds that equaled the sound of the siren she had used to get the attention of the soldiers. She also had to wonder if it would get worse if she saw the soldiers and used the siren again.

She finally came to the conclusion that using the siren once had been a good idea. It had at least gotten the attention of the soldiers. They knew she was there...or they knew someone was there, whether it made a difference or not. She was sure it made a difference, but her second conclusion was that she shouldn't use the siren again. She began to think about what it would take to draw the infected away from the airport, but that would mean she had to climb down out of her safe perch.

Half-awake, she imagined herself sneaking down the ladder and outrunning the infected. Then she would get inside the maintenance building and make a bomb. More running would follow, and she would detonate the bomb a mile or so away to draw the horde away from the airfield. More running...this time, she would run for the tunnel.

Symone woke up to sunshine streaming into the tower, and she started her day the same way she had since sounding the siren. She lifted the hatch a few inches and surveyed the area at the base of the tower. She was disappointed to see it was business as usual. At least a dozen of the infected were milling around below her.

"So much for outrunning them," she said as she closed the door again.

The memory of making a bomb to distract the horde was coming back to her, and she knew she had dreamt it all. For one thing, she had never been an Olympic track star, so she didn't know where she had gotten the idea that she could outrun them. When she considered it, she knew she could outrun them at first, but judging by the numbers she could see on the runway, there were likely to be just as many of them a mile away. She might be able to outrun some, but she would always be running into more of them. That would be more like dodging than running.

She checked her water supply and saw she was okay for at least a week if she rationed a little. Maybe she could stretch it for two weeks if she was careful to drink only when thirsty. That reminded her of Henry, and she wondered, not for the first time if Henry had run out of supplies. She imagined he was hungry all the time, but the hunger was never the worst part. The thirst wasn't either. The worst part had to be the isolation and missing his family. She knew about that firsthand. She had been alone for longer than she could remember, and she missed him terribly, but at least he had the company of his fellow astronauts.

Then there was the agony of missing the children so much. As far as Henry knew, she and the children were safe together, and she was glad for his ignorance of what had happened. If he knew the children had disappeared from their home after she had left them alone, he would not only be worried about them, he would hate her for leaving them.

It wasn't the first time she had found herself sinking into despair that threatened her sanity. One thought would lead to another until she realized everything she knew was right here in front of her, and she knew very little. She knew there were infected dead roaming around under her tower. She knew soldiers came and went from the tunnel, but that was all she knew for sure. The rest was just what she hoped. She hoped Henry was alive somewhere, whether he was still in space or somewhere on Earth. She hoped Emily and Adam were alive somewhere, and wherever that was, she prayed they were safe. Her thoughts always came back around to just how little she knew, and that made her wonder whether or not it would be better to die with hope or to die with the knowledge that Henry, Emily, and Adam were really dead...or worse. Maybe they were like those things below the tower. Maybe they were already down there with the other infected dead. She couldn't live with that knowledge.

"So why not die while there's hope?" she asked herself.

She didn't really remember opening the hatch again, but she must have spoken the question out loud because the crowd of infected below her was moaning and reaching for her with outstretched arms.

"Why not just dive headfirst into them?" she thought. "The fall would break my neck."

She was so far into visualizing the fall and the sound of her neck snapping that she didn't realize she had lost her audience. They were already walking away as if they had something better to eat, but their moaning was so loud compared to before. She didn't understand that the moaning was something much more than what they could do. It was the sound of airplane engines, and the sound was close.

19

Eastchurch

Southern England - Present Day

Henry circled all three prisons to size up the different possible landing areas. If there was an airport of any type on the island, he didn't see it, and it wasn't his first choice to stray too far from the objective. The outer edges of the island were more populated since residential neighborhoods are seldom built near prisons, and if there was a landing strip anywhere close to the edges, it would mean crossing places that were heavily populated by the infected.

All five of his passengers were glued to windows hoping to spot something useful, but one by one, they reported in that there were two choices...an open field or the main road that ran the length of Her Majesty's Prison Swaleside. There was a slight bend in the road just before Elmley, but Henry figured he could have his speed down far enough to make the bend without a problem. Sim was in the seat across from him, and he agreed. He announced to everyone that Brabazon Road was their target and for everyone to remain seated because he intended to drive on the road until they reached the place where the main entrance of Elmley reached the highway.

"Beats walking," said Colleen.

Henry circled back to line up with the highway. As he completed the turn, he told Sim to radio the Chief's plane to let them know they were landing.

"No contact," said Sim. "The last I heard from them was that they had spotted a small runway near Folkestone. It appeared to be a private aero club runway just big enough for the Sherpa, but I've had nothing since."

"Any indication of trouble?"

"No, the transmission began clearly but faded out. My best guess is that the distance between us was increasing at the time. We might regain contact as we approach evening," said Sim.

Henry brought the wheels down near the prison at Standford Hill and decreased their speed as they passed Swaleside. They couldn't help noticing that there was no movement anywhere within the fence around Swaleside. It was a sprawling prison that appeared big enough to hold at least one thousand prisoners, so it wouldn't have been a surprise to see the infected dead wandering in the open areas.

It only took a minute for them to reach the end of the first prison and then the slight bend in the road. Henry was silently telling an unseen force to keep the road clear. It wasn't exactly praying, but it was close enough. His senses were reaching out to find some indication that Symone and the children were nearby, but he was getting nothing in return. He adjusted for the bend in the road, and everyone felt themselves pulling against their seat belts. He straightened out again and began driving the plane like a car as they passed the diamond-tipped end of Elmley.

Sim, Hampton, Colleen, Tom, and Iris all faced the windows on the left side of the plane, and it didn't take a mind reader for them to know what each was thinking.

"Where are all of the infected?" asked Iris. "If these prisons were in operation when the infection arrived, someone either opened the gates and let everyone leave, or they kept the infection from getting in."

"The infection always got inside back then," said Hampton. "Before they knew that it was fatal, they would've opened the gates for someone, and they wouldn't have inspected for bite wounds."

"That leaves the other option," said Iris, "but if they opened the gates and just let everyone go, someone would have stayed. Someone would have felt safer inside prison than outside."

Sim said, "The gates are closed."

His radio crackled, and he put a hand against the headset covering his ears to block outside noise. He heard a fraction of the transmission, but it was enough for him to hear the Chief say they were landing.

Henry had just brought the plane to a stop where the road turned to cross in front of the prison, and he saw Sim react to something over his radio, and Sim raised his own microphone to acknowledge. He gave Sim a hopeful look with his eyebrows raised, and Sim gave him a slight shake of the head.

"Just a partial transmission that they're landing. I gave them our status, but I don't know if they could hear me."

Henry had been forced to keep his focus on the landing, so he didn't know what the others had seen and asked for an update. Iris told him they had seen no signs of life inside either prison. The two fenced prisons could hold twenty-four hundred people between them but had closed gates, and both appeared to be deserted.

The engines were still running, so Henry rotated the Sherpa until it was facing the road where they had just landed, and he put them into an idling speed.

"There's your movement," said Henry.

Out the front of the plane, they could see all the way to where they had touched down near Standford Hill. At least a half dozen infected were climbing from the fields onto the road. They were still far enough away, but their presence meant their group wouldn't be working to solve the puzzle of a hidden shelter without distractions.

"What's the plan?" asked Colleen. "If you don't mind my suggestion, I don't think we should go in even if the gates are unlocked."

Hampton answered, "I agree. It's a big place, and we could search it for a month without finding a clue about the shelter entrance. It might be inside somewhere, but remember that most of the other shelters have an entrance somewhere outside."

"Do you think there's power inside?" asked Iris. "Wait, I can answer that myself. This place is surrounded by wind turbines, and there's a big solar farm to the east. They have power, but there's either no one here or someone is smart enough not to advertise their presence."

Henry said, "If someone is here, then they might have been monitoring our radio broadcasts too."

Tom had been listening to the others, but he was concentrating his efforts on the map.

"We don't have Eddie here to tell us how his uncle would have done this, but we have to think like Titus Rush, and I think we have one clue staring us in the face, and that would be the aviation museum. It won't be easy to figure out, but we have one advantage over the average person. We know it's around here somewhere, and I think we should start with what we know because it's like an arrow pointing the way."

"Okay," said Hampton, "where's the arrow telling us to go?"

"It's not exactly a challenge, but maybe we should at least go to the aviation museum. The name of the road is Wright's Way. That could be read as the right way."

"Too obvious," said Hampton. "I think we need to find something that's stood the test of time...something that's been here a long time and will stand a long time. I mean, think about it for a minute. The aviation museum and the prisons aren't old enough. We need a historical location that people aren't likely to blow up or burn down. England is rich with history, and I think Rush would have used that."

Iris said, "What about the aviation memorial in town? It's marked on the map as being constructed before the Channel Tunnel."

"Not old enough," said Tom. "We need something or someplace that people generally don't paint graffiti or deface. Rush wouldn't want the clues to be destroyed."

Henry said, "Your Titus Rush must have been a clever man. He had to make the clues difficult but obvious at the same time, depending upon how well he wanted the entrance to the shelter to remain hidden."

"I know that look," said Iris. "You've spent too much time with the Chief, and you've figured it out."

The revelation made Henry grin, and the others knew Iris had been right.

He explained, "The Aviation Memorial might not be old enough, but the church across the street from it has been there since around 1430. I remember reading once that the stained glass windows were preserved by the historical society by installing protective panes of bulletproof glass over them. Someone obviously wanted them to stand the test of time."

"How far is the church from here?" asked Colleen.

Sim had already done what navigators do almost as a reflex. He had located the church on his map and calculated the distance.

"It's about two miles back the way we came when we landed. The good news is that it's a straight road all the way. The bad news is that we drew some attention when we landed. The infected are mostly coming from that direction."

"How many?" asked Iris.

From the front windows, they could see a dozen or so infected on the road, and they were considerably spread out.

"Let's not drag this out," she said. "We all know that the church is where we need to go. If we're wrong, we'll move on, but I'll give you one more reason besides the protective glass over the stained glass windows."

Everyone waited for her to savor the moment because her face had become a mirror of Henry's with self-satisfaction. She produced a travel guide that had been in the pocket on the back of a passenger seat. Since the planes had been used by island tour agencies, they had been plentiful at one time. Over the years, the copies had been carried off the planes for various reasons, but one had survived.

Iris held the book open to a page that had a picture of the Aviation Memorial. The picture actually spanned two pages from the left to the right, and it was taken at an angle, so the center of it wasn't in the fold of the book. At the center was a statue of a man from the waist up. His left hand was raised with a finger pointing to the sky, probably in tribute to the men who flew over Eastchurch.

Iris smiled and said, "Doesn't this guy look an awful lot like Uncle Titus Rush?"

******

They left the Sherpa where it was and quickly set off down Brabazon Road. Moving single file with Hampton in the lead, they soon reached the first of the infected that blocked their path. These were slow and wasted compared to the well-preserved infected they had met in some places. Hampton used his machete for each of them until his blade got stuck in the neck of one, and Colleen moved up to take the lead while he used his foot for leverage. By the time they reached a roundabout where the name had changed to Church Road, they had eliminated all of the infected that had responded to the noise from their plane. Despite the fact that the next few blocks would lead them into a more populated part of the island, it appeared to be deserted.

"Anyone notice the lack of infected and the lack of debris?" asked Iris. "It's almost like someone cleaned up."

When they reached the intersection with High Street, they saw the Aviation Memorial and the church across the street.

"Rush would have put his clue on the other side away from traffic," said Tom. "That's what I would've done."

They crossed the street in single file as they watched for movement at any of the windows of nearby buildings, but none of them could resist the temptation to at least glance in the direction of the Aviation Memorial and the statue at its center. With the long hair and beard, it could have been Eddie's uncle, and even though the index finger was pointing straight up, it was also in a straight line with the door of the church.

The door was locked, so they circled until they reached the side of the church behind the altar where the priest would have prepared for Mass. It was the only place where the glass didn't depict a historical scene, but they still felt bad about needing to break it. Tom was the tallest member of their group, so he stretched upward and pushed at the wooden frame about eight feet from the ground. As soon as he did, there was a flurry of activity at the window as an infected dead was drawn to the sound.

Tom jumped backward out of reflex as the face pushed against the glass, leaving a smear of brown grime. Iris reached up with her machete and tapped the glass in front of the face to taunt it, and the move succeeded in raising the ire of the agitated infected dead. It slammed its face harder against the glass, and a crack appeared. It spread to one side but didn't break, so Iris gave it another tap. The next time the face hit the glass, the infected dead came through the glass so fast that it fell to the ground in front of her. She couldn't recall in all the years of the apocalypse she had ever used her machete on the head of an infected that was wearing a priest's cassock.

"Watch the glass," said Tom as he pulled himself up to the window sill. The room was dimly lit, but there was no other movement inside. There was the musty odor of death inside a room that hadn't been aired out in years, and he saw the remains of two bodies strewn on the floor.

Once inside, Tom cleared away the remaining glass and then laid an altar cloth on the sill.

"We should all come in through here in case the church itself is occupied."

At the beginning of the infection, many people sought refuge in churches, which ultimately meant churches were full of the dead by the end of the first day. There were rare instances when retreat to a church was a good idea, but it was never a permanent solution. Someone would always let in a wounded person. Churches would never turn anyone away. Sooner or later, the infected dead were inside, and everyone died.

After they were all squeezed into the small room, Tom gently opened the thick door that led to the altar. There was enough light for him to see two infected near the front row of pews, but he would have been forced to expose himself too much to see the rest of the church. They all knew from past experience that the infected stopped moving if it was quiet for too long in a contained area.

"I'll go knock on the front door," said Hampton.

Before anyone could object, Hampton slipped back out the window and disappeared. Thirty seconds later, there was a loud booming knock on the front door, and the response was immediate. They stood up from virtually every corner and every pew. The church was crowded with the infected, and they moved toward the knocking.

Iris said, "We can't handle that many inside, so let's get them to go outside."

She pushed past Tom and ran across the altar stage to the opposite side of the church. Her goal was the huge twin side doors that were used as a second exit for large funerals and weddings. They faced directly toward the Aviation Museum, and it seemed like a good idea to let the infected out of the church and into the open where they could be killed easier.

Iris knew she was in trouble when she got to the doors because they were barred by an old wooden beam that sat cradled inside a pair of metal handles. The beam must have weighed hundreds of pounds because she couldn't even budge it, let alone lift it from the handles. Several of the infected had already seen her and had changed from their previous course toward her.

Back at the rectory door, Tom wanted to give Iris a chance to get the doors open, and the infected already had their backs to him. He could take them out, but more started in his direction as soon as he opened the door a bit further. His guess was that there were over one hundred of them spreading toward Iris, him, and the knocking at the front door.

Iris gave up her attempts to lift the beam out of the handles and instead went to the right side and pushed it from the end. It slid an inch, then two inches inside the handle. Two more inches later, the right side dropped heavily to the ground, and the door on the right side was free to swing outward. When she did, it knocked heavily into six of the infected on the other side. They had apparently followed the group of survivors to the church, and they were being drawn closer by the chorus of groans coming from inside.

The door was too far open for her to close it, and even if she could, the swarming crowd of the infected inside was focused on her. She felt one pull at her shirt and another tangle its hand in her long silver hair as they crowded against her. Over their heads, she could see Tom's machete repeatedly raise and lower as he chopped his way toward her. Henry, Colleen, Sim, and Tom were all fighting their way to her, but it was too late.

The crush of bodies against her from the inside overwhelmed the few that were outside, and the door was forced open wider. She felt rather than saw the hand that gripped her extended right arm, and she braced herself for the searing pain that she knew would follow. The hand was strong, and it pulled her so hard that she was sure her arm would be ripped from her body. It pulled so hard that she had to follow where it led, and she wasn't sure why there was no bite or how she stayed on her feet, but she was suddenly clear of the door.

Hampton pulled her hard enough to get her away from the door, but he had to let go and start killing. She finally fell to the ground and saw that he had killed the six infected that had been outside and was now trying to keep a large swarm from coming through the door. Thanks to the heavy beam that had one end still in its handle, it acted as a barricade over half of the door and prevented it from opening, but it wasn't enough. They were still overwhelming him. He finally took a few steps backward and unslung his M4. Aiming at their heads, he methodically moved from one to the next until his magazine was empty.

As Hampton reloaded, he realized that his friends inside had worked their way to the door, and the last of the infected had gone down. He turned back to Iris and extended a hand to help her from the ground. She took it and felt the dull ache from her shoulder that hurt badly enough for her to know she might need to wear a sling for a while, but she had lived through the close brush with death.

There was a warm sensation on the back of her neck, and her other hand went to her head. She knew she had lost a handful of hair as it was ripped painfully from her head by the infected. Her hand came back with blood on it, but when she probed the tender area, she couldn't find a bite wound.

Colleen came outside and helped Hampton carry Iris back inside. Hampton lifted the beam back into place in its handle, and Iris could see that Henry, Sim, and Tom were going through the church mopping up the infected that were still moving. Once she was situated on the front row of pews, Colleen poured an antiseptic rinse across Iris' head, causing her to scream. Colleen put pressure on the spot with a big gauze pad. It elicited a wince, but this time Iris bit back the scream. She also focused on the anger she felt about having a bald spot in her beautiful hair.

Henry said, "That's not what I had in mind when we came inside, but now we can search for clues without interruption."

"I wouldn't count on that for very long," said Hampton. "I emptied a magazine out there, so everything within a few square miles is headed this way. Let's pair off and study the stained glass windows. Make like art critics in a museum and figure out what they mean."

They split up into three pairs and began their search. Like most old churches, there was no shortage of art. That included the windows, statues, and engravings into the ancient wood.

"Anyone know any Latin?" asked Iris.

"Of course," said Henry. "Just try to survive private schools without it."

"What's the Latin phrase for being mad about my hair getting ripped out?" said Iris.

Henry said, "That's over my head, I think."

The play on words earned him a general groan from everyone, but Iris had to admit, the laughing didn't make it hurt worse.

"Let's focus," said Tom.

"Here's something interesting," said Sim. He was standing in front of one of the stained glass windows with Colleen, but he wasn't looking at the window. He had his face down close to the side of the pew and was running his hand across an engraved pattern.

Henry walked over to Sim and saw the engraving. An angel with wings spread outward held a sword in her right hand. The left hand held something that at first glance resembled an apple, but Henry recognized the flames coming out of the top of it.

"A grenade fired proper," he said. "We're in the right place."

******

Two hours later, the frustration was beginning to build as the light faded on the other side of the windows. They still had a few hours before the sun would set, but clouds had blocked out the sun as raindrops fell. Henry had gone from window to window and written down the Latin phrases. He sat and translated each of them, but nothing made sense with regard to a clue. They had found the same angel on the ends of four rows of pews, but they were randomly spaced throughout the church.

One by one, the others sat down on the benches and thought about everything in the church. The angels with the grenades were obviously meant to tell them something, but other than making them feel like they weren't wasting their time on a wild goose chase, they didn't know what they meant.

Added to their weary bodies was the smell inside the church. In an attempt to get some fresh air, they had propped open the rectory door where the broken window was. From time to time, a faint breeze would come to their rescue, but the scent of decay was getting to them all. Not to mention the fact that there were still bodies everywhere.

"I hate to say it," said Henry, "but we need to waste some time moving bodies out of the way. It's distracting having to step over and around them."

Colleen added, "It's also disgusting when you step on one. I always feel like they're going to sit up or groan or something."

As tired as they were, everyone forced themselves to their feet to begin the chore.

"Not you, Iris," said Tom. "That shoulder needs to be checked by a doctor. I saw how you've been cradling it with your left arm."

The rest of the group seconded Tom's order, so Iris reluctantly sat down and watched. She also studied the Latin phrases that Henry had translated so she could feel useful. One kept popping out at her. It was the same sensation she got when she did crossword puzzles and got stuck. Then she saw it. One of the windows was inscribed with the Latin phrase, "Noli cito ad judicium movere, cum possis ambulare. Pondus electionis tuae est dux tuus."

Henry had loosely translated it to say, "Do not move quickly to judgment when you can walk to it. The weight of your choice is your guide."

Iris called out to Tom and Colleen as they went past her carrying a body by the hands and feet. "What's a four-letter word for move quickly?"

They kept going with the body, but they both played along just like anyone would when someone asked for help on a crossword puzzle.

"Run? No, that's three letters," said Tom.

"Trot?" asked Colleen.

"Dash," said Tom. "What's it begin with?"

Iris answered, "How about an R?"

Tom and Colleen paused, and then they audibly dropped the body.

"Rush?" they both said together.

"Right," said Iris. "Why can't this be translated, Do not RUSH to judgment when you can walk to it?"

Work had come to a standstill as Henry, Sim, and Hampton realized Iris had found something.

Henry said, "Let's take a closer look at my translation for alternative words."

The bodies were forgotten as the group poured over the phrases, but spotting the name of the shelter master was one thing. Spotting messages from him were another.

"Wait a minute," said Henry. "All of these windows were original masterpieces except one, and that's the one with Rush's name in it. So, we shouldn't find more messages in those phrases."

Iris saw where he was going and said, "There's more to this message. Judgment...walk to judgment...where would you find judgment in a Catholic church?"

Henry's head turned first, followed by the others until they were all facing the confessionals. Four doors in a row were the entrances to the confessionals. Two were for priests, and two were for penitents.

"It can't be that easy," said Tom.

He walked over to the first door and peered inside. When the others joined him, they saw the same angel engraved inside the door, but there were no buttons, no switches, and no levers to pull that would cause a secret door to open.

"There's more," said Tom. "Titus Rush wouldn't make it that easy."

Iris said, "The angels must be the other part of this. Do we count this one in with the others? What about the rest of the translation?"

As a group, they decided the other four angels were meant to lead them to this one, but that meant they had to interact with the others somehow, and it had to be something that couldn't happen by accident. It had to be something that couldn't happen in a crowded church, or the door might pop open during services. After arguing about how it could open accidentally if there was more than one person in the church, it finally came down to one thing. The weight of one person mattered because the only way to interact with a pew was to sit on it.

"Okay," Tom began, "how do we know which order to sit in the pews?"

Henry said, "We can't guess because there are five thousand and forty possible combinations."

"There are four angels because there are four letters in that crazy old man's name," said Sim.

As soon as he said it, Sim thought Titus Rush wasn't really that crazy because he knew someone smart enough would figure it out. He jumped up from where they were gathered near the confessionals and ran up to the altar. The others watched as he stood higher than the rest of them and pointed with his finger while he counted the pews.

When he finished counting, he yelled, "Would anyone like to make a wild guess how many pews are on each side? Twenty-six!"

Henry wrote the name RUSH on the paper with the Latin translations and then assigned each a number from the alphabet... eighteen, twenty-one, nineteen, and eight. Everyone realized that they would have noticed eighteen and nineteen were suspiciously close to each other, so they were on opposite sides of the church.

"How do we do this?" asked Colleen.

Iris was in pain from the burning wound on her head, but she was smiling.

"Everyone, get out of your seats and stand over here."

Iris stood next to the open confessional door.

"To add one more layer of security to this," she began, "the confessional door must be open. Since they're more often shut, it makes sense that it has to be opened to set the unlocking events in motion. Henry, would you like to do the honors? Walk, don't run, to pew number eighteen and sit next to the angel. I think there's a timer on this, but the range should only be a few seconds to allow the seat to weigh you."

Henry did as he was instructed and sat in the proper place. On a signal from Iris, he got up and walked at a normal pace to pew twenty-one and sat down again. He repeated the process by crossing to pew nineteen on the other side, and then he finally sat in pew eight.

They were all holding their breath, waiting for something to happen, but the church remained silent.

"I don't believe it," said Colleen. "We're all so dense! Henry, it's time for you to go to confession, and please be sure to close the door behind you."

All of them groaned and put their hands over their faces while Henry crossed the church one last time and entered the confessional.

He pulled the door shut and knelt on the padded rail in front of the little window where the priest would normally be. Then he waited. When his weight was measured accurately in the mechanism below the floor under the railing, the elevator began its trip downward.

Outside the confessional, they all heard the low rumble that told them something had happened, but when Tom pulled at the handle of the wooden door, he was surprised at how solid it felt. It refused to move even the slightest bit. Hampton gripped the handle with him, and they pulled together, putting their feet against the frame for leverage. When they stopped to get a better grip and pulled again, they fell backward into the pews behind them as the door flew open with ease. The confessional was empty.

******

Henry Tisdal was trained to be calm under pressure. Nations didn't let ordinary people become astronauts because the job took more than education or knowledge. Astronauts had to have that internal switch that allowed them to turn off fear. Fear caused delays at times when fast reactions were critical to survival. Henry turned off that switch and focused his attention on every detail as he descended.

He reached out and touched the walls with his fingertips, and they were as smooth as polished metal, but it was so dark that he couldn't see them even though they were less than two feet away. They were also slightly warm. He lifted his eyes to the ceiling, and it was gone too. It was up there somewhere, but it was lost in the blackness. There was a familiar smell he remembered, but he hadn't smelled anything like it in so long that it was almost foreign. It was the smell of clean air without the ever-present smell of decay nearby. He put his hand to his face snd sniffed. The odor of death and rot was still on him and on his clothes, but the air that rushed up from below him was refreshing.

The sensation of downward motion was like any other elevator he had used, but the only place he had felt something so subtle was in outer space. He knew he was going downward, but in the absence of light, most people wouldn't know they were even moving. It was his training again. The elevator went down for a long time.

Henry remembered in training how they had strapped him into a chair that could spin silently without friction. Next, they put a totally light-proof helmet on his head. Then they told him they were spinning the chair to the left, then to the right, and then to the left again. Someone asked him over a microphone to tell them when the spinning stopped.

Henry replied, "It never started."

Without answering, the technician gently spun the chair in a circle.

Henry said, "That's better."

He was still on his knees because he wasn't sure what would happen if he stood up or even tried to sit, so he focused every bit of his senses on the sensations he felt in his thighs. The elevator stopped descending, and the faint lean he felt in his muscles told him it was now moving laterally to his left. When he stopped moving, there was nothing but silence, but he knew he wasn't alone.

The last thing a survivor would do was speak in such total darkness. In a world where the dead would eat the living, that was usually a bad idea, so Henry waited. If he wasn't alone, he couldn't imagine the occupant or occupants of the darkness could see him any better than he could see them.

Henry felt the burning in his legs caused by kneeling so long, and he realized the years in space had taken a toll on his muscles. When he was younger, he could have knelt there for hours. What felt like an hour was probably only fifteen minutes. He was just about to give in when the soft voice of a woman came through a speaker. He felt like it was behind him, but he wasn't sure.

"Did you complete the entry sequence, or was there a malfunction?"

Henry didn't understand the question at first and almost asked for clarification, but he suddenly understood.

"I completed the entry sequence," he answered.

"Who told you the entry sequence?"

"I...we figured it out."

Whoever it was speaking to him from the darkness, they must have found it hard to believe that someone had figured it out. The voice was insistent.

"State the steps of the entry sequence."

If there was one thing Henry was sure of, it was the fact that he and his friends had figured out how to gain access to one of the doors of the shelter. There would be more doors with different codes, but this one was solved. He calmly recited the steps he took to activate the elevator.

There was a prolonged silence, and Henry didn't doubt the woman was explaining to a superior that someone had entered the shelter by using the proper sequence. It couldn't be accomplished by accident, so it had to be on purpose, and this man claimed he and his friends had figured out the code from the clues in the church. Unknown to Henry, his presence was causing a great deal of excitement before he introduced himself, but hearing his name spoken aloud was cause for celebration.

"My name is Henry Tisdal, and I would like to speak with someone in charge," he said to the darkness.

The lights came up slowly, and Henry saw he had been correct about the location of the speaker. He was facing a blank wall, but as he turned, he saw a bank of windows. Staring out at him were several people in military uniforms. The sound on the speaker must have been turned off because he couldn't hear the applause and cheers that they were giving him.

******

Hampton went so far as to check the other confessionals, and he even lifted the padded kneeling rail and looked under it.

"This must be where the magician shoves swords through the confessional, and the assistant pops out somewhere else."

"He's not here," said Sim.

Colleen tried not to sound sarcastic, but that was the way it came out.

"Ya think?"

She apologized immediately, but Sim wasn't offended by her comment because stating the obvious was something people do when what they're seeing isn't believable. His statement was no more ridiculous than Hampton looking under the padded railing as if he would find Henry neatly tucked into a corner.

Tom and Iris each took their turn to inspect the inside of the confessional. They were sure one of them would find something the others had missed, and it was Iris who found it. She pulled a flashlight from her backpack and aimed it at the seams where the floor met the walls inside the closet-sized confessional.

"What is that?" she asked the others.

Hampton had worked on plane engines and motorcycles enough to recognize the shine from a lubricant. One in a million people might have noticed it, but only if they had been searching for it the way Iris was. He reached past Iris and ran a finger over the shine, then sniffed at his fingertip.

"That's a very refined layer of oil. It's so thin it'll evaporate in a minute."

Iris said, "We used it in our shelter at Ambassador Island."

"I remember," said Hampton. "The doors moved so smoothly on their hinges it unnerved me. I actually tried to make one squeak."

"What do we do now?" asked Sim. "If that's a lubricant, how do we know the floor didn't just drop out from under him?"

Even though Henry was missing, Iris wasn't at all concerned.

She said, "You've been inside enough of the shelters by now. Have you seen any traps in them? Have you fallen through any trapdoors? Okay, everybody…line up at the first pew. We'll go one at a time and hope we don't fall on top of Henry's head."

20

Folkestone

Southern England - Present Day

The original plan was to land at a small runway not far from the Channel Tunnel entrance, but the map must have been old because the woods between the runway and the tunnel were far thicker and wider than the map indicated. He almost decided to turn north before reaching the small airport to search for a clear field or highway on the other side of the woods, but there was something happening at the airport that made him curious.

The Chief saw that the runway was clear enough for them to land, but there were far more infected dead in the area than they had seen anywhere else since their arrival in England. This horde appeared to be interested in the tower that sat beside the maintenance hangar, and it didn't take a genius to know what interested the infected. They were drawn to loud sounds, to fire, and to movement, which was why they had seen small groups of them gathered around the bases of wind turbines. The blades of the turbines had continued to spin, but without maintenance, some had gotten noisy. The infected watched the turbines the way people used to watch interesting airplanes fly over.

There were plenty of things that moved, made noise, and burned, but nothing attracted the infected more than a living person. If someone got cornered up a tree or on top of a building, the infected weren't likely to leave. As a matter of fact, they were more likely to invite their friends by making a fuss. One would groan until another joined in, and before long, the loud groaning from an off-key choir of infected would draw more of them from miles away. From the way they were gathered together and reaching upward, it was an easy guess that some poor soul had been trapped in the tower.

The Sherpa's engines were high pitched and loud enough to draw the infected away from the tower, but the distance between the runway and the tower was far enough that the Chief could land before the crowd arrived. They would have time to get out and begin working to reduce the size of that crowd, but the Chief was worried about the stretch of woods on the other side. Judging by the number of infected in the open, there was likely to be even more in the trees. It took them a while to get from where they were to where they wanted to be, but the mistake most people made was underestimating how quickly they could surround their victims. He wasn't going to make that mistake by letting them come up on the other side of the plane while they worked their way closer to the tower.

"Listen up," said the Chief as he made a pass over the airport. "We don't have enough firepower to take on a horde this size, but someone's trapped in that tower. We need to land, extract them, and get back in the air. Any objections?"

Kathy felt like she had seen enough people become victims, and she knew they were going to help if they could, but over the years, she had never forgotten that the biggest unknown in a rescue operation was the condition of the person being rescued. If they had been bitten already, then it was too late for rescue, and the risk wasn't worth taking.

"I count over two dozen just between the runway and the tower," said Kathy. "We have to get that number down just so we'll have time to get whoever is in the tower onto the ground. Then we have to be sure we aren't loading bite victims into the plane."

The Chief saw the skeptical expression on Kathy's face, but he knew she was right. He didn't like to go into a combat situation without a plan, and right now, he was drawing a blank. Cassandra tapped him on the shoulder and leaned in where the others could hear her better.

"Captain Miller was telling me about how you dumped fuel on a big horde to save him and his men a long time ago."

"Not enough fuel for that," he answered. "We knew we were flying toward a fuel source back then. We don't know where our next gas station is around here."

"Can we spare enough to set that building on fire?"

The Chief got that look on his face that was reserved for moments of clarity. They had all seen it before, and they knew something had sparked his creative mind. It just so happened that a spark was all they would need.

"Yes, we do, but odds are that we won't need it. Everyone ready to hear Plan A?"

The Chief took Cassandra's idea and added a few details, and by the end of their second pass over the runway, they each knew their job. The Chief circled the airport and then came in for a landing on a gravel road on the opposite side of the building from the tower. He drove the plane straight up to the building, sure that the noise from the engines would be drawing the infected away from the tower.

Cassandra and Captain Miller jumped from the plane as soon as it was moving slowly enough, and together they rushed toward the back door of the building. They knew it would be locked, but they weren't planning to stay long, so they destroyed the door frame around the lock with automatic weapons before kicking it open. They expected to find infected inside, so their job got easier when they didn't have to waste time eliminating any.

Kathy didn't leave the plane until the pair had gone inside, and then she took up her position far enough from the building to cover both corners. As the infected from the tower arrived at both ends of the building, she took careful aim and shot them methodically. Behind her, the Chief rotated the Sherpa and was ready for takeoff as soon as the others got back on board.

Inside the maintenance hangar, it took only five seconds for them to locate their targets. Cassandra's target was anything that might contain fuel, oil, or grease. All three were in plentiful supply for their purposes, and it was close together. Captain Miller's target was the mechanism that would open the hangar doors. He was surprised to find there was power to the chain-driven doors, and all he had to do was push a button. He did his job first, and both hangar doors rumbled noisily upward. On the other side of the doors, the infected that were already walking away from the tower toward the hangar were distracted from the sound of the Sherpa and made a detour.

Captain Miller backed out first to help Kathy cover their flanks, while Cassandra took aim with two flare guns. She shot the white-hot flares into the fuel containers a split second before diving into the open with Kathy and Captain Miller, but the explosion was enough to throw the trio off their feet. The side of the building at one corner blew open, and the fireball that followed spread across the infected that had circled in that direction. The rest of them were going through the open hangar doors and walking straight into the flames. The building burned like a huge oven.

The Chief felt the wind from the blast buffet the plane, and he worried that they had overdone "Plan A." The door of the plane opened, and he saw all three of his friends fall through almost at the same time. They were yelling and laughing, and he discovered the reason they were all yelling was that none of them could really hear too well. He pushed the throttle forward and raced the plane along the road, but he didn't take off yet. If they had done their plan as well as they hoped, he would be able to drive the plane in a wide circle around the burning hangar and go straight to the tower.

With the hangar on their right, they rounded the corner and saw that the infected were ignoring everything but the fire. There were secondary explosions that kept their interest, and the groaning and popping of hot metal were too inviting for the infected. It was a bonus that their dried-out bodies also caught fire before they even got to the building.

The Chief called out as loud as he could to his nearly deaf companions, "There's one person climbing down the ladder from the tower. Kathy and Cassandra, get her on board and do a bite-check. Jim, you're up here with me."

The Chief brought the plane as close as he could to the tower, and as soon as he got the signal from Cassandra that their passenger was on board, he drove to the runway and accelerated for takeoff. Captain Miller climbed into the copilot's seat, and the Chief was surprised to see his friend was still laughing.

"What's so funny?"

"What?"

"Never mind."

The plane lifted smoothly into the air, and the Chief banked to the Channel Tunnel entrance in search of a place to land that wasn't infested with the dead. He could already see the tunnel entrance, so he rotated around it, watching for flat fields or straight roads. He saw the perfect spot only a quarter of a mile from their destination and leveled out to land. He felt Kathy's presence at his shoulder and assumed all had gone well with the woman they rescued because Kathy didn't interrupt what he was doing. He relaxed a bit, knowing things had worked out, and gave all of his attention to a smooth landing.

They came to a stop next to a rolling hillside that was the only thing between them and the tunnel. They could climb over their side and practically slide down the embankment to the entrance. The Chief finally cut the engines off and turned to Kathy.

"Well, how is she? No bites?" he asked.

"No bites," said Kathy. "Cassandra is checking her vitals, giving her some water and vitamins, and helping her clean up a bit, but she's in pretty good shape. She's ready to get going, though. She says she needs to get to the Channel Tunnel because she's sure her children are in there with the soldiers, and Chief…her name is Symone Tisdal."

******

It wasn't what Henry had expected, but then again, he hadn't given much thought to actually finding people. He had always believed that his country had somehow prevailed, but he had seen firsthand how it had worked out for the allies. As prepared as they were, they hadn't been able to prevent the collapse of their organized shelter system, perhaps because the shelter for the President had been breached. Maybe it would have been different if that shelter had survived.

England had suffered at the beginning for the same reasons the other countries had. There was no ability to stop the infection from getting inside the shelters unless there were limits to how many people were allowed to enter, and there had to be an efficient method in place for screening survivors. Henry had a thousand questions, and the young lady who was examining him was very forthcoming with her answers.

She was a Royal Navy doctor named Anna Townsend, and she had escorted Henry from the sealed room where he had first arrived. Doors along the hallway were closed, but as they walked from the arrival station to the examining room, faces were pressed against glass panes to get a glimpse of the astronaut who had returned.

Henry had asked Doctor Townsend several questions, and she was doing her best to answer them in some sort of coherent order. He mainly wanted to see if anyone knew what happened to his wife and children, but he quickly learned that the doctor didn't have all the answers. What she knew for certain was that he was inside the shelter built to save the Royal family and the highest members of Parliament. He was surprised when he was told there was another shelter somewhere on the western coast of England, but there had been limited contact with it.

She told him that the shelter was activated early when there were signs that the infection was overwhelming first responders. The reason the infection didn't get inside the shelter was because of a brilliant suggestion from an infectious disease doctor who was visiting from America. He had recommended that the military should evacuate as many people as possible to the Isle of Wight. He anticipated the situation there would be temporary and expected the infection to break free of containment, so he told them it would be their triage and separation center. As survivors were brought in, the bite victims were placed in quarantine while the healthy survivors were evacuated to the shelter under the Isle of Sheppey.

It wasn't a perfect plan, but they couldn't do anything for people who had been bitten, and they had to save as many people as possible. She told him there was no screening process for who was valuable and who was not. If someone made it to the Isle of Wight and they weren't bitten, then they were evacuated to the shelter.

"What happened if people refused to be separated from loved ones who had bite wounds?" he asked.

Dr. Townsend sadly lowered her eyes and said, "People weren't forced to leave their families. Many chose to stay, but they were told what was going to happen. They were told there was no cure, that bites were always fatal, and they should consider the injured as already dead and look out for themselves. It was such a shame because we aren't at capacity yet. That's why patrols go out every day to find survivors."

"You're still finding people and bringing them in?"

"We have over forty thousand people in the shelter, and we have room for ten thousand more," she said.

"Forty thousand," repeated Henry. "So my wife and children could easily be here."

Henry thought he saw a very slight hesitation, and he felt like she was holding something back, but if she had known something and was allowed to tell him, he was sure she would have volunteered it by now.

Dr. Townsend continued answering the questions he had already asked, but she was dying to ask a few of her own. She was surprised by his good health and how he had gotten from the International Space Station all the way to the Isle of Sheppey.

He told her about how they had stayed in space for as long as they could and then landed near the Marshall Space Flight Center in northern Alabama. When she learned others had survived in the shelters, she almost cried from relief. They had come to believe they might be the only survivors because there had been such a complete communications blackout.

After over an hour of blood tests, examinations, and questions, a soldier arrived to see Henry. He introduced himself as Major George Merritt and gave Henry the good news that he had been sent to escort him to the offices of the UK Space Agency for debriefing. Dr. Townsend pronounced Henry as healthy and infection-free and said he was at liberty to join the general population.

Henry was even more excited to meet the Major than he was Dr. Townsend because he was sure Major Merritt would have information about his family, but he hadn't forgotten about his friends he had left behind in the church.

"Major, did my American friends follow me down the elevator?" he asked.

"A very intrepid group of people, your American friends. Who among you figured out the clues to opening the shelter?"

"It was a group effort. They seem to have a knack for such things, but I can take credit for the Latin translation and any historical information. It truly did take more than one person, though. Where are they?"

"You'll get to see them soon enough, Mr. Tisdal. Each came in separately by design, so they were quarantined just as you were. The Eastchurch door is intended for easy isolation to ensure the infection doesn't get inside the shelter. They are all being examined as we speak. I found Iris Barnes to be most enchanting, but she was putting up quite a fuss about having her hair pulled out. I was instructed to give you a brief tour on the way to the Space Agency."

He gestured toward the door and allowed Henry to go out ahead of him, but Henry couldn't hold it back any longer, and as he stepped past him into the hallway, he caught him off guard and took the opportunity to ask the biggest question on his mind.

"Major, do you have any information about my family?"

He saw the hesitation again. The half-smile turned into an uncomfortable, forced smile.

"You'll be meeting with Deputy Chief Executive Holdsworth, and I'm sure he will have information for you. It's my understanding that he did what he could to bring in as many people from the space program as he could."

It wasn't bad news, but it also wasn't what he wanted to hear. Still, the Major had passed the buck straight to Mr. Holdsworth, and Henry resolved to keep his chin up for a while longer. He was close…he could feel it, and he was going to make it back to his family.

The medical wing where he was examined exited into a courtyard just as if he was leaving a building. There was an artificial skylight above him that gave him the impression that he was inside some sort of indoor mall, but he knew they were too deep underground for that to be a real sky above the curved windows.

Across the courtyard was an open area with a row of escalators, and the Major led him past groups of people who all turned to give Henry a smile. Some called out a welcome, and some applauded politely. They stepped onto an escalator and rode up to the next floor. That was when Henry truly understood the scope of the Isle of Sheppey shelter. It was a railway station that rivaled any he had ever seen. As many as eight trains were being boarded from platforms fed by more escalators, and as soon as one would leave, another would arrive.

"Not what you expected, Sir?" asked the Major.

"Not really, and please call me Henry. All these people…they appear to be going about their business as if it's a normal workday," he said with disbelief.

The Major said, "It hasn't been perfect, Henry. The first year was chaos. There were people who wanted to go back to the surface no matter how safe it was down here. There were times when it seemed like it would all fall apart because there was one thing that every single person here had in common with the man, woman, or child standing next to them. Everyone lost someone."

The stark reality of the answer hit Henry like a solid punch in the stomach. He watched hundreds of people going about their business, and he faced the Major with unblinking eyes.

"Who did you lose, Major?"

He held the Major's eyes with his own, and he saw the thin layer over them that glistened when the man remembered a loved one that didn't make it.

"My wife and two of my children," he said with a slight catch in his throat.

"I'm sorry, Major."

"Don't be, Henry. There's one thing that got so many people

through this, and that was our shared pain. We caught on quickly that we could wallow in self-pity, or we could turn to each other for comfort. Forty thousand people is a lot of folks, but that meant there was enough love and support to go around. Men who lost their wives found women who lost their husbands, parents who lost their children found children who had lost their parents. Children who lost brothers and sisters were taken in with families where they had new brothers and sisters."

Henry couldn't take it anymore. He had to know what he had lost. If every person he could see in a crowd of hundreds had lost someone, he had to know who he had lost. Tears sat ready on his eyelids...ready to tumble down his cheeks as he braced himself for the inevitable.

"You have to tell me, Major. I have to know. Who did I lose?"

He could see that the Major knew something, but he couldn't put the man in a position where he was breaking orders. Before he could apologize again, Henry stopped him.

"Mr. Holdsworth should be the one to tell me."

Major Merritt held a palm out in the direction of the trains, and Henry allowed himself to be guided to an open door. The train slid over the tracks almost silently, and Henry marveled at the places they passed. The Major explained that the size of the shelter required some form of rapid transit, but it was still small enough for a person to get from their residence, work, school, or shops easily. There were places where they could walk to those places, but the Ministry of Employment and Relocation had done a marvelous job of creating the illusion of variety. If someone lived, worked, and shopped in the same place, they would get bored.

"You have industries in the shelter?"

"Some," answered the Major, "but we still depend upon what we left behind. Not only do we have teams that search for survivors, but we also have teams that go to the mainland to retrieve equipment and supplies."

Henry had a sudden realization. "This place was in operation before the infection. And it can't be just on the Isle of Sheppey."

"We have some facilities above ground too, but they have to appear deserted to keep the infected dead from getting too interested. The prisons were converted to food processing plants almost ten years ago."

Henry was stunned into silence as he watched the different facilities go by, and he had an ache in his heart when he saw children with backpacks. Some were so young they had only known this life underground. He tried his best to picture his own son and daughter. The last time he saw them, they were four and six years old. Now, Adam would be eleven, and Emily would be thirteen. His brow furrowed as he corrected himself...twelve and fourteen.

"A teenage daughter," he said. He remembered Adam Callaway teasing him by saying, "Just wait until your daughter's a teenager. That's when you lose more sleep than when they were babies."

The Major knew what he was thinking and didn't comment. The train slid to a stop, and the door opened. The Major once again gestured for Henry to lead the way, and Henry saw they were in front of a building that was clearly operated by the government. It was the first one he had seen with guards on both sides of the door. They saluted the Major and held the door for him and Henry to go inside. It was a moment he wasn't prepared for, but it was like ripping off a band-aid.

Deputy Chief Executive Holdsworth stood politely off to one side. Adam and Emily were seated on a couch holding hands, and they regarded Henry with curious eyes. Henry felt like his heart had moved upward in his throat, and he was about to choke on it. His thoughts rushed by faster than he could answer the questions that came with them.

"Where was Symone? Are they really my children? Does this mean Symone is dead? Do they know who I am?"

He didn't speak because he couldn't, but he thought through each question as he stood and stared at the boy and girl who were so small the last time he saw them. They were so small, and they were with their mother. He saw the smile that spread across Emily's face first. She was old enough to remember her father, and Henry wished Adam Callaway was there to see the way his teenage daughter charged from the sofa into his arms. Adam was a split second behind her, and the three of them held each other as they cried and laughed.

Henry held each of them out at arm's length so he could see them better and see how much they had grown, and he saw that Adam had a picture in his hand. He reached for it, and Adam held it out for him to see. It was the last family picture they had done before he went into space.

"Emily told me to look at this picture of you every day, so I would know you when you came back."

Henry could see that Adam was proud of himself, and he mouthed the words thank you to Emily. Then he said it aloud for them both to hear.

He wanted to hold them forever, but there were others standing around them who didn't know what to do. Henry sensed some discomfort and forced himself to face the middle-aged couple who stood behind the couch where the children had been sitting.

Deputy Chief Executive Holdsworth stepped forward and said, "I'm Alfie Holdsworth, and these fine people are William and Sidney Goodwin. They've had the pleasure of caring for your children since they arrived here."

Henry remembered what the Major had told him about parents losing their children, and he instinctively knew the Goodwins had been selected to care for Adam and Emily because their own children had been victims of the infected dead. He also knew it would be difficult for them to lose Adam and Emily now. He stood and motioned for them to come around to the other side of the couch, then he pulled them into the hug with his children.

"It looks to me like our family is bigger now," he said. "Now, let's see if we can find your mother."

******

It was a whirlwind of input even for the seasoned shelter veterans from America. Henry asked to see his friends as soon as they were processed, and Alfie Holdsworth had been pleased to find out there were more people with Henry at the church. He wanted to meet all of them and hear everything about what had happened on the other side of the Atlantic. He was ecstatic to learn that a small group of people had revived shelters, and as soon as they were able to establish satellite connections, he intended to contact all of them. His agency was making that a priority.

Iris, Sim, Tom, Colleen, and Hampton were waiting for Henry in the comfortable lobby of a hotel. They constantly turned in their overstuffed sofas and chairs to take in the people and their surroundings. It was unbelievable that so much was happening underground.

Sim couldn't help but compare what it had been like for him and the survivors who flew with him from Washington to Columbus, Ohio. While they had survived off of so little in an airport, this shelter was in its early days of populating and organizing. By the time they left the airport, this place was functioning as a small city. Now it wasn't so small.

As if she was reading his mind, Iris said, "Amazing, isn't it? We were living underground for years, but we were never on this scale."

"We were fighting off swarms of rats while this place was opening elementary schools and people were eating in restaurants," answered Sim.

Tom said, "This is how the shelters were supposed to work, but the Britons decided to do it on a larger scale rather than a few dozen smaller shelters. The shelters at Fort Sumter, Huntsville, and Columbus were big, and maybe they would have worked if the infection hadn't interfered with them at the start. Can you imagine what this would be like if the infection had gotten inside?"

"I'm curious," said Hampton. "Do you think any other countries did this? When we decided to bring Henry home, we didn't think we were bringing him back to anything like this."

Colleen was leaning back with her head resting on Hampton's shoulder. "Too bad we can't stay."

Something about her comment made their surroundings feel temporary, and it was Tom who filled in the silence with the most sobering observation.

"I don't think they'll be able to keep the infection out forever unless someone finds a cure."

"Why not?" asked Colleen.

"They're too big too soon," he said. "All of our shelters run the risk of being compromised every day, but the risk is lower because they're more compact. I heard there are over a hundred exits and entrances to this shelter. Only one is open all the time, but that's one too many. I think the infection will get inside sooner or later."

"That's disturbing," said Iris, "but maybe Henry can play a role in lowering the risk."

They didn't notice Henry at first, but he heard what Iris had said.

"Lowering the risk of what, may I ask?"

They all jumped to their feet and rushed to give Henry a hug, but they also saw the two children on either side of him. They were holding hands, and the resemblance was obvious.

"Emily and Adam, let me introduce you to some of my American friends who helped to bring me home."

Everyone got their chance to be introduced, and it was a bittersweet moment for them when they were told that Symone wasn't with the children. They each offered their assurances that Symone was going to be found, and they were surprised to find out that the children had absolute faith that their mother was fine even after over seven years.

Emily said, "When they told us our father was safe and that you had brought him home, we said we knew he would be back, and we know you will find our mother too."

None of the group could resist, and they all repeated their promises even though they had just been talking about the flaws they saw in a shelter this size. Even as they made those promises, there was a discomfort growing among them, and Henry sensed it. It wasn't exactly what they said, but they each had that forced cheer one would see on the face of a family member in the waiting room of an Intensive Care Unit, right before they said not to worry to another relative.

"You were talking about me lowering risk," said Henry.

Iris took Henry aside so the children wouldn't hear and said, "When you were in space, you knew it was bad down here, but you didn't know how bad. You had to ensure your systems kept running on the space station, but you didn't have the infected following you down streets, through forests, or falling over you while you were sleeping. You didn't see friends dragged to the ground and eaten while they screamed in agony. You've seen some of it since you got back, but can you imagine what those dark days were like when it first started?"

Henry didn't need Iris to tell him what it was that had the Americans on edge. All it took was for him to take in the crowds of people in the hotel lobby. Through the large windows, he could see the street outside, and hundreds of people walked by without a care in the world. They were blissfully ignorant of the fact that it was still happening outside.

Iris continued, "What your country has done here is miraculous, but it's a house of cards if the people let down their guard, and we think the establishment has done exactly that."

Henry had been surprised by the utopia in the massive shelter, but he was willing to accept it because it had saved his children and kept them safe for years. Iris had laid bare the truth of just how lucky the people in the shelter had been, and the truth hurt. Henry became defensive.

"They made it work here. I'm sorry that things fell apart in so many of your shelters, but you can't deny that this was a success. They have transportation, agriculture, and a continuation of a way of life that's in many ways better than before."

His reaction surprised them, and the anger that stayed just below the surface of his words made her take a step back from him. She felt her own anger rising and threatening to spoil the moment as well as create a public disturbance.

With a slightly shaking voice, she gave Henry a challenge that he couldn't refuse.

"Do you see that TV behind the bar? What is it broadcasting? From here, I would guess it's a movie. Go see for yourself what happens if you ask the bartender to switch to a live broadcast. If there's anything making news besides the fact that a celebrity astronaut has come home, I'll shut up."

Henry hesitated at first, but he hadn't shut out the woman he had come to know as a friend. He also knew why Iris had managed to keep so many of her own people alive. She was intelligent before the infection, but it had also made her even smarter. When she was buried alive, she learned that there was still danger out there that could come at you from any direction.

He told his children to wait with the Americans for a minute while he checked something, and he went over to the bar. The bartender was excited to have the opportunity to meet a real celebrity, and he would be glad to change channels on the TV.

The first channel showed a large photo of Henry in his spacesuit, and then a video clip showed the liftoff of a flight a few years before the infection. Then there was a photo he hadn't realized was taken that showed the reunion with his children. Henry made a hand motion to the bartender to change channels.

The second channel was a children's network that was teaching a lesson about numbers, and the bartender flipped to the next channel without having to be told. An old football match was in progress, so he switched again. The movie came back on, and the bartender said something to Henry that they assumed was a question about what he wanted to watch, and the news channel came back on. It was another story about Henry, and as they watched, it was followed by a segment about production in one of the agricultural centers.

The conversation that ensued between Henry and the bartender couldn't be heard by the Americans, but they could read Henry's body language and saw the stiffness across his back when the bartender shrugged his shoulders indifferently.

Colleen whispered to her husband, "I think Henry just asked him something about the infected on the surface."

Hampton said, "I think the bartender may have asked Henry why he wanted to know. Did you notice that none of the stories about Henry are talking about his experiences or what it's like up there?"

Henry came back to the group but went to his son and daughter first. He excused himself from the others and took them over to the dining area next to the lobby, where he ordered ice cream. After he had them situated, he came back and sat down on the sofa heavily.

"This place has Internet," said Sim, "but it's more like a wide-area network. There's nothing on it about what's really happening on the surface. There's a bunch of stuff about Henry, but there's nothing about the shelters in the US, military movements, China, Russia, or other world news. You can stream games, make video calls, and do social media, but it's all censored."

Tom said, "When I was debriefed, I was asked not to discuss the outside with anyone."

"Me too," said Iris. "There used to be an online database of everyone in the shelter so people could find relatives or friends who had survived, but that's become restricted now. If you want to know if someone new came in, you have to submit an application for it to be researched. They want people to adjust to their losses."

The others all nodded to indicate the same, and Henry saw their point. If the truth was kept from the general population, there would be a mistake sooner or later. It was like people who lived in a hurricane-prone area, but the hurricanes missed them for too many years. When one finally hits, they won't be prepared.

"What do you think I can do?" asked Henry.

"You can start by telling them to seal the exits," said Tom.

Iris couldn't agree more. "Sooner or later, someone is going to open one of those exits. It's going to be someone who got restless and wants to see what it's really like out there. They'll get bitten, maybe bring the infection into the shelter, maybe leave the door open. It could even be a kid who wants to go searching for lost parents on their own."

That hit home with Henry. Ever since the moment of his return, the only thing the kids could talk about was finding Symone. From what he had seen outside, he knew the odds were against finding her alive.

21

Eurotunnel

Southern England - Present Day

Kathy delivered the news to the Chief about the identity of their new passenger with a neutral face and waited for his reaction. It was nice once in a while to see him be surprised, and she wasn't disappointed. His eyebrows went up so high that she thought they would disappear into his hairline.

"Did you tell her about Henry?" he asked.

Kathy shook her head. "No, I wanted to be sure we got her calmed down a bit first, and we needed to be sure about bites. She's been through a lot. She said she's been totally alone in that tower for years. Can you imagine?"

"Did she say why?"

"She's convinced there's a shelter in the tunnel. She's tried to work up the nerve to go in, but she's seen the infected go in and sometimes come out. In the few minutes I spent with her, she told me she had seen soldiers come out of the tunnel, so she rigged up a siren to get their attention, but that backfired. She attracted that horde, and the soldiers haven't come back since."

The Chief grew concerned and asked, "What's your take on how she'll react when we tell her where Henry is? Too bad we needed him to fly the other plane."

"I think she'll be good, but get ready to block the door. She's going be ready to leave for the tunnel as soon as you tell her."

The Chief climbed from the pilot's seat into the back of the plane, where Cassandra was checking Symone's blood pressure one more time.

"How's our patient?" he asked.

He gave her his biggest smile, but Symone could only take in his size. This giant of a man instantly made her feel like everything was going to be okay.

Cassandra said, "It's remarkable how some people got healthier since the infected showed up. Symone was just telling me she used to run for exercise, but running to stay alive took the fun out of it. She hasn't had fried food in years, though, so her arteries aren't clogged."

"That's good to hear," said the Chief. He held out a hand to her and said, "Welcome to the Mud Island family. We have something important to tell you, but I want to get your promise first."

"Promise?" she asked as she shook his hand. "What's the Mud Island family?"

"I need for you to promise to stay calm, and I especially need to know if you can take orders instead of running off to do your own thing. The Mud Island family is a team, and we stay alive by following orders. Do I have your word?"

Symone's hesitation was as much humor as it was curiosity, but she nonetheless gave him her word. The Chief sat down across from her. Kathy and Cassandra flanked her on both sides.

"Why do I get the feeling like I'll want to get out of this plane in a minute?"

To make matters worse, Captain Miller joined them and stood with his back to the door.

"When we realized there was someone in the tower," the Chief began, "we didn't in our wildest dreams expect it to be the person we were looking for."

"You were looking for me? You're Americans...did Adam Callaway send you? Do you have any word about Henry?"

The Chief didn't want to give her bad news when all she needed at this time was good news, so he ignored her question about Adam.

"Henry came to England with us. We split into two groups to find the shelter where we thought we would find you and your children."

They were right to expect a reaction from Symone, but instead of bolting for the door, she stood up to better see the inside of the plane.

"Henry's here? Where is he?"

She tried to shoulder past Kathy to get to the cockpit, but Kathy gently steered her back to her seat.

"We have two planes," said Kathy. "We needed him to fly the other one, and they went to the place where we think the shelter may be located."

"But the shelter is here," insisted Symone.

"No," said Kathy. "There's a strong chance the tunnel is only a way to get to the shelter. All of the shelters have a back door, and we think this is the back door."

"All of the shelters?" she asked. "There's more than one?"

"There are more in America," said the Chief, "but we think you have one here on the Isle of Sheppey."

Symone let it sink in first, then she seemed to remember something. She dug into her pocket and pulled out three business cards. The emblem on the front was already something they all recognized, but it was the row of numbers on the back of them that caught the Chief's eye.

"That can't be a coincidence," said the Chief. "Those numbers are coordinates, and our navigation instruments show we're almost on top of that location. That's the address to the Eurotunnel entrance. You can tell me where you got those when we have more time. Right now we need to get moving."

In her mind, she was calculating the distance between the tunnel and the Isle. It was a long way, but after living in a world where the dead came back hungry for human flesh, she figured anything was possible. Her eyes went back and forth between Captain Miller and the Chief as if she was wondering if she could get by both of them.

"I've stayed alive this long," she said, "but I would have gone into that tunnel a long time ago if I thought there was a chance in hell of finding the shelter on my own. If I understand you correctly, it's going to take more than luck to find it without getting eaten."

Symone watched their reactions and was really awestruck by one thing they had in common. They were relaxed. Some people might have mistaken their posture as overconfidence, but she read it differently. Yes, they were confident, but what they had said about being a team made them different. They had each other's backs. If she went into the tunnel with them, it would be different.

"What would it take to be invited to go along with your team into the tunnel?" she asked.

"Only your promise to follow orders," said the Chief. "Don't leave the group, and do as you're told. Our goal was to find you and your children, so we're halfway there."

"When do we leave?" she asked. "And by the way, you didn't answer my question about Adam. I just hope it happened while he was doing something he loved, not by getting bitten. That's what I would have wanted for Henry."

"He wasn't bitten," said Kathy. She spared her the details.

******

The mouth of the Eurotunnel was so dark it seemed to absorb the light after going only a few feet inside. There were enough rechargeable flashlights in the plane for all five of them, but since they didn't know how far they needed to go or exactly what they were looking for, they were hesitant to use more than two at a time. There were three tunnels. Two of them were equipped with rails, and a service tunnel ran between them. They chose the tunnel on the left side because that was the one Symone had seen soldiers emerge from.

The Chief had asked Symone what she knew about the tunnels as they prepared to leave the plane, and she had told him what had been on the news. The tunnels were slightly more than thirty-one miles long, and each railway tunnel had large, water-tight doors that allowed access from the service tunnel. She said the doors were three hundred and seventy-five meters apart, and the trains were so long that a stopped train could be in front of two doors at the same time.

The Chief did some quick math in his head and estimated there were as many as one hundred twenty-five doors spaced a quarter of a mile apart. That was too many doors for them to open, so they agreed they would inspect the hinges of each door until they found one that had signs of wear. If he was right, the damp air inside the tunnels would have caused rust on the hinges. Soldiers who were opening and closing the door would have caused the rust to break free and flake to the ground.

Symone also provided a piece of information that all but confirmed in the Chief's mind that they were on the right track, literally and figuratively. The tunnel boring machines were big, complex pieces of machinery. When the British and French machines met near the middle of the Channel in 1990, the French machine was dismantled and taken in pieces back to France. According to the official records, the cost of dismantling the British machine outweighed its value, so it was diverted to the side and buried under the Channel.

Symone said, "My husband and Adam Callaway had a theory about that. They suspected the tunnel boring machine was secretly used somewhere else. It was incredibly sophisticated and still holds the records for tunneling faster and further than any other machine. They said it was probably diverted but not buried."

"Is there anything else that would have made them suspect that another tunnel was being dug?" asked the Chief.

Symone almost laughed at the question, not because it was funny, but because her husband had laughed when no one really made an issue of the fact that the debris from the Eurotunnel consisted mostly of chalk, but the debris continued to come out of the tunnel for months after boring was done, and it was more like clay than chalk. There were some incredible fossils discovered in the clay. Geologists and paleontologists argued about how they could have come from the floor of the Channel.

"I think the argument is settled," said the Chief. "Now, all we have to do is prove it."

Kathy was in front of the group, and she sniffed at the air.

"It's disgusting down here. You don't suppose…"

Her question was cut short when her beam of light flashed across the piles of human remains that were literally eight to ten feet deep along the left side of the tunnel. The sloping mass of bodies stretched away into the darkness further than her flashlight would go, and they all reached for bandanas to wrap around their noses and mouths.

"I hope we find the right turn fast," she added.

Captain Miller clicked on his light and played it along the other side of the tunnel.

"There aren't any bodies over there," he said. "Someone moved them all to the other side. I wonder why someone would go to all that trouble. Notice something about the bodies?"

"You mean there are fresh ones stacked on top of the old ones?" asked Kathy.

Kathy wasn't a police officer for long when the infected dead arrived. As a matter of fact, she had been an apocalypse survivor for far longer, but she still saw the mass grave as some kind of crime scene. Hundreds of bodies could be seen under the beam of her light, but she imagined there were going to be thousands as they walked deeper into the tunnel. She moved the beam across the tracks toward the right side and studied the dark streaks that could only have been caused by the blood and other bodily fluids released when the bodies were moved, but the tracks were still clean. She knelt for a closer look at the tracks.

"What do you see?" asked the Chief.

"I can see plenty of things I don't like, and here's how I piece it together. Symone told me there were about four dozen trains per day that made the trip between England and France. That means there were hundreds of people in the tunnels at the start of the infection. The drivers could stop the trains as easily as you could stop a car, and they most likely were surprised to find pedestrians in the tunnels at both ends. Some of the pedestrians were running from the infected, but at speeds over ninety miles per hour, they couldn't tell the infected from the living."

Kathy paused and moved her beam of light back and forth to illustrate her points.

"First of all, these tracks have been used recently by some sort of heavy vehicle that rides on rails. Second, the first people to die down here were pushed to one side in order to keep the service tunnel doors clear. I think it was a vehicle used as a plow at first. Third, there are recently dead people piled on top, which means someone picked them up and tossed them out of the way. Lastly, it's good news for us."

"How so?" the Chief asked.

"The tunnel to the Isle of Sheppey wouldn't be too far inside the Eurotunnel. They already had a long way to go, so they wouldn't add to it by starting from way out in the Channel. Whoever cleaned off the tracks wouldn't have bothered to clean past their door, and even if they did it as a diversion, they most likely wouldn't go as far as the next door. Another quarter mile of bodies would be a big job. I'd also be willing to bet that new bodies aren't moved on a regular basis."

"New bodies," said the Chief. "Where are the new bodies coming from? Even if they're still coming from a stopped train somewhere out in the tunnel, they would likely rot before reaching the end of the tunnel."

"I don't know, but if I'm right, we can at least move at a faster pace just by staying to the right side of the tracks."

They moved over to the right side and increased their pace to just under a jog. With three of their group having military combat training, it wasn't hard for them to tell when they were due to pass the first service tunnel entrance. It felt like a quarter mile to all three, and they reset their mental odometers.

The second door appeared on the right much sooner than they knew it should have, and the Chief threw up a fist.

"Was that a quarter mile?" he asked.

Both Cassandra and Captain Miller shook their heads.

"Less than half that far," said Cassandra. "This must be the one we're looking for."

Kathy aimed her flashlight further down the tunnel and reported that the bodies were still pushed to the left, but there was something on the tracks.

"I'm going to check that out," she said.

Captain Miller fell in behind Kathy to go investigate, and it didn't take long to find their plow. He unscrewed the gas cap and pulled a long knife from his belt. He shoved it inside the tank, and it came back out wet.

"Over half full," he reported.

When they came back to join the others at the door, Kathy said, "I don't like this. There's something wrong, but I can't quite put my finger on it."

The Chief said, "Whatever it is, keep thinking about it while the rest of us figure out this door. It's almost identical to the other service door we passed, but I see some differences. For one thing, that latching mechanism is a decoy."

A steel rod extended all the way from the right side of the door over to the latching mechanism. On the real doors, the rod would pull a flat, metal bar that ran from the top of the door to the bottom. Three large pins were inserted into the door frame on the left, and the bar would supposedly pull the pins out of the frame.

"Did anyone else get a good look at the first door we passed?" asked the Chief.

"I did," said Captain Miller. "The first door has been opened by someone. The pins were still shiny from being withdrawn and reinserted. Also, you were wrong about the hinges being rusty. They were coated with some kind of rubber paint that keeps moisture out."

"What's different about this door?" asked Kathy.

"It's bigger," said the Chief. "We all saw the big vault door on Mud Island, and the one at Fort Sumter was identical. Both were like massive vault doors in banks. If you wanted to make a back door on a shelter tunnel, you would want it to be big. I don't think these doors open like the regular doors in this tunnel. I think the whole thing opens, frame and all. Also, you wouldn't have the latching mechanism on the outside where anyone could get at it."

"Here we go again," said the Chief. "We need to think like Titus Rush."

Kathy shook her head. "One problem...what if Titus Rush didn't have anything to do with this tunnel door?"

"Let's hope it was in his original design, but remember that whoever came out through the door had to have a way to open it from this side, so don't rule anything out."

For the next hour, they sat and stared at the big door. The Chief thought he was getting somewhere when he saw that the big air pipes to the left of the door still worked. The valves all still spun freely, and the large cutoff levers still moved up and down. When he changed the positions of the levers, they heard a blast of air go through the pipes, but the door remained shut.

"You said not to rule anything out," said Symone. "What if the door is operated from somewhere else?"

The Chief pointed at the door and said, "That's what it says on the door. I think it means the door was opened and closed remotely by the Control Center after someone contacted them with the request. The second sign means it's not a good idea to be in front of the door when it opens."

There were warning signs on the door that said, DANGER REMOTE CONTROLLED DOOR, and DO NOT ENTER HATCHED FLOOR AREA.

"What if it's remote-controlled from somewhere else?" asked Symone. "Maybe somewhere like the first door?"

Kathy said, "She didn't even meet Titus Rush, but she thinks like him."

Cassandra stayed at the second door and found herself a dark spot outside of the beam of her flashlight. She propped it under the arm of a body with the beam aimed at the door. She was closer to the pile of bodies than she wanted to be, but it was better to be near them than exposed in the open. It gave her goosebumps, but she knew that was the way her body warned her to stay alert.

The Chief's light faded away as the others went back to the first door to see if it offered any clues. Cassandra watched it until it was nothing more than a pinprick of light, and she was grateful that she could still see it, even if it was faint.

At the first door, there was a consensus that the pins were proof that someone had unlocked the door recently. The shine on the pins still reflected light from the lubricant. Now all they had to do was find out what devious clue Titus had left them about this door.

The Chief thought back to the other shelter doors and how some had combinations based on crazy things that meant something to a crazy old man. Titus Rush came up with some ideas that were so logical when you thought of them, but there always had to be a tipping point. There always had to be something different that made the rest of the crazy patterns fall into place.

"I wonder if Henry's group has had to open a door that was designed by Titus Rush," said Kathy.

The Chief said, "If they did, they might still be standing in front of it. The one in the planetarium in Huntsville was far more logical than most. At least it was based on historical events. I don't see anything on this door that offers a clue."

"What if there aren't any clues on this one?" asked Captain Miller.

The words had no sooner left his mouth when the Chief interrupted.

"I've got it. It was staring us in the face on the warning sign, and it's just the kind of thing Titus Rush would have done."

"Cut the dramatics," said Kathy, "and open the door."

"Wait a minute," said Captain Miller. "I have a strange need to know how you got the answer."

"Don't encourage him...please?" she pleaded.

The Chief wasn't going to spoil the chance to explain it, but he promised to keep it short.

"The signs say it's a remote-controlled door, but given the distance from the control center and the door, the word shouldn't be taken literally. The door isn't controlled by a remote. It's a door that's controlled remotely."

"You promised to keep it short," said Kathy.

The Chief ignored her and went on.

"Titus Rush liked the rock band RUSH, as you all know. One of their songs had the lyrics *Invisible airwaves crackle with life*, and then there's a line that goes, *emotional feedback on a timeless wavelength*. What's the most archaic frequency used in radio?"

"I don't know, but you promised to keep it short."

Kathy wasn't able to stop herself even though she knew the Chief was having a good time with his explanation.

The Chief took out his handheld radio and switched it to the lowest possible setting. Twenty-seven Megahertz was the setting used by CB units and shortwave radios back when the Eurotunnel construction began.

He used the keypad on his radio to type 1979, the year the song was released, and the silver pins of the door were retracted by the locking mechanism. They all took a step backward even though they were outside of the floor area where the door would swing open, but that had become a force of habit as a result of the infected dead. Everyone who wanted to survive knew not to stand too close to a door as it opened.

Inside the door where there should have been an entrance to the service tunnel, there was a simple switch with two settings…OPEN and CLOSE. Without preamble, the Chief pushed it to the OPEN position.

"Classic Titus Rush," said the Chief.

Kathy said, "I would have cut my own throat if there had been another puzzle inside."

Cassandra felt her goosebumps get bigger when a rumbling sound started directly across from her. She stayed in the shadows away from her flashlight and watched as the door moved. It wasn't just the door that moved, though. This time it was the door, the frame, the machinery, and even the pipes. The entire structure moved inward away from her, and then it swung on silent hinges, leaving a massive opening.

A single soldier in full combat gear stood beyond the opening in a dimly lit corridor that sloped sharply downward. If he had been standing only a few feet down the corridor, she would have only been able to see him from the waist up.

"That's how they could put a door on the right side without it opening into the service tunnel," she thought to herself. "It goes under the service tunnel."

The soldier took a few unsteady steps closer to the opening, and Cassandra could see him better but still not very well.

"Why isn't he holding a weapon?" she asked herself.

The answer became obvious when he stepped into the open door. There was a bloodstain on his uniform that she had mistaken for camouflage, and the wound that had caused the bleeding was a massive tear across his right carotid artery. He was still coming forward as Cassandra heard the footfalls of the rest of her group approaching. She would have preferred to do it silently, but she had to end it before her friends arrived. There could be more of them.

The shot caused the others to drop to the floor. It was deafening in the enclosed space, but she had easily hit her mark. She kept her M4 aimed at the new tunnel opening and saw three heads appear over the bottom near the floor. They were walking uphill, so the heads grew into bodies as they came closer. She pulled the trigger three more times and then yelled.

"Clear!"

The Chief kept his Smith & Wesson out ahead of him as he smoothly eased from the floor and moved toward the opening. A groaning sound came from the darkness beyond the door somewhere behind the vehicle that sat on the tracks, and Kathy aimed her flashlight that way. Several more of the infected were moving towards Cassandra's position, and two wore uniforms just like the other soldiers. Cassandra saw them too, and she shot them easily.

"Are you okay?" asked the Chief.

Cassandra walked out to stand next to him and just gave him a nod. He barely saw it in the dim light, but he imagined her heart was still in her throat. As cool as she could be in combat, it had to bother her to see the infected inside the shelter door. It would have bothered any of them if they had seen them in the tunnel of Fort Sumter. It didn't matter that the tunnel entrance was a long way from the actual shelter…they weren't supposed to be on that side of the door.

"We might have more company in a few minutes," said Kathy. "We should get inside and close the door."

******

Just like the service tunnel, there were two lanes, but they were narrow. There were six armored vehicles lined up along the left side of the slope. That explained how the soldiers were able to travel from the tunnel entrance all the way to the shelter. It was almost fifty miles from Folkestone to the Isle of Sheppey by roads, and though the tunnel was a more direct route, it would still take close to two hours to make the drive at a conservative speed. The tunnel was dimly lit, and they didn't want to run into a horde in the narrow confines. There would be too little room to maneuver, and they had come too far for a stupid mistake to end their journey.

They were all eager to get to the shelter, but the fear that grew as a result of finding the infected soldiers inside was wearing on their minds. The biggest fear was that infected soldiers might have already made it back to the shelter. They knew nothing at all about the security measures at the other end of the tunnel, but their hope was that it was good enough to intercept the infection.

They only needed one of the vehicles, and they still had plenty of room to spread out. They were tempted to take two in case one had mechanical issues, but the gas tanks were full, and they appeared to be well maintained. The first one in line started up easily, so they decided to stay together. They had already split up once, and even though they didn't have a reason to be worried about the rest of their friends, anything could go wrong. Cassandra was selected to drive.

There was enough time on the ride to talk about their experiences and get to know Symone better. She didn't really know how remarkable it was that she had survived for so long, but she didn't want to talk about herself. She wanted to know all about Henry. She couldn't understand why anyone thought surviving the infected dead was any harder than what he had done. In a way, she was right, but if Henry was there with them right now, he wouldn't see it that way.

They didn't dwell on whether or not the children were safe. In her heart, she was unwilling to accept anything but the possibility that they were fine. The worry about the infected soldiers was lessened a bit by the fact that the tunnel was almost fifty miles long. Symone had lost track of time since the day she saw the soldiers and sounded the siren, but if she had to guess, that would have been the day when they had been injured. A small part of her feared that she had caused them to become infected. Maybe they had been bitten while trying to reach her.

She told her new traveling partners about her concern that she was at fault, and they understood, but they also wouldn't let her put it all on herself. They told her that three of their group were trained military, and Kathy was a police officer. All of them ran toward danger, not away from it. If they became infected trying to reach her, then it happened while they were doing their jobs.

They didn't tell her how worried they were about the infection getting inside the shelter. The Chief could remember talking with Hampton for hours about how the infection always seemed to get behind the protective barriers. In Hampton's hometown, they thought the rivers and bridges would keep it out, but no barrier worked if the people weren't careful. It had overrun his town when someone kept secret the fact that a family member was bitten.

Then there was the ultimate barrier breaker. The infection wasn't always caused by a fatal bite. Sometimes people just died then got back up. That's why the safest shelters were like Mud Island and the one on the oil rig. Small shelters would have fewer fatalities to worry about and fewer chances for the infection to spread.

A silence gradually fell over the group as they got closer to the Isle of Sheppey. They didn't know if they were driving into a safe shelter or into another breached shelter like the one in Columbus, Ohio. They were all wound like coiled springs ready to be set loose when they realized they could see the end of the tunnel in the distance. There were concrete barriers in a staggered pattern for the last one hundred yards, so Cassandra was forced to drive in a zigzag pattern and slow down to a crawl. They could see sharpshooters behind the last barriers and at a guard post that at first looked like it was blocking the road. When they were closer, they could see that the tunnel ended before the guard post. On both sides of the road, a fence spread along the outermost wall of the shelter, and a gate could be rolled into place if needed. If the infected came through the tunnel, they could be isolated inside the fence.

Cassandra stopped three concrete barriers from the sharpshooters. She knew what she would want if she was on guard duty and an unidentified group of people rolled up on her. She turned in her seat only long enough for the Chief and Captain Miller to agree with her. Kathy didn't need to be told that she should get out first. An attractive woman with long blond hair would be less threatening to the guards. She eased from the door on the left side of the vehicle and lowered herself to her knees. She put her hands slowly behind her head.

"Now you, Symone. Do exactly what Kathy did, and don't speak until they tell you to."

Symone did as she was told, and then Cassandra. Captain Miller followed her, and then the Chief finally got out. The guards visibly shifted their aim to him as he unfolded his tremendous bulk from the vehicle. He saw them glance at each other, and he was even more careful to move slowly. The guard inside the fence was talking with someone over the radio, and it was obvious that this development was something totally new. Not only was the last patrol missing, but a group of strangers had come through the tunnel.

On a signal from the guard inside the fence, one of the sharpshooters left his position and approached.

"Are any of you infected?" he asked.

They all answered, but they knew it wasn't the last time they would be asked if the soldiers were aware of the dangers involved when strangers showed up. It was hard for them to see over the concrete barriers from their knees, but they could hear vehicles arriving at the gate. More soldiers took up positions, but one of the vehicles was an ambulance, and medical personnel went about erecting a tent. They obviously intended to inspect the strangers for bite wounds.

Another vehicle pulled up behind the ambulance. A flurry of activity followed as two men jumped out of the small car and ran right past the medical personnel and guards. One was an officer, and he was waving his arms and yelling something at the soldiers. One by one, they lowered their weapons. The other man with him didn't stop running.

Henry Tisdal would rather take a bullet than wait one more minute to hold his wife. Symone saw him coming and launched herself from the pavement. They collided so hard that they almost fell over, but by then, the officer had yelled Henry's name loudly enough for everyone to hear, and the cheers echoed through the tunnel.

******

It didn't take long for the medical team to clear them all. Symone caused the most concern because she wasn't as well-nourished as the others. The medical team considered the Chief to be somewhat of a specimen and wanted to know if he was immune to the infection because he was so healthy. He was actually amused by their questions and told them he didn't know because he had never been bitten.

The arrival of Henry was the last thing the Chief expected, but unknown to him and his companions, the guards were told there was a strong possibility that someone would come through the tunnel. They were given strict instructions not to shoot without reporting in first. When the guard called his superiors and gave descriptions of the occupants of the vehicle, Henry was quickly located.

All of them were happy to hear that the rest of their group was safe in the shelter, and the Chief couldn't wait to lay eyes on Iris. Kathy and Cassandra hugged each other when they found out their husbands were safe, and the bachelor in the group tried to hug the Chief. It was something the Chief loved to do to Eddie back on Mud Island, so Captain Miller couldn't resist putting the shoe on the other foot for a change.

Symone was the only one who wouldn't calm down with the

medical staff. She had learned from Henry within seconds after their collision that the children were safe and well. He knew that as glad as she was to see him, she had tortured herself for years because she had lost them, and he also knew he needed to prepare her for the shock of seeing them so grown. There was really no way to prepare her other than to tell her the truth, so when she asked through tears how they were, he said she wouldn't believe how much they had grown. He quickly added how proud she would be to see them so healthy and strong.

"If only I had been with them when the soldiers found them," she said. "We could have been safe together all these years. I've missed them growing up."

"We both have missed those years, but that doesn't matter anymore. You'll see it in a few minutes. What matters is that we're back together, and we don't ever have to be apart again."

It was Major Merritt, the officer who had arrived with Henry, who finally got Symone to understand what mattered. He had William and Sidney Goodwin brought to the gate and introduced them to Symone. He explained that they had lost their children at the beginning of the infection, and they were given the responsibility of caring for Emily and Adam, not to replace their parents, but to help them to heal.

Symone was speechless at first, and a small part of her envied them for having the years she had lost, but then she realized the same thing Henry had. They would always be the adoptive parents to her children, and she could see the hurt they were trying their best to hide. They had every right to believe the Tisdals would never be found alive, yet they were genuinely happy for her and Henry. Still, they were aching from the loss of children twice, while she had only endured it once. When she pulled them to her with love, they knew Symone was ready to see her children.

They were reunited in the privacy of the medical tent after a bus arrived carrying the rest of the Mud Island family and the Tisdal children. The Chief had just given Iris a big kiss when he saw Emily and Adam being taken to the open door of the tent. Emily was staring at him and giggling at the kiss while Adam was big-eyed and amazed by his size. He gave them a smile and a little wave that they returned before stepping through the opening.

The Chief thought it might just be the best moment of his life when he heard them shout in unison, "Mummy!"

It had been Symone's greatest fear that her children wouldn't remember her. Sometimes she had even struggled to remember their faces, so she was sure they would forget hers. Now, as she dropped to her knees with her arms spread wide, her fears were washed away. Their bodies were older, but she saw her children rushing toward her with nothing but joy on their faces.

Symone had never given up hope, but not in her wildest dreams did she think it could be this wonderful.

22

A New Life

Southern England - Present Day

The Chief was invited to meet with the Royal family separately and in private, and it had come as a complete surprise. Henry was the hero who came home, and his family was a shining example of the success of the shelter. Where others had failed, the United Kingdom had succeeded. It turned out that was why they wanted to meet with him. They were grateful yet concerned about the flaws that had accompanied their success. The ease with which both groups were able to gain entry into the shelter caused them to wonder if they were secure enough, and the Chief was invited to review their operations from top to bottom.

For his work as a consultant and for his part in bringing Henry home, he was given a gift that they didn't expect. He was knighted, Sir Joshua Barnes. Titus wouldn't have mentioned it to anyone if he had accepted the honor, but the Chief kind of liked the way it sounded and instructed his friends to call him Sir Joshua.

Kathy told Iris he was going to be insufferably pleased with himself for a long time, and she didn't know if she could take it. Iris told Kathy not to worry because the novelty would wear off, but until it did, she was supposed to call her Lady Iris when he was around.

It took almost a month for the Chief to review the shelter operations because the infrastructure was so big. He decided the first priority was the size of the population under the Isle of Sheppey. There were so many people in the shelter that they needed a solid plan for dealing with natural deaths. Iris had encountered the same problem inside the Ambassadors Island shelter, so the Chief turned the problem over to her.

Iris discovered that the shelter occupants had a remarkable record for responding to natural deaths before they led to an outbreak of infection. That meant they had been lucky for almost eight years. Just like the towns and cities that had fallen above ground, too much depended on the honesty of the citizens. Iris worked tirelessly along with the shelter managers to implement a plan. It was far from perfect, but it was better than relying on luck.

The Chief had been right about the number of emergency exits that were spread around the island, and he was amazed that they had never been breached. There were over one hundred ways to open the shelter to the outside world, and some of them had already been used in secret by people who went in search of loved ones. If they had found their families, they might have brought the infection back with them.

The tunnel was supposed to be the back door like the one at Fort Sumter, and it still remained an important link to the outside, but the military was forced to reassess its use to search for more survivors. They had lost a whole squad of men without even knowing what had happened to them, and in the process, infected soldiers had come back inside. Fortunately, they had remained near the Eurotunnel, and it had been a good decision not to send more soldiers to find out what had happened to them. Soldiers didn't like leaving comrades behind, and they may have brought the infection back to the shelter despite their orders.

It wouldn't be the best duty for a soldier, but the Chief recommended that a post be established at the inside of the door and that the door would never be opened unless the Queen herself was outside trying to get in. Since that was so unlikely, they understood his point about the door being for a real emergency only.

Of the remaining emergency exits, all but four were permanently sealed. The one in the church was left open because Henry assured them no one was likely to follow in their footsteps through the confessional. Besides, he considered the puzzle associated with the door to be a work of art. Latin scripts, stained glass windows, wood carvings, weights that were measured in a specific order, and a confessional…the complexity of all those things made him feel almost as if he had known Titus Rush. The other three exits were heavily manned by soldiers who were hand-picked by their squad leaders and promoted. They were all members of the Grenadier Guards, and they took up their posts just as they had at Buckingham Palace.

One of the exits was located in the prison where Henry and his group had left their plane, and the Chief was particularly impressed by the familiar design of the prison. It was truly shaped almost exactly like Fort Sumter, but it functioned much the same as the town above the Green Cavern shelter in Guntersville. The only thing he had them change at that exit was access to the shelter below. It was nearly impossible to get by the guards at the door.

The biggest change that was made was not a physical door but a mental window. It was a necessary change that had to be made in the minds of the people. What the Mud Island Americans saw inside the shelter frightened them because it was complacency. The population wasn't afraid anymore, and if they weren't afraid, people would start to do what is only human nature…they would want to explore. People would leave the shelter and become infected if they got curious about the outside world.

With the help of the entire American group, the Internet was expanded to include remote broadcasts from cameras that were carefully placed by small teams. In some cases, the teams were accompanied by the Chief, but mostly Cassandra and Captain Miller. The views from those cameras were of locations where the infected dead could always be seen. Television programming was changed to include warnings about the infection instead of ignoring what was happening outside.

At the end of the month, the Isle of Sheppey shelter was a safer place to live, but the people in charge knew they would need to evolve to prevent new problems. They established a special office to oversee that evolution so they would think of problems before they happened instead of reacting after they arose. They were safe for now, but whether or not they remained safe would depend upon how many problems they could anticipate.

******

Andi Hartford waited as long as she could for their return, and twice she was forced to run for her hiding place by the submarine that lurked in the open waters between St Mary's and the mainland. She made several runs back to St Agnes to see if Beatrice had seen them, and she had left the dog with her for company. Andi figured she would need to add St Agnes to her list of regular stops to keep Beatrice supplied.

The Allen brothers were getting bored, but Andi kept them busy by exploring the many uninhabited islands around St Agnes and St Mary's. There were also shipwrecks that dated back a few centuries, and they recovered enough old coins made of silver and gold to keep them occupied. The wrecks from World War I and II were fascinating but not as lucrative.

They couldn't stay there forever, though, and they decided they would wait for a turn in the weather to make a run for it. With any luck, they would get fog at night and be able to slip into the Atlantic undetected. If they had any doubts about the intentions of the submarine, they were put to rest when they saw a private pleasure craft making the crossing from St Mary's to the mainland in broad daylight. From their hiding place among the uninhabited islands and rock outcroppings, they watched the submarine surface directly in the path of the boat.

The private craft must have been manned by a security force because they engaged the submarine without fear of the consequences. The response was swift as missiles tore through the sleek body of the yacht. If there were any survivors, the crew of the submarine didn't try to find them. Andi figured the people in the yacht might have met the same fate even if they surrendered.

It took several weeks after that event to finally see a dense fog roll across the islands, and judging by the height of it, she anticipated it would last well into the night. The Allen brothers prepped the tug for departure as they watched the dark fog bank grow closer, but Donnie kept a watchful eye on the open water above St Mary's. The submarine had a habit of showing up in the late afternoon, and if it was north of St Mary's, they would have a good head start before the submarine headed south toward the Atlantic.

Donnie saw the periscope first, but something seemed different. It was moving much faster than normal. It was usually traveling at a slow speed as if it was the master of the English Channel. He reported the sighting, and Andi joined him with binoculars to assess their chances of reaching the fog undetected. They were both surprised by an explosion that made the submarine buckle in the middle as it was forced the rest of the way above the water. It was blown in half, and they watched with big eyes as both halves separated and sank below the surface.

"What could have done that?" asked Donnie.

As if in answer to his question, a second periscope pierced the surface, and it was quickly followed by the sail of a submarine. It had its scope turned toward the spot where the first submarine had gone down, but the heading of the gray hulk was undeniably straight at the Maggie Mae's position. Andi wondered how long it would be before a torpedo would do to them what it had done to the other sub.

The radio burst to life in the wheelhouse, and Andi felt relief wash over her.

"Ocean-going tugboat, Maggie Mae. This is Her Majesty's Ship Ambush. Do you read, over?"

Andi signaled with one thumb upward for Jessie to acknowledge the message, and he put it on the deck speaker for her to hear.

"HMS Ambush, we read you, over."

"Stand by to receive passengers, over."

Andi let her smaller tug move into position along the starboard side of the much larger submarine. At a length that was longer than a football field, her tug would have been used to help the submarine into a berth or when being put to sea, so the HMS Ambush simply waited for her to come alongside. The Allen brothers cast lines across and readied a plank from their deck to the submarine.

There was no mistaking who the passengers were as soon as they came out of the hatch in the deck aft of the sail. The Chief was clearly not made for submarine hatches. Andi counted them as they lined up on the deck to give their thanks to an officer before crossing to the Maggie Mae. The water was calm, so they were able to move quickly. She saw the Chief, Iris, Kathy, Tom, Colleen, Hampton, Cassandra, Sim, and Captain Miller all coming aboard. Henry was gone, and she assumed by their broad smiles that they had gotten him safely home. Being delivered by a British fast-attack submarine was also a good sign.

"Welcome aboard, Chief. It's good to see you."

"Thanks, Andi, but that's Sir Joshua Barnes now."

Andi had her mouth open to ask another question, but the Chief was already past her, so she turned to Kathy.

"What was that all about?"

"Don't ask me," said Kathy. "Check with Lady Iris."

Andi greeted each of them and then thanked the officer for delivering them to her. He called back between the two ships with the welcome news that the HMS Ambush would be escorting the Maggie Mae all the way to Charleston, so they could travel at flank speed. When she joined them at the helm, she wagged a finger at the Chief and Iris.

"If you want me to play your little game, you have to tell me why you're Sir Joshua and why you're Lady Iris...unless...no. You weren't knighted, were you?"

The Chief and Iris both gave her a big smile, but the Chief got serious and said, "We have some unfinished business with some people in Atlanta now that we're done here. Let's make a quick stop to visit Beatrice. The Ambush has a load of supplies for her. After that, are you ready to head for home?"

ABOUT THE AUTHOR

Bob Howard (1951-) was born in New Jersey to an Army Sergeant from Ohio and a mother from Romania. He was moved from one Army base to the next, and before he began high school in Huntsville, Alabama he had lived most of his life overseas in Germany and Okinawa with brief stays in Maryland and North Carolina. He credits his imagination to his exposure to different cultures and environments at an early age. He began reading science fiction and fell in love with post apocalyptic novels. He still has an original copy of the first one he read in 1966, The Furies by Keith Edwards. He joined the Navy after high school and continued to move from one base to another, including a submarine base at Holy Loch, Scotland. He eventually stayed in one place when he got stationed in Charleston, South Carolina. He graduated with a BS in Psychology from the College of Charleston. He married his wife in 1984 and together they raised a son and a daughter.

* * *

It takes a lot of work to get a book of fiction written and then edited. We want the book to flow, but we also want it to be grammatically correct whenever possible. If you see a spot where you think a comma was needed, it may be that I left it out because it interrupted the flow. The same isn't true for typos. If you see one of those nasty little things and would like to let me know, I would be pleased to correct it. I've learned that I've got some really bad habits when it comes to pet phrases, and I make mistakes. I hear from a gentleman in Japan regularly because he has such a keen eye for errors. I'm lucky to have him as an after-editor. That doesn't mean you won't see something that everyone else missed. Please make my books better by telling me.

I would love to hear from you, and I value your opinions and comments. The best way to help an author become better at his craft is to write a review, so please feel free to write one. If you would like to know more about me or get in touch with me, please visit my website at *realbobhoward.com*. You can also sign up for my newsletter and be notified when the next book is released.

With gratitude,

Bob Howard

www.ingramcontent.com/pod-product-compliance
Lightning Source LLC
Chambersburg PA
CBHW020322040726
47494CB00026B/623